"Fredericks spends ample time creating a three-dimensional portrait of Betty. . . . So when it all goes horribly wrong, the reader feels Betty's agony. Fredericks fills in substantial details from real life but never forgets to put the human cost, and its lasting damage, at the forefront of her narrative."
—*The New York Times*

"Author Mariah Fredericks casts doubt on [Gow's] innocence in this propulsive read."
—*Good Morning America*

"Mariah Fredericks takes an ingenious idea . . . and turns it into a compelling book. Fredericks brings humanity to everyone involved, reminding us that they were not just a news story but real people."
—*Montecito Journal*

"Fredericks successfully explores this very public story through a new lens. . . . As the tragedy plays out, the emotional tension is palpable. Regardless of the degree of prior knowledge the reader brings to the novel, this beautifully crafted, gripping tale is an excellent read. Highly recommended."
—Historical Novel Society (Editors' Choice)

"Carefully researched . . . This is a compelling story about a courageous woman nearly forgotten by history, with a bittersweet mix of sorrow and redemption; for readers who enjoy Jennifer Chiaverini, Marie Benedict, or Melanie Benjamin."
—*Booklist*

"Mariah Fredericks is an expert at capturing history's ordinary voices in extraordinary circumstances, and *The Lindbergh Nanny* is her best yet. . . . An eyewitness view of a still-shocking event that makes for perfect historical fiction."

—*CrimeReads* (Most Anticipated Crime Books of 2022)

ALSO BY MARIAH FREDERICKS

The

LINDBERGH NANNY

A Novel

Mariah Fredericks

MINOTAUR BOOKS
NEW YORK

For Fredric Larry Weiss, with love and respect.
Thank you for having the conversation.

Published in the United States by Minotaur Books,
an imprint of St. Martin's Publishing Group

THE LINDBERGH NANNY. Copyright © 2022 by Mariah Fredericks. All rights reserved. Printed in the United States of America. For information, address St. Martin's Publishing Group, 120 Broadway, New York, NY 10271.

www.minotaurbooks.com

Excerpt from *The Wharton Plot* copyright © 2024 by Mariah Fredericks

The Library of Congress has cataloged the hardcover edition as follows:

Names: Fredericks, Mariah, author.
Title: The Lindbergh nanny : a novel / Mariah Fredericks.
Description: First edition. | New York : Minotaur Books, 2022.
Identifiers: LCCN 2022033552 | ISBN 9781250827401 (hardcover) |
    ISBN 9781250827418 (ebook)
Subjects: LCSH: Lindbergh, Charles A. (Charles Augustus), 1902–1974—Fiction. |
    Lindbergh, Charles Augustus, 1930–1932—Fiction. | LCGFT: Biographical
    fiction. | Novels.
Classification: LCC PS3606.R435 L56 2022 | DDC 813/.6—dc23/eng/20220715
LC record available at https://lccn.loc.gov/2022033552

ISBN 978-1-250-88820-4 (trade paperback)

Our books may be purchased in bulk for promotional, educational, or business use. Please contact your local bookseller or the Macmillan Corporate and Premium Sales Department at 1-800-221-7945, extension 5442, or by email at MacmillanSpecialMarkets@macmillan.com.

First Minotaur Books Trade Paperback Edition: 2024

10 9 8 7 6 5 4 3 2 1

You've made an image of me, that's quite clear, a complete and final image, and there's an end of it. You just won't see me any other way. . . . Every image is a sin.

—MAX FRISCH, *I'm Not Stiller,*
a favorite book of Anne Morrow Lindbergh

Only in the sky is there hope, only in that which man has never touched.

—CHARLES LINDBERGH,
The Wartime Journals of Charles A. Lindbergh

In 1932, Charles Lindbergh and Anne Morrow Lindbergh were the most celebrated couple in America, famous throughout the world. On March 1, their twenty-month-old son was kidnapped. Two months later, he was found dead in woods not far from their home. A man was convicted and executed for the crime. But many believe there were others involved who were never identified or held accountable.

Chapter One

Englewood, New Jersey
February 1931

I can see the house. But not all of it and certainly not how you get there from here. It sprawls above us, main house, servants' quarters, garage, those who live there and those who serve their needs. As the car winds up the hill, you get glimpses through the skeletal winter trees that stand like witches' brooms. A window flashes. A stretch of white-painted brick. The dark gray point of a slate gable. All of a sudden, the sun finds its spot through the trees, catching my eye like a needle.

The car turns a corner and I have to look through the back window to keep the house in sight. It's like the start of a fairy tale, and I think of how I'd tell it.

Once upon a time, on a hill in the dark wood, was a house. And in that house lived a mummy and a daddy . . . and who else?

Me, the child would say.

Of course, you, otherwise how would there be a mummy and a daddy? You're the most important person in the story.

But who are you?

"The Morrows brought the living room and the library over from some pile in England."

I turn to meet the chauffeur's eye. He's seen me staring at the house. I feel caught.

"Did they." As if I couldn't care less.

We roll through a high iron gate, stopping to let the guard inspect us. He peers through the window of the little guard box, then raises a hand to the driver. We continue on the gravel path. I can see the whole house now. They call it an estate, but really, it's a chockablock sort of place, a few buildings set this way and that up against each other. Only three stories, it doesn't seem that grand, at least when you consider who lives there. A lot of windows. And funny little doors tucked here and there. How many open? How many are locked? So many ways in, you wonder if they worry.

I'm told it's new. But everything in this country is new.

I take a deep breath.

Colonel. Mrs. Lindbergh.

No, other way round. *Mrs. Lindbergh. Colonel.* Greet the mother first. People fawn over him all the time, she must be sick of it. Show her you know she's the one you have to please . . .

The fingers on my left hand are tingly; no surprise, I've been gripping my wrist the whole way here. I let go, shake out both hands. Wonder how it is the Lindberghs are living at her parents' house. Surely, they have all the money in the world . . .

We've stopped. Why? We're only halfway up the drive, nowhere near the house. And yet the chauffeur is out of the car, he's coming round to open the door. Hastily, I straighten myself, tugging at my gloves, the edge of my jacket, run the heel of my hand over my skirt.

I get out to see a woman standing at the door of a small stone cottage. She's in her mid-forties, wearing a smart suit, dark hair pulled back into a chignon. For a second, I brace myself, Dear Lord, it's *her.* But this woman is too old, the clothes too sensible, the gaze too frank in its assessment.

"Miss Gow?" she says.

"Yes?" I hate the question mark.

"Kathleen Sullivan. We spoke on the phone."

I remember: secretary to Elizabeth Morrow, the grandmother. Strange that the mother doesn't do the interviewing. But of course, she's up the hill. In the big white house. With the baby. It occurs to me: I may never get inside that house, may never get to meet him. This could well be as far as they let me go.

"They'll want to meet you, get to know you," Mary said when she told me she'd put me up for the job. The thing is, she's wrong. They don't. Knowing you, *really* knowing you, is the last thing they want. What they want to find out is: Can you be who we need you to be? Now, standing on the gravel path, I can tell the assessment has started. Am I Miss Gow? Probably. But who is Miss Gow? A name tells her nothing. I've sent a letter; how much of it is lies? The recommendations; are they honest? Have they told her everything she needs to know? Not likely. Everyone wants this job. But do I want it for the right reasons?

Should she let me in?

She waits so long, I think for a moment she's decided, *No,* actually. But then she stands back from the door and I say "Thank you" to the invitation that hasn't been made.

It's a nice office they've given Mrs. Sullivan. Pretty, with curtained windows and a lovely blue-and-white rug. It's snug, low ceilinged in the way of cottages. Her desk barely fits, and the two armchairs are so close they don't leave much room for your legs. I cross my ankles, look appreciatively around the room so I don't have to face her just yet.

She asks if the ride over from Tenafly was all right. I say yes, thank you.

Then add, "Thank you. For sending the car."

She smiles briefly; they'd send the car for anyone. It's not a mark of favor.

When she puts my letter on the desk, I feel a jolt of panic, certain I've made a mistake, spelled my own name wrong, written Sheboygan instead of Chicago. *You didn't give the Mosers' name, nor their telephone number*, I remind myself. *There's no way for her to know you ever worked for them, no way for her to get in touch.*

"I understand you come recommended by Mary Beattie."

Mary works as a maid for Elisabeth Morrow, the sister, but I can't imagine her recommendation greatly impresses Mrs. Sullivan. "Yes, we're good friends."

We're not, but it sounds better than saying I've met her a few times through my sister-in-law.

"We like to trust our people," she says. "How old are you?"

It's a simple question that covers a multitude of others, and I hesitate. "Twenty-six."

A slight raise of the eyebrow. *Some experience, not much for the number of years. Boyfriend? Fiancé?*

"And I have it right, it's *Miss* Gow?"

"It is."

She sifts through papers. My letter, the Gibbs reference, what else could she have about me? "How long have you been in America, Miss Gow?"

Precise, I think. Be elegant and precise. Recrossing my ankles, I say, "I arrived in April 1929."

"From Scotland?"

"That's right. Glasgow. My brother came first. He got me the position with the Gibbs family." No, "got me" is wrong. Sloppy. I should have said "secured." Engaged. *Through him, I was engaged by the Gibbs family . . .*

"And you worked for them . . ." She frowns as if she can't quite make out the dates. "For a year."

It's only the truth, I tell myself. No criticism implied. "Yes. Unfortunately they suffered in the financial crash and couldn't keep me on. I believe that's in their letter."

She doesn't say if it is or it isn't. "You were in Detroit for a time."

"Yes."

"What took you to that fine city?"

I don't know what devil is in the brain that makes you think of the very thing you shouldn't. The right answer, the correct answer, is there, ready to be given. I came up with it yesterday and rehearsed it in the car. Yet now, when it matters, the only voice I hear is myself screaming like a shrew: *You told me to come to America. You said come to Detroit.*

Mrs. Sullivan has noticed the pause, I can tell from the way she's holding the point of her pen to the paper. A moment's more hesitation and she'll scratch me right out.

"I was offered a position."

"You didn't stay long. Only five months."

There are two choices, two truths, both unpleasant. One admits failure as an employee, the other failure as a woman. At least a woman of intelligence. I don't know who Mrs. Sullivan has called, who she might have spoken to.

I may have to be truthful. A little.

"There was a gentleman I hoped to marry. I knew him from back home and . . ."

I shift slightly in my seat. "Let's say I won't be returning to Detroit. Fine city though it is."

Our eyes meet; I feel the question. *Is that all?* No complaints, recriminations? It's something they watch for. You complain about one thing, they think, *Whiner.* Admit you left a position after three weeks because the father thought he was entitled to put his hand down your blouse, they write, *Difficult.* If you get teary because you've had a shock, they write, *Emotional.*

I push the memories down, keep my face still.

She asks, "Is it fair to say you haven't had much experience working for this sort of family?"

"It is." The Mosers were well off. But I've been sure to not mention the Mosers, and I'm not going to now. "But I daresay very few people have."

She sets the pen down. Now I have her full attention; maybe even some respect.

"That is correct," she says. "Colonel and Mrs. Lindbergh are unlike any other couple in America. Her father is a senator. His father was a congressman. These are people not only of means, but distinction. You may have heard of his little flight to Paris. As a result, they and their child are the focus of unparalleled attention from the public and from the press. Anyone connected with them comes under intense scrutiny. That includes members of their staff. Are you prepared for that?"

"Yes."

"You may be offered money for stories or photographs, as much as two thousand dollars . . ."

This Mary warned me about, and I know what to say. "I'm familiar with the tabloid press, Mrs. Sullivan. I think it's disgusting, their lack of regard for people's privacy. I want no part of it." I let a touch of outrage slip into my tone that she would ask such a thing, think me such a person. She listens closely, trying to decide: Am I sincere?

Then she says, "You understand why I have to ask."

"Of course."

"The couple's schedule is irregular. They intend to travel. Extensively. You will be on your own with the baby for considerable stretches of time."

She waits for me to add objections, conditions. I smile. *No objections, Mrs. Sullivan. None whatever.*

She stands. "Well, then. I'll take you up to the house."

It's so abrupt, I'm not sure what's happening. Gathering my things, I ask, "What happens there?"

"You meet Colonel and Mrs. Lindbergh."

Chapter Two

So. Here is how you get to the house. You are driven by the chauffeur, who has been waiting this whole time. You ride in the company of Mrs. Sullivan, who makes pleasant conversation as she tries to find out more about you. You long to say, *Please, I need to think, could you be quiet?* Instead you smile as if this is all quite normal and say, "Yes, it is mild for February."

Mrs. Lindbergh, a pleasure to meet you.

Colonel, an honor, of course . . .

Mrs. Sullivan has said something. I haven't been listening, and it takes me a moment to translate the sounds. "It goes without saying, no autographs for your nephew or anything like that."

I say, "Of course not." Easily and honestly, because my niece in America is not even a year old and nobody else gives a damn. I suppose the Lindberghs do get asked a lot. Still, it's insulting.

But insulting is good, gives me a bit of spine, something of myself to hold on to as we get out of the car and Mrs. Sullivan goes up to the front door and rings the bell.

A butler in tailcoat answers the door. He's dark, tall, with a full, doleful mouth. Heavy-lidded eyes widen to take me in, then slide off in dismissal. The black hair looks like it's had some help from a bottle; there's a dash of powder to cover up those red, broken veins around the nose. Get close enough, I think, and you'd know what he drank for lunch.

Mother once said to me, *"Betty, when you get nervous, you get snippy."* I might say I see what I see and there's no use pretending otherwise. But she's not entirely wrong.

The butler's name is Septimus Banks, and Mrs. Sullivan asks if he would take me up to see the Colonel and Mrs. Lindbergh. In an accent not his own, he says, "If you would come this way," then gives me his back. I smile *thank you* to Mrs. Sullivan and follow, careful not to react because the house is much grander on the inside—not simply designed to impress, but to intimidate. When I was a child, they opened one of the local manors to the public and Mother took me as a treat. What I mostly remember was queuing and shying away from things as Mother whispered, "Don't touch." Easy not to touch here; the entry hall alone is larger than my mother's house. The walls are wood paneled, with two massive marble fireplaces on either side. Vases almost as tall as me and crowded with lilies, roses, and gardenias stand on mahogany pillars. The floor, pale red stone, makes my shoes look quite shabby. I feel my gaze pulled upward and see a vast crystal chandelier overhead.

We reach the second-floor landing. A lovely clock ticks on a side table. Above that, there's a portrait of a handsome steel-haired woman by a fireplace in a heavy gilt frame ten feet high. A gold-fringed runner of green vines and peonies extinguishes the sound of our footsteps. There are doors at either end of the hall, but Mr. Banks doesn't lead me toward either one.

"Please wait here."

He disappears through the door on the right. Now it's me and the lady in the painting. Who is she? I wonder. An actual member of the family or just some impressive stranger's portrait from that pile in England, thrown in with the library and living room furniture?

I hear footsteps below and look over the railing to see a maid carrying a bowl of flowers across the entryway below. She walks quickly, as if those flowers better get where they're going and fast. I lose sight of her as she passes under the balcony. A moment later, I hear a door close.

And . . . still, no one comes.

The chandelier looms near, the endless columns of crystal cascading like fireworks. An unseen disturbance—a rat in the attic, a gust of wind from an open window, a stomped foot in a far-off room—sends a shiver through the crystals, and there's a tinkling, so faint that by the time you've heard it, it's gone. Looking up at the stout chain that holds the massive light aloft, I imagine giving it a shove, watching it sway, come loose, tipping as it crashes to the stone floor below.

The impulse puzzles me; I'm not a destructive person. It's all those delicate crystals, hanging in space—a vision so beautiful, so precious and pristine, you can't help but think about breaking it.

I hear voices. On this floor and getting close. The door on the left opens. And there they are.

At first, they don't quite make sense. I compare them to the images I've seen and find something missing in the picture. Well, the plane, for a start. Always, in the newsreels they show it: the plane so simple it looks like a toy. And other people, the vast crowds surging like so many ants, breaking through barricades to surround him. Then him standing on the balcony, looking down on thousands of cheering faces and frantically waving arms. The next shot him alone with the plane, a long, gangly boy who's done the miraculous and now what?

Here there are no crowds, no celebration, no cheers. Just three people in a quiet hallway. But he's not ordinary. He hangs back, the ends of his arms in his pockets, bright golden head ducking. No aviator jodhpurs or khaki jacket, just a pleasant tweed suit. His smile is brief, nervous. But his eyes, hero blue, stay on you. For a moment, I'm caught by those eyes, then remember: *don't*.

She comes forward, hand outstretched. As I take it, I feel I am meeting an exceptionally poised twelve-year-old girl. When the news of their engagement was announced, some complained Anne Morrow wasn't pretty enough for the great Lindy. True, she's too small to be a great beauty. He's too tall, she too small. Yet they fit. She's got a funny nose, tilted and elfin. Her eyes are a gorgeous violet; you don't see that in the films. But it's her hair that's her glory, cut short and high off her pale forehead. Her smile as we shake is modest, as if to say of the house, *Yes, it's a lot, isn't it?*

Then taking back her hand, she laughs. "It's funny, I can't help feeling we look alike. Do you see it, Charles?"

"No."

I wait for the pleasantry. It does not come.

Then she says airily, "No, of course, you're taller and you haven't got my ridiculous nose."

She resets. "Miss Gow, so nice to meet you."

"A pleasure to meet you, Mrs. Lindbergh. Colonel."

He asks, "How many families with infants have you worked with in the past?"

Here? I think. Standing in the hallway? What about me told them I don't even merit a chair? Never mind. The interview has started and I better catch up. I recount my experience with the Gibbses and one family in Detroit. But I am off-balance, and I sound neither capable nor cherishing. Mrs. Lindbergh asks if I have siblings and I tell her, "Well, I'm the youngest of six, so . . ."

I expect disappointment; no little brothers or sisters looked after. But she says, "*Six.* Were you the darling of the family?"

Grateful, I say, "More the despair."

The conversation turns to habits. How much milk do I think best for baby? How much sleep? Should babies have lots of layers or be free to move? How much cuddling do I think is wise? Do I have a preferred method of potty training? I feel the colonel's interest sharpen and sense strong views. It's a minefield; one area of difference will be grounds for showing me the door.

I say, "Generally, I prefer to hear from the parents what they think best for their child and adopt that routine. It doesn't do to have the nurse and mother at odds."

Mrs. Lindbergh says shyly, "Well, I may be different from other mothers you've worked with. We follow the Watson method." I nod as if entirely familiar. "We want Charlie to be able to manage for himself, to feel confident. The Colonel and I"—she looks up at him—"believe self-sufficiency should be encouraged, rather than dependence. Too much cuddling and rushing to help fosters a needy attachment."

Does she believe it, or he does and she goes along? No matter. One and the same in this house.

I say, "That makes a great deal of sense," thinking, Of course this is how a man the world calls the Lone Eagle would raise a child. The Lindberghs take my words as agreement. And I let them.

"We're planning a trip to the Orient in summer," she tells me. "We'll be gone for a few months at least. Would you mind that, being left on your own with the baby?"

Her eyes are bright with excitement at the prospect of the trip. But something else as well. Anxiety. Her hands are clasped, the grip quite tight, and her voice too definitive: *I* am *doing this.* She's braced for judgment. From me, of all people.

It is strange to feel affection for someone you don't know, protective of someone who has so much. And yet I do.

"Not at all," I tell her. "That's my job, isn't it? To make sure you're able to do what you need to without worry?"

It's the right answer. She glances at him, hopeful. Turning back to me, she asks, "Do you need specific days off? Vacation requirements?"

"No. I only have my brother here, and I'm sure he's seen enough of me."

She laughs. For the first time, I consider the possibility I may get this job. A whirl of pleasurable images. Telling Billy. Writing mother. The news making its way back to Detroit. Let him feel regret. Let him feel . . .

Then I hear the Colonel say, "You speak English very well."

I smile to keep my jaw from falling. Can he even think it's a compliment? He senses my amazement and his mouth goes sullen, his neck red.

Laying a gentle hand on his arm, she says, "They speak English in Scotland, Charles."

She looks at me, knowing very well he's made the mistake. Even so it's my job to make it right.

"Aye, moost of the time," I say, and a round of laughter releases us.

He asks, "Do you like dogs?"

"I love dogs."

"Good."

My face is starting to ache, my teeth are clenched. *Is it good? Why good? Why dogs and not cats, Colonel? Do dogs speak English? Or do you not expect them to—dogs, immigrants, all the same . . .*

My mother's voice: *"Snippy, Betty."* Wiping the complaints from my mind, I ask, "Should I . . . see the baby now?"

There is the briefest pause.

"I'm afraid he's out with my mother," says Mrs. Lindbergh smoothly. He chimes in with, "She likes to walk him around the gardens."

"Of course."

After that it's "Thank you for coming by, Miss Gow" from them and a "Thank you for seeing me" from me. They stay at the top of the stairs while I make my way down to where the butler is waiting to show me out. The chauffeur is already waiting by the car. They have people to bring you in and people to take you out when they're done with you. Kathleen Sullivan is nowhere to be seen. Probably back in her office, interviewing the next candidate.

I shouldn't have asked to see the baby.

"So?"

A pair of eyes watching me in the rearview mirror. The same chauffeur, dark hair, snub nose, ruddy cheeks, and bright, curious eyes. That sharpness—sympathy or gossip?

I shake my head.

After a few miles, the second question comes. "Were you impressed at least?"

"By him? Not really." That gets a chuckle.

What went wrong? I'm sure it was all over my face what I thought when they were talking about independence and no cuddling, but honestly, it's a baby. How much can he do for himself?

When he complimented my English, I should have just said thank you. Asking to see the baby, that was bad, but showing what I thought of him, that was worse. My joke helped. But she saw my reaction, and it's not something she can allow, someone thinking less than the best of him. Even if it was his fault.

I rest my head on the window, see people on the street stop to stare at the limousine as it rolls through Tenafly's runty downtown.

The chauffeur says doubtfully, "You sure you want to be let out here?"

I nod to the Bergen Theatre, where they're showing *Little Caesar*. "Thought I might go to the movies."

"All right then." He stops the car at the corner, opens the door. I wonder, Can I stay, just a moment longer? But it's over and I know it. I get out of the car. With a touch of sarcasm, he tips his cap. "See you at the pictures, Beautiful."

"Well?"

My brother sits dark browed and challenging across the diner table. Hands flat on the surface, shoulders braced, he wants a full report: What have I gone and done now?

"Terrible," I tell him.

The glower gives way to concern. "It wasn't."

"They hated me." Suddenly, it seems funny. At any rate, that's how I'll tell it. *Charles Lindbergh? I met him once. He* hated *me.*

"They can't have hated you." He gestures with his coffee. "You ruined my life and I don't hate you."

Billy often says I ruined his life. He's eldest, I'm youngest, first and last. "There were five of us," he'll say. "Me, James, Alex, Agnes, and Isabelle. Then all of a sudden, this one comes along. *'She's an angel, did you ever see anything so precious. Pretty wee Bessie.'* Father's wee yin, spoiled rotten from day one."

Billy came to this country first. When I wrote to say I was coming, he said, "What's poor America done to deserve that?" Then he met the ship and let me stay with him, Jean, and the baby as long as I needed.

"You did get to meet the great man, at least."

"I did. He's nobody special."

"And knowing you, you said so. 'You, Colonel Lindbergh, are nobody special. Your offer of employment is rejected. You may take your Eaglet and stuff him.'"

It's meant to be funny. Is funny. Still. Billy's imitation of me—prideful, superior, *snippy*—is too sharp for comfort.

He reaches over, takes my hand. "Hey. Just one job."

"I know." I sniff, sit up straight. "I didn't really want it. But . . . would have been nice to have something go right."

I feel Billy's sympathy fade. He told me not to go to Detroit.

Anxious to be back in his good books, I say, "How's work at New Jersey what'd you call it?" Billy works as a lineman, doing electrical wiring, but I always pretend I can't remember.

"Steady and pays well, thank you."

"And my niece?"

"Izzy? She's fine. In fact, Jean and I were just saying, if only we could find a first-class baby minder. We thought we had an excellent candidate. Only the Lindberghs snapped her up."

"Oh, yes . . ."

"They're going to call, I promise."

I want to say, *Truly, the Lindberghs are not going to hire a girl who left school at fourteen, worked in a dress shop, and had five jobs as a nanny in two years. A girl who . . .*

Don't. Forget that.

"*Don't* write Mother," I tell Billy.

Solemn, he raises his hand: *I promise.* In this, we agree: from our mother, who worries, certain things must be kept secret.

"'Oh, but Bessie, the *crime* . . .'" I mimic her hand-wringing over America.

"'Billy, it's so *dirty*.'"

"'All those *gangsters!*'" we chorus, attracting the attention of the waitress.

Afterward, we walk. Billy offers his arm and I take it, resting my head against his shoulder. Looking up at the Bergen marquee, I say, "Maybe *I'll* be a gangster."

"You would," he says. Then: "Was he really not anything special?"

I wrinkle my nose. "Are you a fan?"

"Well . . ." Embarrassed, he looks down. "I do remember it. The flight. The fact he wasn't anybody and he did this incredible thing on sheer guts and brains. Made you feel . . . anything's possible. What *can't* we do?"

Feeling low again, I say, "Should've gotten you the autograph."

He kisses the top of my head. "They'll call."

"They won't." I stand tiptoe, kiss his cheek. "But thank you."

But Billy is right. The next morning, Kathleen Sullivan telephones and says, "Congratulations, Miss Gow. How soon would you be able to start?"

"Right away," I gasp.

We talk about salary—less than expected, but more than I've made in the past. I'm about to thank her again when she says, "Oh."

". . . Yes?"

"One more thing. Any flirtation with the man of the house will result not only in dismissal, but a bad report that will follow you to any family worth working for in America and Europe. Is that understood?"

I am stunned. Is there anything—anything—these people don't know?

Then I realize she doesn't know. It's what she'd say to any woman under forty.

"Of course."

Chapter Three

It's not clear where I'll be living. I am now part of the Lindbergh household, but they have no house of their own as yet, which is why they're living with her parents. They've not even been married two years and seem to have spent most of that time in the air. In a matter of months, they'll be flying off to the Orient. For now, I'm told to bring myself and my things to the Morrow estate and they'll find a room for me.

Life is a very different matter when you're no longer Betty Nobody but the Lindbergh Nanny. Now the bright-eyed chauffeur greets me as Miss Gow as he opens the door to the car. He says his name is Ellerson, and I should call him that because everyone does.

"Told you," he says cheerfully.

"You didn't. You said, *'See you at the pictures.'*"

"This isn't the pictures?" From the mirror, he grins, knowing to me a limousine is just as glamorous. "Anyway, I knew it was going to be you."

"Well, I didn't," I say, stretching out. "I was so nervous. I've never been around people like that."

"Sure, that's what they liked about you."

This time, we barely stop at the gate; just a wave to the guard and go straight up the hill. As Ellerson brings the car around the back of the house, I see a man digging by the hedge at the far end of the garden. It's hard work, he jabs at the earth, pitching the dirt aside. He's wearing an olive-green sweater, and it takes me a moment to place him as Mr. Banks, the butler with the powdered cheeks and withering look. February's a strange time to be planting—and a butler makes a strange gardener—but before I can ask about it, I'm greeted at the back door by Kathleen Sullivan.

"Let's get you settled in," she says as I get out. "Ellerson, take Miss Gow's suitcases to the second floor."

"Junior's old room?" he asks and she nods.

"Junior?" I'm unsure if she means the baby or someone else.

"Mrs. Lindbergh's younger brother. He's away at college. Let's start with the laundry room. You'll be spending a fair amount of time there."

Following, I feel someone's missing. "Will Mrs. Lindbergh be joining us?"

She looks over her shoulder. "I did say you should learn not to expect them."

In the laundry room, Mrs. Sullivan shows me the soap used to launder the baby's diapers, where his pram is kept, and how to dress him for outdoors. In the kitchen, she shows me how to wash his dishes properly, and I am introduced to the family dog, a black terrier named Peter. I give him a pat and notice there are two dog bowls on the floor, two leashes on a peg. I'm about to ask about the other dog, when she says briskly, "Shall we meet the baby?"

"Yes, please."

As we head upstairs to the nursery, she tells me in a low voice that he naps at midday. Bedtime is 7:00 P.M., but he is to be woken up and set on the potty at ten o'clock. Between the hours of seven and ten, he is to be left strictly alone.

"What if he cries?" I ask.

"Then he cries."

It's silly, I tell myself, to be so nervous over meeting a baby. But some take to you right away, some don't, and some never do. It's a test, this first meeting. No one will say so, but it is. If young Master Lindbergh fusses, goes rigid when I pick him up, if I look upset or unsure of myself . . .

With a careful twist, Mrs. Sullivan turns the doorknob and lets me into a large, airy room filled with sunlight. Light white curtains billow by the open windows. I hear "hello" and take in an older woman standing by a handsome crib. From the silver hair and the pearls around her neck, I know this is Mrs. Morrow, lady of the house, senator's wife, grandmother. In person, she's more approachable than her portrait; her face is broad and plain and there's a ruddiness to her cheeks that hints of outdoor life rather than soft conversation in parlors and universities. I'm told she's a poet, a scholar of some kind, but she seems more forthright than her shy, ardent daughter. Right away, she extends her hand, gives mine a good shake.

The baby is sitting in the center of a blue oval rug, dressed in a white romper. Scattered around him are wooden blocks with letters on them and a dog on wheels with leather ears and a pull string. Arms in the air, he's crowing and growling to himself, making his plans. He's about the size of a bed pillow, and soft like one, a little bundle.

Maybe it's his smallness, the way he's all alone on that rug, everyone standing at a distance in this large room. Or maybe it's his noises, the pleasure he takes in the world of toys around him. I immediately want to catch him up and hold him close.

"Isn't he a lamb," I breathe.

Mrs. Morrow smiles. "That's what my daughter calls him. 'My fat lamb.' It's the curls." His hair is baby blond, almost white, like soap bubbles all over his head.

I kneel at the edge of the rug. Charlie notices and goes still; he doesn't like it. So, I move back. His feet are bare; I notice the toes on his right foot overlap. *What, not completely perfect? Well, me neither, so we've got that in common.*

I think of starting with *This little piggy* but decide best not until he's more comfortable with me. At the moment, his chief concern seems to be getting hold of a block that's out of reach. He reaches out a chubby hand, bending forward slightly, frustrated there's so much space between him and that block. I pick it up and hold it out to him. For a long moment, he stares at me, then puts his fingers alongside mine. When he starts to pull, I hold on to see what he'll do. When he frowns, I let it drift toward him till his brow clears. Then I gently pull it back, making it tug-of-war, back and forth between us. Finally, he gets the block, and I get a big scrunchy grin.

We make a tower with the blocks. We knock it down. We make another tower. We knock that one down too, laughing as the blocks scatter across the floor. Charlie and I become a we very fast.

I ask Charlie if he will show me his favorite parts of his grand-mother's garden. Mrs. Morrow thinks it's an excellent idea. I can feel her watching me as I dress him for outside. I do it quickly, giving him no time to fuss. He's not happy that he can't move his arms freely in all the layers and his face crumples. I lift him up high and ask which doggy shall we take for a walk? Peter doggy or wooden doggy? Which one, hey? He grins, puts a finger in his mouth.

After our walk, Mrs. Morrow takes Charlie and Kathleen Sullivan shows me my room, which is connected to the nursery by a small bath-room. This is "Junior's" room and it's very much a boy's space, with a navy bedspread, a ship in a bottle, and pennants on the walls with names like Groton and Amherst. An old teddy bear with one eye sits in a rock-ing chair. My suitcases have been left by the edge of the bed.

I go to the window and pull aside the curtain. From here, you can get a sense of how large the estate is. Mrs. Sullivan points out a building in the distance, tells me it is a school started by Mrs. Lind-bergh's sister, Elisabeth. The family hopes Charlie will go there next fall. Looking down, I see the long hedge, the spot where the butler was digging. One part of the earth is turned over, the dirt patted down, a patch of dark brown amid the sparse winter green.

It's a grave, I realize. And remember the extra leash.

. . .

Before leaving, Mrs. Sullivan tells me that the staff takes their meals in the kitchen. I may eat at six or eight; any other time, I must fend for myself and it's not wise to do so without making friends with the cook. I say I understand. After putting Charlie to bed, I go down to the kitchen to find Ellerson settling at the table with a plate of beef stew. "Ah," he says grandly to the cook, "a place for my friend, Mrs. Hobie." Nice to be called friend, I think. Then I realize it's a joke; I'm to serve myself.

As I sit down, Banks strides through the swinging door, followed by a gawky, dark-haired English girl, who seems to think she's playing the part of a maid in a comedy. As they take up the dessert courses of the Morrows' dinner, he is terse, precise, knows what he's doing. But she giggles, is none too careful with the plates, and drops the silverware. When he corrects her, she rolls her eyes and says, "Sorry *m'lud.*" She winks at me, wanting to share the joke. I pretend not to catch it.

Then as Banks turns toward the swinging door, I'm astonished to see her fling back her hand and give him a great whack on the bottom. Banks stops dead still, fixes her with a killing look. There's a terrible silence. Then she backs up meekly with a small "Sorry, Mr. Banks."

When they've gone, I look to Ellerson. His shoulders are shaking as he laughs silently. I mouth, *What?*

"Septimus Banks and Violet Sharpe—it's a long, grim story for a winter's night."

Grim. I look to the bowls on the floor. "What happened to the other dog?" When he doesn't answer right away, I know it's not the usual story with pets.

He says, "You know how Sullivan warns you about the newspapers trying to get to Lindbergh?" I nod. "Well, it's not only them. Sightseers come to the house, wanting a glimpse or an autograph. 'You're my boy's hero'—that kind of thing. Mostly, they're a nuisance. Some of them, you have to watch out for."

I remember Banks digging and go cold. "How so?"

THE LINDBERGH NANNY   [23]

"Last week, the family was out. A car full of gawkers drives at top speed up the hill to the house. Miss Constance's dog Daffin was out in the yard, and . . ."

"Oh, no."

Ellerson nods. "Left him to die howling."

I look to Peter, who's sitting by my chair, hoping for food. *Poor fellow, you lost your friend.* I reach down to scratch his ears. "Constance is the youngest sister?" Back at his stew, he nods. "And Miss Elisabeth is the one that has the school?"

His eyebrows jump. "With her great 'friend' Connie Chilton."

That, I don't understand, but Ellerson doesn't explain. "And the brother? Young Master Dwight?"

Ellerson takes a moment, then mouths something that looks like *nuthouse.* Startled, I pick at my food, thinking of gates and dogs and thoughtless nosy bodies—and my own nosiness. Not even here a day, and I'm whispering about the family in their own kitchen.

Guilty, I say, "It is awful, when you think about it, how people act as if they're *things* to gawp at."

Ellerson shrugs, unimpressed by my piety. I ask, "Do you like working here?"

"Beats starving. How about you? Where you from?"

"Oh, over the pond," I tell him. "Here and there."

"And now you're just thrilled to *bits* to be working for Lucky Lindy."

"Well . . . beats starving." We smile over our stew. On that small intimacy, I risk the question. "What did you mean, that was what they liked about me?"

"When they told you the salary, was it what you expected?"

"Not exactly, but . . ."

"Days off, vacation time, what'd you ask for?"

Sheepish, I say, "I wanted the job."

He nods and repeats, "Some people, you have to watch out for."

After dinner, I sit on Dwight Junior's bed, listening for the baby and praying he doesn't cry. It would be just my luck to crack and go in when

I'm not supposed to, only to have the Lindberghs crash through the door, him blue eyes blazing. *Aha! We knew you wouldn't follow the rules!* Dwight Junior's book collection isn't much help. He's got *The Wonderful Wizard of Oz* and *Myths and Legends of the American Indian.* You can tell he's read them; the spines are cracked and creased, covers worn at the edges. But a life of J. P. Morgan and an encyclopedia of Western civilization are in pristine condition, untouched. After reading a page of each, I can see why.

Gazing around the room, I think, This boy in a nuthouse. All this and yet . . .

Finally, I hear the clocks sound ten and creep through the bathroom into Charlie's darkened room. Babies are never fully silent when sleeping. They shuffle and snuffle, and Charlie's no exception. He complains when I lift him up, tries to curl into me like I'm his blanket.

I take off his nappy and set him on the small wooden chair that's his potty. He struggles and whimpers at the separation from me, the sudden chill, and I say, "I know, Charlie, I'm sorry." According to Kathleen Sullivan, he doesn't even have to do business. This is to make sure he sleeps until morning. I keep him there for a good two minutes until he starts getting really frustrated. Then I pin up his nappy and croon into his ear, "All right, you've had enough. Back to bed now . . ."

Of course, he can't fall asleep right away, so I stay with him, hand on his back, singing in a low voice. Gradually, he gets less fretful, stays quiet longer. The breathing becomes slow and easy. Then the little jerk of the body that tells you they're deep out.

I let my fingers slip down the fuzzy nubbled fabric of his sleep suit to the silky folds of his neck, damp from the earlier struggles. Then I dabble a moment in those curls, following the swoops and whorls with my fingertip. I can just see them in the dark, white and shining. The endearment comes to me.

Lamb.

Chapter Four

Princeton, New Jersey

A month later, we move to a new house. It's only temporary. The Lindberghs are building a house of their own not far from here in a place called Hopewell. This place is ... well, it was originally a farmhouse, and it wasn't much better when we arrived. No rugs and not much furniture; Mrs. Lindbergh has written to the Colonel's mother to see if she has some to spare. The barn smells of cow and there's chicken mess on the floor. As a boy, the Colonel worked on his family's farm and the roughness of it suits him down to the ground— far better than the grandeur of the Englewood estate with its gates and guards and endless guests. Here he tramps through the woods for hours, coming back with newfound eggs. We're surrounded by open field; some days, you hear the thrum of engine overhead as the Colonel and Mrs. Lindbergh go flying in a blue-winged biplane. Of course if he's happy, she is. "My own house!" Mrs. Lindbergh says several times a day.

"Will there be chickens in Hopewell?" I asked her. Because to be honest, this isn't quite what I expected working for the Lindberghs. She laughed and said, "Maybe!"

I half imagined the Colonel would be getting in a plane every morning, flying off somewhere. Instead, he drives to work like most men in this country. Some days he works for Transcontinental & Western Air. Other days he works at the Rockefeller Institute.

"What does he do there?" I ask Mrs. Lindbergh. "Is it planes or . . . ?"

"No," she says, pleased and proud. "He's working with Dr. Alexis Carrel, who won the Nobel Prize. My sister Elisabeth has a weak heart. The Colonel says the heart is the body's engine, and he doesn't see why you shouldn't be able to replace a valve or even the entire heart if need be. So he's trying to build a pump that would allow you to take the heart out, fix it, and put it back in, good as new. It would be marvelous, wouldn't it? Any time a part was imperfect or wore out, you could simply replace it."

"My," seems the only possible answer.

The Lindberghs hire a middle-aged couple from England, Elsie and Olly Whateley. Elsie does the cooking, Olly the driving and odd jobs. He spends his days following the Colonel around the house and grounds. The Colonel is a man for lists. Long arm waving this way and that, he spots endless points for improvement. He calls them out to Whateley, who stands, hunched over a small notebook, hurrying to write it all down. He doesn't seem terribly handy. Once when he'd bent a dozen nails trying to fix a broken plank in the barn, I carefully asked Elsie where they'd worked before and in a lovely Brummie accent, she said, "Us? We've worked all over. Mr. Whateley was in jewelry for twenty years, had his own shop. Then he worked for my brother-in-law for a little while. Then we came here and . . . oh, we've done all sorts of things."

She smiled: *Rackety but honest, that's us.* I laughed, feeling it was a nice change from the pretentious snobberies of Kathleen Sullivan and Septimus Banks.

She said, "Most families don't want you taking the same time off. Well, how's that supposed to work for a married couple? So when the agency said, the Lindberghs need a pair of caretakers, we said, 'As long as we can take our holiday together, that'd be lovely.'"

Then looking at her husband pounding away at another nail, she said, "Mind you, given Mr. Whateley's carpentry skills, there may not be a house to care for much longer."

It's difficult, what you hear inside a house not your own. Eight rooms. Six people. Narrow hallways, plaster walls, shallow wooden doors; even whispers can be heard. Certainly tears. A scrap of complaint, a spiteful laugh. The ecstatic whine of sex. You know you oughtn't, and yet you can't help it; the ear pricks at the sound of secrets. The sudden snarl of raised voices—*This, this is what I really think of you.* Guilty, you linger, wanting just that bit more of people as they really are.

"If he comes at me one more time with one of those lists of his . . ."

"Can't bear it here, honestly."

"Doesn't know what she's doing, that much is clear."

"For God's sake, are you trying to fail?"

"I am trying, Charles. I don't know how much harder I can try . . ."

And in the morning, it's "Good morning, Betty" and "Whateley, I need you to go into town." "Of course, Mrs. Lindbergh." "Certainly, Colonel."

Still, the six of us find our way. Sometimes I think of us as three and three—family and staff. Other times, I see us as three pairs: the Lindberghs, the Whateleys, and me and Charlie, I suppose.

Dear Mother,

Thank you for your lovely long letter. I am sorry my news of Billy, Jean, and the baby has been so scant of late. I haven't been able to visit, as the Lindberghs are preparing for a trip to the Orient and when they are not at the airfield, they are studying maps and Morse code. (I know you have doubts, but Colonel Lindbergh says there is no reason women cannot pilot a plane as well as a man.) Each may only take eighteen pounds of personal items, including shoes. The other day, he borrowed the baby's scale to weigh a shotgun and bullets. The weight of everything must equal its "value in usefulness." The baby of course will stay here . . .

From downstairs, I hear the doorbell. The Lindberghs are out, but one of the Whateleys can answer it. This letter must go in the mail today. When she last wrote, Mother all but said she'd had a breakdown, she'd heard so little from me, *clearly* something dreadful had happened.

The Lindberghs have hired a nice couple. She is Elsie and so lovely. He is Olly . . .

The bell rings again. I listen, but there's no thud on the stairs or creak of a door to indicate someone's on their way. I feel the nudge of duty, but Charlie's having his nap and this is my only time to myself.

He is Olly and is partial to pipes, cricket, and reading the newspaper . . .

Dear *God,* they're ringing again. Pulling the bedroom door open, I listen in the hallway. No jolly humming from Whateley, no reminder murmurs—"Low on potatoes"—from Elsie. Did they go out and not tell me?

When the bell rings a fourth time, I launch myself down the stairs to the front foyer. Through the window, I see a middle-aged woman, purse held in front of her, gazing up at the house.

I open the door. "I'm terribly sorry."

She accepts the apology with a smile. "I'm sorry to be a bother . . ."

"No, not at all."

"But I'm here to see the baby."

The baby. There's been no call from Englewood to say anyone was coming. I search my memory for mention of an appointment. A special nurse or tutor. I try to take her in, looking for clues, a medical pin on the lapel, a badge of some kind. She is stout through the middle, motherly double chin. Gray-brown curls under a handsome blue straw cloche. Sensible shoes, a few scuffs, and the purse has seen better days, but that's true for most people.

It occurs to me that what she looks like is a baby nurse. Have I been . . . replaced?

"The baby," she reminds me, pleasant, but imperious.

I feel foolish for barring the entrance. Nevertheless I say, "I'm sorry. May I have your name?"

"Mrs. Dorothy Lewes."

Dorothy Lewes, Mrs. Lewes. I sift my recollections of my talks with Mrs. Lindbergh, find no memory of a Mrs. Lewes.

I stall. "The Colonel and Mrs. Lindbergh are out, and they didn't leave word . . ."

A slight frown. "I really do have to see the baby."

And yet, you're not saying why. The oddness of her starts to come clear. Why didn't she give her name right away? Or her credentials? And the way she started with needing to see the baby . . .

Her lips go thin across her teeth. She steps forward. I hold the door partially shut, fill the space with my body. I feel a prickle at my neck. Even in America, women don't try to push their way inside someone's home.

Struggling to keep my voice low and authoritative, I say, "You can't just come in, I'm afraid."

Hand tight on the doorjamb, I wait, pray possibly, for the expected, the normal. *Young lady, do you know who I am?* But the silence has gone on too long; she has no answer for me. She fidgets, craning her neck to see over my shoulder. She's looking for a way in, I realize.

When I see her shoulders rise, a shaft of terror goes right through me: She's crazy. I barely have time to brace before she throws herself at the door, shouting, "I have to see the baby! You must let me see him."

Legs spread, feet planted, I cling to the knob and doorjamb as she puts her full weight against the door. I manage to give it a hard shove, and she stumbles back.

But before I can slam the door shut, she launches herself again; fist and purse fly at my head. I am not a person anymore, just a thing to get out of the way. The heel of her hand slams against my cheek—in the madness, a moment of astonishment: She's actually *punched* me. With rage of my own, I kick at her, screaming, "Mr. Whateley! Mr. Whateley!" Waking poor Charlie, who wails.

For the briefest moment, she goes still, all anger gone, her whole being focused on that cry. Now, I think, *Push the door shut, crush her arm if you have to* . . .

I feel myself pushed aside from behind and hear a curse from Mr. Whateley as the woman tries to barge past. She gets only a few feet before he gets her by the arms. For a moment, the two of them spin in the foyer, him clinging on, her red in the face, hat off her head, hair wild as she screams, "I have to see him! I need to . . ."

Pulling one arm behind her, Whateley gets a hold around her neck, jerking her backward. He barks at me, "Call the police."

I move, then freeze. The phone, where is it? Is there one on the first floor . . . ?

"In the library, go!"

I race to the library, knocking the phone over because I can't stop in time. Righting it, I dial. But wrong number. Hang up. Try again. My hands are shaking. Through the open door, I can see Whateley's got the woman down on the floor, his knee heavy on her back. She thrashes, howls, desperate to throw him off. Then all of a sudden, she goes limp. And weeps.

"Yes, police? It's the Lindbergh house . . ."

Her name really is Dorothy Lewes. She is a wife and mother of three—or was. Her husband had a degree in chemistry, but he lost his job and could not find another. For a long time, he simply sat in their kitchen. Then one day he walked out and didn't return. Whether he ran off or the river took him, it's not known.

She took a job at a Woolworth's. But the pay wasn't much, and they had to move to a neighborhood where they didn't pick up the garbage. Rats invaded the building. One of her children died of tuberculosis. The two others were boarded out. Three weeks ago, she received word her boy was sick. She took a day off work to visit him and lost her job. The police think she came here hoping for money. I don't think that's what she wanted. But no one's asked me.

"How did she get in?" the Colonel asks.

We have been gathered in the parlor, the Whateleys and I standing in a row facing Colonel Lindbergh, who paces before us. His anger is red hot, twitchy, like a glowing poker; you know if it lands on you it will be agony. Mrs. Lindbergh sits on the sofa behind him.

I glance at Olly Whateley; would he like to speak up?

"Miss Gow opened the door to her," he tells the Lindberghs, his voice quick and blaming.

Colonel Lindbergh asks him, "But why did *Betty* open the door?"

Whateley mouths something like, *I really couldn't say, sir,* but the Colonel interrupts with, "Where were you?"

"I . . ." Whateley's face goes red. Embarrassment and anger both. He doesn't like being ticked off by a young American, no matter how famous he is. Elsie looks up at him, her mouth tight with anxiety, willing him to answer the Colonel, and have a *good* answer. Seeing her desperate, him stammering, I'm put in mind of an old music hall team that's seen better days. And I remember that were it not for Whateley, Dorothy Lewes might have made it up the stairs.

I say, "It was Mr. Whateley who stopped her going to the nursery. She was out of her head, I'm not sure I could have stopped her."

I look to Mrs. Lindbergh. "I'm so sorry. I never thought—she was a woman, nicely dressed. She seemed harmless."

"But she wasn't," says Colonel Lindbergh.

"No, sir."

"Charles, I think they understand now," says Mrs. Lindbergh quietly.

He looks at each of us in turn; do we? We nod, frightened and haphazard.

"One of the things Mrs. Lindbergh and I appreciate is that you all come from societies that are less expedient, less degraded. Because of that, it may take some time for you to understand that Americans are a primitive people. We are not a mature country. We lack discipline, have no strong sense of shared purpose or identity. Many people here simply . . . *want* without respect for others. Some of them are sick, like Mrs. Lewes." He looks at a newspaper on a side table. "Others are greedy. They seem like ordinary people because they are ordinary. Ordinary doesn't mean they're incapable of harm."

"Trust no one, sir," says Whateley. "The missus and I understand."

He's drawn a line—the missus and I. The weight of expectation shifts to me. It's been decided this was my fault. The searing rage has passed, but the Colonel wants to hear me admit guilt. Half an hour ago, I would have happily taken the blame, but I resent it being pushed on to me by Olly Whateley. And, if I'm honest, I resent the Colonel's demand that I grovel.

From the sofa, Mrs. Lindbergh is watching. Waiting.

I say, ". . . Of course."

It sounds wrong even to my ears. Petulant. And I've left off the "sir." I need to say something more. But the words crowd up at the back of my throat and will not come.

Suddenly Mrs. Lindbergh asks, "How is your cheek, Betty?"

She comes over as if to take a look for herself. Reaching up to shift my hair with deft fingers, she examines the bruise left by Dorothy Lewes's fist, then says, "No, I don't think she did any real damage, but blows to the head have to be taken seriously. Don't they, Charles?"

So graceful, so lightly done, this transformation of me from disgrace to heroine. I marvel at Anne Lindbergh, who seems to me in that moment truly finer, better than any of us. Her husband often talks of breeding, what science teaches us about genetics, strains, and livestock, as if people are just bits and bobs to be assembled correctly. Well, here's superior breeding for you. I smile slightly to show I appreciate what she's done, and she smiles back.

Chapter Five

Charlie has a basket made of straw and as it gets warmer, he takes his naps on the front lawn, shade and sunlight moving over him as the wind blows through the trees. The first time he slept on the grass, I set down a blanket beside him, thinking I'd read a book or do some mending. But the Colonel said, "You don't need to, Betty. He's fine on his own."

Remembering Dorothy Lewes, I said, "I don't mind, it's so lovely . . ."

"He's fine on his own," the Colonel repeated. "We're far from the main road, pretty hard to find."

And yet, she found us, I think. But this, apparently, is the Watson method Mrs. Lindbergh spoke of. Hard rules, few cuddles, leave the child to fend for himself, so when he enters "the real world," he'll be tough and self-sufficient.

But Charlie's barely walking yet, so at first, I stayed on the porch or by the window at least. But Colonel Lindbergh always noticed. I should take a rest myself, he said, write to my family, do something pleasant. And I did, but always by a window that looked out onto Charlie.

Catching me one day, the Colonel whispered, "He's perfectly safe. I promise."

Mrs. Lindbergh told me the same, adding, "How is Charlie to be a man in the world if he thinks he needs his beloved Betty watching over him at all times?" A reminder that they were the parents and I had promised to follow their rules.

Also, I know it bothers her sometimes, that Charlie calls for me more often than her. He's started saying "Beddy" and even "Gow"— which I tell her is really "cow." He's not got "mummy" or "daddy" yet.

And so I try. It is easier if I stay in my room, which is at the back of the house and has no windows that look over the front lawn. I start *The Good Earth,* which Mrs. Lindbergh admires. Maybe it's the sun, but the book makes me sleepy. I put my head down on the pillow, thinking I'll just close my eyes. The alarm is set, and I always hear Charlie if he cries anyway.

When the alarm goes, I am startled to realize I actually fell asleep. *Oh, dear, not a rave review for you, Mrs. Buck,* I think as I pull on my shoes. I hurry down the stairs, waving to Elsie, who is bringing the sheets in from the line. The Lindberghs' dogs, Skean the Scotty and terrier Wahgoosh, skitter up to me, sensing open doors and outside. The nap has me feeling fresh, happy at the thought of Charlie awake and stomp-crawling across the lawn. He, the dogs, and I will have a good long round of fetch.

"Now, no jumping on him," I tell the dogs, as I let them out. "Let our little man wake up first." Skean is a puppy; last week he scrambled into the basket and scratched poor Charlie. Best not trust him, I decide, picking him up and giving him a kiss between the ears. Wahgoosh runs ahead, barking. He, I know, will stop right by the basket, sniffing, circling around . . .

Gone. That's how I first understand it, the basket is simply not there. Bewildered, I stare out at the expanse of lawn, surrounded by waving trees, no dot of yellow and white to be seen anywhere. For a moment, I wonder, Am I still asleep? It has the feel of a dream.

It seems important to maintain cheer, so I say to the dogs, "All right, men, let's find Mrs. Lindbergh. I'm sure she can tell us where the baby is."

The dogs follow me to the porch but prefer to stay outside. At least I think they do, I'm hurrying, only vaguely aware I don't hear them once I get through the front door. Afternoon, Mrs. Lindbergh will be in her bedroom, practicing signals in Morse code on a buzzer; when they fly, she's not only the copilot, but the navigator and radio operator. She won't like being disturbed, I realize, maybe I should have gone to Elsie. The sheets, is it possible she mistook the basket for the laundry . . .

At any rate, I'm here now. I knock. There is the briefest pause, then I hear, "Yes?"

Opening the door—slow, careful, no panic—I say, "Mrs. Lindbergh, I'm so sorry to bother you. I was wondering, do you have the baby?"

She cocks her head, puzzled. It is absurd, actually; this is her practice time, why on earth would she have the baby?

"Only his basket's not in the yard."

That gets a quizzical look. Limbs stiff from sitting so long, she lifts herself out of the chair. "Well, he can't have gone far."

We go together to look again at the front yard. Then both sides of the house and the backyard. At one point, as we make our way around the perimeter, she says, "Maybe Mr. Whateley was working in the yard and had to move him."

"I wondered if *Mrs*. Whateley . . ."

"Did you ask her?"

"I didn't."

"Oh, go and ask her." We are smiling now. The emptiness around the house feels far less ominous. This entire dilemma has been caused by my rushing to Mrs. Lindbergh. It is, in fact, no dilemma at all.

"I feel so silly to have worried you," I say, moving back toward the house.

She waves an arm, forgiving me and urging me to go to Mrs. Whateley. Meanwhile, she continues her journey toward the high uncut grass in the back.

I find Elsie in the kitchen, where she is chopping turnips. Slightly out of breath, I ask, "You didn't move the baby's basket, did you?"

She stares at me and my stomach drops. "No, no, I didn't." Her voice is fearful; she has not forgotten Dorothy Lewes. "Is he not where he's supposed to be?"

"He is not," I say, trying like Mrs. Lindbergh to sound chipper.

"Oh . . ." She glances fretfully around the kitchen. "Perhaps we should ask Mr. Whateley. He's in the garage."

"I'll do that."

The garage, I think as I circle round the back of the house. Once when there was a light rain, we moved Charlie into the garage until it passed. I glance up. Sky's blue, but maybe Mr. Whateley felt the weather in his joints. Older people do sometimes.

The door to the car is open. I see Mr. Whateley's legs hanging from the back seat; he is cleaning. The Lindberghs are often muddy when they come back from the airfield. It seems polite to wait until he's emerged and I do . . . for all of a minute, at which point I start to feel he knows perfectly well I'm here and he's just making me wait because he thinks *I'm not going to be rushed in my job because of some brainless chit.*

"Mr. Whateley, I do apologize. But have you seen the baby?"

He scrambles out of the car. "What do you mean? You're his nurse."

"He was having his nap," I say evenly. "Someone has moved the basket from the front lawn. I understand: you didn't do it, and you haven't seen him. Thank you."

"Well, you'll have to search the backyard. The nursery, the barn . . ."

He ticks these jobs off on his fingers. I am already tense and his overbearing suggestions make me testy. My mother's phrase comes to mind: Knows the price of tea in China, but not how to make a cup himself. Ruddy English know-it-all. "Yes, Mrs. Lindbergh and I are looking for him together. Thank you, Mr. Whateley."

The nursery, I think as I head back into the house. The most obvious place for someone to have put Charlie. Right next to my room and I never even looked. Certain—thrilled—that this will be over when I open the door and find Charlie in his crib, I race up the stairs. Only to find Mrs. Lindbergh sitting at the edge of his rocking chair, hands clasped and thinking hard. She had the same hope. The same disappointment.

"It doesn't make sense," I whisper.

She stands. "We'll look in every room. You take upstairs, I'll take down."

The Colonel's study is downstairs. "Maybe the Colonel has him?"

"That will be my very first question."

I can't help it. I half follow her and listen from the stairs. I hear a knock. Then the Colonel says, "Yes?" A creak and Mrs. Lindbergh's light, carefree voice, "Charles, by any chance, do you have the baby?"

When I hear, "No . . ." I retreat back up the stairs.

My bedroom. The nursery again. Both bathrooms, pulling aside the shower curtains in each. As the possibilities dwindle, fear chokes harder. As does the stubborn sense that this cannot be happening. There was no sound of a car, no one approaching. I hold firm to this for a moment. No one has come to the house—in that one fact lies Charlie's safety. Then I remember: I was fast asleep. A car could have come and I not heard it. But someone else would have heard it, surely.

"You're his nurse."

I am at the Whateleys' room. I already know, Charlie won't be in here. Elsie would never and much as Olly Whateley irritates me, he's not a man to grab a child and hide him away. Even so, I don't just look from the door. I step inside and have a good look around. It's a small room, but light and airy. There's a wedding photo in a heavy frame on the bedside table. Beside it, a photograph of Whateley, with more hair on his head, solemn and upright in front of a shop, Whateley and Smith. Silver-backed brushes in the drawer. In the closet, Elsie's work dresses and his stout wool suits and a pair of brogans. There's a whiff of tobacco in the clothes. All heavy, old-fashioned things. The thought, Sad, really, comes to me, but I brush it off.

There's only one room left, and that's the Lindberghs' bedroom. Mrs. Lindbergh did say, *"You take upstairs."* In her agitation, did she realize that meant me going into her and the Colonel's room? I put my hand on the doorknob but fail to turn it. Then imagining the Colonel's fierce bark, *"What do you mean you didn't look in our room? Do you want to find him or not?"* I decide this must be a thorough search. I give the knob a wrench and step inside. In the calm, sunny bedroom, tidied by Elsie only a few hours before, Charlie is nowhere to be seen.

And yet, I feel him. Unsure what sense is telling me he's here, I make my way to the master bathroom, hand outstretched as if it were dark. No wicker basket, white blanket, or curly towhead in the cold tile and porcelain. Turning back into the bedroom, I wander carefully around the bed, feeling with my shoe along the underside.

Then I hear it. The rustle snuffle of a baby rolling over. It's muffled, low down. I look to the floor for places that might cover a baby. Large chair, under the bed, closet . . .

As I pull the closet door open, the sudden burst of sunlight breaks Charlie's sleep. Still in his basket, he tucks in on himself before stumbling to sitting. With his whimper, I hear footsteps thudding up the stairs. Weak with gratitude, I call, "Found him!"

Both Lindberghs are at the door. She slumps against the doorjamb, sighing, "What on earth . . ."

He's smiling.

Not a relieved smile. Not a confused one either. In fact, it's not so much a smile as a . . . smirk. He tries to hide it with his hand. But his eyes are gleeful. After a moment, he bursts out laughing.

"Colonel Lindbergh?"

"I told you he would be fine."

On the floor, Charlie is crying. He's not fine. I want to scream it in Lindbergh's smug face: *He's not fine. He's not fine and I can't pick him up because you think it's good for him to feel no one will come for him if he's frightened or hurt. Because . . . why? Why should anyone feel like that?*

Even she, I can see, is unsettled. "Charles . . ."

"It was a joke!"

A joke. To have us tearing around the house, terrified out of our minds, thinking something awful had happened to his son. Staring at him, I try to put it together in my head: this brave, exceptional man, this *hero*, giggling like a nasty boy when his prank ends up with someone crying or bloodied. Insisting it was a joke when the tears and blood were the aim all along.

Lost in my own rage, I barely hear her say, "Well, it was a very unfunny joke."

Seeing the disapproval on her face, he bursts out laughing again. "No, it wasn't."

I think of the time he left Charlie locked outside on the lawn, crying in a wire pen. For hours. All for that asinine "method."

I say, "It was just unsettling. Not knowing where he was."

He makes a vast show of composing himself. "I'm sorry, Betty."

And how, when I asked Mrs. Lindbergh if I could go to him, she said there was nothing we could do.

I crouch, feel the back of Charlie's diaper. "Well, as you say, he does seem to be fine. He does, however, seem to be wet. So . . ."

As I lift Charlie in the basket, she says, "Thank you, Betty."

"Of course."

That night, I remember how I worried about working for Charles Lindbergh. The mistakes I might make. One in particular. How terrible I'd feel. If it happened again.

I'm not so worried now.

Chapter Six

"Charlie, do you know what day it is?"

Seated next to me in the car, he beams, not understanding the question, but hearing the excitement.

"Today's the day your mummy's going to become a pilot. She's going to fly a plane. That's silly, you say, Mummy already flies planes. That's true, Charlie, but today she's going to fly all by herself. She's going to *solo*."

I look to Ellerson, who's driving us out to the Long Island Aviation Country Club. "That's what they call it, right?"

He catches my eye in the mirror. "She's getting her private pilot's license. Four landings, a spiral, and a few figure eights."

A spiral? It sounds terrifying to me. I cuddle Charlie close, more for me than him. He's only interested in pulling off his shoe.

"Say, tell me something," says Ellerson.

Wary, I smile to show my willingness to be asked, making no promise to answer. "You were in Detroit, right?"

My first thought is, Kathleen Sullivan told. Or Mary, she knew I went to Detroit—but that's all she knew. Kathleen Sullivan might have found out more. But if she had, I would no longer be working for the Lindberghs.

I have said nothing about Rob Coutts, I remind myself. Nothing to no one.

"What happened?" Before I can say *Nothing,* he grins. "Man, right?"

Our eyes meet. Gossip, I decide. And, intriguingly, sympathy.

"Why do you say that?"

"Always a man."

It occurs to me to be insulted. But I feel Ellerson's not putting me in any box he hasn't been in himself. Before I can say, *No, it was the job,* or *I didn't care for the city,* or *Oh, yes? Which were you then? Heartbreaker or brokenhearted?* he brings the car to a stop. We're here. They call it a country club, but to me it just looks like a big scrubby field with a few bare strips of ground to take off and land. In the distance, I can see a modest white brick clubhouse, a pool, and some tennis courts. Several planes—with their sloped backs, lifted wings, and propeller tilted to the sky, they put me in mind of strutting peacocks—are scattered around the grounds.

Purposely, we've arrived late. When she told me to bring Charlie, Mrs. Lindbergh said, "He won't want to wait through the whole thing. Better to come when I've finished." But we're not quite late enough; Mrs. Lindbergh is still in the air. In my lap, Charlie has got his shoe off entirely, chortling at his success.

Hearing the buzz of the plane overhead, I say, "I don't know what to do."

"You want me to keep driving?"

I look at my watch. "This is when she said to come . . ."

"Then you better get out of the car."

Our eyes meet again in the mirror. That diminutive lady with her tilted nose and marble forehead in an airplane. For weeks, we've all acted as if it's nothing, of course she can do it. She's flown with him before; for their honeymoon they went all over South and Central America. But this is her alone and it's not been easy. He's made her study late into the night, shouting at her when she got tired or muddled. As if she hadn't been working for hours, days, weeks. I thought it was him being a bully. Now I wonder if he's afraid for her.

A sharp knock makes me jump. Colonel Lindbergh, eager and vital at the window. Charlie crows, strains to get to his father. The decision has been made: we're getting out. Even if it means watching Mrs. Lindbergh crash to her death.

I climb out of the car into the warm spring air. My arms are emptied as the Colonel takes Charlie and points, showing him the plane as it whizzes through the sky. It doesn't mean anything to Charlie; climbing Daddy's shoulder is more fun. I brace, worried the Colonel will be annoyed. Instead, he laughs, and holds Charlie high overhead before swinging him down, imitating a plane's sound as if he were only a little older than his son. Charlie's thrilled, laughing and wanting it done over and over. The Colonel holds him up, examining him. For a moment, their foreheads touch, blond curls brushing, two cleft chins, one large, one small. "He's getting pretty interesting," he says of his son.

The press is here, but they're kept back by the clubhouse fifty yards away. A man in a fedora stands by the Lindberghs' car keeping an eye on them. I vaguely recognize him from the Morrow house. When the Colonel lifts Charlie up, one of the reporters spots him and lifts a camera; immediately, the man in the fedora strides over and takes forceful hold of his arm. The camera is lowered. The Lindberghs have released only one picture of Charlie, taken shortly after his birth. Now that he is almost a year old, people are fascinated to see what the son of the most famous man in the world looks like. To their credit, the Lindberghs want to keep Charlie out of the spotlight, away from public fuss and adoration. Once I suggested taking Charlie to the Jersey Shore; Mrs. Lindbergh said she didn't think it was a wise idea. Too exposed.

Unnerved by the reporters, I turn my back on them and look up to the broad blue sky like a dome overhead. I admit, all the sky's ever meant to me is weather. Even when the world was thrilled by Lindbergh's flight, I thought it a fine thing to do—for him—but I didn't understand the fuss. When I spot Mrs. Lindbergh, the wings of the plane tilting and dipping, I catch my breath and think, Oh, marvelous! The way she weaves through the air, climbing up, gliding down, playing in it like a dolphin in the sea. Meanwhile, we're stuck down here as she glides far above us, free of it all.

The Colonel goes still, wanting to watch this final landing. The blue eyes stay fixed, the chest rising and falling a little, shallow, careful breaths, as if not breathing could hold her aloft. As she descends, the edges of his mouth tick upward, a fierce light in his eyes; she's done it. A smile explodes across his face, pride and pure joy. Entranced, unthinking, he hands Charlie back to me and runs on those crane legs to her and the plane. A thought drifts into my mind: it would be nice to be loved like that.

The wheels of the plane touch ground only to bob up again as if she and the plane can't bear to be earthbound again. The roar of the engine calms as she wheels around on the landing strip. The crowd at the clubhouse surges forward. Men with their notebooks out, cameras held high. No more silence of withheld breath, now there are shouts, cheers, applause. The clubhouse staff and the Morrow man try to keep them back, but they converge on Mrs. Lindbergh. I can only find her in the crush by spotting the bright dash of gold of her husband's hair. Overwhelmed, I whisper, "My, my, Charlie."

A man is at the edge of the crowd around the plane. He slaps a man with a camera on the shoulder and they hurry toward me, the first man calling, "Hey, is that the baby?" Before I know it, there are several of them, bearing down so fast, I'm worried they won't stop in time. They cluster around us, shoving. I sense cameras and pens coming at us and flinch. Worse is the shouting, harsh, vicious like dogs barking before they snap. "What's your name, Miss?" "Are you the nanny?" "How long have you worked for the Lindberghs?" Charlie cringes, scared and squirming; I have to hold on to him with both arms.

Trying to keep my voice calm, I say, "Keep a distance, please. You're frightening him."

It doesn't mean a thing to them. All they know is that it's The Baby and they want him. Not even a him to them, Charlie's an it, a thing, a story. If one gets closer than the rest, they'll all shove in, the ones in the back pushing to the front, the ones in the front shouldering each other out of the way. Frantic to be inside a place with doors that shut, I look around for Ellerson and the car. But he's taken it far down the field. Putting my head down, I start walking toward the clubhouse. In a swarm, they follow. The ones at the back run ahead and in a minute, I'm trapped again. I feel I've angered them by trying to get away; they push closer now, entirely reckless. One of them has got a microphone, and he keeps shoving it at me. Terrified it's going to hit Charlie, I put a protective hand over his head.

"No pictures! No pictures of the baby!" The Morrow man bullies his way through, going from photographer to photographer, checking cameras, pulling film. Then the Lindberghs come and their arrival parts the crowd, silences the shouting. In her flying uniform, Mrs. Lindbergh gives a polite smile now and again to the reporters, but she keeps back from them, like you would with a drunk who's getting fresh. The Colonel just glares, all joy gone. He's not so much a man as a sword as he cuts his way through, shoulder first.

Seeing me and Charlie, Mrs. Lindbergh cries out; she looks dear in her soft pilot's helmet and goggles, the thrill of what she's accomplished in her elf smile. Eager, she reaches for Charlie. But it's just more hands and noise to him. Shrinking into me, small hand closing tight on my blouse, he whimpers, *"Beddy."* Her face, so bright a second ago, goes dull.

Heartbroken for her, I whisper, "It's all these people. Congratulations!" She takes the compliment with a wave of the hand as if her solo flight were no great thing at all.

Chapter Seven

I know a darling thing / Who's one year old today."

In June, Charlie turns one year old. I'm not much of a poet. But I leave the card on Mrs. Lindbergh's dressing table. Maybe, if she wants to, she can put it in a box of Charlie's baby things. So he can read it when he's grown up and remember me.

"Happy birthday to you, happy birthday to you, happy birthday dear Charlie . . ."

Seated in a chair on the lawn of the Morrow estate, Charlie's mostly interested in the candle on his piece of cake. When we clap and cheer at the end of the song, he looks up, startled. What *are* we doing?

His father takes a picture of him as Mrs. Lindbergh teases him with a small wooden bull from Mexico he was given as a present. Charlie's not that interested, but at his feet, Skean is ready to have a go. Mrs. Morrow hands me a piece of cake, saying, "Charlie looks so sweet in that outfit, Betty. Although I think we may have to finally cut his curls while we're in Maine, what do you think?"

I say, "Oh, I hope not. But you may be right."

We're getting a sense of each other, Charlie's grandmother and

I. With the Lindberghs leaving for the Orient, Charlie will be her and my charge for the rest of the summer. It wasn't something I expected, this . . . supervision. But as the trip got closer and closer, Mrs. Lindbergh grew anxious. That's when Mrs. Morrow suggested Charlie and I come up to stay with her and Senator Morrow in Maine.

"That way," she said, "you'll know I'm looking after him and he's safe and loved."

And Mrs. Lindbergh burst out with, "Oh, thank you, Mother. That would take so much off my mind."

Which surprised me. I knew she didn't like leaving the baby, but *"so much off my mind"*? What was on her mind? Did she not think Charlie would be safe and loved with me? Mrs. Morrow sees him once, maybe twice, a week. She's not got the first idea what he eats, what his schedule is, how to pin up his blankets at night . . .

Mrs. Morrow says, "I was so pleased when the Colonel consented to have a party for Charlie. I know he's not *fond* of gatherings." There's a drop of acid in her tone, not the first I've heard from her on the subject of her son-in-law. She turns to watch her youngest daughter, Constance, try a cartwheel. She raises her hands, ready to applaud, but the girl tumbles over and it turns into a single clap of commiseration. Laying a hand on my arm, she says, "Excuse me, Betty . . ."

"Of course."

Gazing around the garden now in the full, glorious bloom of late June, I remember how intimidating this all seemed to me four months ago. This was meant to be a small party, and so it might have been if we'd stayed at the farmhouse in Princeton. But we're in Englewood with the Morrows—and their staff. In a few days, I shall be sharing a house with these people. No more Whateley grumbling about Birmingham's poor cricket performance. But also no more of Elsie's smiles and warmth. Aside from Ellerson, I don't really know the Morrow people. I watch as Mr. Banks helps the Senator into a lawn chair, snapping his fingers for an umbrella. The glamorous Elisabeth Morrow laughs with her friend Miss Chilton, unaware that a sulky Violet is standing nearby, a tray of canapés on offer. Miss Chilton's eyes light on Charlie, and she smiles, gives him a small wave.

The crowd shifts and I see Mrs. Lindbergh talking with Kathleen Sullivan, who seems to be that rare staff member who's also a friend of the family. They're talking of the Orient trip and Mrs. Sullivan has actually taken hold of Mrs. Lindbergh's hand as she peppers her with questions. Intrigued by this familiarity, I draw closer. The Colonel's standing behind his wife, head slightly bent as if he'd like to whisper something in her ear. He glances at Mrs. Sullivan, once, then twice. Then calmly, he takes hold of Mrs. Lindbergh's arm and draws Kathleen Sullivan's hand off his wife. Mrs. Sullivan is so startled, she stops talking. Graciously, Mrs. Lindbergh asks a question to fill the silence. I notice though, she tucks her hand neatly under her arm by the breast.

"She would never have done it herself, but she's pleased he released her," I hear a lightly accented voice say. I turn to see a woman with a large nose, bobbed hair, and a clever expression.

She holds out a lean, strong hand. "Marguerite Jantzen. I work for Mrs. Morrow as a seamstress. It's nice to meet you, Miss Gow."

I like the way she uses my name and her own; she doesn't say *I'm Mrs. Morrow's seamstress,* the way Violet might call herself the Morrows' maid. I try to place the accent. Continental. French? No, *Jantzen*. She's German.

"You're off to Maine soon?" she asks.

"Yes." Conscious anything I say may be repeated, I say, "The baby will love being with his grandparents. I hope I'm not in the way."

"I shouldn't think so. Mrs. Morrow will be busy. She is always busy."

The criticism is clear, but I don't know Marguerite Jantzen well enough to agree. "Will you be going?"

"Oh, no. But the house next door is owned by the Lamonts; they're friends of the Morrows and they always bring their yacht for the season. With a yacht, you have handsome sailors, no? So, you won't be too bored."

She casts her gaze on Charlie, who's trying to catch Skean's pointed ear. "When you get back, let's see each other. You'll tell me what it's like, looking after America's crown prince."

I smile, unsure as she goes if I have made a friend or met someone I dislike intensely.

"Bags all packed? Ready for some fun?"

Suddenly beside me is Ellerson, eyebrows jumping, rattling ice in a cup.

"I'm going to be working," I tell him. "It's not a holiday."

"Sure it is. They get to relax, we get to relax. There's dances, beach parties . . ."

"Charlie's not such a dancer yet."

"Oh, you can take a few nights off."

If Ellerson were a different man, I might think he had specific plans for these dances and beach parties, and maybe he does. But I'm fairly sure they don't involve me. At least not in that way and it's not because of the ring on his finger or the family he never talks about. Ever since that day in the car, he's been keen to see what he calls "Bad Betty from Detroit." No matter how many times I tell him she's gone.

I feel a nudge at my knee. I look down to see Charlie, wooden bull in his hand.

"What do you have there, Charlie? Something special?" He does look darling, all in white, with a proper little man's shirt and shorts that stop at the knees of his sturdy legs. He pushes the bull against my hand. Crouching down, I take it to admire. I poke Charlie's tummy with the tiny horns. He giggles, tries to catch it. I hide the bull behind my back. Charlie saunters around me, looking for it. I switch it back to the front and he follows. I tell him he's clever, guessing the game so fast. Then I fall backward with him, laughing, "Oh, Charlie, you got me. You got me. And the bull. The bully bull." I tickle him with it, running it up his back, letting it prance through his bubble curls.

A shadow falls. Kathleen Sullivan standing above me.

"The family wants to take a photo," she says.

"Oh, of course." I get to my feet. Brush down Charlie's clothes. "Come on, Charlie. Going to have your picture taken . . ."

"I can take him," says Mrs. Sullivan.

Briskly, she picks him up. Too quick, he doesn't like the sudden change and he twists in her arms, wailing and reaching for me. Maybe it's the heat, the strain of so much polite talk, but I feel suddenly miserable. Turning the bull in my fingers, I think, *I'm sorry, sweetheart*, as he disappears around the side of the house.

Then Ellerson taps my shoulder; Banks is gathering the staff to witness the taking of the photograph. I'd rather not, but Ellerson takes my hand and pulls me along, whispering about the others until I'm laughing. He nods to a skipping Violet as she tries to take Mr. Banks's hand only to be shook off. Then points out a girl with a heavy jaw and heavier manner stomping behind them—"Violet's sister, Edna, laugh a minute as you can see." A handsome young man, his sleeves rolled up, gives me the eye, and Ellerson says, "Alfred, the other driver, don't waste your time, leave him to the housemaids." Then as the elegant seamstress passes, "Marguerite Junge . . ."

"She said Jantzen."

He smiles. "Yeah, that sounds like her." As our small group troops around the side of the house, we join a stream of parlormaids, footmen, gardeners, secretaries, laundresses, drivers, cooks, and kitchen maids. Coming to the rose garden where the family has lined up, we take our place at a suitable distance.

There are seven family members present and the photographer takes his time getting the right arrangement. Charlie is at the center in his mother's arms, his father tall and singular enough to stand at the back. On either side, the grandparents, the Senator beaming, slightly unsteady. Mrs. Morrow smooths Constance's hair, messy from her cartwheels. Elisabeth, the eldest, lovely, grave, and appropriate, needs no tidying. No Dwight Junior, he is still "at school." Mrs. Lindbergh, small and dark; I know she regrets not being blond like her sisters. But to me, she stands unique, even if her smile is slightly strained with the effort of holding Charlie still.

I hear Violet giggle behind me, one of the parlormaids as well. Banks shushing. The strike of a match; Marguerite is smoking a cigarette. The photographer moves Colonel Lindbergh to his wife's side, urges Constance closer to her mother. To my right, Edna sighs, "... God's sake." Ellerson elbows me. I elbow him back. Then I catch Banks glaring at us and straighten my expression.

Funny, how we outnumber them.

"Excuse me, Miss, you sound like a sister I used to have. I haven't spoken to her in so long I can't remember her *name* now. Bessie? Bethy?"

I wait while my brother comes up with every "B" name he can think of. When he gets to Brunhilda, I say, "All right, Billy, I'm sorry. Some of us have important jobs, you know."

"Oh, Betty, you needn't feel jealous. Being a lineman for New Jersey Electric is tremendously impressive, but you'll soon find something to write home about."

I hear a squeak in the background, Jean cajoling. "How's my niece?"

"Hungry, she's *always* hungry. Misses you."

"Ah, give her a kiss. I'm sorry it's been so long. I haven't had any time off."

"But you're working, happy . . . ?"

"Well, I am working—so much I don't know about the other. When I get back, I'll come for dinner first thing."

"I'll hold you to that," says my brother.

"You'll keep a diary."

"Yes, ma'am."

"And take pictures . . ."

"Once a month, I promise."

It is not the first or tenth time Mrs. Lindbergh has given these instructions. We are at the railway station, standing on the platform. The Bar Harbor Express that will take us on the first leg of our journey to the Morrow home on the island of North Haven in Maine has arrived. The conductor has called "All aboard." Our trunks have been loaded. All that's left is for me and Charlie to get on. But Mrs. Lindbergh's not quite ready for her adventure to start. She can't stop touching him, tugging at the edge of his shorts, smoothing his hair, checking his shoe to make sure it's secure.

"Not too many toys at once," she tells me.

"No, ma'am."

"And don't . . ." She runs a finger down his nose. "Don't make him fond of you. He is so fond of you already, of course. But don't . . ."

"Don't spoil him and don't hover because I think he needs extra care because you're away."

I've guessed right. Mrs. Lindbergh's shoulders relax. "Yes. Thank you. My mother may try to do things her way, and I suppose you'll have to let her. But . . ."

"I understand, Mrs. Lindbergh. Don't worry."

The whistle blows. It really is time. Tentatively I incline Charlie toward her; would she like to hold him? For a moment, her eyes fix on him, longing. But there's her Lindy and their flight, and she longs for that too.

Her hands jump in the air between them. "All right, my sweet boy. Be good." To me, she murmurs, "I should let you go before the press finds us."

Perhaps it is that worry, that someone is spying on these last moments, that makes her turn casually and leave us without once looking back.

Mrs. Lindbergh has booked us drawing room tickets; quite sumptuous with curtains on the windows and large plush seats that are almost armchairs. I settle Charlie next to me. The dogs have already gone on to North Haven and I wonder aloud what mischief they've gotten up to. Charlie rolls his wooden dog on the seat, makes a whirring sound. I say, "That's more a car than a doggy," and stop myself just in time from calling him Charlie. Outside the house, off the grounds, I'm not to use his name. The fewer people know the Lindbergh baby is in North Haven, the better. Officially, we are traveling as Betty and Mary.

I glance at the other people in the car; they're dozing, looking out of the window, reading newspapers. A mother playing cards with her child. It's funny they don't realize, right in front of them is the *most famous baby in America.* But then, no one's seen a picture of Charlie since he was an infant. It's a long journey. At first, I'm entranced by the sight of water and open sky, the sheer size of this country. But after five hours, the air in the car becomes heavy, a little sick-making. Over and over, I pull my blouse from my skin, wipe sweat from my forehead with the back of my hand. Charlie puts his head in my lap and I let myself fall into a little dream: this is my baby and we are traveling to our lovely summer house in the country. His father's gone ahead with our things and when we arrive, he will sweep us up with a great cry, so happy to see us, and it will be wild and free and utterly secure at the same time . . .

It's late afternoon as the train pulls into the station. Charlie stirs, face red and damp, curls crushed. He's cranky and I have to cajole him to the ferry that will get us to the island. On the ferry, he's manic, the way children get when they're overtired, pulling me this way and that as I say, "No, we must sit down. Look, Charlie, pretty sunset, let's have a sit and look at it." The swell and roll of the water makes me nauseous. When I see Ellerson with the car waiting at the dock, I nearly weep with relief.

"Long journey?"

"Oh, my God."

But the next morning, I wake to a beautiful fresh day, the sound of seagulls and dogs barking on the lawn, the murmurs of the Morrow staff going about their business. I have been allowed to sleep late; I feel I've been granted a miracle. Looking out the window, I see Mrs. Morrow with Charlie on a vast expanse of lawn. Breathing deep, I feel this is a *simpler* place. No houses close by, almost like you're at the end of the earth.

The dogs race to greet me when I come down. Charlie crows, standing up in his carriage. "It's so beautiful," I say to Mrs. Morrow and she smiles. "We do love it here."

With me up, Mrs. Morrow returns to the house while I wheel Charlie around in the carriage. Barking and hopping underfoot,

Skean wants to come along; worried that I might catch his paw with the wheels, I pop him in alongside. They make a darling pair, two heads, one black with furry ears, one gold, peeking over the edge. The air is warm, smells of ocean and pine. "Gentlemen, we're going to have a lovely time here," I say.

Then I hear it, the jagged click and rapid whir of something re-loading. I hear the snap of metal again and my head turns. Before I can place where it's coming from, there's a rustle, branches being pushed aside, twigs snapping. They've run off. I try to slow my heart, tell myself it's over, they've gone, nothing's happened. They didn't get anything. We're safe.

For a long moment, I stare down at Charlie. Wanting out of the stroller, he's got his hands on the rim, bouncing at the knees, making his impatient noises. I reassure myself: he's fine.

But the next day, we're in the newspaper. LINDBERGH BABY IN MAINE. Me, frowning, hair in my face, Charlie worried, as if he's seen the man who took the picture. But we didn't see him. He got what he wanted—us—and got clean away.

Chapter Eight

North Haven, Maine

I like this house.

Still big, mind you. More than thirty rooms. The Morrows built it on land that was once a farm. With the tall dark pines, rocky cliffs, and churning seas, the island puts me in mind of holidays back home. The nursery looks out on the water and every day, Charlie and I watch for birds and sailboats. We race with the dogs on the lawn, tumble through meadows of wildflowers, and search for dragons in the acres of forest. We hold hands as we make our way down the sloping hills to the beach where we collect shells, and I tell Charlie he always finds the best ones—how *does* he do it? Then I lift him high over the waves, watch his footprints as they wash away.

Still, the very first week, Mrs. Morrow comes to me and says, "It's time."

Charlie and I are on the floor of his room; we've built a farm with blocks and we're moving the animals in and out of their pens. Charlie bashes the horse and cow together as if they're arguing. Pulling my finger through a curl, I say, "It is?"

She holds up a little pair of scissors. "I'm afraid so. We have friends coming to dinner. They're dying to meet him." She smiles. "We'll save every snip."

I lie in front of Charlie, trying to keep him distracted with the animals while Mrs. Morrow, kneeling behind him, starts to cut. He doesn't like the sound of the scissors and pulls his head away—a sudden movement, not safe around sharp things. I tell him he's going to look so handsome, a real little man. But we end up having to hold his head still while she cuts quickly all around, the curls falling like snow. "I know, Charlie, I know," I say as he cries.

When it's done, I dust off his neck and back, so the loose hairs don't itch. Charlie puts a thumb in his mouth, and I want to ask why he had to go through that. He'd be just as lovely for the guests with long hair. He does look more like a boy and not a baby; his face thinner, more like his father's.

Mrs. Morrow gathers up the hair in a small cloth bag. When she's gone, Charlie and I go back to our farm. On the rug, I feel something silky and shifting under my fingers. A lock she's missed. I take it, put it in my pocket.

I've started . . . I won't say breaking—bending, maybe—the rules. I don't wake Charlie up at night anymore, I just check on him and if he's sleeping soundly, I leave him be. I felt guilty the first time, but either Mrs. Morrow agrees with me or she never knew it was a rule in the first place. I thought she'd be watching every move, but that hasn't been the case. Marguerite Jantzen, or Junge, or whatever she calls herself, was right about that. The Morrows have many friends in Maine and they like to entertain. When the family has a party, the staff has a party. They've brought twelve people from Englewood and hired others locally. For every five bottles that go out, one gets held back. A lot of food left on plates that somehow never gets packed away for next day's lunch. If there's a band playing, the radio gets turned on in the cellar. More than one visitor's car has been used as a trysting site. My bedroom's near the nursery, but at night I can hear the creaking floorboards and squeaking hinges. Whispers. Giggles. Muffled tears. One of the maids crying because it's her first job and she wants to go home. A knock on a door, Mr. Banks saying, "It's me." I've seen Ellerson slowly roll the car into town after midnight. Seen Alfred the second chauffeur meet up with kitchen maid Sally one night, and Deborah who makes the beds another night. It is a big house. But it's too many people for us not to know things about one another.

One night I'm awakened by the sound of a heavy fall and an explosion of curses, the like of which I've not heard since the Glasgow docks. Immediately, a door opens somewhere in the house, and the light thud of small feet and a feminine whisper joins the fractious grumbling. "Oh, my God, Septimus, what have you done?"

"These fucking people . . ."

"Never mind them. Come on, get up."

"Fucking family. I worked for Carnegie, Lord . . ."

"Just, put your arm . . . I've got you."

But not quite. I hear the crash of his body against the wall, Violet's gasp as he slips. Probably his arm's around her neck, he falls, she does too.

And of course . . . Charlie's been woken. The abrupt wail gets me out of bed. I slide on my robe, open the door to see Violet buckling under Banks's weight. He looks a mess, dark hair on end, pouches livid beneath the eyes, clothes disheveled.

Violet's eyes meet mine. I think, *Better you than me, love,* and go to Charlie.

The next day, Violet turns up while I'm washing Charlie's things. "I'm sorry about last night," she says.

I wring out one of Charlie's socks. "You needn't apologize. You weren't the one falling over yourself."

She plucks at her fingers. "I know. It's just, he's got a difficult job"—I raise my eyebrows at the sock—"and so."

"Nice of you to take the trouble," I say blandly.

She laughs. "I should say, we are going to be married. But don't mention it, not everyone knows."

Does Banks, I wonder? I see no ring on her finger. She catches me looking, covers one hand with the other. "We have to keep it secret since we both work here. You won't say anything, will you? About the engagement, but also last night? I hate to ask . . ."

This is really why she's come. To make sure Banks's drinking remains something known but not spoken of. Still, none of my business. Not as if . . .

I shake that off, say shortly, "No, I won't."

The reassurance makes her cheerful. "We should go out sometime. In the evening after work. We all do, it's great fun."

Yes, I saw last night how fun. "It's difficult with the baby."

Violet, while not bright, knows a snub when she hears it. Stepping away from the door, she says, "Well, all right then. Thank you again."

Violet's not the only one who wants me to join the party. Every few days, Ellerson asks me when am I coming out. It's become a game. I don't like being a game. I don't want people knowing the kinds of things about me that I know about them.

"What am I supposed to tell my friend?" Ellerson asks when I say no to a dance in town.

"What friend?"

He leans on the hood of the car. "One of the crew for the Lamont yacht wants to meet you. He's seen you on the beach with the baby. He's Norwegian. Shy. Very sweet."

Sweet. I think of Violet's delusions about Banks. My own delusions, if it comes to it. "Mrs. Morrow hasn't told me my night off and I don't like to ask. I'm here to care for Charlie, not go to parties."

"Come on, Beautiful. You need a man in your life who doesn't wear diapers. And who isn't just a bad memory. You don't like him, toss him back."

It's a funny thing, when someone lets you know they've seen something about you that you try not to show—and says, *Ah, not so bad. We've all been there.* I like Ellerson calling Rob Coutts a bad memory. I like him seeing me as a woman who tosses men aside if they don't please her.

I say I'll ask.

Mrs. Morrow says, "Of course, you should go, Betty. Don't you worry about Charlie. Take the evening. Have fun."

It makes me feel bad, some of the things I've thought about her.

I'm not sure what to look like. Ellerson told me, "Get out of that damn uniform." But you forget, almost, how to dress like yourself when you wear the same thing day in and day out. I don't seem to have anything for summer, nothing pretty or flirty. No matter what I put on, I see the Lindbergh Nanny looking back at me in the mirror. Proper, efficient, no nonsense. All very respectable, but not what a Norwegian sailor has in mind for fun. But do I want to be what a sailor has in mind for fun? And here's another question: What do I have in mind for fun?

Honestly? A hot bath would do.

Oh, come on now, Betty, I think, wriggling out of my tweed skirt and into a maroon dress with the low neck and ruffle round the skirt. Yes, that's better. Wouldn't wear that to church. I smooth the dress over my hips, appreciate the dips and swells of the line. Turn sideways. Pull my shoulders back, tilt my neck so it looks long and inviting. Smile a little, let the tongue touch the tip of my teeth.

Not felt like this since Rob Coutts.

Forget Rob Coutts.

When I meet Ellerson on the lawn at dusk, he says, "Now *there's* the girl who got up to no good in big bad Detroit."

I'm suspicious: Is he making fun? "You make me sound like a gangster's girlfriend."

He throws an arm around my shoulder. "The way you look, Beautiful, Al Capone would have made different plans for Valentine's Day."

The Morrows have let Ellerson have one of the cars. As we approach, I can see Violet and her sister, Edna, in the back seat and my heart sinks. I feel conspicuous out of uniform and I don't want fuss. Still, I present a smile and say, "Hello, girls" as I climb in. Violet squeals, "Ellerson! You got her to come! Betty, I can't believe it. Isn't she gorgeous, Edna?"

Edna says something like gorgeous that somehow isn't. They're a funny pair, the Sharpe sisters. Both brunette with pale skin, but different temperaments. Violet's the elder but seems younger with her bright mouse eyes, eagerness, and sudden hooting laugh. Edna is dour, with coarse, bushy hair, the sort of person who takes pride in calling a spade a spade—even if it's a rake.

Gunning the motor, Ellerson shouts, "Grab hold, ladies, we're off!"

The car swerves down the road. A flask appears. Ellerson takes his time with it until Violet claps her hands and he has to pass it back. She takes a great swig, lets her sister do the same, then offers it to me. I put up my hand. "I don't."

"Ah . . . ," scolds Ellerson as Violet cries, "Go on!"

I accept the flask, tip it to my mouth. I've not had alcohol in some time. I'd forgotten the burn. And the warmth. I smile at Violet. She could have been standoffish after our Banks chat. But it seems she's not the sort to hold a grudge. Perhaps I should try the same.

The roadhouse is on a different part of the island; you can tell, this is where the people who work for the summer folk live year-round. The main street is dusty, lined with wood planks on either side for walking. As it's night, most of the stores are shut; it looks like some have been shut for some time, their signs hanging loose, windows boarded. In contrast, the roadhouse is blazing with light and sound. I can hear laughter, shouting, the thumping, insistent low notes of a piano, and the blare of trumpet. Violet whoops as we walk in, and we're immediately pulled into a loose crowd of Morrow people, including a well-oiled Septimus Banks, who's already swaying, a bottle held precariously between two fingers.

Ellerson heads to the bar. I follow, asking, "Why do the Morrows keep Banks on?"

He signals for two drinks, then tells me, "The missus likes all those lords and ladies he's worked for and the Senator likes that he can get his hands on a good crate of whiskey. Banks has bootlegger friends from his days in catering."

"Banks is friends with gangsters?" I am thoroughly delighted.

Drinks in hand, Ellerson starts back to the Morrow people. I dawdle, but he gives me a firm look: I am to join. So I do—just in time to hear

Violet shriek, "I'm telling you, it was Miss Elisabeth he was after . . ." even as Edna argues, "The Senator and Mrs. Morrow were never going to let a mechanic near their darling Number One."

Grinning, Alfred says, "Old man was probably too soused to notice either way."

"She's a dyke, anyway," puts in Banks, causing Violet to shout, "She is *not*!"

"I think the old lady would prefer Connie as a son-in-law. At least she graduated university," says Edna.

"Yes, a mailman's not good enough for the daughter of the ambassador to *Mexico*." Banks gives the country's name a nasty twist, as if it were "toilet." As they snipe back and forth, I listen amazed at their gleeful malice and wonder: our night off and all we can talk about is the family? On the other hand, what else do we have to talk about?

Then Violet announces, "It's the young ones I feel sorry for. Master Dwight"—I watch with distaste as Alfred goes slack-jawed and starts twitching—"and poor Miss Constance. After what happened last year . . ."

At that, Edna darts a look at me and nudges her sister, who falls silent. They all do; I sense I am about to become part of their stories. Which I did not want to be. Anxious, I look for Ellerson, but he's left me to talk with some fellow at the bar, damn him.

Because they seem to expect it, I ask. "What?"

"About the kidnapping," says Violet, as Banks brays, "Oh, don't go into all that!"

"Miss Constance," says Edna, ignoring him. "A year ago, she got a letter at school. It said she was to bring fifty thousand dollars and place it by a stone wall near the house. If she didn't, they'd kill her."

They're watching to see how I respond. Trying to sound bored, I say, "And? Did the Morrows go to the police?"

"The family hired a girl who looked like Miss Constance to deliver the money," says Violet. "The police were watching, ready to arrest whoever came to pick it up. Only no one ever came."

I examine Violet's face, then her sister's, not entirely certain they haven't made it up. There's something about the story that doesn't make sense. Fifty thousand dollars is a fortune; you wouldn't demand such a sum, then not show up. Unless you knew the police were waiting. But how would you know that unless . . .

The men drift off to the bar for another round and Violet asks me in a playful tone, "So—what's it like working with Colonel Lindbergh?" She gives the "L" a little curl, making Edna smirk.

My mind half on Miss Constance—that darling girl, wheeling over on the lawn, how scared she must have been, to feel those people out there, wanting to hurt her—I think how to answer. It is what people ask: *What's he like?* To be honest, I don't know. Or . . . I don't know how to put it. People expect you to go all breathless, *Oh, he's just . . .* You could say he's very good-looking. Or else they want to know the secret bad things.

So. What do I know about Charles Lindbergh?

I know when he was fourteen, he drove his mother across the country. He got arrested for not having a license. And being underage. I sense his mother's a bit odd. "A woman of strong emotions" was how Mrs. Lindbergh put it. But I could hear what she was trying not to say.

I know our Wahgoosh is named after a dog he had as a child. One day a neighbor killed it out of irritation and left it in a well. I know "wahgoosh" is Chippewa for "fox."

I know he met President Wilson as a boy and thought him "just a man" even if he was president. I know he's not one to say he's wrong.

I know he's the only man to save his life by jumping from a plane four times. I know he's never wondered what it would be like to go to bed with me.

I've heard his father was against the war. Against big business in farming. I've heard in Minnesota, his father was shot at, chased by mobs, and hanged in effigy.

I know he saw his first flight when he was ten and fell in love.

I know he loves his wife. But thinks she's too weak to become what she should be without him. At least what he thinks she should be.

None of this would I want repeated by Violet Sharpe, and I'm about to say I don't see all that much of him when I feel a hand on my shoulder. "Can I borrow her?"

I turn to see Ellerson and feel relief. Then I see the man behind him and think, Ah, the famous Norwegian. As we move away from the Sharpe girls, the Norwegian smiles apologetically, as if he's taking me from friends. He doesn't demand my attention right away, which I like. And he is attractive. But I feel at a disadvantage. It's not natural, meeting someone who already knows something about you—or else why ask to meet you—and the only thing you know about them is they want to meet you. They've already decided things about you before you knew they existed.

"This," says Ellerson when we've found a quiet corner, "is Henrik Johnson." He puts a hand to his mouth like he's telling a big secret. "Sometimes known as *Red*."

"This," I say, "is Betty Gow. Pleased to meet you, Mr. Johnson."

Honestly, "Mr. Johnson" seems too formal for him. He has red-brown hair and a naughty grin in a sweet face; the little boy hiding something behind his back and you're not sure if it's flowers or a dead frog. After some chat, Ellerson spots someone across the room—or pretends to—and leaves us. Mr. Johnson looks shy, awkward at having put himself forward. Younger than me, I'm almost certain.

To put him at ease, I ask what he does for the Lamonts. If Norwegians are natural sailors, Vikings and all that. He says solemnly that this is so, even in his baby bath, he liked sinking his toy boat.

I hear a burst of laughter, see Ellerson with his arm slung around another man's neck. "Did you really ask Ellerson to meet me, or was this his grand idea?"

"Oh, no, it was mine," he says. "I said to him, I saw this girl on the beach, but she's so pretty and has a baby, she must be married. Then he explains, She's only the nurse, no husband, it's okay. But I should ask you . . . is it okay?"

"Fine so far," I say, with a smile. "Is it Henrik or Red . . . ?"

"It's whatever you want to call me."

That's a bit casual minded for me, but then I remember, at home,

I'm Bessie, here Betty. People can have different names. "And what brought you to America?"

"A boat," he says with a terribly straight face. I nod: *All right,* and he laughs. "No, I was working on a steamer a few years ago. It docked in Brooklyn and well . . ." He twists, hands in his pockets.

"You jumped ship."

He admits it with a tilt of his head. "I like America, what can I say?"

"With no job lined up."

"You can always find a job. Life is short. You take what it has to offer. For example . . ." He looks out at the dance floor. "Right now, life is offering a very good song. Would you like to dance?"

Smoother than you look, I think. "Why not."

He's a good dancer, able to keep up a conversation while moving his feet. As we dance, several girls pass and say hello. "You're popular," I say.

"It's a small island," he says. "You get to know everybody."

"Do you?"

"Yes," he laughs. "Look, now I've even met you."

"So," he says at the end of the evening, "have you decided what you want to call me?"

I don't want to admit that I've thought about it. Or that I don't like either Henrik or Red as my choices. "Not yet."

He leans sideways, as if trying to see me from a different angle. "There's a picnic on the beach Saturday night. Maybe you'll tell me then?"

I mean to keep the upper hand and say, *Maybe.* What comes out is, "All right."

"Really?"

Ellerson honks. I walk toward the car, swinging a bit as I go. When I look back, he's still there.

"Go home!" I shout.

"I'm going to go down to the beach," he calls back. "I'm going to wait there till Saturday."

The next morning, I think, No, I won't be going. A few dances, nice enough. That's all it should be.

Then on Monday as I wipe egg off Charlie's chin, I think, But why?

The answer comes swift and cutting: Because you're stupid, that's why.

Not stupid, I whine, Rob Coutts was a liar.

But no. Not true. He didn't lie, I just didn't see. And a woman who doesn't see what she should is a stupid woman. Sorry, my girl, you deserve the title.

Tuesday and Wednesday, I'm resolved: not going.

Thursday, I'm lying in the lawn, arm across my eyes, drowsy from the sun. The thought oils in: Oh, but this one's sweet. Harmless.

Charlie throws a handful of grass over me. I laugh, demand to know what he thinks he's doing as I pull him onto my lap, rock him side to side. Content, he settles against me, and I think, Well, I seem to have got this not terribly wrong.

Friday—I don't know why—I ask Ellerson if he's going. He says no, other plans. Eyes bright, he says, "So, you like him."

"I don't know him. Other girls seem to, though."

"He's good-looking, sure they know him. It's summer. Don't take it so seriously."

That's true enough. After a month, I'll never see Mr. Johnson again. He'll just be a little . . . Maine adventure.

Then Ellerson asks, "Hey, Beautiful, I got a favor to ask. Lend a guy a couple of bucks?"

I know from the Morrow rumor mill, Ellerson likes to gamble, but he loses. "Unlucky at cards?"

"Hoping to get lucky in love."

I ask, "Is there such a thing?" and he laughs.

Chapter Nine

The picnic is on the beach near the Morrow house; you only have to walk down the hill. A full moon means I can see my way through the grass. The world's gone smoke and silver gray. They've built a fire on the beach. I can hear the faint sounds of laughter. I look over my shoulder, the lights of the Morrow house behind me. Then I keep toward the moon and the darkened figures moving around the fire.

There's a tricky slope at the bottom as the ground gives way to sand and I find myself walking sideways so I don't fall and slide down on my bottom. The grass is tall and sharp edged, catching on my skirt. I keep my arms up for balance, my eyes on where I'm going. I feel someone take my hand, a voice says, "Here . . ."

I slip down the last few feet, find myself face-to-face and just a bit too close. He asks, "So, what's the name?"

I don't mind it, I find, the closeness. "Does anyone call you Henry?"

"Yeah. You do."

It's surprisingly chilly by the water. Henry and I sit on a log just outside the ring of people close to the fire. The light catches us only occasionally; the wind comes off the ocean, and I cross my arms over my lap.

"How's the baby?"

"You can't really be interested."

"It's what you do all day. Yes, I'm interested."

Disbelieving, I pick one or two funny moments to share. He asks questions, makes observations, and I find myself talking more than I usually do. I see Henry smiling and say, "What?"

"You really care for him," he says. "It's not just a job."

It's true, but him saying it feels intimate, and I change the subject.

Like Henry, most of the people at the party work for the Lamonts. A few of the men get up from the fire and wander over, offering drink, glancing at me. Henry keeps his part of the conversation pleasant but brief. He introduces the captain of the yacht, a Mr. Christiansen; for a while, they speak in Norwegian. I draw my foot through the sand, wonder if I'm expected to find other company.

Then I hear Mr. Christiansen say "Nice to meet you" and I say it's nice to meet him.

Henry takes my hand. "Do you want to take a walk? Get away from all the people?"

"Yes," I say, relieved. "Yes, I do."

It's not a long beach, but we're able to get far enough away that the people turn into dark shapes and all you can hear is the odd ripple of laughter. Henry points out the stars and tells me a funny story of getting sick the first time he shipped out. At one point, he turns to walk backward, hands in his pocket, so he can watch me as we talk.

I follow at a small distance.

He says, "You know, Scotland and Norway, they touch."

"Oh, do they?"

"Yes. North of Scotland, the southern tip of Norway. Same latitude."

"Well, that's significant."

He stops walking. I slow, then stop. "What?"

"I'm wondering. If I can kiss you." He wrinkles his nose like he knows he's an idiot.

I smile and he guesses, "Yes?"

"Yes."

He does. Soft and polite at first, but he's better at it than he pretends to be. He puts a hand on my waist, murmurs, "Yes?" I let my head sway *Yes*. After a little while, the hand slides up as the other eases onto the curve of my bottom; he likes that, spends a good long time exploring. I like it too as it happens. At one point, I think, No, too fast. But then: summer.

We lie down and he puts just the right amount of weight on me. Every so often, I catch sight of the stars. Lovely to feel so secure and so dizzy at the same time.

But I'm nervous; all those people, someone's bound to come stumbling by. A few times I glance at the fire. Maybe it's the distance, but the light seems lower, fewer moving shadows around it. Henry lifts his head, I feel his fingers at my temple as he turns my head back toward him.

"Don't worry," he whispers.

So, I don't.

It is nice. Being with someone who enjoys your company and isn't shy about saying so. Ellerson's pleased with himself, and Violet says I'm looking quite chipper these days. I tell her, "He's a lovely boy, and I'm tossing him back at summer's end." I feel bold, pretty, and just a bit careless, the way I used to.

At the same time, I keep track: How many clean shirts and shorts does Charlie need for the time we have left? What has to come with me on the train and what can be packed in the trunk? At the station, who will meet us? Are we to go to the Lindberghs' temporary house in Princeton or stay with the Morrows in Englewood? I hope it's Englewood. I dread having only the Whateleys for company.

One day as I'm carrying fresh, folded diapers to Charlie's room, I pass Mrs. Morrow in the hallway. From her speed, I can tell all she wants from me is a smile. Which I give her and proceed down the hall.

"Oh, Betty . . ."

I swing around. "Yes, Mrs. Morrow."

"As you know, the plan is to return to Englewood next week." I nod. "But I've been told there's an outbreak of infantile paralysis, and I think it would be better for the baby to stay here."

I'm aware of the footsteps all around us, people cooking, making beds, dusting. Is Mrs. Morrow saying all those people will be gone? Just me and Charlie in this enormous house?

"How long?"

"I beg pardon?"

"I'm only wondering how long we'll be here."

"I can't predict the length of the outbreak, I'm afraid. We could leave you Mrs. Barnes. She's a local woman, knows the town."

The Lindberghs aren't due back for months. I want to ask what I should do if it gets cold; I only packed summer clothes for Charlie. Not to mention myself.

The smile is flickering. I'm a thing on the list in her head, already checked off, on to the next. She'd like me to be happy. At least fine. At least pretend to be.

"Of course, ma'am. It'll be lovely to see the leaves change."

"So, you have two more weeks with Red," says Ellerson, washing the car as he listens to me complain. "The Lamonts don't leave till the middle of the month."

"But I can't leave the house."

"Bring Red inside the house."

"I can't do that."

"Why? Who's going to tell?"

I stare at him. "It's not a matter of telling. It's not right to bring strangers into other people's homes."

"Oh?" says Ellerson.

Two nights before they leave, the Morrows host a farewell party. Charlie makes an appearance for the guests, and by the time I get him back, he's tired and cross. I hold him in the rocking chair, crooning, "Did you meet all sorts of important people tonight? Were they all excited to see the son of Lucky Lindy? Are they all going to vote for your grandpa? Well, that's a good night, isn't it?"

After Charlie's asleep, I put myself to bed as well. From the shrieks of laughter from the servants' quarters, I gather the Morrow staff is having their end-of-summer party. As it gets later, I hear the thud of car doors, calls of farewell, sighs of so sad to see the summer end. The house grows quiet.

I'm awoken by a splash, the bright, happy slap of skin against water. A burst of male laughter, then shushing and silence. Agog, I go to the window and see Ellerson in the pool with another man. A waiter from the party, to judge the clothes left on one of the lounge chairs. They're in the deep end, treading water, arms spread just below the surface, their legs and lower bodies ribbons. Ellerson tosses his head as if to shake off the water, then faces the other man with a broad smile: *To hell with it. To hell with it all.*

Opening the window, I lean out, catching Ellerson's eye. *What are you doing?* I mouth. He gestures: *Come down.*

I'm tempted. But it's one thing when you drive the car, another when you look after the children. Instead, I rest my arms on the sill, watch as they swim, feeling mildly shocked, I suppose, but more . . . fond. Envious, if I'm honest. Underwater, their bodies twist, stretch, unravel to nothing, only to become suddenly, startlingly whole when they reappear. I want it, what they have. It's theirs, even if the space is borrowed. And being secret, not allowed, makes it somehow more theirs.

Blowing Ellerson a kiss, I shut the window and return to bed.

But I worry. What if someone sees them? Or the other man says something? I'm not sure how the danger works, if Ellerson, because he works for the Morrows, has more to lose, or if the other man's in the same boat. I think of Rob Coutts, how I was so sure. And so wrong. And how being wrong wasn't a small thing; I was shattered. You'd think, something that dangerous, I'd have felt it. I didn't.

People don't, I find.

. . .

Leaving day. All morning long, people go back and forth from the house carrying trunks and suitcases. I half listen as Mrs. Morrow directs Violet and Edna where to take the linens and china. The sisters start off in one direction only to be told tersely, no, the other car.

On the front lawn, I'm teaching Charlie to jump. I've set up some cushions from the garden chairs so he can launch himself from one to the other. There's one that's just a step too far and he's bouncing at the knees, game but unsure. "Come on, Charlie," I say, taking hold of his hands and swinging him through the air. "England to France, over the Channel . . . Well done!"

A hand passes over my head. I hear, "You take care of yourself, Beautiful."

That night, I lie in bed and listen to the empty house. Charlie snuffling in his crib. I think of all those rooms, hollow and dark. Only the mice and clocks moving at all.

At nine, I listen to the long, solemn bells. I swing my legs over the side of the bed, then leave the room, go out into the dark hallway, and creep noiselessly down the stairs.

He's there on the patio, waiting.

I slide the door open. And let him in.

It's not all bad, having the house to myself. Mrs. Barnes keeps to the kitchen and she's not a woman given to idle chat. At first, I only go to the rooms I was allowed in before. But after two days, I decide, why not? Who would know? Charlie and I play hide-and-seek all over the house. We play detective in the bedrooms and pull books off the shelves in the Morrow library. One rainy afternoon, we get out an enormous atlas and sit on the floor. I turn to a map of the Orient and say, "Where's your mum and dad, Charlie? Can you find them?"

Point to Alaska. "Are they here?" To Japan. "Here? I don't know either, Charlie! I don't know where they are."

. . .

"You have a phone call."

Charlie and I are on the front lawn, trying to catch leaves as they fall. So far, we've had no success, but it makes a good game. When Mrs. Barnes calls from the front door to tell me I have a call, I think for an odd moment she's joking. Henry would never call during the day. At least I hope he wouldn't.

"Is it the Morrows? Or Mrs. Lindbergh?" I ask, going inside.

"No," she says. Then she says to Charlie, "You come with me. Have a cookie."

I watch her as she takes Charlie off, then say absently, "Yes, this is Betty Gow."

The person on the other end introduces herself as Mrs. Ethel Schneider.

The name means nothing to me, and I'm about to say I'm sorry she's gone to all the trouble, but she's got the wrong number. Then she says she is a neighbor of Billy and Jean's. And I don't say anything.

She is sorry, so sorry . . .

I hear myself say, "*No*. Please, no."

Jean is fine, she tells me, the baby is fine.

Without knowing why, I'm falling, arm bent around my middle, everything tight—that's what's bringing the tears, like water from a twisted rag, I'm being wrenched so tightly the only way to breathe is to say, "Oh, my God." I hear the word "accident." She says something about "your brother." She says she's so sorry for my loss.

"I need to talk to my sister-in-law," I say. Talking to Jean is the only way out of this. Because this woman is insane, she's lying. I have never heard her name mentioned once by Billy or Jean, how can she be the one to tell me this? It's all wrong, she has it wrong.

"Mrs. Gow is with a doctor. But she was insistent that I call you. I have the baby, you needn't worry . . ."

The thought of Isabelle, without her father and her mother, shattered, left with this . . . this *stranger* puts me into a rage. Coldly, I ask her to tell Mrs. Gow I will be on the next train, that I will be with her and she's not to do anything until I get there.

I hang up, see Mrs. Barnes is standing at the door, hands bundled up in her apron. "I've put the baby in his pen. Was it . . . bad news?"

The tone is sympathetic, but the question so useless, I walk right past her.

"Where are you going?" she wants to know.

"I have to pack."

"Pack?"

Halfway up the stairs, I turn. "I have to go to New Jersey. Tomorrow, today if possible . . ."

"What about the baby?"

"He'll . . ." I pause for a moment, desperate for her to say she can look after him and I can go to Billy.

She doesn't.

"I'll take him with me."

"But Mrs. Morrow said . . ."

I hurry back down the stairs, stopping two steps above her so I can speak clearly and be heard. "My brother is dead. I have to be with his wife and baby, I have to be with them right now."

My voice is rising. Some might say I sound hysterical, well, let them. If I have to scream in this idiot woman's face to get out of here, I will. I think of my mother. Does she know? Has anyone told her?

I don't even know how he died.

My stomach twists and I have to sit down. The sobbing is like being sick. You want to stop, hold it back, but you can't.

"You can't go anywhere right now," says Mrs. Barnes. "The last ferry goes in half an hour, you'll never make it. You sleep on it tonight. Then in the morning . . ."

She's lying and I'm grateful for it, because it reminds me: They want to stop me and I need to get up now and do what needs to be done. Taking hold of the banister, I lift myself up and start climbing.

She calls after me, "You cannot take that baby where there's disease."

In a searing flash, I think, *He is not my baby and I don't give a good goddamn.*

"Fine, then he stays here."

A creak of stairs; now she's following me, frantic I mean what I say and I'm going to walk out, leaving her with the baby.

"He is your responsibility . . ."

No, he's his parents' responsibility, only they're off flying around the world. His grandparents', only they're in New Jersey, doing their important things. Well, now I have an important thing, a more important thing . . .

"This is your job," she shouts at me.

I wheel on her, slamming my hands against the railings. "Then I quit! *I quit!*"

She stares at me, open-mouthed. Then I hear, "Beddy?"

I pull at my hair, call in a cracked voice, ". . . Coming, Charlie."

A whining grizzle; he doesn't like the pen. My name again, his version of it. *Five minutes,* I plead in my head. *Give me five minutes . . .*

He starts to cry.

I'm not leaving. I cannot leave. It's me. There is no one else.

"It's all right, Charlie. I'm coming . . ."

That night, when Charlie's settled, I leave the house. The moon is bright, washing the land silver. I start marching—stomping fierce and determined—down to the water. Close to the sand, it gets steep and I fall a few times. Good. It feels good to fall, twist, bruise, bleed. If that's all you can feel, at least you feel that.

I look up at the sky, the smeary clouds drifting over the water. Somewhere, the Lindberghs are up there, not knowing, not caring, tapping out their little signals to each other. They'll fly and fly until they float down so all the people can rush up to them, cheering and excited, then they'll fly away again. No way to reach them. Only the clouds and each other for company. Nice.

Where are you, Billy? Are you anywhere?

I find a shell, toss it at the waves as they rush thin and bubbled onto the shore. It feels good to whip my arm through the air. A handful of wet sand. Another. A pop bottle that's washed up. The weight feels right. I want something heavier.

Getting up, I start to search. Bending and throwing—sand, shells, bleached wood, stones. At first, I hurl them into the ocean, swinging wide and wild, to see how far they'll go. But the waves are high and crashing; I can't hear them as they hit the surface. I look up at the stars, throw a fistful of sand. All that light and fire so high above the earth . . . well, here's sand, dirty, dingy, itchy sand, rocks, shells, bones that have been broken and buffeted and crushed until they're nothing. With each handful I fling at the sky, I scream. At first, just sound. Then the words come, from a throat raw and burning, "I'm here. I'm here."

I'm here.

Chapter Ten

I don't think I sleep the night of Billy's death, but it's difficult to tell in the dark. Is that the ceiling or are my eyes closed? Here's what I know: I am in a bed. In a room. In a house I don't live in but cannot leave. Larger than the house is the island; larger than the island, the ocean. I am surrounded by water, miles and miles of it. All those trains, buses, cars, humming along roads, connecting everything up across space without end—they've nothing to do with me. In the silence of the island, I try to recall the crossing from Scotland, that endless stretch of water, the churning of the ocean. But in all those sounds, the promise that you will get there. You've found the path and you're on your way. Now I'm alone in the ocean, the rope that was tight around my waist has come loose, slithered away before I could catch it. And now I'm floating out God knows where.

I guess I do sleep because Charlie wakes me and there's sun. When I understand the noise that's woken me is him calling, all I can think is, *Seven hours. Seven hours* until his nap. I can't fathom it, how I'm going to do seven hours before I can lie back down and not think about anything.

Little ones, they want you all the time. I'm all right when it comes to watching Charlie from a distance. But when he gets close, with his hands pulling at me, I think, I can't. Once, I feel tears start and cover my eyes. But he tugs at my fingers, worried, and I have to say, "Peekaboo!"

I set him up on the front lawn, put his favorite toys on the blanket and hope he'll just let me sit. He's been chatty today. It makes my head hurt.

For a while he moves the animals around the blanket. Then he gets to his feet and brings one of the animals over to me.

"Buh."

"Yes, that's the bull, Charlie."

At least I think that's what he's saying. He's shoving it at me. The wooden bull they gave him for his birthday. Could be ball, though. Could be Betty. Who knows.

I'm sitting folded up, arms around my shins, chin on my knees. Charlie circling. He wants me to get up, chase him. Do something. But right now—as I have said to him—I need to sit.

He pushes the toy into my arm. In a thin, tight voice, I say, "That hurts, Charlie . . ."

But he's not interested in how it feels to me, but to him—the block of wood, the little horns, against the flesh. He's concentrating, a frown on his face, the line and puckered mouth. That's all I am to him at this moment, a soft thing to dig into. Like his father with one of his experiments.

I shrug away. "I said it *hurts*."

As if he talks. Understands. But I'm tired and I don't want to play. I know it's only me, I know I'm all he's got. But I'm tired, frankly, of being all he's got.

"Buh."

"Dear Lord, yes, Charlie, *buh*!"

He waits, not sure. I am loud, I've waved my arm. Will I move again? Get up? Play with him?

He hits me. Hard on the shoulder with the wooden toy. "That *hurt*!" I scream at him, wanting him to feel my voice like a slap. "That hurt, Charlie!"

He's scared now, not so curious. I grab his wrist, pry the bull out of his hand. He twists, whining, trying to keep hold of it. I get it, throw it far into the grass. His cries become bleats of anger. He takes hold of the first thing he can reach, my sleeve, pulling on it, even as he tries to push me. But I won't budge and his head bobs as he hops from one foot to the other in rage.

He's leaning, braced against me. Deliberately, I shift my arm and he falls. Awkward, on his left side. For a moment, he struggles, feet and head raised. Then he collapses, head landing on the ground. Face turned from me, he cries, like he's given up, like he knows he's alone and there's no one to care for him. Immediately I gather him up; I'm hasty, clumsy, and the movement frightens him, makes him wail even louder. Cradling his head in my hand, I cry into the soft, damp creases of his neck. Over and over, I tell him I'm sorry, I'm so sorry, I will never, ever, ever do that again. Does he forgive me? I stroke his back, kiss his ear, nuzzle his curls. I must start to feel like his Betty again because he quiets. But his eyes are dazed and like it's his only friend, he puts his thumb in his mouth.

"It's a good thumb, isn't it, Charlie? Best thumb in the world. Better than ice cream. Shall we find the buh? Let's go find it, hey?"

Mrs. Barnes leaves precisely at five. I warm up our evening meal and eat with Charlie in the kitchen. After I put him down, I sit on my bed in the next room, feeling the emptiness of the place. I grew up in a city, in a full house, other families on either side and voices from the street coming in through the windows. A silence this deep, it doesn't feel real. Doesn't feel . . . right. You feel something must be creeping up behind you; there but staying quiet so you won't know until it's too late.

The ring of the telephone, shrill and sudden, makes me jump. It's an alarm—something's wrong. The something bad, it's happened. I scramble out to the hall, frantic to make the sound stop. Moonlight coming in through the front windows, throwing shadows from the fragile desk, the spindly chairs no one sits in, the frame of the window itself stretching high along the wall.

I snatch up the receiver, breathe, "Yes, Morrow house."

"Betty?"

Henry. *Oh, hello, Henry. I'm so sorry I haven't called. I imagine you've heard the sad news.* That's what I mean to say.

Then he says "Betty?" again, like a worried little boy, and I answer him with tears.

"What did he do?"

We're sharing a deck chair under a blanket. The sky is so full of stars, it's like the universe has gathered overhead to watch us. I look up to see the light left on in my room, it's the only light in the whole house.

"He was lineman for the . . ." That stupid company I could never remember the name of. "He did electrical work for the state. Rigging up the . . ."

He nods to say he understands. "And there was an accident?"

I'm curled around him, cheek to his chest, so I can't see his face as I murmur, "With the wires. He took hold of something he shouldn't and—"

Agitated, I start to sit up. Bringing my head back down to his shoulder, Henry says, "I'm sure it was quick and he didn't know anything." I fiddle with the button of his shirt, thinking this is a good lie, the sort said out of kindness, not meant to cheat you.

He asks if I've written to my mother. I tell him I've gotten as far as "Dear." She never wanted Billy to come to this country. He was so patient with her, listening to all her worries. America was so big, so violent. Something could happen to you there and who would care? She couldn't quite express it, but to her, it wasn't a real country. Just a vast slap of land, filled with lunatics shooting at each other and making money.

Henry's stroke becomes more lingering. It's not what he's asking for—he's not asking for anything, bless him.

Afterward, he says, "So, it's not a good time to say this . . ."

"But you're leaving next week."

"Yes. But the Lamonts don't need me until next summer. After we get the yacht back, I can go anywhere. I was going to stay with my brother in Connecticut. But I don't have to."

I nod, not sure what he's saying.

"I could be in New Jersey," he explains. "When you get back, I could be there. If you want." He looks uncertain. "Maybe you don't want . . ."

It's sudden. What I want has not been something I've thought about for some time. A twist of unease: Henry was supposed to be here, only here. Summer. Not part of anything real. But it's also true that he is here, now, when no one else is.

"I don't know what's going to happen," I tell him. "Charlie and I could be here come Christmas for all I know."

"Then I'll write you."

"I'll write back."

Dear Mother,

I am heartbroken that I cannot be with you and the family at this terrible, terrible time. The Lindberghs are away and there is only me to care for the baby. Otherwise, I would be on the next boat home.

Billy was the best older brother I could have had. He looked after me here, just as you said he should. I don't know what I shall do without him. I hope having Jean and the baby back in Glasgow gives you some comfort. I hope to see you all soon.

Love,
Bessie

September becomes October. The ocean turns rough and gray. Leaves cover the lawns and it gets dark early. I read to Charlie in the library near the fireplace. Knit him a woolly hat. Mrs. Barnes and I search the cottages, get out the heavy sweaters left behind by the Morrow girls. I put one on Charlie, but it's a dress on him. He needs new clothes, but there's no money. I could ask Mrs. Morrow, but it's an awkward letter to write and I keep putting it off, hoping she'll call and say we can come home.

One afternoon, I hear weeping as Charlie and I come in from our walk. An image of that single plane soaring through the air strikes me through. Snatching Charlie up, I hurry to the kitchen to find Mrs. Barnes sobbing.

"He's gone," she says when she can speak. "Senator Morrow. Mr. Banks found him, he had a stroke in his sleep."

I think to say *Best way to go really*. But after Billy, I know, everything people say about death is wrong. The instinct is to comfort, make it smaller, less painful. It's insulting. People don't want words when someone dies. They want to howl.

"The Colonel and Mrs. Lindbergh are on their way back. She wants to be there for her mother."

"Yes, I'm sure."

I thought I said it right. It sounded right in my head. But from the way Mrs. Barnes looks at me, I can tell I missed. I meant to sound caring. But she heard what I was thinking. *Yes, I'm sure. I would have liked that too.*

"Well," I say to Charlie, "I suppose we should start packing."

Mrs. Barnes looks bewildered. "They didn't say that."

"What did they say?"

She thinks, then shakes her head. *Nothing.*

"They didn't say anything about Charlie? If we're to come or . . ."

She's still shaking her head.

"Have they forgotten us?" I mean to say it as a joke. But I can hear my voice go harsh on *got*.

She looks at me with distaste. "They're in *mourning*."

So am I, I want to say. Why doesn't that matter?

I rub my cheek against Charlie's. "Then . . . we wait."

Dear Betty,

Well, I hope you will not be angry with me, but I am now living in New Jersey. Ellerson found me a room at the boardinghouse where he lives. (I thought you said he had a wife?) He says to tell you that he misses you and it's time for you to come back. I agree.

Do you remember Marguerite Jantzen? She says she knows you—but she is really Marguerite Junge! Her husband has come from Germany and he is also living at the boardinghouse, so I hear all the stories of the Morrows. Big scandal: Banks has been left nothing in the Senator's will! Mrs. Morrow has kept him on for now, but Ellerson says he is one too many away from being fired.

How is the baby? Give him a squeeze from me. Give yourself a squeeze as well. I miss you. Please write soon.

I like to read Henry's letters at night. They put a voice in my head, break up the silence. Otherwise, I'm too aware of the dark and the quiet. When everyone was here and we were all crammed in one corner of this enormous house, it drove me mad, all the chatter and footsteps and doors banging open and shut. Now I'd give anything for noise. Human noise.

Lying on the bed, I settle my hands on my stomach.

Dear Henry,

It was lovely to get your letter. Do you know, you're the only person who's talked to me in days? The other day on the lawn, I listened to the trees blow in the wind. It was the only sound except for Charlie and the squeak of the wheels on his wooden dog. I looked up at the big empty sky and thought back to the last time we took a car ride. I thought, maybe there was a crash. Maybe we died. Maybe this is an afterlife only we don't know it. And that's why we're the only ones.

During the day, I give myself little checks. I tap the edge of the table, sing Charlie the cow song, or look at the clock, make sure it's the same time that's in my head. Once I caught Mrs. Barnes looking at me like I'd done something funny. And I couldn't think what I'd done. I mean, I really couldn't remember the last thing I'd said or done.

Turning my head, I look out the window, but the sky hasn't started to lighten, you can't find the horizon. From the next room, I hear the rustle of sheets; normally a sound that makes me start that prayer, *Go quiet, stay asleep, don't wake up* . . . Now I go through the bathroom that separates us. Charlie hears the creak of the door and pops up, peering at me over the bar of the crib.

"Do you want to come in with me, Charlie? Just for tonight?" I get my hands under his arm and backside. "Sweet boy," I whisper as I carry him into my room. I settle him on my bed, drawing the quilt over him and tucking it in around the edges. I lift his head, nudge the pillow underneath. Then very carefully, I lie lengthwise beside him, lining my belly up with the warm huddle of him. His white hair is like a quiet burst of light in the room. His breathing like the tables and clocks, a sign I haven't floated away. He's here. I'm here. In a few hours, it will be tomorrow and Mrs. Barnes will come.

And then it happens. Not the next day or the day after that; I'm not sure really when. But the telephone rings and I pick it up to say, "Morrow residence." And hear Mrs. Sullivan ask, "Is that Betty Gow?"

"Yes, it is," I say, and the answer strikes me as funny.

She is calling to say the Lindberghs will be back at the end of the month. We are to arrive a few days before, which means we will leave day after tomorrow. There will be a ferry ticket at the landing, a train ticket at the station.

"Very good," I say, matching her tone. Then add, "I was sorry to hear about the Senator. Please give Mrs. Morrow my condolences. If you feel it appropriate."

I wait. She doesn't say anything. Either Mrs. Barnes never reported back about Billy's death or it's been forgotten. Hanging up, I look at Charlie on the rug of the library.

"We're going home, aren't we, Charlie? Well, you are at any rate."

"I can see your tummy, Charlie." I give it a gentle poke and he giggles.

I can see his diaper too, through the rip in his shorts. I can see the threads that have come loose on his sleeve, the dangling hem. The grass stain I never could get out. The cuffs of his sleeves are chewed up, some of the elbows out. Some of the shirts got so tight, I had to cut the necks

out. He hasn't worn shoes for weeks, because his old ones have no soles
left and they're too small anyway. I don't think he has anything left
with all the buttons on. I try to sew the buttons back on, but sometimes
they come off in the grass and get lost. Some of his pants are held up
with string run through the loops and tied. You'd never know he had a
haircut. The bubble curls are back, wild and uneven. And he's grown.

"What are we going to do with you, Charlie? I'm not sure your
own mother would recognize you. We could walk right past her and
she'd say, 'Look at that poor child, all ragged and dirty. It's a complete
disgrace.'"

He smiles, pleased to be a disgrace. I tell him boys are all alike and
think what to do.

The fact of it is, there's no money. Mrs. Barnes gets funds for gro-
ceries, I get my wages. But no one thinks of a baby needing anything.
Or if they do, they think well, someone'll manage.

I can't bring him back like this. I suppose that makes me the someone.

I ask Mrs. Barnes if she will drive us into town; there's a store that
sells children's clothes. I buy Charlie new pants, shirts, even a new
sweater and shoes. There's a pleasure to new clothes, the fabric smooth
and even, everything the right length, the colors fresh. Charlie looks
a new boy.

"You have a very handsome son," the saleslady tells me.

"Thank you."

Chapter Eleven

Englewood, New Jersey

It is late October when the Lindberghs return to New Jersey. Charlie and I are marching his little animals, two by two, into his Noah's ark when they find us in the nursery. "Charlie," I say. "Look who's here . . ."

He doesn't recognize them. But he's not afraid, going easily into Mrs. Lindbergh's arms. She pecks at him, her head darting down, mouth here, mouth there. The Colonel rubs his neck, says softly, "Hi, Buster."

"He looks so well, Betty," she says. He says, "*Grown*, my God."

"It was lovely in Maine."

"Yes, it's beautiful there," she says absently, focused on Charlie. "Oh, it's so good to have him *back*."

Well, I didn't take him from you, I think. *And putting your spit on him doesn't make him yours*. Unnerved—these are not thoughts to have in front of them—I search their faces; have they seen?

They have not.

She tells me she and the Colonel want time with Charlie—just them. Lord knows, she says, I deserve the time off. He says, "We feel three months is acceptable."

I stare at him. Three months is too much. Three months is we don't need you. Three months is Charlie forgets me.

"Paid, of course," she adds anxiously. "The Colonel will be traveling, I'll be staying here in Englewood." She glances at him, as if to make sure that this plan is acceptable to him. "The new house in Princeton isn't quite ready, the Whateleys are looking after it. You're welcome to stay at Englewood, though."

Englewood reminds me. "I was so sorry. To hear about your father."

My condolences are unexpected and not entirely welcome. Perhaps she senses the test: Has she been told about Billy? Will she remember?

She says, "Oh . . . yes." Then, "Charles, look at the baby's feet, they're *enormous*."

They turn inward, heads bent, clustered around their son. To their backs, I say thank you. And that they've been extremely generous. I think to explain about the old worn-out clothes, the new things I bought, but then the Colonel swings Charlie around asking, Does he want to fly? When Charlie shouts, "Uh-huh!" Colonel Lindbergh lifts him up so his toes touch the top of his father's head. Too high, I think, and indeed he cries, "Down, down!" But when the Colonel sets him on the rug, Charlie says, "Den! Den!" and lifts his own small arms to be swept up again.

"Best," says Mrs. Lindbergh, "if you go now while he's distracted."

Looking down at the ark, I see the Colonel's knocked over some of the pairs with his flying game; the giraffes and lions are lying sideways and scattered. Tasting grief, sharp and sour, at the back of my throat, I shut the door.

"She's free!"

Unpacking, I look up to see Violet at the door of my room. Not waiting to be invited, she slips in and bounces on the bed. "Was it awful?" she asks. "The house in Maine after they left?" She felt terrible for me, so lonely. Then before I can say anything, she says, "We're going to the Peanut Grill. You must come."

Tired, I think. Or headache. But then she says, "Red will be there. He's missed you *so much*."

I ask what time. Violet says nine o'clock. I'm about to say, *Too late. I'm up at seven for Charlie.* Then I realize, I don't have to be up at seven for Charlie. I don't have to be up for anyone.

"Nine it is," I say.

She squeals, races back to the door—to tell someone the glorious news, no doubt. Suddenly mischievous, I ask, "Will Mr. Banks be joining us?"

Her face darkens. "He most certainly will not!" The smile pops back. "See you at nine!"

They cheer—actually cheer—when Violet brings me into the Peanut Grill. There's clapping and hooting and shouts of my name. Ellerson waving me over, Marguerite smiling as she sips her drink. And Henry, scrambling over people in the booth; it's more a collision than an embrace, he's so excited. He lifts me in the air, the roar rising along with me. From above, I take in his face, thrilled, amazed, as if he can't believe I'm here.

"Hello," I say when he's put me down.

"I'm happy," he says. "Really happy."

I laugh. "Yes, I can see."

"You don't think I'm an idiot?"

"Oh, you probably are. But I am as well, so."

Normally, I'm not one for loud places, but tonight the Peanut Grill suits me. Being surrounded by the Morrow people, Henry's arm around me in the cramped booth, everyone wanting to know: How *did* I survive all those weeks in that huge house? It wasn't easy, I tell them. Sometimes I thought I was losing my mind. Everyone laughs.

I don't tell anyone about Billy. I can't be funny about that, and I'm determined everyone should keep laughing. Every messy, drunken burst of shouting wipes out the memories of those queer moments before dawn when I thought it was going to be dark forever. Henry keeps his head on my shoulder, snuffling against me like a lovely dog. I pat his head several times, *Ah, who's my boy?*

At one point, I catch Ellerson looking sarcastic and give him a stern look. I want happiness, I say. I insist on it. In surrender, he puts up his hands. He's already been drinking with his pals at the taxi stand in town. He also has an ugly bruise under his eye. I brush mine to ask and he says, "Bet on a loser." And before I can think how to say man or horse, he sends Violet up for another round.

When she's far enough away, I ask the table, "What happened with Banks?"

"That seems to be over," Marguerite informs me.

"What *is* it, exactly?"

"He falls into her room when it suits him. I suspect when they got back from Maine, she demanded a ring and he said no."

"And ever since," says Ellerson, "she's been looking for whatever kind of yes she can get."

I look and see Violet, one elbow on the bar, giggling with a young fellow in a flat cap. She's not subtle that girl, I think, with tipsy affection. When Ellerson, irritated by the delay, makes to get up, I say, "No, I'll go. Get a closer look at him."

Violet, it turns out, has not even ordered. The gentleman, whose name is Mike, his profession driving a truck, has bought her a drink. I signal to her that I've got it, she should have fun. Leaning over the bar, I try to catch the bartender's eye.

"Hi."

It's one quick sound in a sea of shouting and laughter; at first I don't quite hear it. Only when he leans into my vision do I turn my head. Take him in. He's good-looking, nicely dressed for the Peanut Grill. I'm about to say, *You don't come here often, that's clear.*

He nods to the Morrow crew. "I said to my friend, all the prettiest girls are at that table, only there's no room."

I pick up an accent, take in the blond hair and blue eyes. Not as singsongy as Henry's. More precise. German, if I had to say.

"All the prettiest girls," I tell him, "and my boyfriend."

He does a long, slow nod of disappointment. Still he waits as I ask for two whiskeys, a Coca-Cola, two beers, and . . . why not, three whiskeys. Sensing his approval of my recklessness, I say, "First night of my holiday."

"What do you do?"

". . . I'm a nanny."

He glances down at my legs but is smart enough not to say he wishes he had one like me.

"How does that pay?" he asks. "My sister is thinking of trying that kind of work."

"Depends on the family, really."

He glances back at the table. "You all work for the Morrows, right?" He peers at Ellerson. "I recognize the driver."

The bartender brings the drinks, starts setting them on a tray. Distracted, I say, "Not all of us."

"Oh . . . you're *that* nanny. Of course. I should have realized."

"Well, not today," I tell him, hoisting the tray. "Not for a few months, actually."

"Here, let me get that for you."

With men, I find, there's a bell, a soft tone inside you that tells you you've been too friendly; they've seen an opening and they think if they get forceful, they'll make it in. It's the point where you keep it cold and short, put distance between you.

I say, "No, I've got it. Thank you. Good luck to your sister."

He smiles. There is no sister.

Behind me I hear Violet shriek, "Oh, you wouldn't believe what some of them get up to . . ." Gossiping on too much beer. Nudging her with my elbow, I murmur, "Watch what you say, young lady."

Returning to the table, I slide back into Henry's eager arms. Ellerson wants to know about Violet's man. Henry puts his hand on my knee. I run a finger down his thigh. "Three whole months," I whisper.

Then I look back at the bar, the crush of people. He was tall, that man. With bright hair that lay close to the scalp, the kind that catches the light. Even the grimy, smoky light of the Peanut Grill. Should be able to see him from here.

But I don't.

Henry buys a new car. A green Chrysler coupe. Secondhand, but I ask, "Can you afford it?"

He shrugs happily. "Not really. But the old one's beyond repair."

Thinking of the times he's taken me out, I say, "Maybe I could . . ."

"No, no." He puts a protective arm around me. "I can pay it, don't worry." Jovial, he pats the hood. "Hey, we'll call it the Depression. Right? Because everybody's in it."

"I don't want everybody in it!" I protest.

"No." He kisses me. "Just you and me."

"This is okay?"

". . . Yes, it's nice . . ."

"You're so beautiful."

I smile down at the top of his head, feel his fingers at my back. He's having trouble with the hooks. I reach around to help him, but a bright light comes through the car window, stinging my eyes, and I put up a hand to block it. For a second, I can't see. I hear the rattle of Henry's belt, feel shifted off his lap. Belatedly, I realize, and take hold of my blouse, pulling it closed across my breasts.

Three rapid knocks. A face under a policeman's cap appears. He rolls his finger, telling us to open the window. I slide off Henry's legs, button up my blouse in the darkness left to me while he does as the trooper says. Because of his lack of papers, any encounter with the police makes Henry anxious. Once I'm presentable, I move to the window, letting the policeman know he can deal with me. He's young with dark curls, shouldn't need to be peeking in parked cars for his fun.

"Is there a problem, Trooper?" Wanting to add, *You know full well there isn't; this is a deserted road near a field, the closest house a mile off.*

"Evening. What's your name, Miss?"

"Betty Gow."

"Ever heard of public decency laws, Miss Gow?"

"Who are we shocking, the cows?"

He recites, "'No public nudity or sexual activity . . .'"

Henry leans forward. "Yes, we're sorry, Officer. We understand."

"Your name, sir?" This time he gets out his notebook.

"Henrik Johnson," says Henry softly, wanting to hide his accent.

"Are you employed, Mr. Johnson?"

Henry is not, except for the odd shift at a local garage; it's the kind of irregularity that gets people asking questions. I put a hand on his arm, to let him know he should sit back. "I'm employed, Officer . . . actually, what is your name?"

"McCann."

I give him a look: *Not surprised.* "Well, Trooper McCann, I am employed. Would you like to know the name of my employer?"

"Sure." He's grinning now.

"Colonel Charles Lindbergh. And his wife, Anne *Morrow* Lindbergh."

The grin vanishes. After a moment, he flips the notebook shut and puts it back in his pocket. Lindbergh is God in this country; the Morrows local royalty. No New Jersey trooper is going to go up against them.

Feeling a bully, I say, "So, since we're not corrupting anybody's morals but our own . . . ?"

The trooper glances at Henry. "Next time, why don't you take her some place decent?" He touches the brim of his hat. "You folks have a nice evening." After a moment, we hear his patrol car start; the sound of the engine fades out as he drives off.

Henry withdraws to the other side, murmurs, "He's right."

I feel the sigh rise, push it down before it can be heard. It's a side of Henry I don't enjoy, one I didn't see in Maine. Probably because he had a steady job in Maine, and there was no reason to feel sorry for himself. Down on himself, I correct the thought. It's himself he's hardest on.

Moving closer, I say, "Well, I'm not bothered."

"Isn't there anywhere else we can go?"

"I don't feel right at the Englewood house, too many people with nothing better to do than talk."

Nuzzling my hair, he says, "It wasn't a problem in Maine."

"That was summer." I don't like Maine being talked about as a lovely time—*oh, if only we could go back there*. Pushing him away, I sit up. "And I don't think your roommate would appreciate me visiting."

Somehow, I've got to the other end of the seat, jammed up against the door. The window's cloudy and I trace some clear lines through the fog. For a brief second, I can see through them to the cold, bright night outside. Then our warmth clouds it up again.

I hear Henry say quietly, "I'm sorry. Police make me . . ." He rubs hard at his stomach. "They make me think of my father."

I shake my head.

"He was a fisherman. Very strict. Religious. He would come home on weekends. Line us up, my brothers and I." He smiles wanly. "Then he would beat us. One by one."

"*Henry*—why?"

"He said it was for something we did that week while he was away or something we would do the next week. I suppose there was a logic to it."

No logic, I say, kissing him. No logic, just meanness. Viciousness.

"Problem's not the policeman," I say later. "Problem's the lack of a place to be, a house . . ."

"They have that new house," he says. "The Lindberghs."

I turn my head, questioning.

"The one they're building. The old people take care of it, the ones you don't like."

"Hopewell. Don't be rude, it's him I don't like, she's lovely."

"Well, if they're living there, it must be a place you can go. You have a room there, right?" I nod. "Maybe we should go see your room. Inspect it."

I don't fancy the idea at all. But Elsie has been asking me to visit; they're on their own out there except for the workmen and the poor thing's lonely.

"I suppose I could ask."

Henry's hand finds my knee, slides to the top of my stocking. "That would be nice, if you asked."

I ask, calling the next day, and Elsie is thrilled. "We've heard rumors of your young man. I'd love to meet him." She laughs. "Oh, it'll be wonderful to have young people in the house. I tell you, if one more bloke with a hammer comes at me demanding coffee, I'll pound his head in."

"Elsie!"

"That's what I've become, honestly. I've missed you. And the baby. I suppose he's growing so fast, I'd hardly recognize him. When would you like to come?"

Chapter Twelve

On the drive to the Hopewell house, I warn Henry. Olly Whateley is English. He will pretend not to understand Henry at times. He will make jokes about herring or whatever he thinks is Norwegian. He will ask what Henry does for work and let him know it's not up to snuff. He will talk about cricket—endlessly. The only thing to do is ignore him.

But isolation has worked wonders on Olly Whateley. He comes out of the house, arms spread wide. Big greeting for me. Firm handshake for Henry. "Lovely to see you."

He compliments the Depression: "Nice looking, these coupes." Then he gestures to the house. "Well, how'd you like it?"

"It's like the Englewood house," I say. "Only smaller."

He points to me. "Clever girl. They used the same architect."

On the outside, the house looks almost finished. Inside, it's fairly raw. The walls are unpainted, the floors unfinished. In most rooms, the light fixtures are just holes in the plaster and wire. But the kitchen is nice and warm and that's where we eat. Whateley asks Henry this, that, and the other about boats and sailing. From there it's on to carpentry and cars. Partly, it's men showing what they know about men things, but for once, Whateley's letting someone else get a word in. Elsie smiles around the table, pleased with all the talk.

After dinner, Henry glances at me. "May I see the rest of the house?"

"Of course," says Whateley, missing the fact that he is not the desired company. "I'll give you the full tour. Come on, Wahgoosh," he calls to the dog. "Time for a stroll."

"I'll stay behind," I say. "Help Elsie clean up."

"Tell me all the news." She likes to hear about the goings-on at the Morrow house. "Is it true the Senator left Mr. Banks out of his will?"

I nod. "While he gave Mr. Springer, his secretary, twenty-five thousand dollars." Elsie's mouth opens in shock at the sum. "Banks does drink. Some say the family thought he couldn't manage that much money on his own."

She sniffs. "So they kept him on wages instead. And Maine? How was that? You were gone a long time!"

I think of the ocean, the gulls, and creaking floorboards. The darkness above me—not knowing if it was the ceiling or my eyes were closed. The brutal talk about the Morrows and Lindberghs—that weird almost-kidnapping. *Dyke. Old lady. Soused*—words hurled like stones.

"I tell you, Elsie, they're a strange crew."

The men return, Henry saying, "That was an excellent tour, Mr. Whateley, thank you." There's the gentlest thread of mockery in his voice, but Whateley doesn't hear it. He and Elsie don't have children, must be nice to have a young man giving him respect.

"Why don't we have a song?" says Whateley eagerly, looking at Elsie. "She has a beautiful voice, studied professionally."

But Elsie says, "Don't be silly. Betty, you haven't seen your room yet. It's just upstairs, why don't you show her, Henrik?" She gives Whateley's arm a slap. "You help me in the other room."

As we go up the stairs, Henry whispers, "Now, this is the staircase. It has fifteen steps and they are all of equal size . . ."

"Was he that boring?"

Henry raises his eyebrows to indicate *very*. "He's a nice man. At one point, I was sure we were lost and he showed me how you find your way in and out, following the electric cables. But next time, you come with me."

I nod, smiling, even as I think, Electric cables, Billy's job at the whatsit.

My room is on a hallway with three others, directly opposite the nursery. Opening the door, I see they've sent over Charlie's things from the Princeton house, his crib and changing table. But no one's put things to rights; the furniture has been pushed through the door and left there. No curtains on the window, just black shutters no one's bothered to shut. Some of his clothes and wooden animals have made it over, but they're jumbled in a box. Upset, I want to set them out properly, but Henry tugs me back saying, "Would madam care to see her room?"

"... Oh, yes, please," I say, playing along as he pulls me across the hall.

You can't really call it my room, there's nothing of me here. It's just a place I'll be in a month. I'm not even sure I recognize the bed and bureau they've put in. There's no light yet, just wires hanging from the ceiling. The moon comes through the bare window, casting Henry's shadow on the wall. He nods. "Look, it's a bed."

"It is." I'm about to add, *Not as nice as the one we had in Maine.* But whenever I think of Maine and Billy, it's like a chill coming through me. I can't be flirty or friendly or even nice. I can't be anything at all.

Taking my hands, he says cautiously, "I like your room."

I don't. I hate it. I hate the emptiness of it, and I hate Charlie's room next door. No blanket or warmth in the crib. His poor things in a cardboard box as if they're about to be tossed out. We shouldn't have come. Not to this neglected place where no one lives and it feels like no one ever will. The car was better than this, I think, remembering the fog of warmth on the windows.

Tentative, Henry puts his mouth to mine, presses gently.

"Better?" he hopes.

It's not, but Elsie's gone to all the trouble. I kiss him back.

I can't seem to be alone. I see Henry almost every other day. We go to the movies, skating, Palisades Park, walk through town, look at what's in the windows. A few times, we go out with Marguerite and her husband, Johannes. He's a dark, acerbic man with one leg shorter than the other and he pulls himself angrily through life on a cane. Henry admires him, thinks he's clever, and he is. But I can't say I enjoy his company. His bitterness infects Marguerite; when she's with him, the talk often turns to her family in Germany, how they lost everything to foreigners after the war, and now she has to work for *others*. Every so often, her eyes linger on Henry and I have to bite my tongue not to say, *I'm sorry you're saddled with a miserable old crow, but this one's mine, thank you very much.*

If Henry's not free, I play cards for hours with the Sharpe girls. Sometimes Ellerson joins us. Violet's not good at games, grows bored when she loses. When she's bored, she asks questions.

"Do you love Red Johnson?" she asks me one evening.

"No," Ellerson and I say at the same time. I laugh, throw the three of hearts at him.

And like that, it's over, the three months that seemed like they'd last forever. When I peek into the nursery at Englewood that first morning back, I marvel at the changes in Charlie. He's longer, more structured. The baby fat's going, his young man face is just there underneath. And he's talking—like he knows what he's saying. *Naw*, when he doesn't want something. *Uh-huh*, when he does. He sounds a regular little cowboy. But he shouts "Betty!" when he sees me. He hasn't forgotten.

"Fair warning," says Mrs. Lindbergh as I catch him. "He repeats *everything*."

"Oh, yes? I love you, can you repeat that, Charlie? I love you."

"Ove!" he shouts, then runs off. "Ove, all gone. Ove all gone."

Mrs. Lindbergh and I burst out laughing. Then she puts a hand to her stomach. Eyes shining, she declares, "So . . ."

It takes me a moment. "Oh, my. Congratulations."

"In August. And I want to thank you. For all the time you've given me with him. It's been lovely, hearing him call for me rather than . . ." *You.* She stops, embarrassed.

Charlie comes barreling toward us. It seems he'll stop when he reaches us, but he races right past, intent on his own journey, and we smile: *foolish expectations.* As we do, I realize with a jolt that I've hated her these past months. But this Anne Lindbergh is so different from the person I had in my head. How did this funny, tiny person make me so angry? I remember flinging the rocks and sand on the beach, screaming at the night sky, and I'm appalled. She can't ever know I felt that way about her; that she trusted someone with that much rage.

"Do you want a boy or a girl?" I ask, desperate to be talking of the right things.

"Oh, I don't care," she says. "Healthy. Safe. Not my nose!"

It's the old joke, how she hates her nose. Here, I can be truthful. "Mrs. Lindbergh, *I* like your nose. I think it's very pretty. You wouldn't look like you without it and that would be a shame."

She accepts the compliment with a pleased shrug. "The Colonel wants twelve children. I hope I can manage."

I say I'm sure she can. And think, Well, our Lord had twelve apostles, no surprise he wants the same.

"They're going to spend weekends at the new house in Hopewell," I tell Henry the next evening. "Just the family. So I'll be in Englewood, and we'll have that time."

He gives me a brief smile. But his mind is elsewhere.

"Something you want to say?"

He takes my hands. "I'm broke. I think is how you say it." He smiles; see it's funny, just another "broke" American. "The garage isn't steady work. When the sailing season starts, I can work with the Lamonts. Until then, I have to live with my brother in West Hartford. But I don't want this to be over."

". . . West Hartford?"

"I'll visit. You'll visit."

Where? I think. Your brother's rooms? My room down the hall from the Lindberghs?

Then I hear him say, "Or we could get married."

I actually laugh. "Oh God, no, I'm sorry. I'm sorry. But . . ." I look around the battered interior of the Depression. "Henry."

Thankfully, he sees the humor of it. "What? It's very spacious. Sitting room there . . ." He points to the passenger side. Tugs me over to him. "Bedroom here. Who knows, maybe a nursery just there . . ." He nods to the dashboard; fondly, I think, *You can't have children, you are a child.*

"When do you leave?"

"I thought March first."

A few weeks from now. And a Tuesday. Not one of my nights off. "Well, if they're in Hopewell that Monday, we can meet then."

"I'm at the garage Monday nights," he reminds me.

"Tuesday, I might be able to get out between seven and ten. I think Mrs. Lindbergh would understand . . ."

Me wanting to say goodbye. Fearful, he waits for me to say it. But it'll become clear enough on its own in time. No need to be brutal about it now.

He says, "West Hartford, it's more glamorous than you think."

"Is it?"

"Oh, yes. Greta Garbo was once seen at a gas station . . ."

On Monday, the day before Henry leaves, Mrs. Lindbergh calls from Hopewell. Charlie has a cold, so they will be staying another night. She sounds exhausted, poor thing. Sick baby and another on the way. "You're sure you don't want me to come?" I ask.

"No, no," she says. "Elsie's here. And we'll be back tomorrow, I'm certain."

"Happy Leap Year!" bellows Ellerson. Off duty, he's been making free with the wine, which is plentiful because Mrs. Morrow is having a dinner party; her first since the Senator died. The staff is a bit out of practice, which has Banks in a temper. He's particularly snappish with the table maids, so I try to help Violet and the other girls keep up. I'm running the dirty plates under the tap when Ellerson says, "Come play with me. I have something I want to ask you."

I give him a reproving look. But then, Edna elbows me to one side with a gruff "*Excuse* me!" so I say "By all means," and let Ellerson lead me to the small table by the window where the staff have a smoke or meal during the lulls in service. In fact, it's where we ate dinner together the first night I came here.

He sets out two wine bottles, opens one, then places the other between us.

"What's this?" I say. "Kissing games?"

"This is truth." With a lazy finger, he spins the bottle; it points to him. He says, "Ask me anything. Fair warning. I'm not always good at this game."

Is your wife a good swimmer? is the first thing I think to ask. But that's too cheeky. How to get at it, Ellerson's . . . freedom? He's always off somewhere. He gambles with everything—money, job, love—as if none of it matters.

"Why do you stay at the boardinghouse so often? Doesn't your wife mind?"

Crushing his cheek against his fist, he says, "My wife is a very nice lady who came to this country in the hopes of becoming a citizen. No, she does not mind." Before I can point out he's not answered all my questions, he spins the bottle, stopping it just before it swings past me.

Right away, he asks, "What happened in Detroit?"

I knew it was coming. Still, I take my time. Assembling facts, tossing what can be told and what can't into separate piles.

"You told me to come."

Grimy streets. Cold rooms. Snotty, whining children. That can all be told.

Softly, Ellerson asks, "What happened? In Detroit?"

Really, he's asking the wrong question. It's not what happened in Detroit, but what happened in Glasgow.

"That's never Bessie . . ."

On Nithsdale Street.

Bessie the Terror? Beastly Bessie? Bessie the Beauty more like.

I was thirteen. Embarrassed. And thrilled. At that age, being called beautiful meant you weren't like everyone else. You were going to have exciting things happen to you. And having an older boy like Rob Coutts—he was a summer day of a man, blond hair, the brightest blue eyes, cleft in his chin—call you a beauty, it was like I'd been welcomed into a special club. At least been noticed. At last.

It's peculiar when you're youngest—unique, cause you're small and people fuss, but also easy to ignore. I was my father's pet, and when he died, there was no one to say *Yes, Bessie, what is it? Everyone listen now . . .* Now when I said something I thought was clever, I no longer got the almost smile before I was told off, I just got told off. "Time to grow up, love," sighed my sister Agnes.

Then one day, Rob Coutts stopped in to borrow something and said I was beautiful and I knew what my life was going to be. I wasn't going to be rushed and exhausted like my sisters, frightened like my mother. My life was going to be better. It was going to be *mine.* Rob lived down the road, raised by his grandmother and there were those who said she let him run wild. Didn't stop girls loving him or boys admiring him, although not Billy, come to think of it, and they were the same age.

Like most, I left school at fourteen. I did look at jobs, a lot of them; even started a few. But none of them were what I saw myself doing for the rest of my life. And when Agnes or Billy said, "Oh, yes, and what *will* you be doing, madam," all I could think of was that special-club feeling. Something that gave me that.

"So picky," my mother fretted a year later when we ran into Rob Coutts on High Street. "She needs to learn she's not so special she can't do an honest day's work."

Solemn, he agreed. Then winked at me as if to say, *On your side, don't worry.*

Then he said, "Actually, Mrs. Taylor, my gran's been ill. I hate leaving her alone when I'm at work. If Bessie could stay with her . . ."

I said I'd think about it. "You'll do more than think about it," said my mother.

I never knew quite what was wrong with Mrs. Coutts, just that she was too sick to go up and down stairs and she rarely left her bed. At first, I was full of enthusiasm, determined to make her like me. I tidied, did meals, read to her from the paper, which she said was all bad news about people not worth her time. It didn't take long to figure out the one joy left to her in life was complaining.

I would sit by her bed for what felt like hours, staring at the wall with its dingy wallpaper covered in faded roses, counting them first lengthwise, then up and down. I gazed at the faces in her picture frames, each one seemingly more tight-lipped than the last. The boredom was bone deep and exhausting. Old people were awful, I decided. Helpless like babies, but not lovely like them. They sagged and leaked, let the food fall from their mouths, their clothes fall open so you saw them for what they were: bags of old skin with broken teeth and filmy eyes. Mrs. Coutts did sleep quite a bit. But whenever I crept out of the room, five minutes later, she'd call for me. "You left," she accused. "You're not meant to leave me alone."

By the end of the week, I was ready to quit and when Rob Coutts came home that evening, I told him so.

"After all the trouble I went to?" he teased. "Stay. Make me supper."

"You make me supper," I said, bad tempered from a long dull day with no attention paid. He laughed, caught me by the hand.

"Stay," he said again, more seriously. His hands moving over me, he said, "You are a terror, you know. You frighten me, Bessie Gow, things you make me feel."

As we started to kiss each other, I understood. Doing things I'd always been told not to—never in words, because they weren't to be spoken of—made this, *us*, more important than anything that had come before.

I started staying later. Sometimes, I didn't go home, telling my mother, "Mrs. Coutts needs me in the middle of the night." At home, I did impressions of her. Agnes gave me an odd look. "Comes to us all, you know. Age."

Rob said, "You're a bold girl, Bessie Gow. Not like most." He also said, "Still, best to keep this secret. I'm not sure your brothers would be pleased." I didn't mind that. I liked it, in fact. I went about town *knowing*. I was beautiful. I frightened Rob Coutts, made him feel things he'd never felt before. We had and were each other's secret.

One day, he turned up with a motorcar, the first I'd ever seen up close. He'd borrowed it from a mate at the docks. "Get in," he invited. I hesitated, looking back to the house. Mrs. Coutts had been fretful that morning, unable to settle. Once, she called me Mary. Another time she asked, "But who are you?" Peering at me, worried.

"She'll be fine," said Rob. "Don't worry."

At first I couldn't enjoy it, bumping along the cobbled streets of Glasgow. Worry over Mrs. Coutts turned to worry that Rob was going too fast, not really looking where he should, and swiveling the wheel too wide. Then he slid his hand over my thigh, said, "Relax." And I thought, Well, if he says. I started to like being whirled through the air, shrieking with glee when we made a broad turn to barrel past someone, making them jump back. *Faster,* I urged him, *Go faster, I dare you.*

We got back late. I slipped into Mrs. Coutts's bedroom, expecting to be shouted at. Then the stink of urine caught my nose and I heard her breathing, strained and irregular. Her frightened eyes sought me out. I took in her hair, gray flyaway strands drifting from her scalp. I'd promised to comb it, braid it nicely . . .

She moaned, as if something hurt. Dropping to my knees by the bed, I took her hand, met those fearful eyes with mine to reassure her: Yes, I was here now. "I'm sorry," I whispered. "I'll get you some dry things. Then I'll comb your hair. You have lovely hair, did you know that?"

I stopped doing my impressions. At night, if she called, I didn't let

Rob pull me back for a laugh. I asked her to tell me about the people in those photographs. Figured out which spoons and cups were easy for her, which caused spills. Once I even made her smile, by saying I thought Queen Mary looked like a kipper. When she got up, her hand would search for me; when she found my arm, I could feel the ease seep through her body.

When Mrs. Coutts died, my mother made it clear she expected me to find other work. Billy said, "At least help Mam at home; no reason for you to stay at the Couttses'." I waited for Rob to mention marriage. Instead he told me he was selling the house and using the money to go to America.

I knew on some level, it was a punishment; I'd been boring rather than bold. Cared for an old woman rather than careen through the city with him. "Suit yourself," I told him. "Don't fall into the Grand Canyon."

I grew up a little, and for a time, forgot. I took a job in a dress shop, saw other boys. But I had no interest in being bold with them and they seemed not to know such a thing was possible. One evening, after a long day of customers and petty complaints, I caught sight of myself in a store window. My mouth was hard, my eyes resentful. I looked exactly like the woman I'd never wanted to be. A few days later, I got a postcard from Rob, a picture of the Statue of Liberty. *When are you coming to America?* When I wrote back, *How does next week suit you?* he sent back, *Dandy fine. Come to Detroit.*

When I got off the train, he grinned. "Oh Lord, I'm in trouble." We still made each other breathless. But I didn't think much of his factory job and thought even less of the fact that he seemed content with it. I noted that the houses on Canfield Avenue were nicer than where he lived. He said, "You've got high expectations, Betty Gow."

I said, "Yes, I have, as a matter of fact. Even in Detroit."

One evening, I was meeting him at the factory after work. I was late and he was already outside. Then a brunette with wonderful legs in elegant pumps left the building, and he grabbed her by the hand. I waited for her to be shocked, whip her hand back. But she just smiled, with those white teeth and bold bright lips they all seemed to have here.

I told myself, this happened to lots of women. Men cheated all the time. But the banality of the moment was the final ruin of any idea I'd had that I was special. Rob Coutts, who'd sent me singing down the streets of Glasgow, convinced of my own glory, had just shown me how ordinary, how much like other women, I was. Not even as good as. Probably in Glasgow, it had been the same. I hadn't been kept a secret because I was special. But because I was one of many. For about five minutes, I considered killing him just to see the shock on his face.

"You told me to come to America," I screamed. "You said, 'Come to Detroit.'"

Just a postcard, he shrugged.

And I was just a girl. Not a terror. Not anything special. A convenience really. Brainless young thing on her back, also does washing. *Oh, did you think it was love? Well, now, that is a laugh . . .*

On the bus back to New Jersey, fists clenched, staring out the window, I told myself that I still had high expectations. I was still a bold girl meant for something different. And fought back the panic that I didn't have the first idea how to be that girl without Rob Coutts.

Until Mary Beattie told me the Lindberghs needed a nanny.

Now, I tell Ellerson, "I had something with a man I worked for." His eyebrows rise and I know he's thinking of Colonel Lindbergh. "Yes, keep that from Mrs. Sullivan, please."

"Was he pretty?"

"Oh, very." I answer his smile, grateful to him for lending me the cover of sophistication. "It's the old story. You think someone's your world and your future and they turn out to be not much of anything beyond a bright smile and a selfish nature. And a cheating bastard, besides." I roll the wine cork under my finger. "Frightening, really, how stupid you can be about people you care for."

"Well, there's your answer—*don't*." He drains his glass. "You know why I like the boardinghouse? Boardinghouse, no one cares. You come, you go. Too long indoors, I can't breathe. Also why I drive cars. Keeps me outside and on the move."

I say slyly, "So no one special? Even at that taxi stand?"

"Well, once a-roaming, I did spy a handsome pair of hazel eyes . . ."

I laugh and for a moment, we sit, companionable in our shared follies. Then suddenly he leans forward. "Boy talk aside, Beautiful, I got a big favor to ask you . . ."

"Games?" Violet appears at the table, pulls up a chair. "How'd you play?"

"You tell the truth," says Ellerson, switching smoothly back to levity. "Or what you think you can get away with."

I try to hold Ellerson's eye: *Are we done with our truth?* It seems so for now. Nudging the bottle in Violet's direction, I ask, "Clark Gable or Fredric March?"

"Gable," she groans.

The door swings open, Edna and Banks bringing in the coffee service and the last of the plates. You can't have truth with this many people about and we go quiet. Violet is almost haughty. But when Banks leaves without speaking to her, I see her bright mouse eyes turn wistful. "Toss him back," I tell her. "Not worth it." She looks at me surprised; I raise my eyebrow: *Yes, I've been stupid too,* and she gives me a small smile. Then Henry puts his head round the door, and she shouts, "Red!"

Edna lands next to her sister, who pronounces herself tired of truth; she wants to play a different game. The cards are fetched from the staff room. We run low on chairs and Henry edges onto my seat.

Now firmly in charge of the festivities, Violet grabs my hand, waves it in Henry's face. "I expected to see a ring!"

"I asked," he protests. "She turned me down." For the next few minutes, I am the villain, Henry the victim of my romantic cruelty.

Violet says, "You're not the only one leaving us, Red. Edna's off to the visa office tomorrow. Everyone's leaving me."

Surprised, I say, "You're going home?"

"Back to England," Edna says calmly. We stay attentive, waiting for reasons. But Edna, being Edna, doesn't give them. Finally Ellerson bellows, "Oh, don't go on and on about it—Christ, can't get a word in edgewise! Who wants another drink?"

When Marguerite looks in on her way to bed, Violet calls out, "It's a goodbye party! Edna's leaving me, Red's leaving Betty . . ."

"Oh, but you must say goodbye to Johannes," Marguerite says, eyes warm on Henry. "Perhaps we could see you tomorrow night before you go?"

I say, "Work," but Henry says that sounds like a nice idea.

Edna says, "I'm just tired of it, is all." It takes me a moment to realize she means this country, her reasons for leaving. Only no one's asked or cared for ages.

Ellerson tells a story about nearly being caught by Mrs. Morrow when he had an uninvited guest. Drunk, he slips, saying he, and I widen my eyes: *Mixed crowd*. But everyone laughs heartily. Too heartily—the swinging door slams against the wall and Banks appears in his robe. We go quiet, waiting to see if he's joining or scolding.

Standing over Violet, he hisses, "Do you realize they can hear you upstairs?"

She flinches. Then, struggling to maintain her dignity, she says, "I don't recall inviting you to this card game, Mr. Banks."

"And I don't recall telling you to shriek like a harpy. For Christ's sake, keep it down."

After he's gone, we play in silence for a few minutes, maintaining the awkward pretense that nothing has happened. Then Violet whispers, "He's upset about Mr. Morrow not leaving him anything . . ."

"Didn't leave me anything," says Ellerson flippantly.

"I didn't expect anything," says Marguerite.

"This is what I mean," says Edna, discarding the four of clubs.

Henry kisses me, murmurs, "I don't understand."

"Disappointed people," I say. "Don't mind them."

It's midnight when I walk Henry to his car. We go hand in hand and at the last minute, he pulls me close and says, "See me tomorrow night."

"They're back tomorrow," I remind him. "I'll be with Charlie."

"After seven, when he's asleep. Just for a few hours. Please?"

"I'd have to be back by ten . . ."

He kisses me slowly. "Back by ten. I promise."

Chapter Thirteen

Hopewell, New Jersey

The next morning, I wake to the wet crunching sound of sleet on the window. I roll over in bed to see gray sky, the tops of the trees swaying in the wind, icy rivulets coursing down the pane. March first, I think, but February's hanging on. I gaze at the storm from the comfort of the covers. It's an awful day. Rolling over, I settle my head deeper into the pillow, put off facing it for a little while longer.

"Betty, call for you."

I'm having a last cup of tea in the kitchen when Violet swings herself around the door. I give her a quizzical look and she says, "Hopewell."

Taking the hallway phone, I hear Mrs. Lindbergh croak, "Betty?" and say, "Oh, no, you've got Charlie's cold."

"I have," she sighs. "We're staying put. Could you come on the next train? Mr. Whateley's looking up the schedule, and he can meet you at the station."

"Of course. Get yourself to bed."

As I hang up, Violet asks, "What's going on?"

"They're staying. I'm going."

The phone rings again. This time I pick up to hear Whateley say officiously, "There's a train that gets you in at three thirty."

I glance out the window at the stormy skies; five hours in nasty weather, going from car to train and back again. "I can get there faster by car."

"I don't have the time to pick you up and come all the way back."

"Let me see if someone here can drive me."

As I hang up, Violet says, "Ask Mr. Banks. He'll know if Alfred or Ellerson is free."

Knocking at Banks's door, I find him going over accounts. "Is there any chance one of the drivers could take me to Hopewell? Mrs. Lindbergh's sick and she needs help with the baby."

He consults a schedule he keeps on the wall. "I believe Ellerson's available. Let me find him."

"Wonderful, thank you."

I call Whateley. He says, "You make sure it's all right with Mrs. Morrow."

As if he knows Mrs. Morrow. As if they have tea and discuss opera. I roll my eyes. Violet snorts with laughter. I wave at her: *Stop.* Even as I think, *Nightgown, change of underthings.* I'm forgetting something. Something I promised . . .

Henry. Hanging up, I wait a second, then dial the boardinghouse. When his landlady, Mrs. Sherman, answers, I ask, "Is Mr. Johnson in?"

"He's at work." Henry manages to charm most people, but I suspect Mrs. Sherman is an exception.

"May I ask you to give him a message? Tell him that Betty can't make it tonight."

Banks appears in the hall, gestures to me. He's found me a ride. Into the phone, I say, "Tell him he can call the Morrow house . . . thank you."

"Ellerson can drive you," Banks calls. "He'll be outside."

"Thank you, Mr. Banks." I hurry toward the stairs. "Violet, will you tell Ellerson I'll be down soon? I have to pack."

"Of course . . ."

I'm throwing things into my suitcase when there's a knock at the door. I shout, "Come in." Stare at the open case, thinking, What else?

Then I hear Marguerite say, "You have to go? Johannes and I were hoping you could join us and Red tonight."

I think, *Really? Here I thought it was me seeing Henry.* "The baby's sick, and Mrs. Lindbergh."

"Oh, so they're staying in Hopewell?"

Biting my tongue on *I don't have time for this,* I nod. "But you have a lovely time. If he calls here, tell Red . . ." I think to correct myself, then decide, why bother. "Tell him I'm so sad this happened and we'll talk soon."

I take a last look at the case. I know I've forgotten something, but it can't be helped. I snap the suitcase shut and run downstairs. It's not until I open the door that I realize of course I've forgotten an umbrella. Ellerson's brought the car around. It's sheeting rain. If it were Mrs. Morrow, he'd step out with his umbrella, shepherd me in. But I'm not Mrs. Morrow, so. Throwing my arm over my head, I run to the car. The wind is harsh and the rain is fat, each drop landing like a handful of water. The ground is soaked. I can feel the wet seeping into my shoes, splashing my ankles. Less than twenty feet, but by the time I fall into the back seat, my clothes are damp, my hair is ruined, and my shoes are a muddy wreck. With the back of my hand, I brush the rain from my face, finger my eyes until they're clear. A chill's gone right through me; fine thing if I get this cold. Pulling myself tight into the corner, I say, "Is there a blanket or something?"

A moment later, a bundle of wool hits me in the face. As we roll down the hill, I notice Ellerson's being quite pointed about keeping his eyes on the road. True, it's not easy driving. The windshield wipers are slamming back and forth across the window, just managing to keep the glass clear. Every so often, the splats of rain are too fast, like bubbles breaking across the window all at once, and you just have to hope that what you saw a second ago holds until it's all clear again.

But Ellerson can be moody, especially when he's hungover; last night, Violet and I had to lay him out on the staff room sofa. "Something wrong?" I ask.

He doesn't answer. I look at the trim rivers of water streaming across the window. When they narrow, all you see is a ribbon of trees and gray winter sky, one long row of the same. Restless, I try, "I'm sorry to drag you out."

"Well, thank you for that." I look questioningly in the mirror: *Why so angry?* "Maybe I wasn't in the mood for three hours of driving in lousy weather."

"I know. I'm sorry. I just couldn't face the train."

He shifts in his seat. "You can make it up to me."

The favor, the one he wanted to ask last night before Violet joined us. Usually, when Ellerson puts the touch on you, he's buoyant, unrepentant. Not this time.

"Lend me a hundred bucks?"

Stunned by the amount, I can only shake my head.

"Just for this week, I'll get it back . . ."

Just this week? I wonder: Is this the gambling or . . . blackmail?

"Tell me how you got the black eye."

I sense him weighing. He wants the money and knows a lie won't get it. With a broken smile, he says, "Know why I like borrowing money from you? You don't slap me around when I can't pay."

Horrified, I say, ". . . You must stop."

"I know. I know." The knuckles on the wheel are knotted, the bone glowing white under the skin. "I will. I just need to pay this guy back. He's getting impatient. And if I get messed up too badly, I'll be out of a job."

At a time when jobs are not plentiful. The route to Hopewell takes us through Princeton. In Princeton, there's a bank where most of us put our savings. There is money in my account and we could stop; no one will question if we're delayed in this weather.

But Ellerson already owes me money. And despite his promises, he won't stop. Once safe, he will go looking for the next big win. I may never get the money back. And today, I feel I need that money.

Because like Ellerson, I might not want to be dragged here and there in poor weather for the rest of my life.

". . . I've not got it, Ellerson. Truly."

He looks back: *Is it truly?* I meet his eye, thinking, *I'm sorry. But you must know you can't be trusted.*

I see that he knows I'm lying—and why. I feel something between us break.

Remorseful, I think to ask how long he has to pay. But he looks back to the road and the time for changing my mind is gone.

I hate not trusting him, hate that I've lied. I put my thoughts on Charlie. If it's a runny nose or gone into his chest, he won't have slept, which means he'll be cranky. And he hates having his nose wiped, fights you when you go after him with a hankie. But you have to otherwise his poor lips get so chapped.

Mrs. Lindbergh will be fretting, busy coming up with things to worry about, but no solutions to any of it. Him all solutions and commands: *Don't like this, change that, I want this better. Everything perfect, because I am.*

Thinking about it makes me cross and I tuck my legs under me.

"You seem blue," says Ellerson.

"I just hate that house," I sigh. "Can we stop at Clark's? I need to get some Vicks."

Clark's is in Princeton, so it's always full of college boys at the soda counter or waiting to use the pay phone. It's crowded and noisy; the counterman ignores everyone. I sway this way and that, trying to catch his eye. Finally, I shout, "Excuse me!"

"Someone's going to walk right out with something one day," I tell him. He sneers and I think, That looks like the day I'm having, no question.

But by the time we reach Hopewell, the rain has slowed. It's been such a deluge, when I step out of the car it almost feels like walking into a summer's day. Hauling out my suitcase, I feel desperate to be friends again. "Want to come in?"

"I should get back."

"Come eat something. Can't go all the way back on an empty stomach."

He looks at the house, apprehensive, melancholy. His eyes are tired, his face creased. The drink's giving him a belly.

Then he reaches for my suitcase. "Give me that."

"Such a gentleman," I tease, happy to be back on good terms.

"That's me."

Elsie gives us lunch in the kitchen. I ask how Mrs. Lindbergh is, and she says, "She'll be better once she sees you. She's run down having the baby to care for and another on the way. The weather's been so poor lately. Cold, wet, and damp for days on end." She brightens. "Charlie's feeling much better though."

Ellerson wipes his mouth. "I should be going."

I see him to the door. "Plans for tonight?"

"Headed to the Sha-Toe," he says, referring to a speakeasy in Fort Lee. "Might drop by the taxi place, see the guys."

The guy, I think, the one who has hazel eyes. But no hundred dollars, I'm guessing.

"Tell me you're going to be all right."

His gaze shifts upstairs; I've been indiscreet, mentioning his problems within earshot of Mrs. Lindbergh. I make a face: *Sorry.* Squeezing my arm, he says, "I'll be fine. Be good, Betty Gow."

I head up to Charlie's room, hearing Mrs. Lindbergh as I come up the stairs. When I open the door, the eyes that greet mine above Charlie's head are shadowed with exhaustion. "Charlie!" she cries. "Look who's here."

They have made changes to the room; it's much sweeter than when I peeked in with Henry. To distract him from Mrs. Lindbergh stepping out, I have Charlie tell me about all his new things. They've put a screen in the room. It's like a little village, with churches and barns and farm animals. "Which one's this?" I point to the cow. Charlie frowns, then shouts, "Moo!" "That's right," I say, "cow goes moo." Then I point to one of the houses, a curl of smoke coming out of the chimney. "Who's in the house, Charlie? Who's in that house? Are you in there? Let's look in the window . . . oh, yes, there you are!"

When I hear a *clink,* I think it's hail or hard rain on the window. Then remember, no, it stopped raining. Tip of a branch, maybe, except there's no trees close to the house. I'm about to ask Charlie where the pig's tail is when I hear it again, louder this time. I look to the window, almost expecting to see a crack. Nothing but overcast sky with the sun struggling behind it. Below the window, a packing case, one of Charlie's Tinkertoys on top.

Charlie wants to know: What am I looking at? I say, "I don't know, Charlie, let's see."

I get up from my crouch, anxiety curling in my stomach as I go to the window. Then I laugh at the sight of Mrs. Lindbergh in her boots and scarf, her small frame swaying as she waves. I bring Charlie up to see and he bursts into smiles at the sight of his mother far down below—such a funny place for her to be—swinging her arm above her head.

"Wave, Charlie. Give Mummy a wave." Tentative, he folds his fingers into his palm.

We play for a while longer, racing Charlie's trucks around the floor, then Elsie looks in. "The missus would like to see him in the living room." To Charlie, she says, "She's feeling better, your mum. Isn't that nice?"

I take Charlie in to Mrs. Lindbergh, then join Elsie in the kitchen. We sit at the table, and she slumps, saying, "Oof, I'm tired."

I make her a cup of tea. "Has it been difficult?"

"*He's* not here, *she's* not well . . ." She waves a hand. "I shouldn't complain. The Lord put us on this earth to care for one another. But it's *lovely* to see you."

Then she laughs because Charlie is peeping around the door.

I say, "Who's this who's come to see us, Elsie?"

"I'm sure I don't know. Let's give him a cookie and see what he does."

Maybe because he's been in bed for so long, Charlie tears around the kitchen, wanting us to chase him. Wahgoosh joins in, jumping and barking. Racing from one chair to the next, I wonder if we're making too much of a racket for Mrs. Lindbergh. When the phone rings, I scoop Charlie up and say, "All right, young man, let's calm down." From the hallway, I hear Whateley say, "Very good, Colonel. I'll let her know."

When Whateley comes through the kitchen, Elsie says, "Let who know what?"

"The Colonel's going to be later than expected." Wahgoosh leaps, pawing at Whateley's battered corduroys.

Elsie frowns. "He's coming back tonight? I thought . . ." She looks to the stove. "Did he say if he'll want dinner?"

"No, he didn't say," Whateley tells her with exaggerated patience. "But I'd rather not hand him an empty plate, so . . ."

He goes out, the dog following, as he says, "Here boy, good boy." Elsie sighs. "Do you need help?" I ask her.

"No, pet, it's fine. I could have sworn the Colonel had some do in the city and wouldn't be home for dinner." She pats Charlie's cheek. "Let's get *you* fed, at any rate."

Charlie eats at the little table in his room while I perch on the other small chair. Every so often, I reach over and wipe his chin, but he's eating really well on his own and I tell him so. Behind me, I hear the door creak open and look up to see Mrs. Lindbergh, a small brown bottle in her hand.

"I'm afraid it's evil Mummy with medicine," she says, in a soft, apologetic voice.

"It's good for him," I say.

Charlie doesn't think so and spits up all over his night suit a few minutes after it goes down. "Well," Mrs. Lindbergh laughs, "that showed me."

But as we look through his drawers for a fresh nightshirt, I see Charlie's low on warm clothing; they only brought clothes for the weekend, and all he's left with are a pair of Dr. Denton's and his sleeveless sleep shirt. The weather's turned cold and blustery again. The wind roars, rattling the shutters.

"I wonder if he doesn't need something warmer," I say. "I've got an old piece of cream flannel I could make a shirt out of."

Mrs. Lindbergh nods excitedly. "I'll see if Mrs. Whateley has some thread. Handsome new clothes for you, Charlie!"

Later, as I cut and sew, she says, "I didn't know you were such a seamstress, Betty."

"I worked in a dress shop back home." I hold up the shirt. I've kept the left shoulder open so it'll slide easily over Charlie's head. Not the prettiest thing I've ever made, but it'll do the job.

Laying Charlie on the changing table, I say, "Almost eight—you're up late this evening, aren't you? Hey, look what I made you." I rub the flannel against his cheek.

"Nice and warm. Now, we're going to put some VapoRub on your chest, help you breathe better . . ."

He scowls, turns his head, and tries to push my hand away. "I know, it doesn't smell pretty." I slide my hand under his arm, dab down the middle of his chest with my thumb. Then before he can wipe at it, I sit him up and pop on the flannel shirt. Startled, he forgets the ointment.

Sliding his sleeveless nightshirt over the flannel, I say, "I made that for you, young man. Blue thread, your favorite color. Now our Dr. Denton's . . ."

I lay him back down so I can get his legs into the suit. When he's all bundled up, I gather his feet and give them kisses. "We ready for bed, then? All ready?"

I lift him up; he can still settle in his old place at my side. But I don't have to tilt my head down to nuzzle his curls anymore and his feet dangle almost to my hip. I rub my nose against his forehead, think how I've missed his smell. Then I see the thumb guards, still on the changing table, two twisted bits of metal like an unwound paperclip with string attached.

"Oh, forgot one thing . . ." I lay him back down. He puts one chubby fist to his mouth. Gently taking his other hand, I slip the guard over his right thumb. "Charlie, my lamb, you like to suck your thumb. It's a delicious thumb, top-notch, but . . ."

Taking his left hand, I give the thumb a kiss, then clip the metal around it. "But your daddy says no. Daddy says you may not eat your thumb. And he's right, I suppose, you only have two, and they are useful . . ."

But Daddy's not satisfied unless everyone around him is denied that last bit of ease or comfort.

Lifting him back up, I bring his head to mine. He's drowsy and heavy, not even bothering about the clips. Mrs. Lindbergh comes in to say good night while I try to catch the shutter and close it. I have to lean far out of the window to reach it, and my hands get cold, making it hard to fiddle with the catch.

"No luck?" whispers Mrs. Lindbergh.

"Maybe if we both try . . ."

I pull on the shutter while she tries to do the latch. But the wood's warped and it won't shut. Mrs. Lindbergh and I grimace: *New house, you'd think the shutters would close!* I make do with closing them on the window to the left and on the French windows. We leave the French windows half-open, so there's a little air and the room doesn't smell of VapoRub.

I don't want the spit-up to set, so I wash Charlie's shirt and dinner bowl in the bathroom. Then I step quietly back into the nursery. Charlie's deep asleep, breathing nice and even. I pin the covers to his mattress so they stay smooth. Then I slip a finger through one of his curls and whisper, "Good night, Charlie lamb."

I go down to the kitchen, where Elsie's putting dinner together. Still anxious about the change in schedule, she's going from pot to pan to dish, and I say, "Sit. Eat. The Colonel's not back yet."

But then we hear it: the crunch of a car coming up the road; Colonel Lindbergh is home. Panicked, Elsie looks at the clock. It's ten after eight. She takes up a dish, then hesitates as the sound that should come next—the honk to alert Whateley to open the garage door—doesn't. Confused, she sets the dish down.

"I heard the car too," I say. "But relax. If he changes his plans last minute, he should understand dinner won't be perfect."

She gives me a look: *Are we talking of the same Colonel Lindbergh?* Then she says, "Oh, remind me after. I've a new dress and I want your opinion . . ."

She describes the dress; it sounds rather daring for her and I'm about to tell her I approve when we hear the honk of a horn and the rasping roll of the garage door opening. Elsie raises her hands: *There he is.* A moment later, Colonel Lindbergh comes in, and she's on her feet and fussing: How was the drive? Is it still so cold? Dinner won't be a moment . . .

The Colonel goes upstairs and Elsie gets the food ready to be served. I glance at the clock. It's almost eight thirty. For a moment, I remember the sound of the approaching car we heard earlier. Why on earth would the Colonel sit in the car outside for fifteen minutes—in this cold? Then again, Betty, I tell myself, there's always a chance you heard wrong.

Only Elsie heard it too.

I try to place that slow crunching sound. Wahgoosh digging outside? He always stays upstairs by Charlie's room at night. A gust of wind? It's been blowing all night, you wouldn't suddenly hear gravel shift outside . . .

I imagine it. A car approaches. No one gets out. For fifteen minutes. Was the Colonel in a mood? He looked tired as he came in. He hates the city. Or maybe they've had a fight. So he wanted to come home and see her rather than go to his event. Only he's angry about missing it and made her wait before coming inside?

He does what he does, I think. Who knows why?

Elsie's just about to call for Whateley when he comes through the door. "Phone for you," he says.

"Me? Did they say who it was?"

But Whateley is busy organizing what goes out first, telling Elsie where she's got it wrong, snapping at her to hurry. Just outside the kitchen, I barely register the phone as I take it up and hear, "Betty?"

Henry. So sweet to call, but . . . why? I can hear voices around him. But only a few and they're calm, not the raucous shouting of the rooming house. "Where are you?"

"Oh . . ." He hesitates and I have a strange thought: That car, was it him? "I'm at a drugstore."

From the corner of my eye, I see the kitchen door open as Whateley comes out with a casserole dish. It's a narrow space, and he's annoyed at having to maneuver around me. Lowering my voice, I ask, "What's the idea of calling me here? I thought you were seeing Marguerite and Johannes."

"I am, I did. I'm . . . with them now. But I didn't want to use their phone; it's expensive."

Whateley returns from the dining room; I pointedly step back as he charges past.

Henry asks, "How's the baby? Is he better? Sleeping?"

"He is. But I don't think I can come out tonight."

"Well, I was thinking, I don't *have* to leave right away."

It's a bad time and place to talk and I don't want to get into a discussion about the future. "No, go. Your brother's expecting you. I'll come up soon. We'll find Greta Garbo in that gas station."

He laughs. "All right."

"Have fun tonight. Be a good boy."

"Yes, ma'am."

I hang up just as Whateley comes back, make a great show of holding up my hands. *Look, no boyfriend.*

After dinner, Elsie and I go up to their apartment, which is over the garage. Elsie's made it pretty and snug, but the cold air and smell of oil comes up through the floor. It's only space for a bed and a small sitting area. It feels like a spare room, not a home. I ask her if she minds and she says, "Not so bad. Roof over your head." She moves to the dress, saying, "Now, tell me what you think and be honest."

That I don't want this life when I'm fifty is what I think, if I'm being honest. I always thought I wouldn't have to work when I married. Yet here's Elsie excited over a cheap dress that's already coming loose at the hem. Guilty, I push away the sulks, exclaim "How pretty!" But my mind keeps picking at the thought. The Whateleys aren't young; they came to service late. Elsie's a proper homemaker, she must have imagined better than this. And she deserves it. The Lindberghs should build the Whateleys a cottage of their own.

I think of my room that's used by guests on weekends, and that blue empty feeling takes hold again. Restless, I look at my watch.

"Oh—it's ten. Time to look in on Charlie."

The garage is on the other end of the house from the bedrooms. Coming off the stairs, I can hear water running in the bathroom, feel the warmth of steam. Mrs. Lindbergh is having a bath. I look for Wahgoosh. He likes to sleep outside Charlie's door and I don't want him running in after me. But he seems to be elsewhere tonight. I put a careful hand on the doorknob and turn.

Too cold, is my first thought. Too much air, too cold. Poor Charlie, with his chest and three layers. In the dark, I can see the French window, still open. Didn't want the room stuffy. And the ointment had smelled, and I wanted the odor out of the room. Well, now *too* cold . . .

Making my way in the dark, I go to the French windows and close them tightly. Still too cold. *That warped shutter,* I think. *Lets in too much air.*

Bending, I feel in the dark for the sharp metal edge of the electric heater. My fingers find the knob and I give it a turn, hearing the hum of coils as they warm to life. I put my hand in front of the grille, feel the heat. Better. The room'll be better now, window closed, Charlie warm and tucked in. My mind catches hard on that image, Charlie on his tummy, head turned. I seem to need it because . . . my heart's pounding. I feel inside for the cause of anxiety. The open window—but I opened it myself. Only not that wide, surely. How was the room so cold? Too cold for a sick baby with a bad chest.

I listen, fearful of hearing that wet, ropy breathing, the little bark of a cough. Nothing. Quiet. Silence. But silence is wrong. I know the sounds of a sleeping child, those sighs and scratching of sheets that tell you baby's fine, fast asleep, all's well, he hasn't died . . .

Why silence? It's a cold, just a cold, he can't have stopped breathing . . .

I grope my way to the crib, hand landing heavily on the railing. But I don't care if I wake Charlie. Crying would be the most welcome, joyous sound in the world right now. But I'm careful when I put a hand in—poor thing, woken up by silly Betty in a panic. I stretch out my fingers, waiting to brush silky hair, warm scalp, the fold of his neck.

Not there.

I feel lower down for the nubbly cloth of his blanket, the rise and fall of breathing, the lump of him. *Please breathing, please, God . . .*

In a rush, I drop my hand on the bed where his head should be. Cold, flat sheet. Lower, the blanket lying thin and lifeless. Frantic, I stamp my hand over the mattress, even as I think if Charlie were here, he'd be up, he'd be wailing. Even so, I feel at all four corners, run my hand along the bars. Nothing. The word "gone" comes to me and I reject it. Not gone. Here. Somewhere. He must be.

I back into the hallway just as Mrs. Lindbergh comes out of the bathroom in her robe, her hair slightly damp, cheeks flushed from the hot water. She rubs a towel along the side of her head. I ask, "Do you have the baby, Mrs. Lindbergh?"

Our eyes meet, the same memory comes to both of us. She says carefully, "Maybe the Colonel has him. He's in his study."

The study is just below the nursery. I hurry down, enter without knocking. "Do you have the baby, Colonel?"

From his desk, he stares. Pulling at my fingers, I say, "Please don't fool me."

"Isn't he in his crib?"

Before I say no, he gets up so fast he practically overturns the chair. Shoving past me, he races up the stairs. He is rough with the crib, pushing the blanket here and there, rattling the mattress. Finally, he knocks the crib itself against the wall in frustration. I flinch, feel dangerously close to weeping.

I hear Mrs. Lindbergh's voice, vague, almost dreamy, "Do you have the baby, Charles?"

How absurd we all sound, I realize, asking over and over. The three of us in the empty nursery. But when Colonel Lindbergh says, "Anne, they have stolen our baby," my mind puts up a block. Closets, under beds, behind couches . . . so many spaces Charlie could be. We must look in those places, all of them. How silly we'll feel when we open the kitchen cabinet and there he is. *Stolen*, for God's sake . . .

I shiver, think irritably, *Still cold.* I've closed the window, put on the heater, how is the air still getting in? I look to the other window in the room, the one with the shutters that do latch.

The envelope on the window ledge is small and white. The Colonel says not to touch it and I never would. Because I immediately understand it for what it is: a changeling, left in the place of our beautiful boy. It is proof that someone has been here and it hits my heart so hard, I know with a strange certainty that it will stop beating. It will have to. Otherwise, I will exist for who knows how long with the knowledge that someone crawled in through the window with the unlatched shutter and . . .

The Colonel and Whateley go out to search and call the police. Elsie comes, asking Mrs. Lindbergh if there is anything she can do, anything she can bring her. With unfathomable politeness, Mrs. Lindbergh says "No, thank you." Then she goes to the window, opens it wide. In the last five minutes, self-extinction has become a rational choice to me. I move closer, prepared to grab her round the middle.

"I need air," she says distantly.

Miserable, I'm about to say she must come away from the window, she'll get a chill when Mrs. Lindbergh's face grows light with joy and she cries, "I heard him! Just now—crying!" She spins around to face us. "Did you hear it? You must have."

I'm about to say I'll run down and tell Colonel Lindbergh, but Elsie's sorrow at being unable to lie is clear, and Mrs. Lindbergh's happiness dies the moment she catches sight of her face.

Elsie says, "I think it was a cat, Mrs. Lindbergh."

Chapter Fourteen

The house is full of people. Outside as well, men all around the house, tramping the ground, calling to one another, the beams of their torches swinging through the dark. The house is overwhelmed with voices, men shouldering through the hallway, crowding the stairs, climbing in and out of Charlie's window. Every so often, some of their words break through—*over here, which window?*—even laughter. That is how many people are here, some of them can actually laugh when one of them slips in the mud outside or when Wahgoosh, manic, skitters around legs, barking ferociously. It is three in the morning and every light in the house is on.

There are twenty rooms in this house. Each of those rooms has four corners—eighty in all. There are seventeen closets. More than thirty drawers. Fourteen cabinets. I have looked in every single one of these spaces, no matter how ridiculous. I have searched for Charlie in a silverware drawer no deeper than three inches. I have looked for him behind curtains and under beds. Beneath piles of shirts and behind dresses. Charlie is nowhere, *nowhere*, in this house. In his place, all these shouting, murmuring men. There's no room they won't enter, save the Lindberghs' bedroom, where Mrs. Lindbergh is hiding. I should go to her. But I can't face her. I can't.

Instead of Charlie, we find more proof that someone was here. Dents in the mud below Charlie's room, scratches on the paint alongside the window. Yellow clumps of dirt left on the packing case in his room, the first place they stepped as they came through the window. A chisel, dropped on the ground. And the ladder itself, hastily discarded in pieces less than a hundred yards from the house. The side rail has split, Whateley tells us. "Likely the extra weight on the way down caused it to break, so they left it behind." For once, he is not pleased by his own knowledge. Pale and hollow-eyed, he pulls his hand over his face several times as if willing himself to wake up.

And near the spot where the ladder stood, footprints. The pattern doesn't look like a shoe sole, more like cloth. "Took his shoes off, they think," says Whateley. They found another set of prints as well, smaller than the first. Possibly a woman. I remember Mrs. Lindbergh, tossing pebbles at the window to catch our attention, Charlie bending his little fingers.

I can't think of that. So I don't.

At four, I creep into my closet, curl tight into the corner. I don't deserve a bed and I need to cry, partly in anguish, and partly because I'm so tired. At some point, I open my eyes, feeling I have been away. Beyond the door, I hear Elsie calling my name.

I nudge the door open with my foot. Her face collapses at the sight of me.

"Nobody blames you, Betty."

"Of course, they do. They should."

She sticks out her hand—not an offer, a command. "Come on, young lady. Nothing's helped by your self-pity. All these people in the house, I need help in the kitchen, so you get washed and dressed."

Briskly, she sets out a washcloth and hairbrush, starts rifling through my clothes for a fresh outfit. Her hand hovers a moment over the uniforms, then she pushes them to the side and chooses a plain navy dress.

Then she says, "The Colonel wants us in his study in ten minutes. So, quick about it."

According to Elsie, the Colonel has not slept. But you'd never know it. He's taut, focused, almost pulsing with energy, like a dog, leaping, desperate to give chase. The three of us gather at the door, watching as he circles his desk, one hand in his pocket, addressing two other men, as if they were his subordinates. He shifts papers, glances at notes, taps his finger on various points of a map. The two men look on, nodding in agreement. One is the aristocratic Colonel Breckinridge, a family friend. The other a police officer with a bristling mustache and high, swept-back hair. Colonel Lindbergh introduces him as Colonel Schwarzkopf, chief of the New Jersey State Police. Then, indicating each of us one by one, he says, "Mr. and Mrs. Whateley, our butler and cook. Miss Gow, the baby's nurse." Colonel Schwarzkopf nods politely, but I'm aware he's taking our measure.

Colonel Lindbergh tells us the kidnappers have demanded $50,000. It is a vast amount of money—to me, inconceivable. "The police feel, judging from the ransom note, that we're dealing with professionals. This is about money. We and they want the same thing: the baby's safe return. It's just a matter of waiting for them to make contact and paying the ransom."

"Forgive me, Colonel," asks Elsie, "but how will they contact us? Should we be watching for anything . . . ?"

"It will be another letter, like the one left in Charlie's room. The signature had a distinctive mark. Two circles overlapping, a red circle in the center oval. Three holes punched through. The kidnappers said all communication from them will bear that symbol."

I can see, the other men are uncomfortable with his candor. As if to remind him we are not above suspicion, Colonel Schwarzkopf says, "We will need statements from everyone in the household."

Colonel Lindbergh turns on him. "I interviewed each of these individuals personally before bringing them into my household. They have the complete trust and faith of Mrs. Lindbergh and myself. They'll give you any assistance required. But I do not want them interrogated or investigated as if they were criminals. Their private lives are to stay private. They are not to be touched."

I could fall at his feet. Maybe it's the haze of exhaustion and crisis—or maybe it's just him. That he should think of us at such a time. Protect us when some would say he has every right to order me out of the house. For the first time, I understand why Charles Lindbergh is the idol of millions. I've seen him tired, apathetic, resentful any number of times. Petty, even cruel. But perhaps it's the day-to-day that gets him down, the commute from the city, the family parties, the "What shirts do you wear, Colonel Lindbergh?" questions from reporters. Here we are in the midst of a catastrophe, and he's entirely calm.

And, strangely, so am I. Colonel Lindbergh *will* get his son back. In a few days, Charlie will be home. We only have to last a few days.

The house, which was not quite yet a home, becomes a police station. Whateley moves the car out of the garage so that a twenty-line switchboard can be put in. Elsie and I gather all the spare bedding and lay it out in the living room where the officers will sleep. There are guards posted at every door. Inside the house, police crowd the hallways, monopolize the telephone, and sort through the flood of mail coming in like beefy, suit-clad secretaries. In every room, the clamor of talk.

"Yes, ma'am, if you could just give me a description of the car . . ."

"Lieutenant, phone. Some guy calling from the Elks Club says the baby's in a farmhouse off 95. Said he read it in a Russian newspaper."

"Elks? I know that guy. Every time he gets loaded, he starts calling around with cock-and-bull stories . . ."

"Sergeant? A waitress at Nemitz says three guys ordered sodas, then asked how to get to the Lindbergh house."

"Woman in Teaneck says there are baby clothes hanging on the line at the house next door—says they were never there before."

"Will Rogers sent a telegram," Elsie whispers. "And so did the president."

With daybreak, people have come. They have read it in the papers, heard it on the radio, and hundreds of them have simply . . . come. Their cars line the road, parked hastily at odd angles. They tramp through the woods, wander around the grounds calling to one another, *Look here! Over there!* Some of them gather to chat as if at a picnic. They drop sandwich wrappers, cigarette butts, pop bottles.

Pictures from Charlie's birthday are given to the newspapers. The little boy we hid from the public eye is going to be seen by the entire world.

Mrs. Morrow arrives and is given my room. I am given a mattress in the staff sitting room; Whateley puts a hook on the door where I can hang the next day's clothes. Mrs. Lindbergh writes out a list of Charlie's diet to be printed in the newspapers in the hopes that the kidnappers will see it. I recite and she writes: one quart of milk, three tablespoons of cooked cereal, morning and night, two tablespoons cooked vegetables. Baked potato or rice. Half cup prune juice. Half cup orange juice . . .

At one point, she pauses, distressed. ". . . How many drops of viosterol?"

"Fourteen, Mrs. Lindbergh," I tell her.

We are considering whether or not to put the time of day for the juices when we hear Colonel Lindbergh talking in the hall. Mrs. Lindbergh lays down the pen, hurries out to see him. He is speaking with Colonel Breckinridge; tentatively, she draws close. But he doesn't acknowledge her, except to wince as if her need is painful to him. After a few moments, she comes back inside, shutting the door behind her.

I make my statement in the sitting room, surrounded by three policemen. I say who I am, where I was born, and how I came here. I give them the names of my employers. When I mention Detroit, one of the officers asks why I went there.

"I went to see friends," I say.

Heart pounding, I wait for them to ask, *What friends?* But instead, they ask how many times I have been to the Hopewell house; still flustered, I say just the once. Then remember, no, it was more than that. But they are so . . . alert, so eager to hear things, I think it best not to change my answer.

Colonel and Mrs. Lindbergh trust me, I keep reminding myself. He has said my past is my past and nobody's business.

Still, when I finish, I ask, "Is that all right, then?" Because they're not saying anything.

The one doing the writing looks up. "Oh, yes, that's fine. Thank you, Miss Gow."

I write Mother. I don't want to; writing it makes it true in a way it hasn't been. But they'll be reporting it over there and I can't have her seeing the news before she hears from me.

Dear Mother,

You will have heard long ago about this terrible thing that has happened to us. It is the most cruel thing I ever knew. I do not feel the least like writing, but I knew you would be anxious to hear from me.

I give her the details that were printed in the paper, careful not to add anything.

I hope to goodness we have him back by the time you get this letter. I just feel numbed and terribly lost without that darling. I love him so. Reporters are just swarming around the house. The whole country is roused. Mrs. Lindbergh has been very brave about it.

As I write "very brave," I remember cutting poor Charlie's hair. "*So brave you're being, brave little man.*" I look to the window, see the light dying, think of Charlie being put in a strange bed by someone not me or Mrs. Lindbergh or Elsie. I imagine him standing in the crib, crying for us. Then I stop. Because I can't think of that.

Then I think of that little person just down the hall, with another person-to-be tucked inside her. Is she lying on her bed? Sitting in the rocker?

I imagine as if it's happening, Anne Lindbergh flinging herself at me, small fists battering my head, tearing the hair from my scalp, fingernails at my throat, clutching until the fragile bones snapped and breath stopped. She'd have the right.

I am just writing *She is wonderful* when there's a knock on the door. A tall, thin pale man—looks as if someone's rolled him in their hands like a piece of dough—says, "Miss Gow?"

"Yes, I'm Betty Gow. Do you want coffee or . . . ?"

"No, no." He smiles, showing his teeth. "But thank you. I'm Deputy Chief Brex of the Newark Police Department. I was hoping you could help me straighten out a few details."

I think to warn him, it's been a long day; details could be difficult. Also, I'm not sure who's doing the asking. This man is different from the ones before.

He says, "We don't want to put Mrs. Lindbergh through more questions if we can help it."

"No, of course not. Please come in."

Chapter Fifteen

There are three of them. Brex, the thin man with the smile I don't quite believe.

Then a dark, squat man with a red face and belligerent manner. Finally, a third man in glasses, carrying a notebook. As he sits, he gives me a brief smile as if to say, *Just pretend I'm not here.*

Brex jabs a thumb at the cross-looking fellow. "My boss, Chief of Police McRell." The ranks don't mean anything to me. But even I can hear they're more important than trooper. I smile tentatively. Chief McRell does not smile back. He leans against the wall, watching.

Brex sits, hands clasped. "Now, Miss Gow. Anything you can tell us about last night."

"From when I put the baby to bed or . . . ?"

"Further back if you can. You were at the Morrow house Tuesday morning, is that correct?" I nod. "And you got the call from Mrs. Lindbergh at what time?"

I struggle. "It was after breakfast, but late. Ten? Ten thirty? I was drinking a cup of tea."

He nods as if that's fascinating. "So, Mrs. Lindbergh calls, you answer . . ."

I'm about to nod, then I remember. "No, I didn't answer the phone. Violet Sharpe told me I had a call. I don't know if that matters."

"Everything matters, Miss Gow. Violet Sharpe is . . . ?"

"She's a table maid for the Morrows."

"Did she tell you what the phone call was about?"

"I don't think so, just that I had a call from Hopewell."

"Okay, go on. Oh—did you talk with anyone else from this house besides Mrs. Lindbergh?"

"Yes, Olly Whateley. He looked up the train timetable for me."

"And who in the Morrow house knew you were leaving?"

How on earth should I know? But I'm here to answer questions, so I reach for names. ". . . Violet Sharpe, she took the call. Mr. Banks, the butler, he got one of the chauffeurs to drive me."

"So, the chauffeur knew," Brex clarifies.

"Yes." As Brex and I speak, McRell stands behind him, arms crossed, lips thin over his teeth. Uneasy, wanting to please, I add, "There are two chauffeurs, by the way. Mr. Ellerson is the one who drove me."

"Who else did you tell?"

I'm about to say *No one else.* Then I remember Marguerite. "Oh— Mrs. Junge. She's a seamstress for Mrs. Morrow."

Brex says to the notetaker, "You get all those names?" The man nods. I will myself not to ask, *Why do you need all those names?*

Told to go on, I recount everything I remember of yesterday. As I do, Brex and sometimes McRell interrupt with little questions: What did I do when I arrived? When did Ellerson leave? When I went to check on Charlie, was the light on or off? Window open or not, shutter open or not? They start speaking at the same time, making me unsure who I'm to answer, forgetful of the other question. The details pile up, the demands—and trying to figure out what's behind them—become a loud buzzing. Some things, they ask over and over, as if they've never asked before. When they come back to the shutter for the third time— did I try to close it or did both Mrs. Lindbergh and I try—I cry out, "I'm sorry, I can't think . . . please . . . stop."

The room goes silent. I wait for an apology. *Gee, I'm sorry, Miss*

Gow. It doesn't come. I'm about to tell them that the Colonel prom-ised we wouldn't be interrogated, when Brex asks, "Your brother, he died in an accident?" His voice goes up at the end, skeptical, as if someone might have misinformed him.

Disoriented by the change in subject, I nod.

"What was the type of accident?"

I cannot imagine how Billy's death has anything to do with Charlie being taken. It feels like an ugly trick—this whole thing does—and for a moment, I feel I might burst into tears. But I remind myself, these men are looking for Charlie, it is their job to find him. My comfort doesn't matter.

"He was employed by the public service, working on high-tension power wires, and was electrocuted." How strange, I think. I finally remembered what he did.

Brex pulls a face like he's sorry. "And you spent some time in De-troit, is that right?"

"I don't see the significance—"

"Is that right?"

"Yes, that's right. I wasn't aware it was a crime to go to Detroit."

McRell steps forward, inserting himself, "Depends on who you know in Detroit. Tell me, when you're the baby nurse, is it your job to clean the nursery?"

He's speaking fast; I steel myself to keep my head clear. "Yes. I tidy, clean Charlie's clothes. Elsie Whateley does the dusting and things like that."

"Because one thing that puzzles us is fingerprints." I shake my head. Raising a finger, McRell continues. "You say you and Mrs. Lind-bergh wrestled with that shutter, and yet we can't find any fingerprints on it. Or anywhere else in the room. It's almost like somebody wiped it clean."

"Or the kidnapper wore gloves. In any event, I assure you it wasn't me."

"What brought you to Detroit?" says Brex, as if McRell hasn't been talking about fingerprints.

I struggle to remember what I said before. ". . . I visited friends."

"And your brother was living when you came here?" I nod. "You lived with him?"

"For a few days. In Bogota. Then I worked for the Gibbs family in New Jersey, and then I went to Detroit."

"Of your own free will?"

It's a bizarre question and I stare at him. "Yes."

"When you worked in Detroit, you were always known as Betty Gow?"

Brex slows on the word "always," making sure I hear it. Fear curls in my belly. I add a "sir" to the "yes."

"How old was your brother?"

"He was thirty-two."

"You ever hear of a man called Scotty Gow?"

"No."

"How long is your brother dead?"

Why do you keep coming back to Billy? I want to ask. He's nothing to do with this. "Several months."

McRell steps in front of Brex as if it's his turn again. "While you were in Detroit, you also went to see a boyfriend you were keeping company with."

The breath goes out of me. As I fight to pull it back into my lungs, I wonder, How do they know? How can they know this?

"Yes."

"What was his name?"

In my mind there is a shift; they have talked to someone about me. That someone has told them a great deal—enough that they know when I am lying. So I give them the name. "Robert Coutts."

"Where did he live?" I shake my head, I can't remember, other than I hated the neighborhood. "Where was he employed?"

You must know, I think. *You know everything else.* Again I wonder how. Then I remember: Ellerson. That drunken night with the spinning bottle, pointing.

He . . . told. A thing he should have known never to tell. Because a friend would know. Did he remember I said it was a man I worked for? Has he told them that as well? Like a child, I sit stunned, stuck on *But*.

Then anger freezes my nerves, and I answer the last question. "The Ford automobile plant."

Eyes narrowed, McRell says, "But you had known him some time before you went out there. You were sweethearts . . ."

As if he hasn't been listening, Brex asks, "Who is that boyfriend she's talking about?" McRell tells him, "She has a boyfriend out in Detroit that she kept company with in Scotland." It's another ploy, I realize. Embarrass me. Wear me down. *Sweetheart. Boyfriend.* Sneering at endearments, the way men do.

Then McRell says, "What became of Robert Coutts, Betty?"

"I don't know him anymore."

He spins a pudgy finger in the air. "You two had a little bit of a quarrel?"

Is that what it was? I wonder. But say, "Yes."

In the same accusatory tone, McRell asks, "When was your brother electrocuted?"

Hating him, I say slowly, "Fourth of September, 1931."

"Have you got a boyfriend now that you . . . go around with?"

It's the pause before "go around with." Letting me know he'd like to use a different word, but to be polite he'll say "go around." Not even pretending not to know but asking so I have to say it. And the way they go back and forth between brother and boyfriend. The other ones—Brex and the notetaker—with their little smiles, this part they like, this they want to hear more of. There's a tall bookcase right behind them. I'd like to bring it down, crack their skulls and snap their necks.

"Yes," I say. "A boy named Johnson. He's employed on a yacht owned by the Lamonts." At the mention of the Lamonts, they exchange looks.

Brex asks, "So you didn't know you were coming here from Englewood until that morning?"

"That's right."

I am proud I've got used to the sudden changes in subject. Boyfriend to travel and it hasn't fazed me. Only it's not a change.

"And your boyfriend knew that too, right?"

"He didn't know it until the evening. I left a message." As I say it, I realize I don't know if that's true. I have no idea when Mrs. Sherman might have told Henry. Or what time Henry called the Morrow house and found out I'd left.

Brex asks, "In your message to the landlady, you told Johnson to call the Morrow home?" I nod. "Well, why'd you do that if you knew you were going to be here?"

"I was thinking how much it would cost him to call me here. So I told them at the Morrow house to tell him I was not at home."

"That was still making him spend five cents to call the Morrow house."

"I am Scottish, but not that Scottish, to save him five cents."

That gets a little smile, then Brex asks, "Did he call you that night?"

"He called here at nine or . . . ten minutes to nine. I was surprised."

Brex frowns. "How did your boyfriend know the number here?"

Our eyes meet. I see the full question: *when you've only been here once.*

"I had been here two or three times," I tell him, not adding that I brought Henry with me. "Possibly someone at the Morrow house gave him the number."

There is a long pause. The man taking the notes looks up: *Are we done?* Please, I think, please, please let us be done.

Brex asks, "You have any relatives still in this country, Miss Gow?"

Barely keeping my tone civil, I say, "I have an aunt and uncle. In Ohio."

"What's your address in Glasgow?"

I give it.

"Your mother and father live there?"

"My mother and stepfather."

"Brothers and sisters?"

"Two of each."

"But no one *here* by the name of Gow—is that right?"

Once again, they're back to Billy. Frustrated, I say, "No," about to add *Except for my dead brother*, when Brex says, as if to get it straight, "No one in Detroit named Gow?"

Startled, I say, "No. No one in Detroit."

McRell calls out, "Your boyfriend who worked in the Ford factory. He ever get into a jam?"

Unsettled, I say, "What does that mean?"

"Trouble."

In my mind, Rob tearing through the streets of Glasgow, my idiot younger self shouting "Faster!" If he's done something, will they blame me?

I steel myself. Whatever Rob Coutts has done in Detroit, it's nothing to do with me.

"No," I say. "No trouble."

"What was the cause of you and him breaking up?" McRell asks.

The girl with the big teeth and bright lips. Me standing there . . . obliterated. These are not feelings I can give to strangers.

"I didn't care for him anymore."

I give a little shrug as I say it: *I'm a pretty girl and when I'm bored with a fellow, I don't waste my time.* It seems to work. Brex moves on to other questions, ridiculous questions. Do I like shows? Dances? Cabaret? Did I date anyone else? I tell him I'm not actually that keen on meeting people.

Then McRell barks, "What was the *real* cause of your breakup with the boyfriend?"

I exhale sharply. My stupidity over Rob Coutts has nothing to do with Charlie; they've no right to hear about it. I think: Something better. More specific. True, but not the truth. "I found out he was not the man I thought he was."

That gets raised eyebrows, side glances. "Found out" was a mistake. Makes it sound like something happened. Which it did. But. I want it to be him and not me at fault. If I tell them the truth, they'll snicker and that I can't bear. Also, I don't want them digging into how I know Rob Coutts. It's not a time for the family to learn I once took up with my employer.

Why do women fall out of love? I have a sudden memory of Henry in the back of the Depression. *"I'm broke. I think is how you say it."*

In a rush, I say, "He had been spending his money as he made it. I don't want to work after I'm married. I just saw that he was not thinking of it as seriously as I thought. He wanted me to keep going around with him and he had no thought of getting married. He just didn't seem to have any push about him."

McRell goes to the table, flips one of the files open, then snatches up a piece of paper. Swinging back to me, he says, "You have an unusual name."

"Not in Scotland."

"There's a man out in Chicago that seems to be your brother. Has a sister, same age as you, weighs a hundred and twenty pounds. That about what you weigh?"

"One twenty-five."

"This paper also quotes that your brother worked in the Ford factory and that's where your sweetheart worked; that's a funny coincidence."

It is funny, being completely untrue, and I say sarcastically, "Yes, sir."

"Wasn't it peculiar that you and your boyfriend loved each other so much and then you broke off with him because he didn't save his money?"

He drawls "so much," my first impulse is to say *No, not* so much. But they'll just say, *If you didn't love him that much, why did you go to Detroit?*

"Didn't you really go out there to be married?" McRell asks.

The contempt in his voice, as if he's caught me out. Astonishing, how stupid men can make you feel about hope. Stretching my lips across my teeth in some sort of smile, I say, "Yes."

He asks it again. "You went out there to be married."

"Yes."

"And after that, there was some misunderstanding, the wedding didn't take place?"

Wedding. I have a scalding memory of sitting across Rob's thighs, laughing as the nightgown is lifted over my head, blinding me. It's not even the nakedness, it's the things I said, felt—all that love and need showered on a man who saw me as just a bit of fun.

"Why didn't the wedding take place?" McRell presses.

I blow the air from my lungs and with it, the memories. Keeping my voice low and even, I say, "There wasn't any date set. When I left for Detroit, I didn't have another position, so I thought there was a chance to go and see what I thought of this boyfriend. I was feeling restless and wanted a change. And I thought I would do that and see if I really liked this boy well enough to marry him."

"Does he drink?"

"No."

"Smoke?"

"No."

"The only reason you didn't marry him was because he didn't save his money?" He sounds incredulous, as if I said the reason was the way he parted his hair.

"I didn't think he cared enough for me because he didn't seem to want to give me as much time as I thought he should. He was different and he didn't have any money saved and he didn't have any serious intentions of getting married to me right away or in the near future."

His voice kind, Brex asks, "What was so different? What was the change in him?"

No change, that was the problem, I want to scream.

"I just didn't care for him anymore."

"Did you quarrel?"

"Yes."

"But what was he doing that didn't please you? He led an upright life?"

Jesus, upright life. But it will have to be told. They won't be satisfied until every drab, ugly part of my life is strewn out on the floor in front of them. Teeth clenched so tight my head aches, I say, "When he told me to come to Detroit, I didn't suspect he had any other girlfriends there. I, of course, was not going to stand for that. *That's* the reason."

Without realizing it, I've slumped, forearms on my legs, head down, arms close to my body. I think to say, *Was it painful enough? Humiliation enough? Do you believe me now?*

Then Brex says, "Okay, Betty. Okay." His voice is soft. The silence stretches. I start to feel light with hope that I will be let go.

McRell asks, "You ever know a Scotty Gow?"

I shut my eyes. "I've told you. No."

"Ever heard of the Purple Gang?"

I shake my head.

"Rob Coutts, you ever introduce him as your brother?"

"No, I never did."

"Was he dark?"

"No, fair."

"So he looked like a Scotsman?"

"Yes."

"So there would be some reason for calling him Scotty."

No one has ever called Rob Coutts such a thing, but to this man, all Scotsmen can be called Scotty and it's not worth the argument. "Yes, sir."

"What does this new boyfriend of yours look like? He Scottish too?"

"Norwegian. Reddish hair. About four inches taller than me."

"Where did you meet him?"

"In Maine," I remind them. "He works for the Lamonts."

"Oh, that's right."

Then all of a sudden, McRell thrusts the piece of paper in my face. I jump as if he's actually slapped me.

"This here"—he rattles it—"comes from the Department of Justice. This means a lot of work for us. This is true. I am not saying that this is you, but this is a true record from Washington, taken over the telephone. We are going to check this out whether Gow is still in jail or in Detroit. There is no question in my mind, but that this is Scotty

Gow of the Purple Gang. I am a little inclined to believe this is your sweetheart. The fellow out there in Detroit."

I almost smile, because it must be a joke. *This* was why they were so interested in my breakup with Rob? They can't actually believe it.

Sensing my incredulity, McRell raises his voice. "You know what the Purple Gang does, Miss Gow? They snatch babies. That's how they make their money. Funny thing, you seeing this fellow in Detroit, then coming to work for the Lindberghs. Don't you think?"

Brex holds up a hand, as if holding McRell back. "Now, we don't think you were in on it, necessarily. Maybe he just took your name to get out of a bad spot. Is that what you quarreled about? Him wanting to use your name?"

I say, "No." For all the good it will do me. Because I can see: They don't care what the truth is. They've got a story in their heads, the woman on that piece of paper. Her boyfriend—or is it brother?—Scotty Gow. Of the Purple Gang. I remember my mother fretting: *"America, it's a place for gangsters,"* and now, it seems, I am one.

But . . . I'm not. The Colonel himself told them I was not. Struggling to keep my voice under control, I say, "Colonel Lindbergh said I wasn't to be touched."

"Colonel Lindbergh has other things on his mind right now," snaps Brex.

Enraged, I fling my arm toward the window. "Someone came into this house and took Charlie. Why aren't you out there looking for them? Why all these questions about Detroit, my brother, or when I called Henry, or who I told . . ."

McRell shouts over me, "Because the Lindberghs weren't supposed to be here."

Supposed to? It's their house, of course they're supposed to. I shake my head.

"Colonel and Mrs. Lindbergh come here on weekends, right?"

"That's right."

"Have they ever stayed later than Monday that you recall?"

"No, but Charlie had a cold, Mrs. Lindbergh got sick . . ."

"So, anyone watching this house would have seen that the Lindberghs aren't here during the week."

He waits for me to agree. "I suppose so."

"Then why did the kidnappers strike on a Tuesday? How did they know to come *here,* to the house in the middle of nowhere, that has no protection?"

Mrs. Lindbergh's father hated that, I remember. He told the Colonel it was madness not to have guards at the gate like they do at Englewood.

Brex's voice, low and urgent, "Who told them the Lindberghs were in Hopewell with the baby on a Tuesday night?"

"No one *told* . . . they just changed their plans."

"No, Betty, *you* changed your plans."

I shake my head, uncomprehending. I don't change things in my life, the Lindberghs do.

McRell says directly into my face, "No one outside the family knew Mrs. Lindbergh was staying here except *you.* You and the people you told you were going to Hopewell."

Me. And the people I told. The mad scramble of that morning. The names and faces: Violet. Banks. Ellerson, Marguerite . . .

Henry.

Childhood memories: *I'm telling! You told! I hate you!* That awful betrayal, of turning private fun into a crime by telling people you shouldn't.

The kidnappers didn't just . . . find us. Someone—one of us—told them where we were.

I fasten a hand over my mouth, hold my arm tight across my stomach. The words "Excuse me" form in my head, but I don't dare open my mouth. I shake my head slightly, then wrench open the door and run to the hall bathroom. Gripping the sides of the sink, I put my head down and open my mouth as it comes out in one painful retch.

Chapter Sixteen

The house is never quiet, even at night. Tossing on the mattress in the staff sitting room, I listen as one shift of policemen goes, another comes in, and the exchange of information starts. People in shacks and farmhouses from miles around are being questioned. Every carpenter, plumber, and electrician who worked on the house is being interviewed. Scores of policemen have tramped the surrounding woods, beating the brush for any signs of the kidnappers. As the hour grows late, they become indiscreet. One is annoyed that the Colonel is in charge, ordering Schwarzkopf about. Another says, "You have to let the family handle these things. It's their kid." They sure feel sorry for Mrs. Lindbergh.

Punchy, laughing, they read through the phone records for the day. Everyday citizens wanting to help by reporting a German couple who quit their jobs on the day of the kidnapping. A barber turned bootlegger, a mechanic who suddenly shaved his beard. A woman who heard a child crying next door; she'd never liked the couple next door, always thought them suspicious.

Everyone is suspicious. Everyone.

I recall the swirl of voices and faces from that morning in Englewood. Violet, giggling and excited by the change in plans. Marguerite, curling around the door. Ellerson, glancing, terrified, in the mirror. Banks at his desk. Henry. *"I was thinking, I don't have to leave right away."*

From the other room, I hear "nanny," someone joking he'd like to get me into an interrogation room. Another says, "She's too smart for you," another agreeing, "She's the coolest of the lot."

A crude joke is made. Men, what they look for in nannies. One trooper says he heard Charlie's not normal, Mrs. Lindbergh flew when she was pregnant and now something's wrong with him. That causes offense. The trooper is told to shut up, get back to work.

No, I decide. I will not do to other people what McRell and Brex did to me. I won't take their secrets, the places they are weak and vulnerable, in order to pinch and mold them to make an entirely different person, the way the police have made me some Detroit criminal's girlfriend and accomplice. They muddled me, Brex and McRell. There are lots of ways the kidnappers could have found out we were here. They might even live nearby; plenty of poor desperate people in the area. The Lindbergh baby has been kidnapped. The police want us to turn on one another. If Colonel and Mrs. Lindbergh can give me their trust, I must do the same for others.

All the same, the next day, I go outside and look at the house. I stand a fair distance from it, trying to get a sense: If someone wanted to know what went on inside, where could they be—and not be seen themselves? What would you watch for? Arms folded, I turn, take in the scrubby winter fields, the ring of gnarled oaks that surround the property. Only one road goes in and out; you can't see the house from the main road, it's blocked by trees. You might watch for cars coming and going, but the Whateleys do drive to town and workmen are always around. You couldn't go by that. We are on a high hill, though. Colonel Lindbergh is clearing space for an airstrip and people have said that actually the best way to get to the house is by air.

Which means we can be seen from a distance. When the lights

are on, the house must shine in the darkness like a small burning star. And the Whateleys are always here; perhaps it seemed the Lindberghs were in residence all week long? Except . . . the Whateleys are frugal with the Lindberghs' money and Elsie is careful to use electricity only as needed. When Henry and I came, the lights were on in the kitchen and the parlor—that was it. Whereas at the weekend, the place is lit up with guests, the road humming with cars. The difference would be obvious to anyone watching the house.

But—again I turn, frustrated by the expanse of wilderness—where would you watch *from*? We're surrounded by forest. Even for the local people, this spot is hard to find; that was part of its appeal for the Lindberghs. Miles off, there are farms, run-down houses, abandoned shacks. But would a kidnapper camp out in a shack or the woods night after night, hoping to see signs of the family?

Also, I realize, there are shutters on most of the windows and Elsie keeps them shut, especially in cold weather. Making it even harder to know if people were here—and how many. I look at the windows of Colonel Lindbergh's study, directly below Charlie's nursery. The ladder would have been visible from the study, had the study shutters been open—were they? Perhaps it doesn't matter. The Colonel didn't go to his study until after nine fifteen and the police think Charlie was taken at nine; that's when the Colonel heard the snap of wood that would have been the ladder breaking. When I was on the telephone with Henry.

How would someone *know* that the family was here? I ask myself. How, unless someone else . . .

"Say, have a look!"

I've been so lost in thought I jump as three troopers crowd round me. There are too many at the house, I think, irritably, and not all of them have enough to do. I know these three. It's the joker with freckles and the one with a weak chin who gulps whenever I come near. The bold-eyed one with dark curls is the "leader." If I had to guess, I'd say one of them made the joke about me and the interrogation room last night.

I'm about to wave them off and go inside when the freckled one holds up a newspaper. There, right in front of me, is . . . me. The awful shot of me and Charlie, from that first day in Maine. Only they've smudged it somehow, made it look like a painting or drawing; Charlie's features are blurred from the nose down, my face is flatter, as if I'm wearing heavy powder. It's us, but not us.

Below,

Authorities today questioned Betty Gow, shown above with the missing Lindbergh heir. It was she who left unlocked the shutter thru which the kidnappers entered the baby's room. Police were also seeking "Scotty" Gow, a Detroit gangster—perhaps related.

I clutch at my mouth, still the words escape. "Oh, my God."

Me, but not me, a smudged me, an ugly me on the front page of an American newspaper. With the accusation, plain, the words no one's said till now: *It was she who left unlocked the shutter thru which the kidnappers entered the baby's room.*

Horror-struck, I gaze up at the shutters at Charlie's window. Here I've been trying to see how the kidnappers would have known we were here without someone inside telling them, and all the while, America is calmly opening the morning paper to learn that the someone was me.

Sensing their prank has gone wrong, the troopers are quiet. The one with the curly hair snatches at the paper. "Hey. Forget that."

I stare at him. Forget it? This is out there. It's what people will see, what people will think. It *is*. What they mean, what I mean, who I am, none of that matters anymore. To most people, this is the only Betty Gow that exists.

It was she who left unlocked . . .

My mother is going to see this. James, Agnes, everyone on Nithsdale Street.

Frantic to escape, I run inside, ignoring the calls of "We're sorry . . ." I rush to the sitting room—my room—but it's crowded with troopers and officers. I pound my way down the stairs to the cellar. Once I've heard the door slam behind me, I press my mouth to the crook of my arm and shriek until it feels like my throat is going to split.

I hear the rap of knuckles on wood, the creak of hinges as the door opens. The dark-haired one leans halfway in. It's the way he bends, putting his shoulder down, ducking his head, that makes me recognize him. It's the trooper who caught me and Henry in the Depression at the Palisades. *It's you,* I think. *Of course it is.*

"I'm sorry."

McCann, I think. That's his name.

"We all are," he says. "We won't do it again."

The next day, Elsie, rushed and exasperated, says, "Betty, could you go to the store for me? I'm out of milk, bread . . . everything." She glances around the kitchen, almost in tears. I say "Of course" and get my coat while she writes out a list.

Whateley drives me to the little main street of Hopewell. I get out on the corner, head to Karlson's Market. A woman jerks her head as I pass. For a moment, she's simply astonished by the sight of me, then her mouth sets as she gives me a long, hard stare. Two men coming down the street catch sight of her anger; they look to me, as if to say, *What's up?* Then grin as they realize. *Oh, it's you.*

I tell myself Karlson's does not go quiet as I enter. That heads are not turning, people aren't slowing, looking back to see: Is it her? Making my way down the aisles, I concentrate on putting things—anything— into the basket. That way, I don't notice the woman who pointedly removes herself from my presence, the gentleman's disapproving cough, the boys peering around the door of the stockroom. They've all seen the papers, I realize. Every one of them is wondering, How can she be here, when she did what she did?

I think to stop, announce, *It's not true. What you're thinking, none of it . . .*

The shove comes from behind, a supposed accident in a narrow space. It upends my basket, spilling what I've gathered on the floor.

There is no apology. As I crouch to pick it up, a man's foot edges into view. I sense someone behind as well.

Leave it, I think. Go.

Scrambling to my feet, I hurry to the exit, no longer bothered if people see my fear. When I push through the door I am confronted by several men waiting just outside. At first they make no sense—police?— then I realize: the papers are in town to cover the story. Someone's made a phone call: *The nurse just turned up at Karlson's.* They surround me, jabbing questions, pens, and camera lenses at me, making me flinch. I wonder: How is this allowed? How can people get this close, do these things to you? Are there no rules? No one to stop them?

Putting my head down, I flail wildly to make space as I hurry to the car. Frantic to get in before they catch up, I throw myself in the back seat and yank the door shut.

"What on earth?" Whateley asks, staring. I've not got a single thing Elsie asked for.

I push the list at him. "Can you go? I'll stay with the car."

Is this my life now? I wonder on the ride back. Who I am? Hard stares everywhere I go, only feeling safe inside a spare room in some- one else's house? I remember it, how proud I was when I got that title, the Lindbergh Nanny. But what the people at Karlson's saw was a child snatcher, gangster's girlfriend, *she who left unlocked*. You wanted to be special, my girl? Congratulations, now the whole world knows who you are.

They may as well arrest me, I think, when we return to the house. What difference could it possibly make?

After that, I keep to the kitchen, doing dishes, filling cups, and cutting sandwiches. Elsie says small tasks, endless and speedily done, keep the mind quiet, and she's right. I'm relishing working my way through a mountain of mugs and plates, the feel of my arms up to the elbows in warm soapy water, when I hear a tentative knock. Looking over my shoulder, I see a plump blond man at the door. He's not brash like some, asks politely for a cup of coffee and is it all right if he takes it in here. He puts me in mind of a pig; cheerful, straightforward, no malice.

"Of course," I say, handing it to him.

He sips, raising his eyebrows to indicate pleasure. "Oh—I'm Lieutenant Keaten. New Jersey State Police. Yes, like the actor. My friends even call me Buster."

"You might need new friends."

He turns the mug in his hands, as if trying to warm them. "I hear the local police gave you a hard time. I'm sorry. Everyone we've talked to says you're devoted to the baby. Mrs. Morrow was, uh, very firm on that point."

He smiles, indicating a tongue-lashing, and my heart sings a private thank-you to that lady.

He adds, "Mrs. Morrow informed us you were alone with the baby for some time in Maine. It's her view that if you had wanted to kidnap Charlie, you had every opportunity then."

Astonished this was noticed and remembered, I nod. "Truly, all I want is Charlie home safe. And . . . if that's what the officers felt they had to do, well." I risk a smile. "I wouldn't waste too much time on Scotty Gow, though. I have no brother named Scotty. Nor boyfriend of that name."

"That's right, your fellow's named Henry. Henrik?" I nod. "I hear you missed a date that night. I bet he was disappointed."

Thrilled to no longer be a suspect and hungry for good news, I sit down at the table. "Colonel Lindbergh says it was professionals and that means we'll get Charlie back soon." I remember Dorothy Lewes, pleasant and sane-seeming until she wasn't. "Not . . . crazies."

"We don't think it's crazies," he says.

Wanting more, I press. "After all, he's just a baby, not as if he can identify them later. They've no reason not to let him go."

"We're doing everything we can to bring the baby home safe and sound," he assures me.

There's something rote about his responses. I'm about to say "everything" they can do is not enough when Officer Keaten puts a postcard on the table. "This came today, as a matter of fact."

BABY STILL SAFE. GET THINGS QUIET.

I cry out in relief at that wonderful word "safe." Keaten asks, "You wouldn't recognize the handwriting, would you?"

His tone is casual, but it's like someone stepping too close. Still, wanting to be helpful, I take a close look, then shake my head. "It's all in capital letters. This came to the house?"

"No. Postmaster in Connecticut spotted it and sent it over. West Hartford, as a matter of fact."

It takes me too long to respond, I can feel the mistake even as I think, Say something, anything, don't just sit still and shocked.

"West Hartford mean anything to you, Miss Gow?"

He knows, I realize. He wouldn't have shown me the card if he didn't. I straighten. "Yes. Henry was on his way there yesterday. His brother lives there."

A small nod, as if the information is as boring as it sounds. He takes another sip of coffee. "Where's he from, originally?"

"Norway."

He wants me to ask why. I won't. Let him do the talking.

"Reason I ask, is the ransom note was written in a way that leads us to believe the person who wrote it, English might not be his first language. Certain words were misspelled in a way that indicates maybe a German accent."

He waits, then adds, "German, Norwegian . . . not too far off."

"Quite dissimilar, I'd say."

"We're just trying to get the baby back to his mother, Miss Gow. When did you last speak with Red Johnson?"

"Red" Johnson. They've been talking to someone who uses Henry's nickname. I don't. Neither do the Whateleys. Ellerson or Violet. Or Marguerite, she uses it too.

"The night it happened. Sometime after dinner."

"May I ask what you talked about?"

"That he was sorry not to see me. He asked if he should put off going to Hartford, I told him no."

"Did he say where he was?"

Instantly, I remember Marguerite at my door. *Johannes and I were hoping you could join us and Red tonight.* At the time, it just seemed a pleasantry, the sort of thing you say. But it was strange, her interest. She even asked, I remember now, *"They're staying in Hopewell?"*

Did she want me . . . out of the house? Away from Charlie?

Henry's sudden invitation, his tongue at my neck. *"See me tomorrow night."* And when I reminded him of Charlie, he insisted I come between seven and ten, the hours no one is to go into the nursery. Henry knows that. He knows because I told him.

But then I think, No, this is ridiculous. "He was out with another couple all evening," I tell the lieutenant. "Marguerite and Johannes Junge. She works for the Morrows. Talk to her, she'll vouch for Henry, I'm sure."

Keaten takes out a small notepad, writes this down. Then unexpectedly, he smiles. "That's a very nice dress."

"Thank you."

"Nice color. I admire people who know color, style, that kind of thing." He looks down at his rumpled uniform. "I sure don't."

I can't tell what the right response is: pretend I have no idea what he's doing or show that I'm perfectly aware this is all a clumsy lead-up to a new attack?

"No, you sure don't." Mimicking his folksy manner.

He laughs. "For example, when you and Mr. Johnson were caught parking at Palisades Park, I can't remember the color of the car. I swear it was in the report . . ."

"It was night. Color doesn't show in the dark."

"What color was it, Miss Gow?"

"Green. Henry drives a green coupe."

"Would you be surprised to hear that a green coupe drove up to the house the day of the kidnapping?"

"I'd be surprised to hear there was only one green coupe in all of existence." I keep my voice light. Remind myself that Henry was working at the garage most of that day; his boss could tell the police he was there. Someone is telling a lot of stories about Henry. Someone wants the police to suspect him. I search the lieutenant's face for a clue as to who that might be.

Keaten offers, "The chauffeur said he had to drive around a car matching that description after he dropped you off."

Ellerson. Again. And he's the only one who could have told them about Rob Coutts.

Staying quiet is the right move; it forces Keaten to say more.

He does. "Also—Mr. Whateley told us he chased off a man and a woman who drove up in a green car. They were taking pictures of the house. They seemed particularly interested in the nursery."

A man and a woman. Whateley has never met the Junges, so he wouldn't recognize them.

"How would they even know where that was?"

"Well, *that's* what we can't figure out, Miss Gow. How did the kidnappers know which room was the nursery? Sure, the papers printed plans for the house, but those were general blueprints. There are shutters on the windows. Makes it tough to see in. Not as if they could just wander around the house, putting the ladder up to every window."

But one set of shutters wouldn't latch. I assume Keaten knows that. Does he believe that it wouldn't latch? Or does he believe along with the rest of the country that I left it open as some kind of signal: *Look for the window with the open shutter . . .*

"Did you ever bring Henry to the house, Miss Gow?"

I have a flash of raw memory, Henry and that awful, empty room, me hating it but trying to act like it was lovely. I feel my neck go hot, and I know Keaten's spotted it. He may know Scotty Gow is a fiction. Henry is a different story.

He says, slow and quiet, "I know how much you love Charlie, Miss Gow. I know you'd never do anything to hurt him. But you need to tell me: Has Red Johnson been in this house?"

". . . Yes."

And he asked to come here. It was his idea. The horrific possibility is starting to take hold. No, I think, he's not . . . *that*. Feckless. Young. Needs to grow up . . .

The car. The green coupe. That I wondered how he could afford.

Even at the beginning, how he wanted to hear about the baby. *"It's what you do all day, yes, I'm interested."*

I hear Keaten ask, "Did Red Johnson ever meet the baby?"

"A few times."

"So, the baby would have known him? Felt comfortable with him . . . ?"

"No." In this matter, I can defend Henry and tell the truth. "Charlie didn't like strangers. He was at that age, he knew his mother, father, and me. Maybe a few others, like the Whateleys. But not Mr. Johnson."

This, he believes. But I can tell, it is not good news. "What?"

His brow creases as he deliberates whether to tell me. ". . . The blankets were still pinned."

"Yes, I pin them to the mattress so they stay on."

"Yet the baby didn't cry."

"He was deeply asleep. Just getting over a cold . . ."

He explains: "The window opens when the kidnapper climbs in, there's a blast of cold air. Someone pulls Charlie out of bed—he had to pull hard because of the pins—and carries him down a ladder, slipping when one of the rungs breaks—"

He pauses, breathes deep.

"And he *never* cries?"

He's trying to scare me, pushing me to say, *Yes, Charlie knew Henry, wouldn't have cried if he picked him up.* Or: *Yes, I went up to his room when no one was looking and handed him to my boyfriend who was waiting on the ladder.*

Because otherwise . . .

"They could have put something over his mouth," I stammer. "A cloth or . . ."

"Chloroform?" It's not what I was thinking, but I nod frantically.

"It has a very strong odor, and we didn't smell it in the room. What *time* did you break your date with Red Johnson, Miss . . . or may I call you Betty?"

I shake my head, too upset to care what he calls me. "I called his landlady that morning."

"But you don't know when he actually found out."

"No. I had to leave a message . . . I've told you all this before."

"And he called you when?"

"Nine in the evening. Around then."

"And he was calling from where?"

"A drugstore."

"A drugstore," he echoes.

". . . That's what he said."

"But you don't know for sure."

For sure—somehow that phrase makes me feel everything I don't know for sure. There is nothing about Henry Johnson I know for sure, except that he works for the Lamonts and he doesn't even do that anymore. I only know what I've felt for him and feelings lie. Henry, Red, Henrik, I can't even say for sure I know his name.

"He's not that man," I say, limping back to a truth. "He'd never do anything to hurt a child." I think of his father's fists. "He wouldn't . . ."

Keaten doesn't believe me. So many desperate men in need of money, so many desperate women who believe them when they lie.

"He wouldn't do that to *me*," I say, foundering.

"Because he cares about you."

"Yes."

"Why hasn't he called, Betty? If he cares about you? Cares about the baby—you say he does. Why hasn't he called?"

Because phone calls are expensive, I think helplessly. *Or maybe he has and your men never told me with so many calls coming in. Or . . .* I don't know. *Why are you making me answer for him?*

The truth is like a dull knife, brutal and wounding: Because you brought him in, Betty. Inside the house. You let him meet Charlie, see his room. You told him the baby was not in the well-protected Englewood house, but in Hopewell, surrounded by forest and deserted farms, with only the one lonely road leading in and out.

You brought him in. And told him everything.

Keaten says, "Betty, if there's someone else we should be looking at—someone on staff, here or at the Morrow house—all you have to do is give me a name. I know they're friends, people you work with. But good people can get into trouble all sorts of ways. Money problems. Resentment over time off. Fear. Frustration, unhappiness. The desire to protect someone."

"That's just life. I can't accuse ..."

I stare at him, unsure: Does he suspect Henry or not? Is this a trick to get me to say the sorts of things about others they've said about Henry? About me?

Then I look at the postcard, the one from West Hartford. BABY STILL SAFE. What matters most comes clear.

"Just tell me ..."

"If I can."

"Tell me that note is real. That Charlie's safe. I keep thinking ... he must be so scared. An older child, you could lie to, say they're going home soon, but he's a baby, he'll be wanting us, wondering why we've not come ..."

I nod at the note. "Is that real? Please tell me what you think."

I meet his eye, begging: *Tell me yes. Make me believe that's what you believe.* The card doesn't have the circles on it, I realize. Three circles with the red one in the middle ...

"Hundreds of children are kidnapped every year," Keaten says dutifully. "Mostly by organized gangsters. The majority of victims are returned unharmed once the ransom is paid."

"Henry Johnson is not a gangster, I swear."

"Okay. But who are his friends, Betty? He ever talk about them?"

I shake my head.

"His brothers, you ever meet them?"

Another shake. "One is in Brooklyn, the other ..." I wave at the note.

"How'd you two meet?"

"In Maine. He saw me on the beach." With the baby. "Asked to meet me."

"Who'd he ask? Who introduced you?"

"... Ellerson."

He waits for me to say more about Ellerson. I let him wait.

Then he asks, "With brothers in Brooklyn and Connecticut, how'd Henry end up in New Jersey?"

"He wanted . . ."

"What, Betty?"

I smile sadly. "He said he wanted to be near me."

And I, because I am a stupid, stupid woman, believed him.

"Talk to the Junges," I say, voice shaking. "They'll tell you. Henry was with them. He's not the man you think he is."

The lieutenant nods. But I can tell: It's his view that I'm the one who doesn't know who Henry Johnson really is.

Chapter Seventeen

That night, I call the Englewood house. Marguerite sounds surprised to hear my voice when she comes to the phone. "Betty, I am so sorry—" and I cut her off with, "Yes, thank you."

"Are the police being terrible?" she wants to know.

"They've been all right. Have you spoken with them?"

"No. I can't think what they think I would know." Her casual entitlement to stand apart from this nightmare infuriates me.

"Well, they may see it differently. That's why I want to ask—"

"Yes?"

"When he called here that night, Henry said he was with you."

"That was the plan."

And that's what happened? I wait for her to say more, but she doesn't. I press, "So you were with him the whole night?"

"Except when he went to make a telephone call."

I shut my eyes, savor the relief. Henry is not guilty. I am not guilty.

"And . . . I'm sorry, I have to ask, you weren't anywhere near the Hopewell house. You didn't come thinking maybe I could join you for a little while or . . ."

"No. We went to a coffeehouse, then drove along the Hudson Drive. Red drove me back to Englewood at around eleven."

"And then what?"

"He drove Johannes home. I think."

Is Johannes Junge, just arrived in this country from Germany, a good man to be with on the night Charlie was taken? He uses a cane; how many disabled men commit crimes that involve ladders? Squirming children that must be kept quiet? But of course the police would say, keeping Charlie silent would have been Henry's job. Or mine.

It doesn't matter, I tell myself. If what Marguerite says is true, Henry was with her and Johannes in Englewood when Charlie was taken, so he did not take Charlie. I try to restore that sense of breathless relief I had a moment ago.

Only . . . Colonel Lindbergh said a little after nine, he heard a knocking sound, as if someone had dropped a crate. The police think what he heard was the ladder snapping. And Henry called here around nine. If that's the time Charlie was taken, Henry wouldn't have been with the Junges. He would have been at the drugstore calling me.

That call didn't make sense. I try to push the thought away. It won't go. Henry knows not to call me here; if I'm here, I'm working. And there was no reason for him to go to a drugstore to call. He could have called from the boardinghouse. If that's where he really was. If he and the Junges were really in Englewood.

Still. Wherever he called from, the call means he was not the man placing a ladder outside Charlie's window.

But was he deliberately distracting me? Making sure I was nowhere near the nursery when someone else was climbing the ladder, sliding the window open . . .

If so, who would the someone else be?

I listen to the silence over the phone. Not for the first time, I wonder why Marguerite used her maiden name for so long, keeping her husband a secret. Why she stays so often at the Morrows', rather than live with that husband. Why has he come to America, if not to be with his wife?

She was the first one to mention the Lamonts to me now that I think of it. She put the notion of handsome sailors into my head.

I have known Marguerite—Jantzen or Junge?—for a year. I remember my first thought, that she would be good company. Smart, sophisticated—not like the others, calling themselves by what they do for the Morrows: table maid, valet. She expected more of her life, and at times, I saw her as the one woman who might understand certain things I feel. Her sly comments, those small enjoyable disloyalties, have been freeing. But now she terrifies me. Because I do not know what she will do. Or what she might have done.

And she is not the only one Henry was friendly with at the Morrow house. There are others I can see climbing that ladder. Even if it makes me sick to think of it.

"Who introduced you?"

Ellerson. Who told me to bring Red inside the house.

"How is everyone there?" I ask lightly, as if we are changing subjects and must no longer be gloomy.

"Oh, you know. The customary antics."

"Violet and Banks?"

"Still not speaking."

"Mr. Ellerson? He was looking poorly when he drove me here. I suppose he was hungover . . ."

I wait for her to say he has had an accident. Or was found beaten in an alley.

"Didn't stop him going to the Sha-Toe that evening," she tells me. "Mr. Banks saw him and said he was in high spirits. Actually paid for drinks, for once. A friend said he was short, and Ellerson peeled off a twenty-dollar bill from a large roll. Just like that."

There are two nightmares. I have them wide awake, at two, three in the morning. One is about Henry in jail. Henry, whose father beat him. I imagine him, the youngest, cowering, arms up to protect his head, *I didn't do anything! Oh, but you will, one day you will and this beating is for that.* I have heard things about the police in this country.

If they do arrest him, thinking he had something to do with the Lindbergh kidnapping, what will they do to him?

The other nightmare is a past I understand differently now. Henry sweet and shy at that dance, a boy who took what life had to offer, and you could take him as you pleased. Which I did because I thought it was safe. This was no Rob Coutts.

But this is when I remember: I had no idea what Rob Coutts was. Because I am a woman, who looks at men and does not see until it is too late.

Now I see the threat with Henry. That undercurrent of doubt, tugging, that I ignored. The questions about the baby. *"It's what you do all day. Yes, I'm interested."* The move to be near me, when I never asked. That time in the car, *"They have that new house. . . . The one they're building. . . . Maybe we should go see your room."* Prowling around the upstairs like children: *Oh, look in here, the nursery!*

The sulks about money. The plan to leave. And that pointless last-minute call. *"I don't have to leave . . ."*

But why stay? If he knew what was going to happen? If he really was that man.

Because he knew I'd be blamed. And part of him cares.

If he cares, why didn't he call me after?

Why didn't I call him?

Because I don't know. There's the truth of it. Or I know two things. I know Henry Johnson is a kind, soft man at ease in the company of women and children. I know he's a man who drifts. Who can't quite take hold of life. He's not a man to plan something like this, then carry it through with cold-blooded calculation.

But for the person who could do something like this, Henry would be useful. He is handsome. Women like him. And he likes us, knows our bodies. If you wanted to find your way into the Lindbergh household, he'd be a good man to pick. The people who kidnap children work in gangs. Henry, always relying on his brothers, not picky about who he spends time with, can be talked into things by other men, harder men, and not see the danger. It almost calms me, this point of the nightmare, because it makes sense, resolving both Henrys into one.

Find someone lonely, they'll have told him. *They don't ask questions when they're lonely.*

The clock ticks on, and at some point, the weary realization: *Henry did not do this. But he could have and you were careless. His innocence does not make you less guilty.* The truth of it weighs on me so heavily I think it would be best to not keep living. I'm not sure how to manage it. Easy enough to get poison, but it would be a hard death. I have long arguments with myself: I deserve pain. To squirm while Charlie is in a strange apartment with careless, callous people who see him as money. Just buy it, I tell myself. And swallow it. In the woods. Not in the house where Mrs. Lindbergh will have to see.

Isn't this dramatic, is the thought that comes around 4:00 A.M. Having a nice old wallow in self-pity. But self-mockery doesn't save me.

I roll over, think, Of course Henry is guilty. Of course he has done this.

Either way, whichever nightmare proves true, the plain fact is my life has stopped. There's no future for a woman so fond and foolish that she let this happen. In the daylight, I can pretend otherwise. But at night, I know.

One night I remember that the Colonel keeps a gun in the house. A rifle, too long for my arms, but a pistol as well. Lying on my back, I think of a life of cowardice where I fail to make the choice that might redeem me. I go down to the kitchen, more to be somewhere else than any real hope that Elsie will be there or that warm milk will do the trick. I remind myself, I do not know where the pistol is. Then think, No, I do. In his study. Center drawer.

As I feel my way in the dark, I hear voices. Light, familiar, a man and a woman. They're murmuring, so as not to wake the house. Not so much out of consideration, I realize, as they want to be left alone.

She asks if the eggs are all right. He says they're just great. Best he's ever eaten.

It is one in the morning. The Lindberghs are having dinner together.

I know I should return to the sitting room, leave them be. But just as I lingered to hear the pettiness and gripes long ago, now I yearn to take in more of their gentle, fragile pleasure in each other and scrambled eggs. There's a long silence. I hear a shaky inhale, the quiet shriek of muffled tears. Him whispering, only the word "back" audible. Her first "I know" is breathy. The second strong, full of faith.

On that, I go back down the hall. And sleep. And in the morning, I realize, my life has not stopped. And there are things I must do.

Another note from the kidnappers. They are angry, saying that the Lindberghs were warned not to make things public and now they must take the consequences. They raise the ransom to $70,000 because they have had to bring in two ladies to take care of Charlie. They say they are following the diet and that Charlie is well. They say they have planned the kidnapping for years.

Whateley says the letter is filled with misspellings. "Gut" for "good," "anyding" for "anything," and words in the past tense ended with a "t" instead of "d," like "holt."

"Obviously Germans," says Whateley. "Scandinavian, maybe." Elsie shoots him a look. He chews on his pipe, embarrassed and resentful.

The note, the one from West Hartford that says Charlie is safe, is not real. It's a lie, written by some boy who's sick in the head and wanted his name in the papers.

The Hartford police arrest Henry anyway.

Chapter Eighteen

When the police arrest Henry, they take his car, the Depression. They find an empty milk bottle on the rumble seat. He tells them he's on a milk diet. Officer Keaten asks me if this is true. To me, it sounds as if Henry is joking; I can almost hear him, nervous, offering a shaky smile, trying to please. *Yeah, sure, milk diet.* I say if it is, I never knew it.

The newspapers howl the news of Henry's arrest, slamming me back onto the front page. Under the headline HER FRIEND HELD, an enormous photo of me, wearing a tight dark cloche, chin tucked into a fur wrap. Marguerite took it when we went skating and gave Henry a copy. Of course the newspapers call him Red. Or "sailor friend of nurse." "Betty Gow's sweetheart." The stories are brutal. RED JOHNSON HELD FOR TAKING BABY. MILK BOTTLE FOUND IN AUTO. LADDER POINTS TO SAILOR, SIMILAR TO THOSE FOUND IN LAMONT SHIPYARD IN THE BRONX. SUSPECT GRILLED FOR HOURS.

I ask Trooper McCann what "grilled" means. Before he can answer, another trooper says cheerfully, "Oh, those Hartford boys can get rough."

The kidnappers send another letter. Because the Lindberghs have let the police interfere, they say they will not accept any go-between chosen by the family. They will choose their own intermediary; through him, they will inform us "latter" how to deliver the money in exchange for Charlie.

With that letter, a realization comes to me, a very simple thing I had not thought of before. On the day the Hartford police release Henry to the Newark police, the simple thing presents itself, clear and sharp as the view out a freshly washed window.

Trooper McCann has been stationed outside the door in order to stop any vehicle or sightseer from reaching the house. Since the incident with the newspaper, he has been kind. I sense he wants to make amends, and possibly other things. His shift ends at eight, and he brightens when I come outside.

I ask, "If Henry's in a Newark jail cell, how did he write that last note?"

His shoulders slump slightly as he realizes this is not a flirtation. He nods down the road. "You want to walk me to my car?"

When we're far enough away, he says, "So you think Johnson in jail while the notes are still coming means he's innocent."

"I think it's a reasonable question. In fact," I add defiantly, "I don't see what you have on the man. The Junges say he was with them in Englewood that night. Isn't that enough?"

"Might be." He drags his brogan through the dirt. "But what would you say if I told you a tollbooth operator says on the night of the kidnapping a green coupe stopped at Perth Amboy and asked directions to Manhattan between ten thirty and ten forty-five. The license plate he could remember is pretty close to Johnson's. In the car, there were two men, one woman, and a baby. Not what you expect to see, right?"

Perth Amboy is maybe an hour's drive from Englewood. Henry may say he dropped Marguerite off at eleven—Marguerite says so as well. But at that late hour, who at the Morrow house would be able to say otherwise?

I ask, "Have you talked to Johannes Junge?"

"He's giving us a hard time, refusing to talk, either to us or the Connecticut police. Says we don't have the authority."

I can imagine that prickly man refusing to cooperate with the police on a technicality. Or for other reasons. But anything that incriminates Johannes incriminates Henry, and I dismiss it from my mind.

Trooper McCann says, "If it means anything, a lot of the guys like Johnson. And he's said all along, loud and clear, that there's no way you would be involved."

He opens the door to the police car, swings halfway in before adding, "But even he thinks it was an inside job."

More stories emerge about Henry. About me. People read something in the paper, add their own bit to it. A history we never had, lives we never led, are created for us in an endless avalanche of black type. Jimmy Bistany, a restaurant owner in Connecticut, says he sold hot milk to a man driving a green coupe at 11:30 P.M. The man said he wanted it for a baby. The Royal Canadian Mounties discover a Betty Gow who is a chorus girl with a criminal record. A Mrs. J. Vanderweg and her husband, a wrestler known as "Tiger Jack White," claim to know that the kidnapping was planned two years ago when Henry and I met because the Lamont yacht was docked in Vancouver. The papers print a photograph: a pert dark-haired girl in a cloche hat standing coyly next to a car. Even to me, she looks like a girlfriend of the infamous Scotty Gow.

People who call themselves reporters suggest that Henry called to tell me he'd be there in a few minutes with the ladder so I could be in the room and hand him the baby before the Colonel noticed anything from his study below. Such a terrible, simple image: even I can see it. Me carefully gathering Charlie from the crib, having dressed him extra warmly because I knew he'd be out in the cold night air. I hear the quiet thud of the ladder against the house, the tap at the window. I see Henry—Red—the man who's said he's going to marry me if he can only get the money.

I hand Charlie into the darkness.

The eminent Colonel Schwarzkopf, with his even more eminent mustache, takes questions from the press. He says no one in the household has been eliminated as a suspect. Except one individual: Wahgoosh. The dog, says Schwarzkopf, was in the butler's pantry at the time of the kidnapping. There were four closed doors and a ceiling between him and the nursery. He could have no more heard the break-in than could Colonel Lindbergh in his study below. Hence his failure to bark is no longer considered suspicious. Under the headline TERRIER VINDICATED! the papers report, "Colonel Schwarzkopf made it clear an injustice had been done to the dog."

If the Lindberghs are aware of this other Betty Gow, they give no sign of it. Mrs. Lindbergh remains hidden with her mother, keeping the baby-to-be safe from the horror of the baby who is missing. Often, it is me the Colonel turns to when he needs someone to describe the baby's routine or recount what happened that night. This is how I meet my first gangster.

Since the police believe a gang has taken Charlie, the Colonel has decided that gangsters can get him back. One day he comes to me with a dark good-looking fellow and introduces him as Morris Rosner. ("Call me Mickey," he says.) Would I show Mr. Rosner the nursery? Tell him what I remember of that night? I say of course. And think: I am talking to a gangster. A real one. Not pretend from the movies. He does dress the part with a gray suit and a flashy white silk handkerchief. If I just focus on that handkerchief, I can just about forget I'm talking to a gangster. Well, bootlegger, really. Like the people Banks knows.

Colonel Lindbergh has asked Mr. Rosner to be his intermediary with the Mafia. Apparently, many people have offered. Joe Adonis, Abner Zwillman. Even Al Capone. But it is Mr. Rosner, along with Mr. Spitale and Mr. Bitz, who will be negotiating with the underworld to see if anyone in the mob dared kidnap the Lindbergh baby—and if so, demanding he be returned immediately because snatching the child of an American hero is a step too low.

I show Mr. Rosner the nursery, the window with the shutter that didn't close, the crib, Charlie's animals, the Tinkertoy that still sits on the packing case. He says, "Ah, that's sweet," and I say, "Yes, it is."

And think, I am talking to a gangster.

Charlie has been gone a week.

The day after Schwarzkopf's press conference, I'm helping Elsie hang clothes on the line when one of the Morrow cars drives up to the house. Expecting to see Mrs. Morrow or Miss Elisabeth, I'm surprised when Violet gets out of the back seat, flanked by two policemen. Like a child, she dawdles, prompting one of them to take her by the arm. She twists away from him, furious and purposeful, saying, "*Don't* touch me."

I say, "Oh Lord, Violet, not you as well."

Actually, I would have expected Violet to be excited about being interviewed. She hates being left out of things and it will make a good story. But she looks unusually stormy. "I didn't want to come. But they said I had to."

"I'm sure they just want to know about the phone call that morning," I reassure her. "Watch it when they try and change up the subject." I look pointedly at the detectives. "They like to try and muddle you."

Only when they go into the house do I notice Ellerson getting out of the car. He keeps his back to me, fishing in his pocket for his cigarettes. He takes his time, finding those cigarettes. Then as if he knows he can't avoid it, he turns.

There is not a mark on him.

"Are you staying to drive her back?" I ask.

"Oh, no. I'm next."

He keeps his attention on the business of a smoke, the lighting of the match, the first inhale. The morning air is chilly, the sun is an apathetic spot through the trees. Arms folded, shoulders braced against the cold, I say, "But you're all right?"

He shakes his head, not understanding.

"It seems you got your hundred dollars." He frowns and I give him a look up and down. *No broken bones. No black eyes.*

Tetchy, he says, "Things worked out."

"Yes, I hear you were celebrating at the Sha-Toe. Drinks all round . . ."

"*One* drink. For a pal I owed. Where are you getting this?"

"Septimus Banks was quite impressed with your bankroll."

I wait to see if the news that he was seen forces some honesty. He says, "As usual, Banks was seeing double. There was no big bankroll. Don't I wish."

"But someone bailed you out." He shrugs, admitting it. "Who was the Samaritan?"

He holds out his hand. "Here, you want to break a few fingers?" He nods at the house. "Go get a lamp, shine it in my eyes."

I know: Ellerson hates accounting for himself. He takes it as a point of pride to get away with things. The prospect of being interviewed by the police already has him on edge. There *are* benign explanations for his refusal to answer my questions.

Pitching the cigarette to the ground, he takes a swift step toward me to whisper, "What are you telling the police?"

"*Me?*"

"Someone . . . put them on to me. They're talking to people."

A flicker of anxiety in the eyes tells me: "people" means the friends at the taxi stand. *The* friend.

"No," I say. "Not me." I am about to say *I'd never* when I remember, Ellerson has not kept my secrets. I needn't be kind.

"But maybe I should have, given that you told them about Rob Coutts. Henry's car . . ."

"I just said I saw a green coupe by the house."

"*Knowing* he drove a green coupe."

He steps back, coughing in amazement. "I don't know what you want from me here."

"You introduced us," I remind him.

"For a summer *fling*," he says. "Who knew the guy was going to move to New Jersey?"

His agitation unnerves me. Does he think Henry is guilty? *Know* Henry is guilty? They live at the same boardinghouse. And Ellerson more than introduced us; he practically insisted we meet. Why?

Or is Henry just a useful scapegoat?

Now it is my turn to step close, speak low. "If you know who did this, tell me. I'll keep you out of it. But a name, *anything* . . ."

Two police officers exit the house, calling out roads and streets they mean to cover. Ellerson turns away, hastily lights another cigarette. And I retreat inside the house.

As I make my way around the house to collect bedding, there is time to consider: Can this be true?

No, I think. Not true, because this is something a monster would do and Ellerson is not a monster. He introduced me to Henry because he knew I was lonely. Because lonely people recognize each other.

But this is lazy thinking. Sentimentality. There are perfectly logical, horrible reasons this could be true.

Ellerson was irritable that day—annoyed by a long drive in poor weather. Badly in need of real money, the kind that's hard to borrow on the promise of "I'll get it to you next week." And he owed it to people for whom violence is business. People who no doubt knew he worked for the Morrows, even sometimes drove the Lindbergh baby.

It is very easy to imagine the proposition. Easy to imagine it being made more than once. Ellerson pretending not to understand or take it as a joke. Until he couldn't anymore.

He didn't want to drive me to Hopewell, I remember. Didn't want to come inside. Perhaps he was reluctant to visit a house he knew was about to be . . . my mind tosses about words like "attacked," "invaded," "ransacked." He would have had time to make that phone call. I kept him waiting while I packed. I can see it. Ellerson on the staff phone: "Yeah, I'll be late, I got to drive the nurse gal to Hopewell. Family's staying over." Anyone hearing him would have thought he was calling his wife or his pals at B&M Taxi.

But . . . no. Because he tried to borrow money from me on the drive there. Which he wouldn't have done if he'd already sold Charlie. He was desperate when he asked me, that I believe.

So it happened afterward. After I turned him down, ruining his last chance of escape. Not just from the people he owed money to. But a life of driving here and there, a life that once seemed free, but really was just day after day of being at others' beck and call. Feeling trapped, suffocated because your home is the wrong one and there is no place you can truly *be*. It could lead someone to think that money, the kind most of us don't bother to dream of, would buy real freedom.

This I can imagine too. Ellerson veering off the road on his way back, stopping at a gas station, finding a pay phone. "Look, that thing we talked about. Say I could tell you where the family is right now, what would that be worth?" Ellerson got back to Englewood at five. More than enough time for the kidnappers to put their plan in motion.

Should I tell the police? Do I have the right? Or is it responsibility?

Also, if I had given Ellerson the money, would Charlie still be here?

"You have no business prying into my private life!"

Passing by the Colonel's study, I hear Violet's voice, shrill and distressed. Then a man murmurs, "Relax, we know you're nervous. Just think. His name will come to you."

"I am not nervous and I can't remember his name," Violet says, airily.

Hovering by the door, my arms full of sheets, I wonder: What is she playing at?

The officer asks, "Well, if you can't remember the man you were with, how about the movie you saw that night. What'd you see?"

"I can't remember," she says in the same la-di-da tone. *Call me a liar*, she seems to be saying. *I dare you.*

There's a long pause. Then another officer asks carefully, "Did you have anything to drink, maybe . . . ?"

"Coffee. I had only coffee to drink that night."

Here, I raise an eyebrow. Violet's a girl who likes her pint. And there's a note of doth protest too much in that *only* coffee.

On the other hand, telling them to go to hell is an interesting strategy. Part of me wishes I'd thought of it.

That evening, Trooper McCann stops by the kitchen before leaving. I'm trying to think how to nudge the conversation toward Violet when he murmurs, "Handwriting's not a match."

"What do you mean?"

His lips move: *Henry*. "You were right. They compared the ransom notes to his written statement. No match. Also Junge says when they arrived at the Morrow place, another car drove up and let a woman out. It had a noisy motor. Violet Sharpe says she returned around then—in a car with a noisy motor. She made a joke to Mrs. Junge about getting in so late. So, it looks like it wasn't Henry's car at Perth Amboy."

"Thank you. Truly."

"Not out of the woods," he warns.

"I know," I say, giddy. "Still."

The news that Henry is innocent—that I have not been guilty of criminal misjudgment—is heady.

"And they sure didn't get anything out of Violet Sharpe. Is she—?" He twirls his finger by his temple.

I laugh. "Not that I ever knew."

I hesitate. If I want to tell the police about Ellerson's debts now is the time.

"And . . . Mr. Ellerson? How did he get on?"

He shrugs. "Fine, so far as I know. Says he had a few beers with some guys at the B&M Taxi company and went home."

Chapter Nineteen

It has been days since we heard from the kidnappers. They have said they will choose someone to be the go-between for them and the Lindberghs. But no one is named and no one comes forward. The silence is terrifying.

But soon after Violet and Ellerson's visit, there is a new energy in the house. I see Colonels Lindbergh and Breckinridge moving suddenly into rooms they've not used before. I hear them talking in low, urgent voices to unknown people on the phone.

At 3:00 A.M., I'm awakened by the sound of a car approaching—it will always be sinister to me, I think, that crushed-gravel sound. Going to the window, I see Breckinridge get out of the car with an older man with an impressive white mustache. The older man keeps a hand on his hat, moves with a fussy self-importance as if he were not a stranger to the house. But I don't recognize him.

I hear the front door open and then carefully shut, listen with growing surprise as their murmurs come closer, until they're whispering just outside the sitting room. Thinking they can hardly object, I open the door to see Lindbergh and Breckinridge with the older man.

I brace for curt dismissal, but Colonel Lindbergh says, "Betty! This is Dr. Condon. He'll be staying the night. Could you make up a bed in the nursery, please?"

His voice is eager, the way it is when there's action, boyish things to do. I look to the gentleman, say, "Of course." He thanks me by inclining his head. I have the sense he's matching what he sees with ideas of me, and those ideas are very important to him. He gives me a smile that's meant to be grandfatherly, but the eyes are cautious.

In the morning, Dr. Condon is taken to meet Mrs. Lindbergh. From the hallway, I can tell he is doing much of the talking. I hear Mrs. Lindbergh say, "Thank you, thank you," and his answer: "If one of those tears drops, I shall go off the case immediately!"

"Who on earth does he think he is?" I ask Elsie. Even though the Colonel has also told his wife she must control her emotions.

"He's an admirer of the Colonel's. Lives in the Bronx, a former headmaster. Apparently, he put an ad in the paper, offering the kidnappers another thousand dollars in ransom money. And the kidnappers answered! He got a letter with another envelope inside, addressed to Colonel Lindbergh. It had the same symbol on it as the first letter, with the three holes. The kidnappers have said he's to be the intermediary between them and the family."

"So, he'll deliver the ransom money?"

She nods, suddenly excited. "Our little boy is coming home. Finally!"

"I want something of the child's," Dr. Condon tells me that afternoon. His voice sounds strangely put on, as if he's imitating a soldier or some other leader of men. "We won't be handing over the money until I see him, but they may try and show me a different child. So I need something Charlie would recognize. Colonel Lindbergh said you would know which toy he favors."

The way he says "we" and "I" as if he's anyone important irritates me. But the idea that Charlie will be seen, that he'll be shown a toy and reach for it, that he won't be just a crude, misspelled sentence in a ransom note, excites me so much, I nearly tip the chair as I get up. "I know just the one."

"I want more than one," says Dr. Condon as we head up the stairs. "Children change significantly over time."

God, you're unbearable, I think even as I smile in agreement. I glance at Colonel Lindbergh; three-hole symbol or not, how does he know this isn't just some nutter?

In the nursery, I offer the gray cat Charlie sleeps with. "Loves this one, won't sleep without it." Dr. Condon shakes his head. Again I look to the Colonel, but the doctor is in charge, it seems.

The wooden lion meets with approval, as does the camel. "How would he respond to this?" Dr. Condon asks, holding up the lion.

"He would say, 'Rawr.'" My throat hurts and I have to swallow. "We do the animal sounds. Charlie likes to roar, it's his favorite."

Then I spot the old elephant sitting on the packing crate. "And there's this fellow."

Dr. Condon puts a hand to his chin, peering at the doll.

"Elepent," says Colonel Lindbergh suddenly. He gazes at the worn animal with its loose threads, chewed trunk, and missing eye, letting the memory of Charlie as not a mission or a task or a phone call but a child, his child, into his awareness for just a moment. Watching, I worry it's too much. The memories can be a twist of gall right down your middle, bending you double, sorrow too strong.

Breaking the moment, I say, "Charlie's not quite got the word 'elephant' yet."

"Then Elepent shall come too," Dr. Condon tells the Colonel.

Saturday, a note arrives at Dr. Condon's house in the Bronx. At nightfall, he is to go to the last subway station along Jerome Avenue and walk one hundred feet. There he will find a hot dog stand with a porch. On the porch, there will be a stone with a note under it telling him where to go next.

The Lindberghs haven't been able to gather the money yet, but Dr.

Condon insists on going anyway. He says it is important to find out if the people who wrote the notes actually have Charlie. That night, as we wait, I cling to that hope. Charlie will be seen. He will be that much closer to us. Real again.

But that's not what happens. The note under the stone directs the doctor to Woodlawn Cemetery. There Condon meets a man in a soft hat pulled over part of his face. His voice is German; like the notes, he makes mistakes like "gotted" for "got." But he doesn't bring Charlie with him.

"It's good news, Mr. Whateley says," Elsie tells me as we ignore the radio in the servants' sitting room.

"I don't see how," I rage, for once not caring who hears. "He didn't get Charlie back. He didn't see him. We don't know where they're keeping him. Condon sat with this man for over an hour. If he'd let the police come with him, they could have arrested the man right there and then."

"And what happens to Charlie if the other kidnappers see that man arrested?" she says sharply. "At least we know we're talking to the people who have Charlie. That's what Mr. Whateley says."

I exhale sharply so I don't scream, *For God's sake, who cares what Whateley says?*

Before I can think of anything civil to say, there's a knock on the door. Lieutenant Keaten looks in and says, "Miss Gow, may I speak with you?"

No doubt happy to get clear of me, Elsie rises. "I'll be out of your way."

Keaten sits. "I come bearing good news. The man Dr. Condon spoke to in the cemetery—Condon asked him what he knew about Henry Johnson."

Because Condon thinks Henry and I are guilty. I knew it. "And?"

"The man said Red—he used the nickname—he said, 'Red Johnson is innocent.' He said you were innocent too."

I think how horrible and astonishing it is that the kidnapper mentioned Henry. Mentioned me. Even to say we are innocent. I hate that we exist in that man's mind, that our names were in his mouth. Knowing the police could well hear this as the kidnappers trying to protect their own, I ask, "Is there a 'but'?"

"The man Condon met at Woodlawn—we're calling him Cemetery John—also claimed to be a Scandinavian sailor." He looks at me. "Anything to say to that?"

"Yes. The Scandinavian sailor you have in jail isn't guilty."

Keaten nods. "Colonel Schwarzkopf has come to the same conclusion."

"And the Junges?"

He looks at me oddly. "Mr. Junge has only been in the country a little while, not really long enough to get tangled with gangs. They don't go in for men who use canes. Her background is solid. And if Henry was with them, they were with Henry."

I nod.

"We're bringing Johnson to Hopewell tomorrow. Deputy Chief Brex wants to sit down with him one last time. After that . . ." He shrugs.

Brex, I think. The nice one who let McRell do all the nasty work when they accused me of being the girlfriend of Scotty Gow. The prospect of seeing Henry again should make me happy. It doesn't. Searching my mind, I find resentment; even before he was arrested, he didn't call to see how I was. Also anxiety; I never called him either. Because part of me thought he was guilty and I didn't want to be associated with him.

"Why does it have to be here?" I ask.

"I'd like to interview the two of you together. We're pretty sure you weren't knowingly involved. But maybe by talking, one of you will spark a memory that could be helpful. That happens with my wife and me all the time. She remembers so many things I don't."

I smile as if I appreciate this homey detail. Even as I think *pretty sure you weren't knowingly involved*" leaves a lot of room for a change of opinion.

"Wouldn't it be better for us to meet at the police station? The Lindberghs won't want to see Henry."

"Colonel Lindbergh does want to speak with him. Privately."

"May I ask why?"

"You'd have to ask the Colonel."

Knowing full well that is something I cannot do.

Hunched, Keaten swings his clasped hands between his knees. "Betty, I'd like to trust that if you know anything about the rest of the staff—here or at the Morrow house—you'd tell me. Anything that might help us find Charlie."

And I'd like to trust you won't destroy people's lives over things that are none of your business. I also don't like that he says "might." We are supposed to be close to getting Charlie back, yet I don't feel hopeful. Quite the opposite.

On impulse, I ask, "The kidnapper said something else, didn't he?"

I can tell from his face I've got it right. "I can't divulge the full details of the conversation, I'm afraid."

You can tell me why you're still asking me about employees who could lead you to the kidnapper when we're supposedly talking to them directly, I think.

Then he says, "I'm also sorry to say we'll be sending Mr. Johnson back to Norway."

After everything they've put Henry through, this seems spiteful and punitive. "Is that necessary? He's a good man, wants to work . . ."

Nothing in his expression changes, but there's a stillness that takes me back to that conversation in the kitchen. When I insisted Henry was a good man and without words, Keaten told me I had no idea who Henry Johnson was.

Now there's a pause as he makes up his mind. "Well, presumably, his child will be glad to see him."

"Child." I register the word. Note that it has not been joined by "wife." All those times I talked about Charlie. And Henry never said one word about a child left behind. And I sense this is not the worst of it.

Quietly, I say, "Clearly, there's something else you want to tell me."

He brings his foot across his knee, takes a moment to adjust his shoelace. "Forgive me for being intrusive. But may I ask if you've seen a doctor recently?"

My neck goes hot. "I assure you, I'm not expecting."

He nods: *Good.* "Just some of the things you hear about sailors are true."

Striving for lightness, I say, "What? Girl in every port . . . ?"

"Things you can pick up from such girls. And give to others." Now he meets my eye. "Prisoners undergo routine medical examination. Johnson says he's been in treatment. But I felt you should know. As you might be affected."

"Well . . . I'm not," I say stupidly. At least not in the way he's implying. I was terrified of falling pregnant. Losing my job. And, I can admit this now, after Rob Coutts, determined never to give that much again.

Now that I know, I am saddened, but not surprised that Henry had his secrets. It is not in his nature to confront difficulties. If you find early on that transgressions—even imagined ones—lead to beatings, you learn to say nothing. I remember when he said I could pick his name. Henrik, Red, Henry. I thought it charming. Now I think, Clever. Easier to have separate lives when you're different things to different people. What was Henry Johnson to me? The boy I was going to toss back because, *Well, just a summer adventure.* Never thought I'd be sharing the front page of newspapers with him. Also never thought he would make me feel quite this . . . sad.

"I am sorry," says Lieutenant Keaten. "I hope I was right to tell you."

"Tell." That word again. A bit of breath from the lungs hums through the vocal cords, meets up with thoughts and feelings, everything from *I love* to the cruelest accusation. It can be a vicious business, *telling.*

But of course, Lieutenant Keaten knows that very well.

The next day, while Henry is interviewed by Brex, I sit in the servants' sitting room with Keaten, me on the sofa, him leaning against the wall by the door. Every so often, another policeman blunders in and Keaten says, "Room's in use" and shuts the door on them.

It would be nice to talk. But after what the lieutenant told me yesterday, there is nothing to say. At one point, it becomes rather unbearable and I'm about to suggest a game of cards. Then there's a knock at the door and Henry is brought into the room.

He is thin, so thin; an old sweater hangs loose on his frame and from the unevenness of his pants, I have a sense of a belt, notched well beyond the last hole. There's a purple-yellow bruise under his eye. His jaw is swollen, giving his face an odd shape. Still he smiles with his ruined mouth. And when he says, "Hello, Betty," I know he doesn't hate me. Which was something I feared.

Nor do I hate him, even after yesterday's news. Because another thing I know, looking at him: Henry Johnson is guilty in some things. But he did not kidnap Charlie. And he has suffered. Badly. The police believed he had the Lindbergh baby. They haven't stopped at much to get him to say so.

"Henry, I'm so sorry."

My distress distresses him, and he rushes to sit down beside me. But then, fearful, he looks to Keaten. "Is . . . this okay?"

"Yeah, sure," says Keaten, embarrassed by Henry's terror.

"Betty, I'm so sorry about the baby. They'll get him back, I'm sure." I notice he keeps his arms close to his sides, his hands tight in his lap, as if in handcuffs. There are bruises on the back of his hands. In a moment of revulsion, the word "burn" comes to me. Henry slides his arms back so the sweater cuffs hide the marks.

He gazes at my face in his old way, intuitive, anxious, loving, like a child trying to understand why Mummy is sad. From his expression, I know: I look dreadful. I say so, and he says, "No, no. Just tired. You could never look dreadful."

Keaten asks if we're ready. We both turn, sit up, and say yes, we are.

We go through the old story, the details so worn and familiar, we can recite them without emotion. Henry remembers what we did Monday a little differently; I remember the time of his call as being later than he does. Wearily, as if he too is sick of it all, Keaten asks about our friends. The Junges. A couple we met ice-skating and went to the movies with a few times. Did we talk about the baby? Of course, we did, I say. It's what people ask about.

"And what do you tell them?"

"That he's fine, thank you."

As I say that, the prayerful thought comes to me: *Please be fine, Charlie. Please be fine.* I think of him in the care of some German woman and beg her, *Be kind to him. Play with him. Give him smiles.*

Tears come so easily these days. I apologize. Say that I'm tired. Henry takes my hand. The touch reminds me and I take it back.

"Well," says Keaten after a while, "I think I've asked pretty much everything."

He stands up, goes to the door. "If you want some time alone . . ."

Henry says, "Yes, thank you, Lieutenant," before I have time to decide. Keaten goes through the door, leaving us beside each other on the small sofa. Henry reaches for me. I stay pointedly still. He sits back into his shabby, overlarge sweater. This is not a joyous reunion. Too much has happened, we've harmed each other too much without meaning to. We are strangers who regret ever having known each other.

"They're going to deport me," he says. "But because I am leaving willingly, they say I can come back if I apply and do all the papers." He tries a smile. "Maybe you will wait?"

I nod, as if considering it. "Your child would miss you though. Wouldn't she?"

He nods, as if exhausted. "Ah, that's why you're angry."

"I wouldn't say angry." I pluck the edge of my skirt. "I wish you'd told me."

But Henry's child is not important now. Nor is the other thing he failed to tell me. Only one secret matters.

"Henry?"

Like a dog, hopeful at the sound of his name, he looks up.

"You owe me this." He nods: *Anything.* "If you know anything about the people who have Charlie, you must tell me. Now."

Shocked, he looks to the door. "Betty, we just told the police . . ."

"That's the police. I don't care what you told them. You said what you had to . . ."

"No, I told the truth."

"But this is me and if you ever cared about me, you'll tell me the thing you didn't tell the police. I know there's something. You spoke to someone. Someone at the garage, the boardinghouse, or that damn roadhouse you go to . . ."

He shakes his head. "I went through all this . . ."

"The house. You showed someone the house."

"No."

"You needed money, Henry. Seven dollars, that's all you had, that's what you said."

Despairing, he asks, "Why do you think this was me?"

I beat my knees with my fists. "If this is in any way my fault, you have to do this for me. It's my one chance to make it right."

"I don't know anything."

"That's not an answer."

He shouts, "I didn't tell anyone anything, I swear it."

His eyes are wide, his voice desperate. The words come so fast, they have no meaning. They're the sounds he thinks will make it stop. Men do lie when they're frightened. But I see his terror—and his heartbreak. That I, like his father, believe him guilty. Of something for which he can never atone. He doesn't understand why I am angry; he only knows it hurts. And that, sadly, I believe in. If he knew something to make the questions stop, he would tell me.

In a gentler voice, I ask, "Did you talk to Colonel Lindbergh?"

Confused by the abrupt change in subject, he says, "Yes. He was very kind. He apologized for . . ." He gestures to his body.

"Was that all?"

"He wanted to know what I thought."

I feel uneasy. The only subject Henry could speak to with any knowledge is me. Do the Lindberghs trust me? Or do they only pretend to?

I ask, "And what did you say?"

"I said I don't think anything."

No, you don't, I think sadly. *You do what you want in the moment you want to do it and you don't* think. *Just as I didn't think when I brought you into the house.* Getting up from the sofa, I lay a hand on his bright, brass hair as a goodbye. Keaten has been waiting halfway down the hall. When he sees me come out, he gestures to the door. I say, "Yes, I'm done."

In my room, I stare at myself in the mirror. I see a small, stylish girl with enormous dark eyes. She's lovely, this girl. So neat and put together.

I haven't the first idea who she is.

Henry is detained at Ellis Island, awaiting deportation. He tells the papers he is not bitter, that he loves the country and wants to come back. He says he will miss me. "Goodbye, America. Thank you for all you have done for me. And my hope is that you will give me a chance to show my appreciation by becoming a hardworking American citizen. Goodbye, America."

Chapter Twenty

On March 16, we get the closest thing yet to Charlie when the kidnappers send Dr. Condon a gray Dr. Denton sleeping suit. It is size two and has been laundered. A note with the three circles says that eight hours after getting the $70,000 they will tell Dr. Condon where to find Charlie.

Dr. Condon puts an ad in the *Bronx Home News*: I ACCEPT. MONEY IS READY, JOHN. YOUR PACKAGE IS DELIVERED AND IS OKAY. DIRECT ME.

And then . . . we hear nothing.

Colonel Lindbergh asks the newspapers to limit their coverage; the attention may be scaring off the kidnappers. He and Colonel Breckinridge gather the ransom money. Once again, the Colonel argues with the police and for once, the police win. The serial numbers of the bills will be written down. And the money will be gold certificates, which have a round yellow seal.

"Mr. Whateley heard them say the bills are going to be discontinued, as the country's going off the gold standard," Elsie tells me over her knitting. "Shopkeepers will notice them."

I find myself in agreement with Colonel Lindbergh. This sort of game playing takes time, and I want Charlie back now. Catching the spenders of the ransom money later feels far less important.

Every day, Dr. Condon runs the ad: MONEY IS READY. Still, we hear nothing.

Then suddenly, the Colonel goes to stay at the Morrow house in Manhattan. We are told he will be there several days.

Hand on her belly, Mrs. Lindbergh looks out the window and says, "The tulips will be up soon. I love tulips. So pure and fresh."

She looks at me and I see the bright, secret hope in her eyes; the Colonel's departure means something is about to happen.

I say, "Nice to have something to look forward to."

"Come on, pet."

Elsie slips her arm through mine, starts walking toward the door. I look at her: *Where are we going?*

"Out. Both of us walking in circles around the house, might as well get some fresh air while we do it."

What, I wonder, as we stumble outside, would the world do without the Elsie Whateleys? Homely, cheerful Elsie, always knocking her hand to her head, saying she's forgot this or can't remember that. When all the while she's keeping me running up and down stairs, so busy I don't have time to worry.

"Penny for your thoughts," she says as we trundle through the muddy yard.

I venture a smile, dare to say, ". . . Tomorrow he'll be back?"

She squeezes my arm with hers. "Tomorrow he'll be back."

At last, we have heard. The Colonel and Dr. Condon are to have the money ready by tomorrow night. Another note will tell them where to leave it. Whateley says it's madness to hand over the money when no one has even seen Charlie. This time, Elsie herself told him to be quiet.

Tomorrow this will be over. I've thought about it, so many times, what it'll be like to see Charlie again. To have the Colonel carry him through the door, hear Mrs. Lindbergh cry out. He might be shy with us, after all this time. I have to be prepared for that. I can't stand to think of it, what he might have been through. They say they've cared for him, but . . .

No, I'm going to stay on that image: Colonel Lindbergh coming through the door, Charlie in his arms. Before that, a telephone call. Jubilant. *I've got him, we're coming home.*

I think it through again, the happy scene. This time I move myself and the Whateleys to the kitchen or upstairs, because really, the Lindberghs should be alone when they're reunited. We'll hear the car first, rolling up the drive, the crunch of gravel . . .

In my head, it turns to night. That night. That long, strange silence when we thought Colonel Lindbergh was home because we heard a car, only it wasn't him.

Another squeeze from Elsie. "I was thinking of making a cake, what'd you reckon?"

He's not coming back. The thought drifts through my mind. I try to black it out, replace it with the happy images of before. But it feels so much more real.

"Hey . . ." Elsie's tone is unusually sharp; she senses what I'm thinking.

I'm about to apologize—you can't lose hope; if you lose hope, you lose Charlie—when I see it. There on the driveway, silver gray, easy to miss in winter. But now the light catches it, glinting off the metal. Because it's April—very first day of the month—and there's sun again. That's why we missed it before. Charlie's thumb guard. Bent, as if someone stepped on it. Muddy after all this time in the dirt, the string crumpled, no brightness to catch the eye. Bending down, I collect it carefully in my hands. The horrible little twist of metal I so hated. I can't stop crying. Behind me, Elsie's saying, "What? What is it?" When I show it to her, she still doesn't understand.

"It's Charlie's," I tell her. "All this time, right here, this close. We just didn't see it."

"And now he's back," she says.

I search the thumb guard for any sign of someone not Charlie, a fingerprint or a thread from cloth I don't recognize. I don't see anything—but maybe the police will. I look from where we're standing on the driveway to the house. Remember the car we heard, the one we thought was the Colonel coming home. How close could it have come to the house without the Colonel seeing it when he came home? Beyond the pool of light from the house, but close enough that they wouldn't have to carry the ladder too far? Because they carried Charlie from his window, past this very spot, to the car.

Could we have seen them? If we'd only looked?

I can't think like that. Finding something of Charlie's feels like a sign, a promise.

"He's coming home," I tell Elsie.

Joyful, we link arms again; on impulse Elsie launches into song: "I love my baby, my baby loves me . . . Don't know nobody as happy as we . . . I'm only twenty and he's twenty-one . . . We ain't got money, but ain't we got fun?" Her voice is glorious and I say, "You're better than the radio, Elsie!" Then join her for a final shout of "I love my baby, my baby loves me!"

"Another cup of tea, Mr. Whateley?"

"No, thank you."

He turns the page of his paper. Crosses his legs the other way.

"I think it's your go," Elsie tells me.

"Oh, sorry." Hastily, I lay down a card.

She glances at me: *Are you sure?* Then takes it and says apologetically, "Gin."

As she deals another round, I look at the ceiling. "Do you think we should check on her? See if she needs anything?"

"No," says Whateley, as Elsie says, "She has her mother."

I half rise from my chair, then realize: there's no reason to.

"Why don't you go for a walk?" Elsie suggests. "They may not be back for hours."

They can't be gone too much longer, I think, looking out the window. It's getting dark. Whateley starts on about cricket. Some team has done poorly and he's irate. "Game's not been the same since G. A. Faulkner. Best all-rounder there ever was. I saw him once at Leeds. 1907. Extraordinary bowler, unlike anything you've ever seen. Trained under a Birmingham man for a time . . ."

"Olly," says Elsie in her quiet way that means he's to hush.

Yesterday was supposed to be the day. The Colonel and Dr. Condon went to the cemetery with the money. Instead of Charlie, they got another envelope with instructions on how to find him. They were told not to open it for six hours.

The note said Charlie was on a boat near Martha's Vineyard. So that's where they are now. With half the United States Navy, Mr. Whateley says.

I don't know how long it takes to find a boat when you've got the navy helping you. Seems like it shouldn't take this long.

I can't stop moving. Running my hand over my knee, bending in the chair, crossing my arms. Nothing feels right. I fix that image of the thumb guard, the bright glint, in my mind. That's the truth of what's going to happen. Not this . . . unease. It's an exchange, I tell myself. We have shown Elepent and Rawr. We have given the money. Changelings have been offered, the real baby will come back.

An irritated rattle of paper. "For God's sake, take yourself outside," snaps Whateley.

"Let her be," says Elsie.

Whateley throws down the paper, announces he's going for a smoke. He likes his paper and pipe in the evening; guilty that I've spoiled it, I say, "No, let me go . . ."

We hear the approach of a car. Everyone goes still. My heart is pounding; this is it. It's about to be over. From upstairs, we hear the door to Mrs. Lindbergh's room open, hurried footsteps on the stairs.

I glance at Elsie, tears welling in my throat; she nods reassuringly. My hand reaches out and she takes it, as well as her husband's. After a second, I stretch my hand toward Whateley—stupid, like children, but it must be the three of us—and he takes it, calmly, rather like a father.

THE LINDBERGH NANNY   { 187 }

The thud of the car door. No talk between the men. I strain to hear Charlie; it's been so long, I can't remember his noises, what he sounds like.

The front door opens. There is no glad cry, no commotion. No wail of a child overwhelmed and confused, the tearful laughter of his parents. The silence is heavy, almost crushing.

"I'm sorry," says the Colonel.

Now we do not know what to do. Our last offering is gone.

The house is empty. The police have left, the reporters no longer trespass. Most of all, the one person who should be here is not, and that makes the few of us still here feel sluggish and meaningless. We wander through the halls, cower in quiet rooms, the bare scraps of the old life—prepare meals, wash clothes, dust, turn the pages of a book—picked over, with less to savor with every repetition. I even hate the radio now, all that cheerful, self-important chatter. Life is dry, hollow, nothing but the wind blowing through once noisy, expectant places.

The switchboard has been dismantled and moved out of the garage. The home phone rarely rings. Even the flood of letters has dwindled. They do still come, most of them of the "Send a hundred dollars and I'll tell you what I know" variety. People don't even feel they have to promise Charlie's safe return anymore. Nine days after the ransom is paid, one of the bills turns up in a bakery in Connecticut. A well-dressed woman in a green car, driven by a chauffeur. When she saw they recognized the bill, she took it back and walked out. No one wrote down the license number.

People are out there, spending the money that was meant to bring Charlie home, with apparently no thought of what it was for. It's theirs now, to do with what they like. I spend a day walking the woods, thinking about that woman. The horror of her.

Dr. Condon places another ad: PLEASE, BETTER DIRECTION.

A new man comes to the house: John Curtis. He says he has been in touch with the kidnappers. He says it is a gang of five Scandinavian men and that they are working with an employee inside the household. Charlie is safe, but they want more money. This is not uncommon, says Curtis, extorting families for a double payment. The baby is being held on a boat, the *Mary B. Moss*. First the boat is off the coast in Virginia. Then it is in Cape May. Together, the two men make eight trips, searching for one small boat.

To me, Curtis's story sounds pieced together from the headlines. Scandinavian men, inside help. Once again, I can feel suspicion curling like chokeweed through the house. Who has he named? Have the Lindberghs started to doubt? In May, when the Colonel goes with Curtis on a sailing venture off the Jersey coast, I wonder: Does he believe him? Or does he just want to escape?

When the Colonel is out of the house, the patterns change. People shift direction, drift to different spots. One day, I see the door to the nursery open a crack. It has been shut since the police left. I peer through the few inches of visibility, see Mrs. Lindbergh standing at the crib, hands on the railing, her growing belly touching the slats.

I want to leave her be. But I don't want to leave her alone. Gently, I push the door open to let her know I'm here. I sense her awareness of me . . . and her determination not to look up from the last place Charlie was in this house. For a long moment, we stand together and apart in this child's room that has been fractured into pieces of evidence and points of entry. There the warped shutter, there the sill where the envelope lay, the spot on the floor where they left a muddy print. The empty crib.

"I feel sometimes," says Mrs. Lindbergh, her voice thin from disuse, "that they could keep him." She frowns, aware she has not expressed herself clearly. "I would let them have him, if I could just once . . . comfort him. Hold him and say it will be all right. If I had known that night that it would be . . ."

Even without the Colonel here, words like "last" are forbidden and she shakes her head. As if to excuse her lapse, she says, "It's not that I'm giving up. But it's been so many days of missing him—it's the monotony. The fear, the wanting, hope, disappointment, you can't help but feel, Oh, this again? For the rest of my life, this?"

"Mr. Curtis . . ."

She shakes her head; Curtis is nothing.

She raises her hands off the rail, a conjuring gesture. "I just want to see him again. One more time. I want to breathe him in, get the feel of him in my arms, heavy and wriggling, so that . . ." She looks at me, bewildered. "I think that's all I want now."

"Oh, and it will come," I say, hurrying into the room. "It will. Right now, Colonel Lindbergh could be this close to Charlie. He may already have him, for all we know."

I am not saying things I believe, but I am saying things I think possible—so as, or so I tell myself, to give Mrs. Lindbergh hope. But she closes her eyes, as if my words are crude, hurtful.

She doesn't believe, I realize with shock. In her brave hero husband who has promised to bring the baby home . . . the faith isn't there anymore. I thought it was him keeping her from falling. Other way round, I see that now.

She says, "I keep thinking . . . it was the wind."

"Ma'am?"

"You remember? The day was so rainy and damp, and at night, the wind was just *howling*. It was almost hard to think." She frowns at the floor. "And of course Charles insisted on stone walls and reinforced concrete because he worries about fire. So he wouldn't have heard the footsteps."

I wonder: Does she realize her breath is coming shorter and shorter? *What have you been thinking, Mrs. Lindbergh? What sort of nightmares do you have?*

"We none of us heard it," I say.

"And the dog," she bursts out, as if I hadn't spoken. "That is the one thing I *don't* understand"—as if the rest of it were perfectly understandable—"Wahgoosh barks at a feather falling. How could he not . . ."

She stares at me. Waiting. As if I can tell her. As if I know.

She is not sure, I realize. *Who you are.*

That is why she keeps the door shut and does not let me in. Her husband may insist I am innocent. But in her heart, she has felt me take her child from her before. And now she wonders if I have done it again.

"The Colonel will bring him back," I tell her. It is the only thing any of us have left.

That afternoon, I write to my mother.

We have new hope as to the baby's whereabouts . . .

Leaning my head on my hand, I think of what else I can write. The newspapers have started coming to Nithsdale Street, and Mother doesn't think what she says to reporters is "talking to the press." She sees it as being polite. Or defending me. *"Well, Betty, when they ask, I can hardly say mind your own business, can I?"*

Strangely, the old throb of irritation with my mother brings with it the thought: *I want to go home.* The need seeps inside me like vinegar, sour and curdling. I want to hear Agnes laugh, want to roll my eyes at Alex's deadpan teasing. I want to talk about Billy. I even want to listen to my mother worry. I press the heel of my hand against my eye till it hurts.

A knock on the door. I don't manage a yes, just an "erm."

Elsie looks in. "Could you come to the Colonel's study, Betty?"

Chapter Twenty-One

It's Lieutenant Keaten; Elsie must not have wanted to say with Mrs. Lindbergh in earshot. Seeing him, a wild, eager thought comes and I ask, "Have you heard from Colonel Lindbergh?"

The question embarrasses him. Colonel Lindbergh hasn't told the police anything about the new developments, wanting to follow the kidnappers' instructions to keep them out. "No. We're tidying up some reports on the case. Now that it's more than two months out, I wanted to go over some things. Mostly what we've covered before."

It's the clothes again, what Charlie was wearing that night. I go through it all: nappy, sleeveless sleep shirt, the extra shirt I made him, and the Dr. Denton's. "Size two," I finish. "But I suppose you have that back."

"Yes," he says. "Thank you. What color thread did you use on the shirt you made?"

"Blue." I've said it so many times it's almost funny. He smiles, but there's something in the smile. For a moment I wonder, has John Curtis said something more? Does Keaten suspect me again?

"Will you be around today, if we need you?" he asks.

"Of course," I say nervously.

An hour later, Colonel Schwarzkopf comes and asks if we can talk in the room we've made into his office. He's never asked to speak with me alone. Something has happened, I can feel it. Whatever it is doesn't seem to require the Whateleys. It's me, I think, Curtis has named me. And the Lindberghs believe him. I want to ask if I need a solicitor. But I can't quite get up the nerve.

His manner is kind, though, almost apologetic as he invites me to sit. "This is difficult, I'm afraid."

He has an envelope with him, large, plain brown. "I'm going to show you something. You tell me if you know what it is."

I nod, eyes on the desk. When Colonel Schwarzkopf slides the contents of the envelope over the leather blotter, my first instinct is mild fussy disgust. Filthy, I think. Ragged. Who let this happen?

Carefully, Colonel Schwarzkopf handles the mess, separating it out until it's two things, not one. Smoothing them so the full size and outline are clear. Only it's not, being so old and worn, parts torn off . . .

Clothing. I hear my own breath, harsh and sudden.

"You recognize them?" he asks.

Knuckles to my mouth, I nod.

"Would you state what they are for me, please?"

". . . Oh, my God . . ."

"Remember Mrs. Lindbergh."

I breathe the panic down. "They're . . . I think they're the clothes Charlie was wearing." I point to the thing on the right. "That's the shirt I made him. I left the collar open on the shoulder. Where did you find these?"

"You can say definitively, this is what the baby was wearing the night of March first?"

"It is. I mean, I can. Those are the clothes."

He gathers them up, puts them back in the envelope. Then after a moment, he takes out a handkerchief and wipes down the surface.

"Betty, you've been extremely helpful."

"I've not done anything."

"You have. But I need you to do one more thing for Charlie and his parents."

He explains what has happened, how two men stopped their truck by the side of the road only a few miles from here. What the driver found when he went into the woods to relieve himself. As I listen, I feel a terrible pity for Colonel Schwarzkopf; he's got it so wrong. It's been difficult for him, not getting Charlie back, all the pressure and criticism in the press. The Lindberghs have set him aside for the likes of Condon and Curtis. It must be humiliating. Still, there's no point in me going with him.

"No, you see . . . ," I explain, "Charlie is on a boat near Cape May. Colonel Lindbergh's gone to bring him back."

It would be a great help to them, he says, if I would come.

It is a half-hour drive. I sit in the back. Colonel Schwarzkopf sits next to the driver. I want to ask what will happen, how I'm meant to decide. But if they wanted me to know, they would tell me. As we drive into Trenton, we start to slow on Greenwood Avenue. I look up at the building, see the name Swayze and Margerum Funeral Directors.

"Why?" I ask. But it's a question without an answer.

They take me out of the car, lead me into the building. That feeling again, that no one is saying anything because they don't want me to know what's really going on. I find myself acting like my mother; elaborately grateful and polite. "This way, Miss Gow." "Yes, thank you."

We walk down a long hallway. At the end, tucked into the corner, I can see it, the door I will go through. With every step, I expect someone to explain what is beyond that door, how this will work, what I'm meant to do. How I'm supposed to . . . know. I glance at the men on either side of me. They're looking straight ahead, as if I am not here between them.

"Are you ready?" the one who was introduced as Mr. Swayze asks.

Absurdly, I say, "Yes."

As we walk into the room, I feel revulsion. This place is so cold and antiseptic, all steel and tile, the acrid smell of astringent. From the corner of my eye, I see the one bit of softness in the room, a white sheet. Then far quicker than expected, Mr. Swayze says, "All right," and whips it away.

I don't see it. I don't understand the noise I make—a strangled whoop, as if someone's driven their fist into my belly. And yet I spin, groping for the door. But the policemen block my way.

Am I all right? they want to know. Can I continue? Of course I can't, but I nod, knowing they will not let me out until this is done.

I breathe into my gloved hand. Fix him in my mind. Stern face, bubble curls, the dimple in his chin. It's an image from a photograph, that's easiest.

I turn.

This is not a child. This is a thing of dirt.

No, I tell myself. *This is my Charlie.* I can't just see what the world has made of him and be horrified. He has to be seen. Has to be known. He must not be . . . left alone.

My eyes dart from one spot to the next. And then I see them: the toes. One curling under the other. His peculiar little . . . *What, not perfect? Well, me neither.*

I try to speak, "there," but the word catches in my throat. I gesture to the foot and nod.

"You're doing very well, Miss Gow."

I'm not, I mourn. *How can you even say it?*

But I can see him now, head turned, as if asleep. I point. *Here, there.* Then ask, "Is it done? Can I . . . ?"

I sense them looking at one another. I stare down at the table—unbearable before, now I can't look away. It's goodbye when I do. *What did we do to you, Charlie? How did we let this happen?*

I'm not even sure of the words, but I hear permission and turn sharply toward the door. Someone pulls it open and I hurry out into the hallway. Through a gaping window, I can hear there's a crowd outside. People have found out. They're gathering. At the far end of the hall, a few policemen, other men in suits.

The length of the hallway makes me dizzy. The walls are too close, the ceiling feels lower. I feel it all pressing on my lungs. Is there gas, somehow? So hard to breathe.

The men at the end of the hall have noticed me. One starts toward me. I panic; he'll make me go outside, into that crowd, with the shouting and accusations and wanting me to say it out loud. Half-turned, I start back down the hall. He lengthens his stride. I think, I'm going to have to run.

"Miss Gow? Betty . . ."

He stops, puts out a hand to reassure me. Look, not coming any closer. The panic eases and I see that it's Trooper McCann.

"I'm so sorry," he says, his voice low and rushed. "Really . . . sorry. Would you like to sit down, take a moment?"

I glance at the open window, the shadow people moving in the dark, waiting with their cameras and questions. My head bobs and McCann takes me by the arm and leads me down a flight of stairs, a long hallway, and several corners, where he finds an office, dark and abandoned for the night. Turning on the desk light, he tilts the light low. "No third degree, I promise." Then he puts a paper cup in front of me. "Compliments of the New Jersey State Police."

It's a small, cramped space, the two of us huddled at the desk. Sitting with his elbow on the edge, he lets me take a sip. Then a gulp.

"If you have questions, I can try to answer them."

For a moment, I stare at him dumbly, my mouth stiff and unworking. Then I manage, ". . . *Why?* I don't understand. They had the money, they *said* . . ."

"If it's any comfort, it was probably an accident."

"Accident" is offensive; I shake my head.

He explains. "You remember, on the ladder, one of the rungs was broken? We think the extra weight caused the ladder to break on the way down. The wood snaps, the kidnapper falls . . . It happened fast. Charlie wouldn't have known a thing."

I take this in. What I have never been able to bear is the thought of Charlie frightened. That he called for me and I never came. So—that did not happen. It gives me no comfort whatsoever.

Remembering my sense that Keaten knew something he wouldn't tell me about Dr. Condon's meeting with the kidnapper, I said, "You all knew. You've known for some time Charlie wasn't coming back."

He nods, admitting it. "When Dr. Condon met Cemetery John that first time, he asked Condon, 'Would I burn if the baby is dead?'"

"He will, won't he?"

"You bet." He holds my gaze a long time, and I feel we are conspirators, planning murder, which I suppose we are and I am glad of it. I think of the child who was tossed into the woods in a burlap sack and left. For the person who took him, I want claws. Teeth and blood. Nothing stainless steel or antiseptic. Nothing clinical. I want him to burn.

But how will we find "Cemetery John"? There is the money; it is already being spent, but it has not brought us to the man who took Charlie, the man who should burn. That man and I have something in common besides Charlie, though. *"Scotland and Norway, they touch."* John and I touch too. In the lives of the people running through the corridors, up and down the stairs of the Morrow house.

With Charlie gone, I think long and hard on what Keaten said: *"Good people can get into trouble all sorts of ways."* I remember my question: If someone wanted to know who was inside the house, where could they be—and not be seen themselves?

Answer: inside the house as well.

Let Keaten and the rest look for Cemetery John. I will look for the person inside.

Chapter Twenty-Two

Englewood, New Jersey

With the news that Charlie did not survive that night, Mrs. Lindbergh gives up. For days, she weeps, heedless and unstoppable. Before, in the time of waiting, we had wondered: How can she stand it? Why does she not cry? Now we wonder if her body can withstand the grief. The new baby is still four months from coming, both longed for and dreaded. She spends hours in the nursery, touching Charlie's things. His Peter Rabbit tam. The music box, and his cart of wooden blocks.

"I'm happy I spoiled him," she tells me, her fingers pulling at one of his shirts as if she might mold a new Charlie from its fabric. "That last weekend. I held him on my lap, I rocked him, sang . . ."

"That's right," I say uselessly. "That's right."

The Colonel does not cry. He sits close to his wife as she weeps. He goes through the notes and charts he and the police made. He walks aimlessly around the grounds, head down, the dogs trotting after. Always there is a frown, as if he is thinking and rethinking: Where did his plans go wrong? He viewed the body, pronounced himself "perfectly satisfied" that it was his child. After a photographer got into the funeral home and snapped a last picture, the Colonel had his son cremated, flying alone to scatter his ashes over the ocean. When I heard, I thought, Oh, now he is nowhere in this world that we can see him. I suppose that was the point. Sightseers crowd the Mount Rose road where Charlie was found, and with them, people selling food, drink, trinkets.

The stories on which we built hope fall to pieces. John Curtis admits he never saw the ransom money. Then he admits he never met the kidnappers. In fact, he made the whole thing up. In a statement, he says, "At the present time I am sane, but I honestly believe for the last seven or eight months I have not been myself, due to financial troubles. I became insane on the subject of the Lindbergh matter, which caused me to create the story in its entirety which was untrue in every respect."

People begin to wonder if Dr. Condon stole the ransom money. Of the many letters he receives, one says, "Enclosed you will find a picture of 'John,' the kidnapper." The picture is a small mirror.

Curtis is guilty, Condon is guilty. Red—long out of the country, but still guilty. I am guilty. Some people think Dr. Condon and I did it together. It doesn't matter what the police say. Once people have suspected you, they don't stop. They simply think there wasn't enough evidence.

Once again, the Hopewell house is taken over. The police return. The reporters flood back, creeping through the woods, past the checkpoints, scattered and calling on the lawn. The phones ring nonstop, shrill and demanding. The letters—every day an avalanche of sympathy. And requests. Always requests. For the usual things, but also, you can't help thinking, a lot of these people wrote these letters hoping the Colonel's or Mrs. Lindbergh's eyes would rest on their words for a moment, connecting them somehow to the only thing anyone is thinking about in America right now.

A different kind of letter starts to arrive, from people who also want to be part of the only thing the country is talking about. But they don't offer sympathy. They talk about the new baby. What will happen to it. What they will do to it.

That is when we leave.

And so it is back to Englewood, the house on the hill where people are stopped at the gate by the guards and escorted to the door if their arrival has been planned and Mrs. Sullivan finds them suitable. Here, Mrs. Morrow is in command. Her other daughters come, Elisabeth and Constance, and the Morrow women surround Mrs. Lindbergh as if wanting to reabsorb her into their orbit, a time before marriage and motherhood. Before loss. Colonel Lindbergh goes back to work at the Rockefeller Institute for Medical Research. Reporters ask workers in the building their impressions of America's hero. Older, they say. Thinner.

Mrs. Lindbergh, it seems to me, spends as little time in the house as she can. She takes long walks with her mother and sisters. Settles herself under trees and looks up at the sun through the leaves. After what's happened, I find myself thinking: Houses are a lie. I wonder if she feels the same, but it's not something I can ask her.

She and the Colonel take long drives at night. One evening they come back, their faces drawn and miserable. And I know they have visited Mount Rose. The next day, I overhear her tell Mrs. Morrow, "Never, never, will I say, *You are mine*. Or *I have you now*. It's pointless."

Then she starts to write. Letters to the Colonel's mother, entries in her diary. There is a small, particular frown when she writes in her diary; she is exacting with her words even as she records the bleakest or wildest emotions one can feel. It's a rigor, a deep purpose I don't always see in her. When she is with others, she is pliant, sensitive, adapting herself endlessly to their expectations. But on that blank span of paper, she can—and will—feel what she needs to, say what she must, and be honest. She does love flying, I've seen it. But I think that paper is her sky.

I would like to grieve with her. But she is the mother. I am not.

Seemingly deferential to my loss, the Morrow staff keep their distance, offering glances and polite condolences. As we pass in the hallways, I look at people I once considered friends and coworkers and, remembering my bond with Trooper McCann, think, *Did you do it? Was it you?* It was one of us. And yet here we are, in the same house, under the same roof and no one is punished.

Without a child to mind, I am shifted to Marguerite Junge's department: the care of clothes. She and I form a fragile, suspicious partnership. She and Johannes hope to return to Germany. "He loathes this country. Says it is both a madhouse and a police state." In the evenings, we sit at the gazebo near the tennis court. She smokes, while I look out at the house and the gardens and try to remember that it once seemed marvelous to me. I also remember: *Two men and a woman.* Of all the "good people" it might be, I would prefer Marguerite and her husband, so bitter over their financial loss and reduced status. But I believe in Henry's innocence, and he was with her. So I must accept her innocence as well. Plus, she is a woman who observes things and does not mind speaking ill of others. In fact, she relishes it, making accusations in the same languid way she turns a cigarette to ash. That makes her the sort of company I want right now.

One night, we see Ellerson as he comes out of the garage. He walks stiffly, and his arm is in a sling.

"What happened to him?" I ask Marguerite.

She takes her time, surveying the night sky. "A car accident. Not one of the Morrows', his own. It went over an embankment and burst into flame. He was lucky to get out in time."

"When did this happen?"

"May. Around the same day." She gives me a pointed look and I understand she means the day Charlie's body was found.

"Was it reported to the police?"

"I imagine so," she says blandly.

Guilt? I wonder. Horror? Even now, I cannot imagine Ellerson as a man who would knowingly kill a child. He is, in his own way, tenderhearted. But he might have been able to deceive himself that Charlie would be returned, with no real harm done. The news of Charlie's death could easily have sent him over the edge.

As could a bad night at cards. Or a nagging partner. Or a lost friend. "Such a disordered life that man leads," says Marguerite Junge.

Sympathy is a strange current, not easily controlled. It flows through the chill of dislike, the tension of mistrust. You can have your mind set: *I don't care about this person.* Even, *I hate this person.* And yet, in a moment—they turn their head, the shoulders slump—the heart inclines toward them. One evening, I see Ellerson by the pool trying to light a cigarette with his arm in a cast, face red, arm unsteady, hair shaken loose from the effort. And I think, Maybe we could have truth. If I ask right.

I am standing on the other side of the pool, the blue water still as a mirror between us. Ellerson twists, his reflection wavers. I look down. My own reflection is shadowy, easily dispersed. When I look back up, I see he has noticed me. And is waiting. With hope or dread—I can't tell.

Did you? The question comes in many versions with many answers. Did you tell the police about the green coupe? Certainly. Tell them about Detroit? Possibly, but Kathleen Sullivan knew it too. Give them the story of Rob Coutts, the boyfriend who did something wrong, you're not sure what, in Detroit? Yes, I think you did. While your man with the hazel eyes, I held back. Because I think that is your needful side, your open heart, and nothing to do with this cruel and terrible thing. It is the side we showed each other and I can't quite forget that. We needed someone to know who we were. And now we're heartbroken that those truths have been shared with others to use against us.

His silence is an accusation. He believes I gave the police everything.

Or . . . he's wary because he is guilty. Because he was broken and desperate and made that one phone call in exchange for the roll of money at the Sha-Toe. A win the like of which he'd never had before.

The police know about his gambling. The roll of money the night of the kidnapping. He is being closely watched, his friends sought out and questioned. And yet Mrs. Morrow makes a point of being kind to him. Thanking him in front of the police. She does not know what she would do without him, she says. Is it goodness on her part? I wonder. Or arrogance?

Not once has he approached me to say he is sorry about Charlie.

Did you?

We leave each other without asking.

The next day as I am taking down the curtains in the library so they can be cleaned and hemmed, Violet comes in to empty the ashtrays. She is much changed. Despite the police telling us we could not leave the country, Edna returned to England. Violet, once the lady of misrule, is quiet and listless without her sister. Apparently she has been ill, something to do with her tonsils. From my perch on the ladder, I can see she's lost quite a lot of weight and her hair has gone dry and brittle.

From below I hear, "You know we're not going to North Haven this summer. Because of all this trouble with the baby."

"Trouble"—the word is so hideously inadequate. I stare down at her, reminded of how childish she is, how selfish.

I spit, "I couldn't care less."

I expect her to flounce off. But she takes her time with those ashtrays, dawdling as she makes her way from one table to the next. Her idleness agitates me; I fight the impulse to shout, *There are five ashtrays in this room. Pick them up, empty them, and get out.*

Then as I push the last ring over the bar, I remember, *"You have no business prying into my private life!"* How she knew she'd had coffee but couldn't remember the name of the movie she'd seen. At the time, I admired her defiance, however brattish, of the police. But that was before we found Charlie. Now that I think of it, they never did learn who she was out with that night.

Violet was the first person at the Morrow house to know I was going to Hopewell.

Climbing down, I gather the fallen curtains off the floor. "I expect you miss your sister."

It's all Violet needs to set down the bin and throw herself onto one of the sofas. Planting her feet on the table, she says, "I do. She's more clever than I am and I can't stand not being able to talk with her. Especially when I'm in such a mess."

She looks at me with a mix of yearning and resentment. Settling on the fat leather arm of the sofa I ask, "What sort of mess?"

"The police won't stop questioning me!" she cries. "When Edna left, they were furious. 'Why did she go home? We told her not to!' Because she wanted to, what do you think? Who would want to stay here?"

Edna Sharpe applied for her visa a few days before Charlie was taken. "And when did she leave?"

Interrupted, she has to think. "I don't know. Early April?"

Around the time the ransom was paid, I think.

"They *will* not stop asking me about men," she says, returning to her grievance. "Where I went, who I saw, did this one buy me a drink, did I let that one make love to me? I told them, you've all got dirty minds, you should be ashamed."

As she says this last, her voice goes oddly flat. Her eyes are fixed on the cold fireplace opposite the couch, as if her thoughts have drifted elsewhere. There's a way she's not looking at me, as if she's considering telling me something, but she fears I will judge her harshly.

Leaning in, I confide, "They wanted to know how far Henry'd got with me in the famous green coupe. And of course, all about my gangster boyfriend in Detroit."

She smiles, warming to friendliness, as she always has.

"But it's not as if you'd have anything to tell them," I add, fishing. "You and Mr. Banks have an understanding . . ."

She gathers a pillow to her belly, sinks her chin into its side. "Yes, but since we'd quarreled, I was . . . maybe seeing some other men."

"Oh, that's right." I give her an approving rap. "Like that truck driver from the Peanut Grill. Is that who the police want to question?"

"No," she says, scornfully. "They want to know about this other fellow I met, I think it was February. Edna and I were walking on Lydecker Street. This bloke drives up and says, 'Give you a lift into town?' I thought *maybe* I knew him? Then when I saw him up close, I realized I didn't. But he seemed nice and we let him drive us . . ."

Of course he seemed nice, I think. Two English girls in uniform, in the vicinity of the Morrow house. Just the sort of girls a certain man would be very interested in meeting.

"He asked me out—of course. I said all right and he said he'd call and let me know when. Such a scandal, eh?"

"And did he call?"

She hesitates, then says boldly, "Yes. We went out the night it happened as a matter of fact. With another couple."

"Oh, that's nice," I say, as if my vision of those two men and a woman had not radically, horribly shifted.

I wait, willing her to say more. But it seems she's done.

I say, "Well . . ." meaning it's time to get back to the curtains.

But as I rise, she grabs hold of my wrist. ". . . Be my friend?"

"We are friends, Violet."

"No, I mean really. Edna's not here and I need someone to talk to. Someone on my side."

I give her a smile. "Of course I'll be your friend, Violet. Come to me anytime."

That evening, I tell Marguerite, "Violet says the police are giving her a terrible time."

"Well. That's hardly surprising." She looks at me, eyebrow raised.

"There does seem to be quite a lot she doesn't remember about the night Charlie was taken."

"Not only that," says Marguerite. "But three days before he was found, she went into the hospital with tonsil trouble. Of course that meant she couldn't talk, which was convenient as the police wished to interview her again. Then, two days after they found the baby, she released herself—against doctor's orders—and came back here. Where she knows Mrs. Morrow will protect her."

This reminds me of something important. Unlike Banks, who sees the Morrows as a comedown in prestige for him, Violet has always liked the family—and they her. And I've never seen any malice in her toward the Lindberghs; she's starstruck like everyone else. That argues against her doing anything so deliberately cruel as to conspire at kidnapping.

On the other hand, she is scatty. She leaks like a cracked cup, spreading her thoughts and feelings here and there, making you marvel, *Oh, what a mess*. More than once, I've reminded her to watch what she says. And as I once imagined the kidnappers instructing Henry to court me—*Find someone lonely. They don't ask questions when they're lonely*—I can imagine that man on Lydecker Street seeing Violet and knowing, yes, she's lonely.

Remembering what Trooper McCann told me, I ask Marguerite, "You and she returned to the house at the same time that night. Did you get a look at who she was with?"

"No, it was dark and I never care to talk to Violet Sharpe."

"Seems we'll never know who it was then," I say lightly. "If you didn't see him and she can't remember . . ."

"*Says* she can't remember," Marguerite corrects me. "Back in March when they took her and Ellerson to Hopewell to be interviewed, the police searched their rooms here. Do you know what they found in Miss Sharpe's bureau? Six business cards. A man by the name of Ernie Brinkert. She has six of these cards—but she doesn't know who she went out with that night? It seems very odd to me."

Chapter Twenty-Three

"They want to talk to me again."

Violet has come into my room without knocking. Breathless, she leans against the door as if someone will try to bash their way in. Setting aside my magazine, I say, "Who?"

"The police. Will you be with me? Stay while they ask questions?"

"I don't know that they'll allow that, Violet."

"They will. If I say I need you. I've been sick, I'm still sick, honestly. They know they have to be careful with me or they'll get into trouble with Mrs. Morrow."

Mrs. Morrow had a doctor look at Violet. He said her pulse was slightly elevated and she had a temperature of ninety-nine. Hardly a raging fever.

Crouching beside me, she pulls on my hands saying, "Please. *Please?*"

Why do you want me? I wonder. *Show of solidarity? A reminder to the police that they have accused one woman and got it wrong? Or are you really so simple that you just need a friend—and believe me to be one?*

"All right, Violet."

. . .

The police choose what must be the smallest room in the house. I have to think it's on purpose: six of us—Colonels Schwarzkopf and Lindbergh, me and Violet, Lieutenant Keaten, and a new man, Inspector Walsh—crammed into a space meant for three at the most. The colonels stand back. Walsh takes the chair opposite Violet, Keaten sits nearby at the desk. It's not a pretty picture, the two of them leaning in, poking at her with questions. I take the place behind her; instantly, she takes hold of my hand. Walsh sees it and looks irritably at Schwarzkopf. Why am I here?

"She's my friend," says Violet fretfully. "I'm not feeling well."

As always, the men look to Colonel Lindbergh, who says I may stay. Violet gives him a tremulous look of gratitude.

Walsh is a heavy man, red in the face with thick fingers; you feel he could start shouting at any moment. He begins by asking Violet to repeat her story of how she met Ernie Brinkert. Violet speaks in a low voice, her head down, so you have to strain to hear her. First Walsh asks her to speak up, then Keaten says, "I'm sorry, Miss Sharpe, but if you could raise your voice a little." He is both a kind man, I think, and a man who believes kindness is effective, especially when paired with brutality. As Brex had McRell do the shouting, he has Walsh.

Violet's hold on my hand intensifies. She looks to Lindbergh. He nods, encouraging her to go on.

Nervous, she exhales. "Ernie called me at one o'clock that afternoon."

Keaten and Walsh exchange glances. Keaten repeats, "One o'clock."

". . . yes."

Walsh inches forward on the chair. "Before you said he called you at eight o'clock in the evening."

Violet's nails dig into the side of my wrist. "I did?"

"Yes, you did."

At first I don't understand the importance of the timing. Then I realize: one o'clock was two hours after Mrs. Lindbergh called. This man, Ernie, whoever he is, could have known the Lindberghs were staying at Hopewell before I even got to the house.

With a cough, Violet recovers. "He picked me up around eight thirty that evening and we went to the Peanut Grill—"

"Now that's another thing," Walsh interrupts. A warning look from Keaten; he's going at her too hard. In a softer voice, he says, "When we first spoke, Violet, you said you went to the moving pictures."

She gazes at the ceiling as if the answer is written across it. "Maybe I thought we were going to?"

"You said you *did*. You said you were at the movies that night. For two hours, starting around nine."

The time Charlie was taken. No wonder Violet couldn't remember the name of the movie, she never went. I feel Keaten's eyes on me and will myself not to react.

"*Now* you say you were at this roadhouse." Violet gives a shaky nod. "Why did you lie, Violet? Can you explain why?"

"I could not explain why, I don't know."

"Were you upset when you found out you weren't going to the movies?"

"I didn't know about it then."

I can't decide: Is Violet brainless, the sloppy way she speaks—using words in a way that makes you wonder? "It"—does she mean not going to the movies or something else? What time is "then"? Or is it clever because your own brain goes foggy trying to fathom what on earth she means. She seems to have Inspector Walsh stymied at any rate, because he barks, "Are you in the habit of going out with people you don't know and having a drink with them?"

Violet glances anxiously at Colonel Lindbergh. "No, I don't know why I did it."

"Are you in the habit of picking up strange men on the street?"

"No, I don't know why I did it. I just did it and that is all."

Her voice is rising; I can feel her wanting to get up out of the chair. I tighten my grip, a warning to stay put. Running out of the room will not help her cause. And—she must answer.

The men let the silence stretch, giving Violet a chance to compose herself. Then Lieutenant Keaten slides a slip of paper across the desk, asks in a neutral voice, "Can you tell us what this is, Miss Sharpe?"

"Where did you get that?"

"We found it in your room."

I recoil. Marguerite had told me, but the proof that these men have gone rummaging through our closets and drawers, put their hands on our things—only to lay them bare on the table as if they had a perfect right—appalls me.

"Would you read it, please?" he asks.

Tearful, voice shaking, Violet reads, "'Banks promises to try and be straight for twelve months.'"

Despite everything, my heart melts. I squeeze her hand.

"What does that mean?" Walsh wants to know. I glare; they know what it means, why put her through it.

"It is a private thing," says Violet. "Something I don't wish to answer."

"Are you acquainted with Septimus Banks?"

"Well, I work with him."

"I mean, are you *intimately* acquainted with him?"

"I don't know what you mean," she says.

It's well done; her tone is simple, her face unreadable. If Walsh wants her to say she's sleeping with Septimus Banks, he's going to have to be vulgar.

Walsh backs off. "'Get straight,'" he repeats, as if he'd never heard the term. "What do you mean by that?"

"It is a thing I don't wish to answer."

"We know he drinks," says Keaten.

She looks at him, unsure, then at me. I give her a reassuring smile; everyone knows Banks has a problem, she's hardly telling secrets.

"Well, that is what I meant." Then, before they can ask what concern it is of hers, she adds, "It's not so much for him I mind. But I want Mrs. Morrow to have a fair deal."

This she says loudly, wanting Colonel Lindbergh aware of her loyalties.

Walsh looks lost in thought. Then he says, "You deposited five hundred dollars in your account in October. Then another two hundred and forty in January. You've got more than sixteen hundred dollars in that account. That's a lot of money, Violet."

It is a lot of money, more than what she earns in a year. And I know she sends money home.

"I save," Violet tells him. "And Mrs. Morrow gave me a hundred dollars as a Christmas present."

"I guess she pays pretty well, too," says Walsh sarcastically. "This man, Ernie—what was his business?"

"I don't know."

She's back to lying. I fight the impulse to crack her hand.

"Can you . . . give us a description? Tell us what he looks like?"

Violet frowns. "He's fairly tall. Thin. Wore a navy suit, a soft felt hat. And a dark gray overcoat." Then, realizing she's mostly described his clothes, she adds, "I'd say more dark than fair."

I try to picture the man. All I come up with is someone not noticeably short or fat. Violet's not one for noticing, but this is vague even for her.

"Did he make any attempt to make love to you?"

"No," says Violet, embarrassed. I fight the temptation to roll my eyes, unable to see how the question relates in any way to Charlie.

"Really?" The disbelief is meant to be flattering. "Not even a kiss?"

"He did try to kiss me when he left," she admits.

Then Walsh goes back to Banks. How much does he drink? Where does he get his liquor? At first I think this is just more bullying and shaming. Then I remember what Ellerson said about bootleggers. They ask again, she drank only coffee? Violet admits she had a cocktail as well.

Finally, Walsh tells her she can go. She is slow to rise, as if she's expecting another attack. She gives one searching look to Colonel Lindbergh, reassurance he doesn't think she's a drunken slut—or worse. But his eyes are fixed on the floor.

"What he must think of me," she whimpers when we're back in her room upstairs.

"Oh, what he must think of them," I scoff. "Honestly, do they not have wives? Are they so desperate for excitement?"

This is not entirely false on my part. Walsh's badgering has brought up spiky memories of Brex and McRell's bullying over Scotty Gow. What does it matter if this Ernie tried to kiss her? And why don't the police say straight out liquor means bootleggers, bootleggers means gangs, and a gang very likely took Charlie. Violet might help if they'd let her, especially if it meant Colonel Lindbergh saw her helping.

But it occurs to me, Violet has had chances to be helpful. And she has not taken them.

"Violet?"

"Um?"

"This Ernie fellow—he called at one o'clock?"

A fraction of hesitation. Then she goes to her bureau, opens the top drawer as if looking for something. "I forgot before, what time he called. It's not like I knew I'd have to remember."

Or, I think, at the earlier interview, you didn't know the police can trace phone records. Now you do so you thought it best to come clean about the time.

I ask the question Walsh didn't. "But you didn't mention me to Ernie?"

"How do you mean?"

"My going to Hopewell. You didn't say anything that would tell him the Lindberghs weren't coming back to Englewood that night?"

It's an easy question. Or should be. It's one she should have gone over and over again in her mind. Lord knows I have.

She pushes some scarves from one end of the drawer to the other. Refolds some underthings. Then shuts the drawer with a push of her stomach. "I don't recall."

"Maybe it was . . . you could go out because the Lindberghs weren't going to be back for dinner, and the other girl could manage on her own?" I wait. "Maybe you said something like that."

"I don't remember," she says. Too fast. She made the plan to say it before I'd even finished.

Charlie is dead, I seethe. *You owe him better than a careless "I don't remember."*

I think of kinder ways to say it. *It would give the family peace to know . . .* But Violet's too frightened—and resentful. Any suggestion that she's being less than truthful and she'll shut me out completely.

I take a deep breath. "Violet, I've made mistakes. I trusted people I shouldn't have. And they did harm. Not to Charlie, but . . . I was careless. I regret it. Terribly."

I watch her face. She might be listening to a radio program that's not very interesting.

"If you're the person who can do what no one else can—find the people who did this—then how can you not? Please, Violet."

"I don't think I feel well," she says distantly.

I let a beat pass. When I see that she's fully retreated behind the facade of ill health, I say with contempt, "Why don't you have a rest?"

"I think I will."

Going back downstairs, I pass by the study, where the men are still talking. I hear Walsh say, "I'm not satisfied. She's hiding something."

Colonel Lindbergh's voice, surprisingly apathetic. "She's scared. She's upset about the baby. She's also been ill."

After that, silence. Neither Schwarzkopf nor Keaten seem to challenge him. It's left to Walsh to say, "That's true, sir. But she wasn't sick when we talked to her in March and April and she lied then. I'm sorry, sir, but I still have my doubts. I'm sorry."

I hear the groan of wood across the floor as a chair is pushed back. As the Colonel comes out of the study, he stops short at the sight of me. I think to say, "It's good of you to defend Violet, sir." It would please him, that show of gratitude.

Certainly, he would resent being called a fool.

Violet is cool to me for the next two weeks, preferring to keep company with the younger maids, who I can tell find her somewhat silly if occasionally good fun. They don't see that her eyes never settle, how she speaks in a rush until she runs out of breath. They don't see the way her fingers move restlessly along the edge of the table. How her broad, big-toothed grin doesn't match the fear in her eyes. She remembers *something*, I think. Something she's taking great pains to hide.

One afternoon, as Marguerite and I take Mrs. Morrow's summer clothes out of storage, I say, "Violet's hardly a criminal mastermind. Seems more likely that she's lying to protect someone else."

"If so, she's risking a great deal to protect someone who did an awful thing. No?"

Our eyes meet and I know we are thinking of the two people Violet would protect.

One evening at dinner service, Violet drops a stack of dirty plates and bursts into tears. When Banks tells her to stop crying and clean it up, she wails and runs from the room.

"She's not well," I tell him as we sweep up the shards.

He glances at me over the dustpan. "You're the new savior, are you?"

"She's not got her sister." I stand, dump the broken pieces in the trash. "Nor you, apparently."

"Word to the unwise: you only hear part of the story with that girl."

The protest of all guilty men; he's worried about what Violet's told me about him. Wanting to provoke, I say, "I wouldn't say Violet was one for holding things back."

"And you think she always tells the truth."

Not by any means. But I am interested in the opinion of Septimus Banks. Banks, friend of bootleggers. Banks who grows less and less steady by the day. He will not be able to work forever. Violet hopes—or hoped—to marry him. Perhaps she or even they were counting on that money from the will that never came. Instead, more work. Endless work. In a place where they are not allowed to be together. She probably minds that more than he. But being left out of the will of a man he had such contempt for, that's an insult Banks would find hard to swallow.

Standing, he slaps at his trousers to be rid of any debris from the floor. "If you think Violet Sharpe's not one for secrets, ask her if she knows a Mrs. George Payne."

Chapter Twenty-Four

That night, I knock on Violet's door, call, "Violet? I just want to see you're all right."

The door opens and Violet pulls me into her room. Shutting the door as if it removes us from the house altogether, she whispers, "The police say they've got a photograph. They want me to say whether or not it's the man I went out with."

"All right," I say soothingly. "So you look at the picture and say yes or no."

"He's got a police record," she whispers. "I didn't know that. I didn't, I swear."

I think, *What* did *you know, Violet Sharpe? Just tell us that.*

"I didn't want Septimus to find out I was seeing other men," she tells me. "That's why I didn't want to say a name before. I thought as long as I didn't give a name, I could tell Septimus the police made it all up. They say they've found this man's business cards in my room. I didn't take any cards, I swear it. Why would I?"

She falls onto her bed, wraps her arms around her knees. Staring up at me through tears, she asks, "Would you lie down with me? Please? Edna used to and I miss it."

It feels impossible to refuse. At first I sit down on the edge of the bed. Then ease myself onto my back, hands laced on my stomach. In that instant, I have the strongest memory of lying next to Agnes, insisting I would never, ever speak to our mother again. Agnes saying, "I'm sure it'll be a great relief to her." When Violet pushes in close, putting an arm over my middle and laying her chin on my shoulder, I let her.

"Violet?"

She murmurs against my hair.

"Who's George Payne? Or . . . Mrs. George Payne?"

The rustle of cloth as she pulls away.

"I am, I suppose."

For all her attempts to surprise and enthrall, she has finally succeeded. "*You* are."

"When I was seventeen. He was much older, more than fifty. We worked in the same house, he was the butler and I was a parlormaid. You know how that goes."

I nod into my hand. "I do. Was he attractive?"

She squints, trying to remember. "I suppose not. But he was kind. Gave me advice—it was my first proper job, I didn't know anything. He took me to the movies. Out for tea." She shrugs. "I just fell in love with him. I don't know if that makes any sense . . ."

I think of Rob's room, staring up at the ceiling in the dark, fantasizing about the time the Coutts house would be my home, Rob mine for everyone to see.

"Oh, yes."

"But . . . ," she sighs, "turned out he was already married. Had a daughter older than me. Still, I couldn't stay mad at him, even after we split up. I'd write to him. Sometimes, we'd meet."

"What did the wife have to say about your letters?"

"Oh, she never knew. He set up a separate address where I could send them."

She explains this as if it's a normal thing to do: seduce a seventeen-year-old girl with a pretense of marriage, then correspond with her using a fake address. My own resentment at being a secret, at being tricked into thinking it was because I was so precious, surfaces. "And you kept seeing him? Weren't you furious?"

"...A bit?" she says as if trying for the right answer. "The real problem was I'd taken jobs as Mrs. Violet Payne, because some women don't like unmarried girls under their roof. And when I applied for a passport, I had to have recommendations from employers. They wrote them for Violet Payne, because that's how they knew me, so I applied as Violet Payne. Only..."

"No such person."

"Such a scandal. My mother shouted at me, 'Who's this Violet Payne?' I said, 'It's me. I got married.' She said, 'Oh, I don't believe it,' and I told her, 'Fine, it didn't happen then.'" She makes a face. "I don't get on with my mother. Rigid stuck-up old thing. Always says about me, 'I don't know what's wrong with that girl.' I want to scream, *You! You're what's wrong!* My poor dad drinks just to get a bit of peace. What's your mother like?"

"She's all right. Found herself a new husband, he makes her happy. She worries too much though."

"I'd like someone to worry about me," Violet says. "So tricky, isn't it? Finding someone to take care of you properly."

She settles in beside me again, head on my shoulder, arm across my stomach. I ask, "Is that what you like about Mr. Banks? You think he'll take care of you?"

"Ended up taking care of him, didn't I?"

I laugh. "Well, he is only twenty years older than you, that's better than thirty. And he probably hasn't got another wife somewhere."

"He did have a wife once."

"Did he?"

The pressure of her chin as she nods. "She died young. Drank too much."

And look at him, I marvel, even though he knows where it leads. Perhaps it's where he wants to go.

Violet has started fiddling with one of the buttons on her blouse. "He's still angry with me because of the baby."

"What baby?"

She rolls onto her back, draws circles on her belly. "One I didn't have."

"Banks?" She nods. "Did he make you get rid of it?"

A tear runs down the side of her nose. ". . . I didn't want to . . ."

Without thinking, I sit up. Immediately she curls into my lap, bunched fist to her mouth like a thumb. She weeps, saying *It was just* and *I couldn't* and *He said*. Until I tell her it's all right, she needn't explain, I understand.

After a long while, she murmurs, "Betty? What did you want? Before . . ." She waves a hand at the little room.

A strange question. Yet it immediately brings an image: myself at sixteen, strolling down the High Street, clear blue sky above the chimney tops, the bright certainty I was going to matter. I was going to do things. I didn't think so much about what things, only that they would be things no one else had done. Because I had Rob Coutts. I had all this energy and specialness. What Agnes would call being sixteen.

"Oh Lord, Violet, who remembers?"

As I stroke her hair, I think of young Violet, the wife who wasn't, sending letters to an address that's not a home, to protect someone who took advantage of her. She keeps secrets for people, I realize. Older men . . . or clever sisters. The people she hopes will take care of her if she sacrifices for them.

Settling a lock of hair behind her ear, I wonder, *Whose secrets are you keeping now, Violet?*

Later, after I leave Violet's room, I knock on Septimus Banks's door. There's a short pause. Then I hear, "Come in."

He's seated at a butler's desk. There's an open bottle on the desk, a highball glass with an inch of whiskey. In the far corner of the desk, there's a photograph; it takes me a moment to recognize the forceful young man in uniform, back straight, dark hair smooth and slick, as Banks. Beside him, a lovely woman with a wide-brimmed hat trimmed with silk flowers, a vision from another age. She leans shyly into him, as if embarrassed to be caught being so happy. It must be said, she looks a bit like Violet.

I shut the door, turn away from the picture. "I asked Violet about George Payne."

"Oh, yes?"

"A dirty old man tricked her into marriage so she'd go to bed with him. I don't see that she's the one who should feel ashamed."

"The real Mrs. George Payne might feel differently."

His neat maneuvering to make Violet a slut while the older man escapes judgment angers me. I say, "Perhaps if you had made her Mrs. Banks . . ."

My use of the past tense alerts him I know about the abortion. The hooded eyes turn sharp, accusatory. "Do you think I haven't asked her?"

Startled, I sift for notes of truth. Violet, Banks . . . one of them is lying. I remember the note in Violet's room. *Banks promises to try and be straight for twelve months.*

She doesn't want to marry a drunk, I realize. Doesn't want to raise a child with one either. What did she say? Not, I realize, that Banks made her. Only that she didn't want to, although she didn't contradict me when I made the assumption. I believe Banks when he says he asked. But I don't have to imagine his nastiness when he's drunk because I've seen it. Violet wants him—but she wants him sober. Despite myself, I feel a grudging admiration.

"She needs help," I tell him. "She's lying to the police." A short humorless laugh. "Because she's afraid—either for herself or for someone she's protecting."

I wait, watching for a crack of humanity. Or guilt. I see only weariness with the troubles of Violet Sharpe. Sitting back, he rubs his eyes with thumb and forefinger. "She needs a decent solicitor. Probably a doctor."

"If you stand by her, it might give her the courage to tell the truth. Unless you think she had something to do with it."

He pours himself a drink, the neck of the bottle landing hard on the glass. "I think she's a lonely, foolish girl who is too easily attached."

THE LINDBERGH NANNY   { 219 }

Too easily attached . . . and yet he came time and again to her room. "What *is* she to you?" I ask him. "Is she anything?"

He scowls at the whiskey, tosses it down his throat as if he wants to be rid of the sight of it. "Better to ask her what I am to her, other than a way to quit work. She's bedding men all over town. Five by my count."

Hearing the whine of hurt vanity, I ask, "And are you angry because you're number six or is it the mess you despise?" I look pointedly at the whiskey bottle. "We're not the Morrows or Lindberghs, Mr. Banks. No one cleans up after us. We're left to spit on a hankie and rub off the dirt as best we can."

The eyes roll up to meet mine. "You want to help her," he says. "You can't. People like that—they're poor swimmers who go out too far because they're not paying attention. Then when they start to founder, they thrash about, scream, and cling on to whoever's nearby. In the end they pull them down too." His gaze settles on the photograph, as if to admit he too is a poor swimmer. And drowning.

"Some might say Violet's helped you when you got in too deep." *In fact, some might wonder if she's helping you now.*

But I doubt it. Septimus Banks doesn't seem like a man who's about to flee the country with thousands of dollars in ransom money. He seems trapped. He might have contempt for Violet's attachment to him, but he also knows she's the only person willing to fight the bottle for his affections. And, I realize with a twist of sorrow, the one person for whom he is willing to try, if that promise note is anything to judge by. But he knows she'll lose. Violet, his job, his health. Nothing can compete with alcohol—and the grief for that lost self—for his devotion.

"Why do you *care*?" The drink is getting to him, making him petulant. "The mechanic stood by you. Police are off your back. New baby, you'll be in work . . ." The hooded eyes bulge slightly, and I feel his contempt for that status: *Be in work.* I look at the photo. The bold young soldier with his pretty bride—where did he think he was going? Not a dark, cramped office, holding on to his livelihood through the indulgence of an old American woman.

"I worked for Andrew Carnegie then," he says of the photo. "Lord Islington, too." Defiant, he repeats it, "Lord. *Islington*."

"I know," I say. "You've told me."

"You'll say it one day. 'I once worked for Charles Lindbergh.'"

"Oh, I very much doubt it," I tell him and leave the room.

The following afternoon, I accompany Violet as she looks at the photograph of the man she may or may not have been out with that evening. When Inspector Walsh lays the picture on the desk, I brace myself for the sight of the man who took Charlie.

Only to see a small, ordinary-looking fellow, soft in the belly, losing his hair, dark brushy mustache. Exactly the sort that gets nervous when he asks a girl to the Peanut Grill—but does it anyway. At dinner, he laughs too loud at her jokes, calls her honey and sweetheart, winks when he says something that could sound dirty, then watches to see her reaction; has he got a live one? Or will she pretend to be a good girl? After two drinks, he puts his hand on you like it's an accident. If you pretend it's not there, he keeps going.

This man did not take Charlie. Or perhaps I don't want to feel someone so . . . recognizable, so mediocre, could cause such agony.

Walsh asks Violet, "Is this the man you were with at the Peanut Grill?"

Violet flicks a glance at the picture. "Yes."

She's barely looked at it, is what we're all thinking.

Walsh asks, "Is this the Ernie you were with that night?"

"Yes. Yes, that's the man."

I try to catch her eye; does she understand that she sounds like she's lying?

Keaten asks, "Why didn't you tell us before that you were out with Ernie Brinkert?"

"Because I didn't know who he was." She says it boldly, like a child in front of a spill.

"You had his business card in your room." Walsh enunciates every word.

"I did not."

Not caring if Walsh and Keaten see, I stare at her. What game is she playing now? Whatever Walsh says, she's putting up no after no as if they're bricks that can build a wall to protect her. But she can't simply deny reality.

Although it seems to have worked, because Walsh doesn't press her on the business cards. Instead, he taps the picture with his index finger. "Just tell me again, is this—or is it not—the man you were with that night?"

He's given her a choice this time. I can tell from the way she hesitates, Violet wants to say no, put up another brick. But she knows she's said it is him just minutes ago.

"Yes," she stammers. "Yes, it looks like him."

Looks like him. Different from *that is*. Walsh hears it too, and I feel a moment of sympathy seeing his disappointment. More than trapping Violet, he wants the right man.

"Are you sure?" he asks.

Violet is not sure, that much is clear. But to her, it's all just more punishment. She's done what he's asked, told him that's the man. Now it seems he wants her to say perhaps it's *not* the man—why else ask her if she's sure? She can't comprehend his distrust, doesn't understand the damage she's done herself by lying so brazenly.

Then all at once, it seems she does understand, because she claps her hands to her face and screams, "Yes, it is!" She starts to sob, hoarse cries of despair racking her body. She doubles over, shoulders heaving. The men look at one another and I want to snap, *For God's sake, you've broken her, congratulations.* I remember when I didn't know if I was Betty Gow the Lindbergh Nanny or Betty the kidnapper's girlfriend, because what did it matter, if the police and the whole world said I was the girlfriend, the dupe, the accomplice, she who left unlocked . . . that's where Violet is now and it's a terrible place to be.

I say, "I think we should call for the doctor." Then I sit beside Violet. I rub her back, take her hair away from her face. I tell her no one's going to hurt her, she'll be all right, the doctor is coming. Gradually the sobs slow, the shoulders ease, and she's able to unfold. Her face is red and damp with crying; one look at Walsh, standing disturbed but suspicious by the door, and her mouth starts to wobble.

I take her face in my hands. "No, you don't look at him, lovey, you look at me. Just me, all right?" Blinking, she nods, taking me as seriously as a little girl would, making sure her eyes stay on mine. Thumbing the tear streaks and strands of hair from her cheeks, I say, "There now, pretty girl, got yourself into quite a state, haven't you?"

At that she tries to smile, but the effort is too much and her jaw starts to shudder and the tears well up again. I'm reassuring her nothing is bad, nothing will hurt her when the door opens and Dr. Lawlor steps in. One look at Violet and he gives Walsh a filthy look. His arrival seems to unnerve Violet even more; when he takes hold of her wrist, she whines as if she can't speak and frantically tries to tug her arm back. I take hold of her shoulders, tell her he's only trying to help, but she can't distinguish help from harm and twists hysterically, trying to throw us both off.

"Her blood pressure is very high," says the doctor. "This interview is over."

Watching Violet closely, Walsh says, "Fine. But tomorrow we're bringing her into the office for questioning."

Violet wails, and I say, "Don't think about that, tomorrow's tomorrow. For now, you're done."

Walsh opens the door to let the doctor out, then takes a moment to confer with him. With neither of the men looking at her, Violet seems calmer. I'm about to suggest she have a nice, hot bath.

She glances at the two men. Then back to me.

And winks.

Chapter Twenty-Five

What was that?"

Violet's sitting on the edge of her bed in her bathrobe. There's a stray thread on the hem and she pulls at it, a frown coming over her face when it won't come loose.

"The wink, Violet."

She looks up, seemingly astonished that I don't know. "Just . . . got him to shut up. Leave me alone."

"They're not leaving you alone, Violet. They said you're to come down to their offices tomorrow. It won't be so easy to get hold of the Morrow doctor then."

A small shrug. "Well, that's what they think."

"Yes, that is what they think, Violet. Because that is what they will do."

I sit down in the chair nearest the bed. "You must stop playing these games. Whatever it is you're hiding, *whoever*, the Lindberghs, Mrs. Morrow, they'll understand."

"No, they won't."

"Won't." The word implies new things to know, and it brings me up short. Cautious, I say, "About the roadhouse and Ernie Brinkert?"

"About . . . talking to people."

I try to guess what she means. "We're not nuns, Violet."

"No, I mean about the baby."

Thinking of the one she didn't have, I'm about to say no one needs to know about that when she adds, "Telling people about him."

I wait until I'm certain my voice will be calm. "You said something about Charlie."

". . . It's not as if I know anything."

Again, that habit of hers, making statements that confuse rather than inform. "If you told someone about me going to Hopewell, about the family being there . . ."

"I didn't."

Then what are we talking about? I wonder. *You've got something to say, say it.*

Exhaustion and dishonesty make my voice flat. "If you didn't say anything about Charlie on the day of the kidnapping, then you've nothing to worry about."

Setting her knuckle between her teeth she mumbles, "But what if you did? Before?"

"Did what?"

She frowns. Then it comes out in a rush. "It was just boy or girl. When he was born. This fellow from the papers, I was seeing him. And he said if I found out, he'd . . ."

Make it worth your while. Appreciate the tip. Sure be grateful. All sorts of ways to talk about money while pretending you're not getting paid.

"So you told him it was a boy." Eyes averted, she nods. "And he gave you some money to say thanks." The hefty savings account none of us could understand.

"It was bound to come out," she says. "Wasn't like they could keep that a secret."

"This fellow you saw that evening, did he ask about Charlie?"

". . . Everyone does."

"So, perhaps you said he has a cold? The family's not back yet so you can get away, only Mrs. Morrow for supper? Something like that?"

She doesn't deny it. I want to ask, *When did you tell him, Violet? When you spoke at one o'clock? That evening at the restaurant? Did he get up to go to the bathroom afterward? Make his own telephone call? Only the nurse, the caretakers, and the mother at home . . .*

I think of what the police said to me when they were trying to get me to point the finger at Henry. "Violet, no one thinks you knew they meant to take the baby."

The tears start. But they're private tears, falling because we're close to the truth now and she has to look at what she's done. She's frightened—and she's guilty.

"If someone approached you, tell the police. What they looked like, what they said. Who they pretended to be. Everyone understands . . ."

"No, they don't," she says, voice raw with grief.

"*I* do. It's not fair, the position they put us in. 'Run our lives, but keep our secrets, talk to no one, say nothing about your work.' They cut you off from normal life, give you a . . ." I look around. ". . . drafty little room and same mess to clean, day and day out. Then you're thirty, forty . . ." I think of Elsie. ". . . fifty, you think, that's been my life?"

"I just want them to leave me alone," she says hopefully, as if I can make that happen.

"They can't do that until you tell them the truth, Violet."

"Why *not*?" she cries. "They can't get him back now."

You bitch, I marvel. *You absurd, selfish, self-pitying bitch.*

But anger will not get me the truth. And so I lie, saying, "I understand. They're men and they don't know what it is to be on the other end of those snickers and looks they give each other. When they're just as bad, only they're men so they get away with it. If it weren't Charlie . . ." I hadn't prepared myself to say his name and my voice catches. Clearing it, I say again, "If it weren't Charlie, I'd say tell them to go to hell. But you may have seen the man who took him. Think of what that would mean to the family. Nobody has to know about the reporter from before, I won't tell a soul."

"But the money . . . I took money."

Thrown by the change of subject, I falter. Which time did she take money? From which man? The pause is too much; the thumb goes back to the mouth and the tears start again.

"Tomorrow, you'll go to the police . . ."

"No."

"Get Banks to go with you. Make him help you for a change. You'll go to the police and you'll tell them . . ."

"No!" She clambers off the bed and for a mad moment, I think she means to run away.

"They'll never take me from this house again," she shouts. "I'm not going to Hopewell ever again . . ."

Hopewell? I wonder. But before I can ask why Hopewell has such terror for her, there's banging on the door, cries of "Violet? What's going on?" I open the door. Gretchen, another table maid, and Delia, a parlormaid, stare into the room.

"And I'm not going to the police department, either!" Violet cries. I can't help thinking the girls at the door are a fresh audience, and she's playing it up.

Swinging a fist around the room, she screams, "They're not going to question me ever again! Never!" Then with a sob, she collapses on the floor.

Seated at the kitchen table, I sip a cup of tea. Wahgoosh comes over, jounces my hand with his head. He'd like a run. I'd like company that can't talk. "Come on, boy, let's go out."

It's dusk, a lovely mild June evening. The horizon glows pure gold, streaking the clouds pink against the faded blue sky. The trees that ring the estate are already in shadow. In the distance, far from the house, I see the Colonel. He's watching the sky, as if homesick.

Wahgoosh, of course, makes straight for him. I follow, slowly, unsure of welcome. Since we found Charlie, Colonel Lindbergh has been rigidly correct toward me. Not once has he mentioned his conversation with Henry.

His back to me, he says, "How is Violet? Mrs. Morrow tells me the police pressed her hard today, and she became hysterical."

Certainly acted up a storm, I think. "She's better now. But the police want to see her again tomorrow."

He frowns, disapproving.

"She's her own worst enemy," I insist. "If she would stop lying . . ."

"She lied about going to the movies because she didn't want Mrs. Morrow to know that she'd been to a roadhouse." He sounds weary as he says it; why are we all so foolish that we do not see the obvious?

I want to say, *And the six business cards from the man she supposedly doesn't remember? And her sister leaving the country, getting her visa just before Charlie was taken? The same sister who was with her when the mystery man approached Violet?* I think to tell him Violet Sharpe sold Charlie the moment he came into this world. The press that he and Mrs. Lindbergh blame for Charlie's death, Violet tossed bits of their son to them, the way you'd throw bread to ducks.

"She's not got a lot of sense," I say shortly. Nothing changes in his expression, but I can tell I have his attention; sense matters to him. "She drinks when she goes to those roadhouses. And she talks about things she shouldn't."

His brow contracts in distaste, but it's me he disapproves of, not Violet. I've been sloppy. Said too much, felt too much, the very things of which I often accuse her. *There are things you have feelings about*, I want to scream. *He was your son. Why do you not cry?*

Abruptly, as if sensing the threat of emotion, he says, "If Violet did pass information to the kidnappers, she wasn't aware of it. She had nothing to do with the kidnapping."

I stare at him, astounded that a man so demanding and meticulous can care so little about a moment of carelessness that has cost him so much. He ignores my stare, reminding me in his lofty way that I have also enjoyed his protection. And Henry. One word, one note of doubt from him, and it would have been us.

"When you met with Mr. Johnson," I say, "may I ask what you discussed?"

That event, so long ago and *before*, it takes him a moment to recall.

"We talked about sailing. How the sea is like the air in its power. It supports you, and it can turn on you. Once you understand how . . . unfeeling . . . that power is, there's a peace to that. A clarity. If you lose yourself in sorrow or fear, you'll founder. Better to understand it. Respect it. Work with the craft to make your way through."

There is something terrible in his words, although I can't say what. Back home, the Reverend Reid might call this submission, but it isn't. Colonel Lindbergh is not just accepting a power that is random, even cruel. He embraces it. Because it feels right to him. Or . . . true. I think of Mrs. Lindbergh and me, when the Colonel hid Charlie or let him tumble in the bath, how we insisted he see Charlie's tears, feel pity or remorse. He would laugh. Turn sullen or irritable. Why, he seemed to wonder, were we always asking him to *care*?

On some level, this horror has confirmed something he always believed about people. They fail. Real hearts are weak, they wear out. Machines, pumps, and engines do not—or if they do, they are easily repaired or replaced. He does not hate Violet for her carelessness or greed just as he does not hate Wahgoosh if he chews up a shoe. He has been vindicated, I think. No—liberated. Not to care. My mind goes to my brother, when he spoke of Lindbergh's triumph. What *can't* we do? So hopeful and triumphant. The words sound different now. I look above the darkened trees, for those bright, sun-rose clouds of a few minutes ago. They've gone a fiery orange, tinged with gunmetal gray.

"But you believe Henry was innocent."

"Yes."

And me? I want to ask. *Do you believe I was innocent too? Forgive me as you forgive Violet?* Because I don't. Ever since we found Charlie, I have wanted to . . . confess. Atone in some way. Say that, no matter what I did or did not do, it was my job to care for Charlie and in that, I failed. Maybe I'm no longer a suspect, but I am guilty. Because I was given a beautiful little boy. And I let him fall.

But I am all but certain Colonel Lindbergh will say *Yes*, in that simple cruel way of his. And that I can't bear.

"You should get out more," he tells me. "Get away from this . . ." He waves at his mother-in-law's estate. It is not a place he likes. Too formal. Too social. Too many people.

And go where? I want to ask him. But it hardly seems fitting to complain about being the infamous Lindbergh Nanny to a man who has already learned to despise fame. So I say, "I don't like to ask the chauffeurs to do extra work."

"You don't drive?" he asks.

He seems genuinely concerned by this. Strange man, I think as I shake my head. Strange, strange man.

"You should learn," he tells me.

The next morning, the police telephone to say Lieutenant Keaten will be coming at eleven to take Violet to the station. Banks takes the call, and I say, "Do you want to tell her or shall I?"

"Be my guest," he says.

I knock on her door, say, "Violet?"

There is no answer. On instinct, I wrench the knob to the right. The door opens and I see that she's sitting fully dressed on her bed. Her breathing is labored, her lower jaw rattling with nerves. She stares at the wall as if the sight of the pale pink and blue flowered wallpaper is the only thing she can bear.

"They'll be here in an hour," I tell her.

Her fingers close tight on the bedspread. "I'm going to see Mr. Banks."

As kindly as I can, I say, "Truly, Violet, I think it's best if . . ."

Violet seems not to hear. Launching herself off the bed, she runs past me, crying, "No, I have to . . . I have to see Septimus."

Half an hour later, I am pacing in the staff sitting room. If Violet hasn't returned in five minutes, I will go find her. If Banks won't go with her to the station, I will. And if Colonel Lindbergh himself tries to stop me, because he doesn't believe the Violet Sharpes of the world can touch him, I will tell him that carelessness is not an excuse—he of all people should know that. Violet Sharpe must be made to answer for what she has done. No more evasions. She is not a little girl, no matter how much she pretends. She is a grown woman who . . .

Then I hear the scream. A man's voice, wild, gibbering. I run from the room, down the stairs, and push my way through the staff already crowding into the hallway that leads from the dining room to the kitchen. From the corner of my eye, I see Mrs. Morrow step sideways out of her study, her body tilted as she tries to make out *what* is going on. There are calls for a doctor, for help, for anyone. Banks starts to moan, call on God. I make out a series of muffled thuds, like someone bouncing a tennis ball rapidly and repeatedly on the floorboards. Later, I will find out it was Violet's heels pounding the floors as she convulsed.

When I am almost at the swinging door—its round window gazing at me like a warning—Ellerson puts himself in front of me. The door swings wide and I catch a glimpse of dark hair on the black and white squares of the kitchen floor. Violet's face, upside down, eyes rolled. I shout something that sounds like "No," and Ellerson grabs hold and drags us both out of the house. Past the gardens, past the pool and the statues, deep into the woods, where the branches strike your face, the brambles tear at your legs and there is no path. Leaves and tree roots under my knees, I press the heels of my hands to my eyes and rock silently, mouth open, jaw rigid.

Later, in whispers behind closed doors, the story of what happened. Violet did go to Banks to ask for help. He said he had none to give her. She went to her room and filled a cup with water. In the water, she put cyanide crystals she kept for the polishing of silver. She stirred it. Then she drank it. Being a woman with some sense of occasion, she made it all the way back down the stairs to the pantry to die at Banks's feet.

It all comes out. Her strange marriage that wasn't a marriage. The abortion, although the identity of the father remains in doubt. Amazingly, her suicide is not seen by most as proof of her guilt. Violet has powerful defenders. Edna, her sister. Mrs. Morrow. The public outcry against the police is strong. They failed to save the Lindbergh baby. In their need to shift the blame, they have driven a blameless young woman to kill herself. Violet, so close to being the most hated woman in America, is now a martyr.

But Violet's parents, as she herself might have predicted, do not share this view. Appalled by the scandal, they refuse to accept the body, so Mrs. Morrow has her buried at Brookside Cemetery. Not far from Mr. Morrow, in fact. The staff from both houses are allowed to attend. The Whateleys arrive, he standing tall, proud of their inclusion and determined to impress. She, nervous, ill at ease; she all but curtsies to Mrs. Morrow. At the service, Marguerite and I stand next to each other, but do not speak. That time is over between us. I look down at the coffin, purchased by both families, and grieve, *How could you? You stupid girl.*

We leave the cemetery severally, the family going first. It is raining lightly and Ellerson walks beside Mrs. Morrow, holding an umbrella. He is deft as he opens the door for her, and I have the odd thought that he is moving with new purpose. He catches me looking and nods slightly. I nod back.

Of course the reporters have come, but they stand at a distance through the burial. Waiting for my ride back, I watch as Elsie puts an arm around a kitchen maid, who's not been able to stop weeping. Whateley, never a man to miss a chance to give his opinion, is talking with a reporter.

"Oh, well, it was a bad business," he says. "Bad business. Girl was very high strung."

"Got around some too," says the reporter.

Hands in his pockets, Whateley rocks on his feet. "Couldn't say, couldn't speak to that." But the way mirth tugs at his mouth suggests he could. Then he coughs himself back to seriousness. "It's hard on some of these girls. Far from home. Lonely. No real prospects. It can end badly, no question . . ."

I think of Violet on the pantry floor, neck arched in agony, body twisting to escape the pain, eyes rolled back, jaw wide, as she gasped for breath like a fish caught on a hook. She brought the cyanide herself from England. She shook the crystals into a spoon, sank them in water, and stirred. Then she swallowed it into her body. I told Trooper McCann I wanted Charlie's killer to burn. I still do. But only Charlie's killer deserves such agony.

Whateley's pomposity has always irritated me. Now it feels like his clumsy potato fingers are plucking at a raw nerve. What Violet did, what happened to her, is not a thing for him to blather about. A thing for people to snigger at, *Got about some.* Violet was . . .

My anger has become so intense, it's breaking my thoughts, making the words fly and spatter like a hard rain on mud.

The thing with Violet is . . . she was . . . the mistakes she made, I could have made. And for all my grand thoughts of swallowing poison in the woods when I thought I might be in some way guilty, I couldn't have done what she did. That should earn her some grace.

I call, "Mr. Whateley!" Startled, he looks over. "It's time to go."

"Died for our sins," quips Ellerson that evening.

"Don't be awful."

"Sorry."

We are sharing a lounger near the pool; Ellerson is stretched out, hands clasped on his stomach, I perched on the end of the lounger. His feet rest on my lap, my folded arms on his shins. Our time in the woods has made us close again. The knowledge that no one else would have brought me there, no one else would have stayed rocking against me as I wept, makes the complaints about who told what seem pointless. Violet's fatal confession has, in the most terrible way, absolved everyone.

"Why?" I manage after a time. "Why do you think she did it?"

As I say it, even I am not sure: Do I mean what Violet did to Charlie or what she did to herself?

Ellerson answers the first question, saying, "She wasn't a bad person, but she wasn't smart. Probably she didn't even know she was doing it."

"She could have just said that. Instead of changing her story time and again."

"She did say she couldn't remember," he says softly.

"She was protecting someone. She must have been."

"Who? Banks? The Morrows are all he has. He wouldn't take the risk. And gangs don't hire a drunk for this work."

Once a drunk, I think, now a wreck. Banks has been committed to a sanatorium. Some might say it's convenient, hiding from the police. But anyone who saw him after Violet's death knows otherwise; he simply fell apart.

"Edna's not a drunk," I argue. "I always thought it strange she applied for a visa right before it happened. And then left the country, even though she was told not to."

Ellerson arches his neck. "Violet blabbed to the wrong guy. Maybe to get him to like her, maybe for money. Maybe because she wanted to think her life was more interesting than it was."

"And now she can't tell us who that guy was."

"No, she cannot."

Does it even matter? I wonder. None of it brings Charlie back.

Then I hear Ellerson say, "I'm sorry, Beautiful. He was a sweet kid."

I nod. "He was . . ."

I can't say all the things Charlie was. It occurs to me, I still don't know who gave Ellerson that hundred dollars he needed so desperately. I suppose it doesn't matter now. I think of Violet's coffin, how she'll never go home. Buried with the Morrows forever.

"Had enough of the picture show?" he asks me.

"I think maybe I have."

He puts a hand over mine; it's surprisingly heavy, strong fingers, well-developed knuckles. It is his way of saying he will miss me.

Chapter Twenty-Six

I never think of going out these days, so when Trooper McCann calls to ask if I'd like to have dinner, it takes me a moment to understand. And another to accept. But I insist we eat at a place far from Englewood or Hopewell. He says perhaps I could call him Joe. I say I'll try.

Glancing at me over his menu, he says, "I've never been out with a celebrity before. Guys at the precinct are going to be pretty jealous."

"I'm hardly that."

"You kidding?" He lowers his voice. "The Lindbergh nurse? I bet we'd get free à la mode for that."

The waitress comes to the table; I brace for recognition, but she just takes our orders.

The subject of the crime having been raised, I ask, "I heard you found the people Violet was with the night Charlie was taken."

After Violet's death, it came out that she wasn't with Ernie Brinkert that night. She was with another Ernie who looked nothing like him. As well as another couple—just as she had said.

He sighs. "We did. Nice ordinary people with solid alibis."

I share his frustration. If this couple and Ernie Brinkert are not the "two men and a woman," when and how did Violet make her slip to the kidnappers? I hate that her death means we may never know who she helped, even unwittingly. And if she was protecting someone, I don't want that person unpunished while she's in the ground.

I ask, "You've looked at all the calls from the Morrow house?"

"All of them," he confirms. "*And* the pay phones from the local businesses. But if you don't know what number you're looking for . . ."

"Maybe someone remembers Violet using the pay phone . . ."

"We showed the local businesses pictures. All your pictures."

I remember the madness of Clark's drugstore, the counterman who never looks up, the crowd that's always around the telephone. How would anyone remember one face on one exact day? The Morrow staff would be in and out of any number of stores, on business for the family or their own amusement. Difficult to say if you saw Violet Monday or Tuesday or . . .

"You showed him my picture as well?" I ask, smiling to let him know I'm not angry. Well, no longer angry.

He shifts uncomfortably. "We had to. Even though *I* knew you hadn't done it."

"Oh, yes? How'd you know that?"

Surprised, he takes a moment. "Instinct."

The waitress brings our dinners. McCann takes up his knife and fork, then sets them down again to say, "We're going to catch this guy. The ransom money's already turned up in Manhattan. We're giving out booklets with all the numbers to stores, gas stations, banks. One day, he's going to spend one of those bills in the wrong place and we'll get him. And when we do?" He takes up his knife, points to me. "I'm going to recommend that instead of the electric chair, we turn you loose on him."

He means it as a compliment, so I smile. It's that cheerful, hopeful American savagery, the belief that brutality is always in a higher cause. Let the grieving woman tear the baby snatcher apart while the men stand back and laugh over his double defeat—caught by them, destroyed by a girl. There are still parts of Scotland, you'd say that and you wouldn't be joking. It would be the whole town. They'd come with stones.

Hesitant, he says, "I know it doesn't bring Charlie back . . ."

"No, it'll be good, when you catch him," I reassure him. "It'll be . . ."

What's the word people use?

". . . justice."

Even as I say it, I have the empty feeling that justice is not possible. Or even what I want. Justice for the Lindberghs, perhaps. But for Charlie?

All Charlie wanted was hands. Lifting him up, flying him through the air, holding him close. He wanted Buh—bull or Betty. He wanted Elepent and Rawr. And to run, oh to run. He did not want prunes. Or Vicks VapoRub. Or hands that pushed him away. He did not want school—not yet. But he would have; he would have wanted everything. Life. The wonderful terrible up-and-down tumble that should have been his life.

Justice? That's for grown-ups.

McCann—no, Joe—says, "New baby coming soon."

I agree to the change in subject. "Any day now."

The waitress takes our plates, asks if we'd like coffee or dessert. Joe has coffee, I ask for tea. Then he says, "So, you'll be staying around." Shy now that he's come to the point.

I consider instinct. Instinct tells me this is a good man. He'd pull out my chair for me, insist on paying for me, notice when I bought something new, and say, *You look pretty today.* He'd ask me to meet his mother, stammer when he proposed. And he'd be proud, so proud and happy, when I said yes.

All these things feel true.

Feel true.

But I can imagine other "truths." Every so often on the street, *Hey, that's Betty Gow. The Lindbergh Nanny. How's the sailor, Betty?* Jokes at the precinct. *I hear you two met when you busted her for public indecency.*

Most of the time, he's able to ignore it; maybe his jaw tightens and he's quiet for a while. Later, an argument over nothing. Tears from me, exhausted reassurances from him.

One vision is no more true than the other. But Joe McCann thinks instinct shows him the better side of people. My instincts are different now. Among the thousands of letters that came to the house in Hopewell, some were to me. The police kept them from me, but the words slipped through, poisonous and dizzying. This is a new country. But its people's notion of what should happen to a woman who is welcomed into someone's home and does harm is dark and ancient. These people savor violence, luxuriate in their righteousness. In their letters, they assure me—and themselves—I will burn in hell. Many of the men and a few of the women vividly describe what they will do if they ever see me in the street.

My mother was afraid of America. Too big. Too new. Too young. There would be gangsters here, guns, fast cars, tall buildings the desperate could leap from or that might collapse on people walking far below. What I would tell her now is it is not the gangsters or the cars. It is the quiet, terrified people—angry because they are abandoned in this land of the free and home of the brave. Something has gone wrong, terribly wrong. Their jobs are gone, their homes are gone, even the person who promised to be theirs, for better or worse. But worse came and promises rotted to nothing. What happened? Who took it all away? Is it . . . their fault?

Then they read about the Lindberghs, the baby stolen from them. They are told this terrible crime occurred not when someone broke into the house, but when someone on the inside let them in. *It was she who left unlocked.* Well, if it can happen to the Lindberghs, America's best! Now they know who to blame. They know who is stealing their children, their hope, their future. And they know what that person deserves.

I cannot live in a country with those people.

And, I realize for the first time, I do not want children.

Perhaps "want" is the wrong word. I simply . . . can't.

I tell Joe, "I've learned it's best to keep quiet about where you'll be and when."

"That could make it harder for a guy to find you."

"I know. I'm sorry."

"I think, perhaps . . ."

Mrs. Lindbergh and I are standing in what will be the new baby's nursery. Mrs. Morrow has decreed the new baby shall be a girl. A lovely new cradle has been brought back from England, along with several pink dresses. Chintz furniture coverings have come down from the attic. A heart-shaped mirror goes on the wall, then paintings of birds flitting merrily through the sky. A pretty bureau, its drawers lined with sweet-smelling cedar. All fresh. All new.

Then the old things. The wooden animals. Elepent. Charlie's wagon of blocks. The bully bull from Mexico.

"It may be time," says Mrs. Lindbergh, "to put them away."

We pack them carefully, wrapping each toy in tissue paper and laying it gently in the boxes. I arrange Elepent's trunk down the center of his belly, smooth his ears over his eyes as the words "Night night" come to me. Rubbing the bull's worn wooden sides—so many fights with that camel!—I feel the tip of one horn has broken and think, *I'm sorry, Bully*. Then put him away.

The next day, I tell the Lindberghs I am going home. A small part of me waits for them to say, *No! Oh, Betty, you mustn't. The new baby—how can we trust our child with anyone else?*

But they don't. They say they understand and that they are sorry. I see her shoulders relax. I look to him, those eyes, the calm impassive face of a man who will not pretend. And I know: there will be a new baby, with new things and new people. The rest will be put away. They are glad to see me go.

The day of my departure, I go downstairs, expecting to see Ellerson with the car. Instead, I find Colonel Lindbergh. Who says, "I'm going to teach you how to drive."

"What, now?"

He opens the driver's side door: *Yes, now.*

It is not a kindness, I realize. It's something he feels is missing in me, something he wants to correct. A test is the last thing I want as a farewell, but it seems impossible to refuse.

My trunk is already packed in the back. I sit down behind the wheel, which seems impossibly large and unwieldy. I feel not big enough to drive. I have to sit as straight as I can, lift my head to its highest point to see out. The key is in the ignition; hesitant, I reach for it. The Colonel barks, "No," and I jerk my hand back.

He looks at me for a long moment, then asks, "What do you know about this car?"

It has four wheels? A joke would provoke violence. ". . . That I don't know what I should?"

"Good. What's the first thing you might want to know?"

I gaze at the dashboard. What does a car need to go? "Petrol?"

"That's right. Check your gas levels. Do you have enough in the tank to get where you're going? Say if you don't know."

"I've no idea what it takes to get to the Anchor Line in New York."

He thinks. "Twenty-Fourth Street, West Side? Takes about a gallon and a half of gas."

I look at the fuel gauge. "It says three-quarters full." I try to think of the right thing to ask. "How many gallons in a tank?"

"Say ten."

He waits for me to say so out loud, to commit to an answer. "So, we have enough."

"What else?"

"I don't know how cars work," I tell him.

"I know." He seems pleased by the admission. "But think: What could go wrong? Remember, it's the unforeseen."

"If it's the unforeseen . . ."

"Then you have to imagine what could go wrong. And the things that can be foreseen, you have to prepare for."

I think. "Tires?"

"Yes, you check the air pressure in the tires."

I feel foolish getting out of the car. But I am aware of him watching me as I make my way around, looking at all four, pressing each with my thumb. Then I think, What if . . . ? And ask, "Do we have a spare?"

"Don't ask me. Look for yourself," says the Colonel.

We have a spare. Only partly kidding, I say, "What if more than one goes flat?"

"Then you take the next ship. Keep looking. There are five other things."

I think to check the lights and the brakes. But he has to tell me to check the oil and water. Then he says, "All right. Now what?"

Again I reach for the key. This time all he has to do is put a hand up. "Why are there mirrors in the car?"

"To see who's behind you."

"And who's behind you?"

I'm about to say no one when he points to the two mirrors. I look in each—and see Alfred inching a car out of the garage. I ask, "Should I let him go first?"

"No," he says firmly. "You go first."

Making my way to the winding road that leads to and from the house, I am frantic with nerves, stopping and starting in a herky-jerky rhythm. I glance at the Colonel, expecting him to say this was a bad idea and take over. But he simply watches the road, as if our awkward progress is completely normal.

"I'm worried I'll miss the boat," I say.

The Colonel shakes his head. It is only noon. Missing the boat is not something to think about now; it will only be an excuse for me not to do it.

As we wind down the hill, I am aware of the house behind me, the twists of the road ahead. Turning the wheel, I am unnerved by the differences between how I think the car will shift direction and how it does. First I turn too hard, then too timidly.

"It's difficult," I complain, half hoping he'll take over.

"Good." It's a small measure of praise; if I had said fun, he would have told me to stop the car.

Finally, we crawl through the gate at the bottom of the hill. I exhale and he almost smiles. For a time, it is open road and straight enough that I begin to enjoy the sensation of being carried along. No, I correct myself, not carried. The car is listening to me, even though it is far bigger and heavier than I. It's my hands on the big, ungainly wheel, my foot on the pedal that's propelling us here and there. Looking at the dashboard, I see an array of circles, almost like stars. Large one speed, smaller one with an "E" and "F" on either side, petrol. There are switches, buttons, even a clock. Everything you have to know, displayed in numbers, arrows, and slashes in a space less than six feet. It is immensely pleasing in its clarity.

"If I take my hands away," I ask, "what happens?"

"The machine doesn't know where to go. It'll go straight for a while, then a bump or dip could send it off course. It's not made to think. You are. That means you have an obligation to."

The stately houses and bustling stores give way to farmland, miles and miles of space with not a soul present and the only signs of people rude wooden fences and the occasional house. We don't even have other cars for company; the road is mine. I let my foot be heavier on the gas, panicking slightly as we speed up. But I become accustomed to it. Then thrilled. I find myself laughing. The improbability of me, Bessie Gow, racing through America. Although here, whizzing past fields, under a sky that could not care less, I feel I am no longer Bessie Gow, or Betty Gow. I am free even of myself.

"Eyes on the road," he says.

"Yes, I know."

As we approach the Palisades, the traffic increases. I see a flash of light in the rearview mirror. ". . . Car."

"That's right."

The other driver is going faster, gaining on us, making himself known. I'm too slow and he wants me to hurry up or he'll pass me.

"What do I do?" I ask the Colonel.

"Are you where you're supposed to be?"

I look to my left. From what I can see, I am driving on my side. "I am. But he's going to pass me."

"Probably."

I edge over to the right. "There's a ditch on this side," says the Colonel. I edge back left. The car is now just behind us.

"Steady."

I feel the presence of the other car pulling at me like a magnet. Our turning wheels so close, it seems we should be joined. I have to fight to keep the wheel in its place, not yank it so we turn straight into the other car's path. As it is, I feel the lure of drifting, connection, collision.

The other car suddenly speeds up, charging ahead, then disappears up the road.

"Always look out," says the Colonel, "for the other damn fool."

Is that an admission, I wonder, that we are also damn fools? That he is as well? Is this forgiveness or rebuke?

Before we cross the bridge, the Colonel takes over. I think of the house I have left behind, think of people still moving through its rooms, caring for its owners. For all its luxury, it is a world small and numbingly familiar. Instead of the roar of wind and engine, silence and the polite, empty phrases from people crammed in and sick of one another. They call America the land of the free, but I've not felt that at all until today. That is, I suppose, a reason Lindbergh means so much to people. Freedom is a thing he understands.

At the wharf, he finds a porter to take my trunk. Waits as I check to make sure I have my ticket in order. Before I head to the gangplank, I hesitate. Most people would say it is a moment that requires something. A farewell of some kind. Charles Lindbergh is not most people. He is not someone I have liked, and with good reason. But if Mrs. Lindbergh welcomed me into the house, he has shown me how to get free of it. And for that, I say sincerely, "Thank you."

It is a long voyage, a rocky voyage. I am not seasick, but I stay in bed just the same, letting myself rise and fall with the waves. I dream of a wave so large, it overturns the boat, sending us all spinning slowly to the bottom. I think that would not be terrible. To spin in darkness and hear nothing more of what goes on above the surface. This is the same ocean Lindbergh crossed. No swells and rolls for him, no lying deep in the rhythms of a storm. He was far above, so high up the world was all just lines and shapes.

It is not until I see the coast of England that I realize, I am no longer the Lindbergh Nanny. There will be no car, no Ellerson with his cheeky salute. I'll have to drag my things through myself. Find trains, find taxis. I can't remember now, the exact way home, and the routes might have changed. I'll have to find people, ask questions. The thought of it makes me feel cranky and tired.

As I wait on the dock in Glasgow for my trunk, I take a deep, self-mocking whiff of fish and salt. The buildings here do not challenge the sky, except perhaps the cathedral. Old voices shouting all around me, I start to adjust my ears to the accents of years ago.

"Bessie?"

The woman coming toward me is fuller than I remember. The iron-gray hair has silvered in places. But my first thought—*Oh, Mum, that dress!*—does not surprise me. Nor does her faintly anxious look, the hand held out, but only partway in case I don't take it.

It startles her, how fast I come to her, how hard I hold on. I don't think she's heard me cry in ages. But she steadies herself, keeps on her feet, and doesn't let me fall.

Chapter Twenty-Seven

Glasgow, Scotland

Agnes says I have an accent. James wants to know, did I ever meet George Raft? "Were you away?" says Alex. "I never noticed." I do sound different, but it's not an accent, it's my domestic voice: clipped, less Scottish, bland. All you hear is the efficiency; the feelings and particulars are scrubbed out.

I settle back into my mother's house and wait for the other, harder questions. But they don't come. My family talks of my time in America as if I'd been on holiday. Billy and Jean's wedding photo has been moved to a central place in the parlor, but no one ever refers to Billy.

One afternoon, my mother has friends over. She calls upstairs, "Bessie, come down and say hello." Taking a cup of tea, I smile politely at the circle: Mrs. Bright, Mrs. Maxwell, and Mrs. McWhorter. The talk is of people I haven't seen, occasions I missed. *Do you remember Doris Stephens, you should pay a call, she married the McBride boy.*

I hesitate, trying to remember Doris. As I do, Mrs. Maxwell asks, "Do you hear from them at all?"

"... The McBrides?"

"The Lindberghs."

Before I can say no, my mother says, "Now let's not," even as Mrs. McWhorter says, "Awful thing, *awful*."

"Bessie, dear," says my mother, "would you bring in some more cream? We've run low."

We haven't, but I take up the jug and flee to the kitchen. Through the door, I hear murmurs, stern, instructional. My mother letting her friends know we will not be speaking of *that*. When I return, it's to a ring of pleasant faces. I set the creamer down, say, "It's been lovely seeing you. I'm afraid I have a dreadful headache."

A few days later, my mother says gaily, "Letter for you from America!" And while I grumble inside, not *that* exciting, she needn't make a fuss, I tear open the envelope, eager and wondering, Elsie? Ellerson? Perhaps Mrs. Lindbergh, although the stationery's not first-rate . . .

The letter is oddly folded, the paper packed into a tiny square. I unfold it, see that the handwriting is large, sloping. All capital letters.

YOU KILLED THAT BABY
I HOPE YOU DIE FOR WHAT YOU DID

I crush it, wringing it between my fists. Then tear it. Over and over, until it's confetti. I fight the impulse to toss it high in the air, let the ugliness flutter all over my mother's entry hall. But the thought of her distress at the litter—*What on earth is this?*—makes me teary and I leave the house, walking down the road to throw it away.

More letters come. From America, but England and Scotland as well. I should hang, I should burn, I should be in prison. They know what I did, they know what I am, they know the truth. *Do you?* I think wearily looking at one. *Well, bloody good for you.*

The newspapers find me. One day as I'm coming back from the market, a fellow from the *Daily Mail* calls out, "Red Johnson says he means to marry you." I tell him, "It's ridiculous," and refuse further comment.

Next come the suggestions. The bright ideas that suddenly occur to my family—as if they hadn't been discussed privately over the phone or with a cup of tea. My mother says why don't I stop by Little's, where I used to work, they'd be so pleased to see me. James observes that the family down the road from him just had their fifth baby and could use some help. Alex says it's a shame I'm so useless, perhaps I should teach?

One afternoon, Agnes recounts her trip to the High Street, mentioning, "They're hiring at Darby's." Darby's is a small dress shop that caters to older ladies and younger women browbeaten by their mothers.

"Darby's," my mother echoes, glancing at me. This time, I won't be permitted to ignore the hint.

"I can't work with customers," I say flatly. "The store would be overwhelmed with gawkers."

"Gawkers buy things," says Agnes.

They also scream at you and spit on you. But my mother and sister have no idea how badly some people need to hate; to them it will sound like an excuse. Perhaps it is.

I say, "Fine. Tomorrow, I will go down to Darby's."

Carefully, I make my way through the crowded streets. I become aware that no one is looking at me. No glances or hard stares. One gentleman crosses my path awkwardly, touches the brim of his hat in apology, and moves on. As I approach the shop, I find myself praying that the position has been filled. But the HELP WANTED card is still there in the window.

I tell the lady behind the counter I am interested in the job. She reacts warmly, letting me know the clothes I put on this morning were well chosen. As I answer her questions, I remember, I do actually know things. How to talk to women about clothes, handle difficult people. She asks for my most recent job experience and I say, "I was in America, working as a nurse."

At that she narrows her eyes, as if she's mislaid her glasses and needs to refocus. "Isobel Taylor's daughter."

"Yes, that's right."

"Well, then." She smiles. "We'll be in touch."

A week later, the sign is still in the window, but even Agnes must admit, they are not going to call. It is the same at the Rose Café. And at Frobisher's Market and Argus Chemist's. Mr. Talt at the bank takes one look at my typing test and says, "I'm sorry, love." Even the family on James's street seems to have found someone to help with the baby. It doesn't stop my mother from pointing out every single child-minder position in the entire city of Glasgow.

One morning over breakfast, I say, "No one is going to hire me to look after their child. No one."

My mother has prepared for this argument. "I don't see why not. If you were good enough for Charles Lindbergh . . ."

After months, her persistent idiocy is enraging. "'And look what happened to that baby!' That's what they say."

"No one blames you, Bessie."

"They do," I say bluntly. "And even if they don't, so many girls wanting work now, you don't go out and hire a woman whose last charge was . . ."

Kidnapped. Murdered. I don't want to say the words. Thankfully, my mother interrupts. "You're just scared, is what it is."

She says this as if it is irrational for me never to want to work with children again. Caught between denying it's true and defending the way I feel, I throw up my hands.

Then my stepfather says, "Bessie's right. It has to be something else." He looks at me, repeats, "It has to be something else."

But everywhere, it is the same. *We'll call. We'll be in touch.* Or: *Oh, that position's filled, I'm afraid.*

Or as one woman puts it, "I'm sorry, love, I just can't see it."

One day, I am sorting through my purse, cleaning out the rubbish, when I come across a small white envelope and think, *What on earth . . . ?* I wave it, too light for a letter. Opening the flap I see nothing at first. Then tucked in the corner, a wisp of yellow. Charlie's hair from when we cut it in Maine. I touch it with my pinkie, remembering not the horror, but the chubby, stubborn, merry boy laughing as he leapt from cushions, offered seashells, or settled heavy and yawning against me. A bit of him still here.

There you go, Charlie. Can't stop you.

After a year, the hateful letters have dwindled. Still, my mother sets my post aside so anything suspicious can be sent to the police. Jean leaves Izzy with us a few days a week now, so we are especially careful about what comes into the house. A month after the anniversary of when Charlie was found, I come downstairs to find her holding an envelope. "It's from America," she says. "McCann?"

"Joseph McCann?" She nods and I take it from her. "Oh, my goodness."

I read it at the kitchen table. He starts with "Dear Miss Gow" and I smile at the formality.

I hope this letter finds you well. Well, I hope this letter finds you, period. I figured your mother's address was a good place to start.

He writes that he has had a promotion. A wood specialist has traced the ladder back to the Bronx. They're finding the ransom money all across New York's Upper East Side.

Apparently, our guy likes the Lexington Avenue train. On the last day to exchange gold bills, a man turned up at the Chemical Bank in New York and exchanged $2,980 of the ransom money. Gave the name J. J. Faulkner, said his address 537 West 149th Street. Funny thing— nobody by the name of J. J. Faulkner lives there.

The name J. J. Faulkner ripples through my memory. But when I try to put a face to it, I can't; perhaps it is one of those names that just sounds as if you've heard it before.

I do have two pieces of sad news. Olly Whateley died. He went into the hospital a few weeks ago for stomach pains. It was an ulcer that turned into peritonitis. By the time they opened him up, it was too late. His wife was in England when it happened.

I feel my fingers at my lip, hear my mother say, "What? What is it?"

"Someone I worked with died. His wife—Elsie, I wrote you about her. She was very kind to me."

Ellerson has skipped town. Took the Morrow car and rode off one day. His wife says she hasn't heard from him. Even his mother says she has no idea where he is.

This time I make no gesture, no noise. I sense I have learned something important, but I'm not clear on the meaning. Like when you're swimming and you reach down with your toes, feel nothing. And wonder, Wait, how did this happen? I was so sure . . .

No, I think. No. Really, this isn't surprising. Ellerson hated being stuck. Couldn't be home, couldn't be at the boardinghouse. Happiest when he was living on the edge of a playing card, tipping back a bottle, or riding around with his friend. And he was always borrowing the car. One day he took it too far and thought just keep going rather than face the consequences. He went on a gambling spree, got drunk . . .

Or he crashed. Again. Maybe broke more than his arm. Or . . . or . . . he and that fellow from the taxi stand decided finally *to hell with it* and went off somewhere.

I like that last vision. But it doesn't feel true.

I try to tell myself: Ellerson may be gone. Fix that in my mind so I can mourn. But all I hear is that joke he made about Violet. *Died for our sins.* Banks, telling the police he saw Ellerson at Sha-Toe, throwing twenty-dollar bills around . . .

But the memory of Banks takes me to memories of Violet—that wink—and the fierce feeling she was *guilty*. She was a selfish girl, always looking for someone to take care of her, mean something to her. Maybe she lied to protect someone else, but that someone certainly wasn't Ellerson.

I know you're lying low these days, so I'll understand if you don't write back. But we're going to get this guy, I promise. If you come back for the trial, maybe you'll let me buy you dinner.

Dear God, I think, folding the letter. So much loss. Violet dead. Whateley dead. Marguerite and her husband back in Germany. Ellerson . . . gone. And Betty Gow? *Whatever happened to her?*

Sitting down, I write two letters. First to Joe McCann, thanking him for writing. And then to Elsie, saying how very sorry I am to hear about Mr. Whateley.

My family makes quite a fuss on my birthday, gathering at the house— all the siblings with their families. "You must celebrate!" says Agnes. "Just an excuse for a party," says Alex. Izzy helps me blow out the candles, because I am very old now, I tell her. Thirty. A wonder I'm still breathing.

It's the girl next door who tells me. Claire. She's fourteen. Bored at home and likes to talk. About boys, films, clothes—she's at that age where every new dress is a new self, every conversation a chance to shine, every nice-looking boy a possible future. I can remember it. Being like that.

I suppose it's because she's young, she's the one who dares. Catching me as I head to market, she says breathlessly, "Did you see, Miss? They've caught him."

I've no idea who she means. "Who?"

"The kidnapper, Miss. In America."

She shows me the newspaper. LINDBERGH KIDNAPPER IN JAIL: BRUNO RICHARD HAUPTMANN ARRESTED IN LINDY CASE.

"That's you, isn't it, Miss?"

Izzy has questions. Am I really going to America? Will I be on the radio? Can she listen? Why do I have to travel with a different name? Most important, will I bring her a present? I say I will and she's to think about what she wants.

She's not so clear on why I'm going; she's asked several times, but our answers haven't helped. We've told her I'm going to help put a very bad man in jail. But when she asks why he's a bad man, what has he done, it's hard. Finally, because she'll hear it somewhere, I tell her that this man took a child from his mummy and daddy and now they don't have their little boy anymore. It will never, ever happen to her—these are things that happen in America. It's a small lie, but necessary.

Izzy, whose father was taken from her in America when she was a baby, understands death better than we think. But she looks at me, upset, puzzled, and in a flash, I sense why.

"Do you remember that I was a nurse in America?" She nods. "He was one of the children I looked after."

"What was his name?" she asks.

"Charlie."

He would be four too, I realize. Suddenly long and lanky, fast like Izzy. She runs everywhere, no one can catch her. Running off to the future, says Jean. Charlie never got to outrun us.

I swallow the ache in my throat, tell Izzy to make me a list. No more than three things and something I can put in a suitcase.

I am packing when my brother Alex comes into my room. Plump and slope shouldered, Alex is the cleverest of us. He'll say things others won't and doesn't give a toss about things that worry most. He and I never had much to say to each other before; but somehow since I'm back, I've appreciated him more.

Now he says, "D'you remember the Morrisons down the road?"

Just like Alex. You can be racing around, trying to get actual things done, and he'll want to start a conversation about the moon's impact on the tides or some such. But the Morrisons ring a bell. He was a loud, beefy man who made the same jokes over and over; she was a tiny thing who never spoke. I can remember thinking, *I don't want that when I'm married.*

"Do you remember Stevie, their little boy?" I don't and shake my head. "Maybe it was after you left. He died when he was two. Tragic accident."

So, this is not one of Alex's moon conversations. I'm about to tell him if he's trying to make me feel philosophical about the loss of children, it is not the right time. But then, swaying against the doorjamb, he says, "The thing is, everyone knew Fred Morrison did it. Couldn't prove it, mind. If the parents say the child had a bad fall, well, have to believe them, don't you? But Fred Morrison was always one for . . ." He raises a fist.

Uncomprehending, I shake my head.

Shutting the door, he murmurs, "Someone loses their temper. Bit of discipline, goes too far. Generally what happens, isn't it? You always said he was odd."

"Colonel Lindbergh?"

He nods. "One of your letters, you called him a sadist."

I remember that letter. Written after the Colonel hid Charlie in the closet. I was in a rage and needed to say what I felt for once.

"Careless with the baby," Alex adds.

He was. I can't deny it. Still, I say, "No."

"You're not in America anymore, Bess. You can say what you like."

It's not what I like, it's the truth, I think. But Alex has made me wonder: Why did I never suspect the Lindberghs themselves? Because when a child dies, you do think of the parents first. And yet I never did. Why? Because they're rich? Famous? It's true, I have some ugly memories of Colonel Lindbergh with his son. But there are others: him flying Charlie through the air, gazing at him, wondering, his voice soft as he said, "Hi, Buster," as if he couldn't quite believe this little person who so resembled him was his.

But this is sentimentality, of course. Things I feel. How do I *know*? I think back to that awful night. The stories I told the police so many times. The stories I will have to tell again in court.

"Do you think I'm a liar, Alex?" I ask my brother.

"Course not." His round face is endearingly indignant.

"Then you believe me when I say I put that child to bed at eight o'clock." He nods. "The Colonel didn't get home until afterward: eight thirty. That's when we heard his car. Charlie was already asleep. There was no . . . Fred Morrison moment."

"Still leaves an hour and a half until you found he was missing."

"From eight twenty-five to nine fifteen, Lindbergh was in the house, eating dinner with Mrs. Lindbergh." I think of that car we heard earlier, what I now think of as Hauptmann's car. "But let's say he arrived a little earlier, say eight ten. In those fifteen minutes, he gets a ladder none of us had ever seen before, climbs through the window, murders his son, puts him in the trunk of his car to bury later? Then has dinner with his wife?"

Briefly stymied, Alex thinks. "Maybe it was another joke, a kidnapping prank like he pulled that other time. Only it went wrong."

"There's a lot I'll say about Colonel Lindbergh, Alex, but no man drives for nearly two hours and decides to go climbing through windows before he's even had dinner for a joke."

"After dinner then. According to the papers, there was nearly an hour no one knew where he was."

"It was his own rule that no one go into Charlie's room between bedtime and ten o'clock. But all right, according to you, he broke that rule and went and murdered his son, sleeping just down the hall from his wife, *and* he wrote a ransom note on the spot, making it sound German, to confuse the police, devising a fairly complicated symbol to go with it. He got the baby out of the house without any of us noticing, hiding the body until he could put it in the woods later. And not because he lost his temper, but because . . . ?"

Alex shrugs. "Maybe he wanted to be rid of the baby. You said he was keen on breeding, superior genes and all that. Maybe he felt his namesake didn't quite measure up."

It is the old ugly rumor. Charlie was deaf, Charlie was brain damaged. Because Mrs. Lindbergh flew when she was pregnant with him. His head was too big, his knees too wobbly, the fontanel hadn't closed.

"There was nothing wrong with that little boy. *Nothing*. He was strong. Talking. He knew the names of animals, he knew . . ."

My name. My throat tightens.

"He was perfect," I manage.

"Not everyone would judge perfection—or imperfection—the same way."

"If the Lindberghs wanted to hide an imperfect child, they could have done it without involving the police forces of two states, the U.S. government, and Scotland Yard. Not to mention the press. If secrecy is what you're after, why create an event that will draw the world to your door? They had all sorts of medical connections through his work with the institute. The Morrows have been hiding Dwight Junior's illness for years. If Fred Morrison can get away with it, you think Charles Lindbergh can't? If he had killed Charlie, he wouldn't have put on a fake kidnapping for all the world to see. That would have . . . demeaned him. And he wouldn't have needed to. One doctor's certificate stating tragic accident would be all he needed."

Alex peers at me. "I thought you didn't like him."

"Liking doesn't come into it. I've had too many stories made up about me by people who wanted me to be guilty because it made a good story. It's a cruel thing to do to anyone. Even Charles Lindbergh."

It is a much nicer crossing than the first one I made to America. The Lindberghs have paid for a second-class ticket. My own cabin. A better dining room with proper silverware.

I'm almost certain the woman at the next table has recognized me. Twice now when I've looked up from my tea, she's made a great show of looking for the waiter. Even then, her eyes have flicked back to me, checking: Can she go on staring?

I turn the page of my book. Just as she wants to give the impression she has not noticed me, I want to give the impression I've not noticed her. They're like dogs, these people. Meet their eye and they can turn nasty.

Douglas, you'll never guess who's on board! The Lindbergh Nanny!

Only I've not been the Lindbergh Nanny for two years now. That girl in the white uniform with the big dark eyes and heavy brows. "Pretty Betty Gow." On this trip, I'm down as Elizabeth Mowat.

I dab at my mouth with the napkin, say to the waiter, "May I have the bill, please?"

Did I imagine it? I wonder as I leave the dining room. Agnes would be laughing. Alex saying gravely, *That seagull's got his eye on you, Bessie.* Billy gruff and teasing, *Always thinks she's the one they've come to see.*

"Let's have a look at you, then!"

My head lurches, not by my will. My first thought is that a gull has flown too close, its wing striking my face. I feel a clumsy gripping at my jaw. A gust of warm breath, the smell of someone else's lunch.

Someone has taken hold of my face.

The woman peers at me. "You're the nanny, aren't you?"

I swing wildly, knocking her hand away. She makes a noise of outrage; how dare I? And I find I am ashamed, desperate to be out of her sight, out of everyone's sight. As I walk hurriedly to my cabin, I think, I can't do this. I can't. In America, it'll be worse, so much worse. Then the trip back. Everyone seeing it in the papers.

Well, I won't get off the ship. I'll simply stay. Say they have to take me back, I won't get off.

It's absurd, of course. They'd never allow it. Besides, I have to do it. I can't, but I have to. If I don't, it'll never end. People will say, *Well, she didn't come back for the trial. Must have been afraid of what they'd ask.*

And Charlie. I have to do it for Charlie. Justice is a grown-up thing.

Chapter Twenty-Eight

Flemington, New Jersey

He doesn't look a thing like Charlie, the new baby. He's dark like his mother, long and watchful where Charlie was stocky and noisy. Mrs. Lindbergh and her mother greet me at Englewood, embracing me warmly as if I've just come back for a friendly visit. She and the Colonel, she says, have been traveling. They have been to California, Greenland, North Haven, of course, Iceland, Russia, Switzerland, Spain, Portugal, South America, Africa. They have even been to Detroit. She recounts all this as if it were just what she needed, highly diverting, great fun. But there's a blankness in her eyes, an anxiety under the gaiety, as if she can't quite remember who she is and, with only a few clues, she's trying to sound like the lady she's supposed to be.

A large German shepherd trots into the room. I ask, "Who's this lovely boy?" and hold out my hand. He growls, his lips trembling above his teeth.

"That's Thor," says Mrs. Lindbergh with a sudden smile. "He follows me everywhere. It's quite thrilling."

. . .

"They want to destroy you" is the first thing Attorney General David Wilentz tells me. The prosecutor in the case, he has come to Englewood to prepare me. He's a slight, dark man, given to quick movement—an agitating presence, which I suppose works well in court. As he paces in front of me, hand on his chin, I can feel my breathing speed up to match his steps.

"Hauptmann's lawyer, Mr. Reilly, has nothing," he tells me. "The police found thirteen thousand dollars of the ransom money in his garage. One of the ladder rails matches wood cut from his attic floorboards, his handwriting matches the notes. He's German, lives six blocks from Woodlawn Cemetery. He quit his job right after the ransom drop, and he's been spending money ever since. Even had Condon's telephone number written in his closet; when the police asked him why, he said he was reading about the case in the paper and jotted it down."

I nod: *Not terribly believable.* And think: $13,000? Can he have spent all the rest in two years?

"Reilly's going to try and confuse the issue. Any mud he can get to stick to you is less mud on his client. He's going to bring up Detroit, the Purple Gang. Show you to the jury as a gal who runs around with a sailor named Red, a man she's not engaged to, a man not in the country legally. She brings him into the family home, the family that's trusted her with the sacred duty of caring for their child. Red Johnson—are you in contact with him?"

"I had a letter from him a few months ago, telling me he'd married. I wrote back congratulating him, but otherwise, we've not corresponded."

He nods; this is an acceptable answer, and I've delivered it well. Then he says, "You're going up right after Mrs. Lindbergh. I want to see calm, composure—a pillar of respectability."

I only see the Colonel once and that is, I think, by accident. He comes out of the library as I am passing, says, "Betty! How's the driving?"

"I don't get much practice in Glasgow." Or call for it, as I rarely leave my mother's house.

He nods, faintly disappointed. It had been on some list, I think, of things that I needed to learn. In order to be better. Also now, we have nothing easy to talk of. He is older. The hair is darker, thinner, the bright blue eyes have narrowed. You wonder if they take in the whole of the horizon these days. I suspect it has been some time since anyone has seen the cockeyed, boyish grin of 1927.

Casting about for anything to speak of other than the trial, I smile at a newspaper, neatly folded on a side table so that a family member or guest might take it in with them to the library. A Banks touch, I think. Then remember Banks is no longer here.

The Colonel, sensing the shift in my attention, looks at the headlines. One catches my eye: SUPREMACY IN AIR IS HITLER'S ANSWER TO BRITISH.

He asks if I am an admirer of the German chancellor, allowing almost puckishly that I may not be, given that I am British. "Scottish," I remind him. "Hitler seems a bully to me. My brother James does a very funny impression."

He nods in a way that lets me know he doesn't think much of my brother and his impressions. Then declares, "I think he's doing a great deal for Germany. Rebuilding on one of the strongest foundations there is."

"What's that?"

"Defeat," he says. "Loss."

I nod politely, thinking, *Humiliation. Rage.*

Then with a brief grip on my arm, he says, "Thank you for coming." And leaves me in the hallway, recalling when we first met and I compared him to the newsreels of the hero, that singular figure standing on the balcony, above cheering, hysterical crowds.

The night before my testimony, I stand at the window of the Morrow house and gaze down the hill, trying to see the little guard box at the gate. Waiting for the man inside to step out for a moment. Have a cigarette. As he used to.

I saw him as we came in. Alfred slowed as we drove past, and there he was. Only he looked . . . quite different.

But perhaps I only want to think it was Ellerson.

Actually, I don't want to think so. I desperately hope it wasn't.

The town of Flemington is seventy miles from Englewood, but only fourteen from the old Hopewell house. In ordinary times, it's a place where chicken farmers come to sell their goods: eggs, meat, feathers for fishing lures. By sundown, the town is quiet. Everyone is in their homes, tending to their lives, minding their own business. Many young people leave for better opportunities elsewhere.

On January 1, 1935, America comes to Flemington. It is the only place anyone wants to be. The streets are heaving with people, the hotels full, the restaurants open from 7:00 A.M. to midnight. Before dawn, people line up in the frigid cold to get tickets of admission to the courthouse; some of the more enterprising sightseers sell theirs for vast sums. Everywhere, people are buying, selling. "Signed" photos of the Lindberghs. Tiny ladders on green string, meant to be worn around the neck as jewelry. Bags of yellow hair, supposedly Charlie's. The hotel serves Lamb Chops Jafsie, named for Dr. Condon's initials, and Lindy sundaes. It is a carnival. It is a den of thieves. As Alfred tries to navigate the car through the streets overrun with people, I am terrified of the car windows. They are only glass, easily smashed.

I can't do this, I think for the hundredth time. I have to do this.

I feel Elsie slip her arm through mine. Pull me close. "You look lovely," she whispers. "They'll think you're a movie star, wanting to see the trial."

I nudge her. "Pair of movie stars."

But this is just brave, silly talk and once it fades, I struggle to stay calm. I keep forgetting to breathe. Then I have to take these great gasps that leave me dizzy. I watch the back of Alfred's head as he assesses the crush around us. He's frustrated; I can sense his foot on the pedal, wanting to push down hard. Every time the car stops, people crowd around, peer through the windows; a few of them even rap on the window or bang on the car. I see their mouths move, hear my name muffled through the glass.

Suddenly, I can't stand it, the inching forward. "Shall we get out? It might be better to walk."

"In this?" Alfred jerks his head to the crowd. "You'll never make it."

I inhale deeply, stretch against the back of the seat. My heart's gone still, it's stopped beating. I put a hand to my chest, pinch using my nails. I can't do this. I have to do this.

For a moment, I'm back with Charlie as Ellerson drives us to the airfield in Long Island. Him pulling at his shoe as I babble at him, *"Today's the day your mummy's going to become a pilot. She's going to fly a plane. That's silly, you say, Mummy already flies planes . . ."*

Someone—me, I suppose—says, "I can't . . ."

Alfred tries to look back. "What'd she say?"

Elsie puts a firm hand on my arm. "She's fine, just keep going."

Elsie doesn't understand. I'm not fine. I want to be, so much. But I can't control my heart, which is about to explode. "No, truly, I can't."

"You can," she says. "Think of Mrs. Lindbergh. She's speaking today. Think of what it is for her."

Alfred gets as close to the courthouse as he can. Then there's nothing left but for me and Elsie to get out. As we do, I hear the hum of the crowd rise in fury, sense a shift in the wave of people toward us. The weight of hundreds of bodies pressing in. The police step in between us and the crowd. Elsie and I lock arms, put our heads down, our feet moving swiftly one after the other along the ground.

Once we're inside, the noise ebbs. We separate. I adjust Elsie's hat, which has been knocked askew. She straightens my tartan scarf. "Now," she says. "Big smiles."

We turn as a camera flashes in our eyes, capturing us for the public.

My first impression of the courtroom is that someone's left a door open and the crowd outside has found its way in. I've seen more organized prizefights. Far too many people, chairs askew, people standing at the back, by the windows, leaning over the gallery. Men wearing hats, jackets on, off, ties straight, loosened. At every window, faces peer in from outside. From the back, I see Colonel Lindbergh's head, still and neutral. He's simply present while everyone else turns and twists to get a look at him. My eyes drift to the other side of the room; I catch a glimpse of fair hair; it's the man who took Charlie from us. Panicked at the thought of seeing him, I jerk my head skyward. People must think I'm having a fit. Elsie and I take our seats. Calm, I remind myself. Composure.

I keep my eyes firmly fixed on the front of the room. The judge, the wooden chair where the witness sits. When Mrs. Lindbergh walks swiftly to the stand, my long-ago impression of her as a poised young girl returns. She is dressed in a black suit with a pink blouse and wearing a black beret. She sits immediately in the chair and is asked to step down again to take the oath. As she raises her hand and recites, "I swear to tell the whole truth and nothing but the truth . . . ," she looks so tiny, yet resolute, the buzzing frenetic courtroom goes silent. When she's repeated, "So help me God," she climbs back into the chair.

The first questions Mr. Wilentz asks are simple. Dull. Who she is, where she lives. I suppose it has to be in the record, but it's almost as if he's giving her a chance to get comfortable. She sits bent forward at the waist, shoulders tight, her hands bunched in her lap. Her voice is quiet, you have to work to hear. But she's composed. I can't help thinking she knows everyone here wants something big and dramatic, and she's determined not to give it to them. For one thing, the Colonel has told her not to. In a rare unguarded moment, Mrs. Morrow has told me of a terrible fight—attack, really—in which Lindbergh told his wife she lived too much in her feelings, that she lacked discipline. That she was a failure.

When Mr. Wilentz asks who else was in the house that day, she answers, "Betty Gow." Hearing my name for the first time, I flinch, as if accused.

He asks Charlie's age. She says, "Twenty months."

Two words, a measurement of time. But they conjure that bustling, babbling time when you're not quite ready for "years." Ready tears and easy joy, peekaboo your only notion of deception. I taste salt at the back of my mouth. Behind me, I hear a woman let out a high, thin keening sound. A man up the row has his mouth buried in his handkerchief.

Mrs. Lindbergh is candid. She is precise. When Wilentz's questions are vague, she asks that he clarify. Charlie is never mentioned by name, always referred to as "the child." When asked the color of his hair, she says it was light golden. He asks if the child was normal and she says he was. She says he called all the members of the household by name. Wilentz asks if he understood when he was addressed, did he understand what was being said to him. I think of his last night, how little he would have understood of what was happening.

At one point, there is commotion at the back of the court; someone is sobbing. The judge asks if everyone will remain as quiet as possible. I set my gaze to the floor. I grip my jaw with my fingers to stop it shaking. Bury my teeth in my lower lip, intent on that small, sharp pain.

Finally, Wilentz asks her about her return to the nursery, now empty. "Now when you went in there, who had preceded you in there, do you know?"

"As far as I know, only Miss Gow."

A low rumble of outrage. Mrs. Lindbergh has simply said what was true. But for some, the meaning is plain. Only I could have handed Charlie to the man who took him. Does she know that is what people hear? Does she mean for them to hear it?

The judge asks Mr. Wilentz if he is through. He says yes. I feel a lurch of panic, then remember, the lawyer defending that man gets to ask his questions. I am not next. There is still time.

Mr. Reilly stands. "The defense feels that the grief of Mrs. Lindbergh requires no cross-examination."

I look to Elsie, unsure what has happened. Mrs. Lindbergh steps down; she keeps her head high, avoiding everyone's eye. I cannot be as she is. Calm, precise—I look blindly at her husband, he is proud of her now, most proud when she shows the least feeling.

A few moments later, my name is called. Once, then again to be heard over the outburst of murmurs, people shifting in their seats in anticipation. The mood in the room has turned cold. Hostile. They are waiting for Betty Gow, the nurse who was the last person to see the baby alive. *She who left unlocked . . .*

"The prosecution calls Betty Gow," Wilentz says for a third time.

"You have to go up, love," Elsie whispers.

I walk swiftly to Mr. Wilentz, surprise him by stopping at his seat. I shake my head. I can't. Not today. Not after Mrs. Lindbergh.

Thankfully, he has another star witness. "If the court please, I will call Colonel Lindbergh instead."

Because it is Friday, it will not be possible for me to appear for two days. But it is understood, on Monday, there will not be another excuse. They have paid for me to come here. They expect me to do the job. I wait for someone to say, *Everyone understands,* so that I can say they should not understand, I know my failure was cowardly and despicable. But no one does say it.

Then on Sunday, Elsie says, "Your mum's in the paper."

"Oh, God." I take it from her. "Is it awful?"

"Very nice, I'd say."

I look at the headline, just one of many covering the trial.

TELLS OF DEATH THREATS
*   Mother of Betty Gow Says Girl Got Hundreds of Letters.*
Mrs. Taylor is quoted as saying her daughter had been under a tremendous strain for two years. "Betty told me she has received hundreds on hundreds of anonymous letters many of them threatening her life.
*   But despite these she never hesitated to return to the United States to give evidence and answer all questions."*

I can see her, round little chin raised, feather in her hat quivering, eyes bright with indignation. You might think her ridiculous, old biddy drawing attention to herself, harping on and on about her daughter. Another time, I might have thought her ridiculous myself.

"But despite these she never hesitated . . ." Oh, Mum, I did hesitate. More than hesitate. I ran.

I'm amazed to see she speaks of Billy, calling him "a good, steady, reliable, hardworking lad." She hasn't said his name once since I've been home.

Well, I think. I can't very well go home and tell my mother I couldn't.

Sunday night, I find myself thinking of Violet. She died just down-stairs. In this house. She must have known it would never end. No matter what she said, who she gave them, even if the Lindberghs stood by her, telling the world, *She didn't mean to.* The only way not to be the woman who murdered the Lindbergh baby for the rest of her life was to end it. I can remember thinking: Clever Violet, switching it all up so we feel sorry for her.

She was twenty-seven years old.

Now I think, *You shouldn't have let us do that to you, Violet. Take your life. You made a mistake. Went out with the wrong man. Said the wrong thing to the wrong person at the wrong time. Maybe it was this Hauptmann, maybe someone working with him. But I feel sure you had no idea they would take Charlie. How devastating that must have been. No wonder you were half out of your mind.*

You shouldn't have sold the family's secrets. But there you're no worse than the man who snapped that image of Charlie and me in Maine.

I look to the door, remember her putting her head round, coming in when you didn't ask her, talking till your head hurt. She . . . admired me, I now realize. Wanted me as a friend. I wish now I had been.

I forgive you, Violet. I hope you forgive me.

Chapter Twenty-Nine

My black suit. Dark hat, feather small and straight. Fur stole. In my bag, one of Mother's handkerchiefs.

The papers always call me a girl. This is not a girl, looking back at me. This woman doesn't walk with her head down, mouth sulky, eyes uncertain when she looks up. This is a woman who does not hesitate to return. To give evidence. To show herself and say, I am not the pretty nurse, not the sailor's girlfriend, not Scotty Gow's mistress, not the duped woman desperate for marriage, nor a woman who would have done a single thing to harm a little boy who called her Beddy.

When Elsie knocks, I say, "Yes, I'm ready."

"Sit up straight, girl." Something my mother always says.

So I do. And Mother is right. It does put air in your lungs. I sit in the same chair where the Lindberghs sat on Friday, faced with a sea of people, all waiting for the truth of Betty Gow to be revealed. I look down. In my hands, Mother's handkerchief is a white curl of cloth, like the flame on a small candle.

My mouth is dry though, so dry. I hold my arms tight at my sides so no one sees that I am shaking all over. My body is convulsing, tremor after tremor racking me from knees to jawline. Stop it, I think, trying to be amused, as if my nervous system were a child in a tantrum. But it will not stop.

As he did with Mrs. Lindbergh, Mr. Wilentz begins with the easy questions. How I spell my name, where I am living. Then we move to the events of that night. Oddly enough, the details I was terrified of forgetting are a comfort, stones where I can put my next step and feel secure. The numbers are useful. They keep Charlie as he really was far away. The cloth I used to make his shirt is Exhibit S-29. The woolen shirt he wore over it, S-14. The hateful thumb guards, S-16. Only the thread borrowed from Elsie—*"Blue, your favorite"*—strikes me silent for a few moments.

My heart starts pounding as Wilentz comes to the journey to Trenton on the twelfth of May. His voice neutral, he asks, "And when you got to Trenton, did you go to the morgue?"

"I did."

"Did you see a body there?"

The same two dull little words. "I did."

"Whose body was it?"

I have every intention of answering. It is important. Some people say the body was another baby's, that this is all a hoax. But I am frightened, genuinely, that to say the name will make me fly apart. I look down at the handkerchief, think of my foolish lovely mother. *"But despite these, she never hesitated . . ."*

I look up. "Charles Lindbergh Junior's."

I see the shadow of satisfaction on Wilentz's face. He glances at the defense. "Take the witness."

Edward J. Reilly looks like a trout, I tell myself. Portly, bald, egg-shaped head resting on a ring of fat, he has round black glasses and a belligerent, pouty mouth. A pompous, ill-tempered old fish.

"They want to destroy you."

Well, he won't, I tell myself. He's just an old fish. But the tremors have started again. I stiffen my throat, arch my tongue to keep my jaw from trembling.

He asks if I prefer to rest a minute. I tell him I am all right.

He starts with my employment history, stressing that I am to go all the way back to the beginning. Rather than mention Rob Coutts, I say I started with a cooperative society in Glasgow.

But after only a few questions, he gets to Detroit. How long did I live there?

"About six months."

"You were single at that time?"

"I was."

"And are you single now?"

Never been married, have you, Miss Gow? is the point he's making to the jury. Why is that? I wonder. Could it be the quality of men you associate with?

"Yes," I say lightly.

"Did you associate with any young men in Detroit?"

If I show even a fraction of offense, the jury will sense controversy. Even shame. As if I've been asked if I ate breakfast this morning, I say, "I did."

"Can you give me some of the names?"

Wilentz stands. "Oh, I object to that, if Your Honor please."

"Cross-examination," pleads Reilly, spreading his hands, the picture of innocence.

They argue over it. I do not want to bring Robert Coutts's name into this courtroom. It's been four years since the police spoke to him. But if there's anything to find out, Reilly will find it.

The judge overrules the question. Reilly has to be satisfied with asking, "Have you communicated with any of these young men since you left Detroit?"

My heart eases at being able to give an answer that is both honest and honorable. "No, I haven't."

Curled finger to his lip as if he's trying to recall, he says, "You found employment with the Morrows first, or was it with the Lindberghs?"

"With the Lindberghs."

"And was that through an agency?"

This is to let the jury know I wasn't cleared by a reputable firm. "No, I was recommended by a lady's maid in the employ of Elisabeth Morrow."

"How many brothers do you have, Miss Gow?"

"I have two brothers. Alexander and James." I think to add, Neither is known as Scotty, but I'm not to give any information Reilly doesn't ask for.

Reilly peers at me. "Where is Alexander now?"

"In Glasgow, Scotland."

"And James?"

"In Glasgow, Scotland."

Reilly looks to the jury. "When did they *return* to Scotland?"

I have a sudden image of James, too tall and broad to fit through our mother's door without ducking, Alex, plump and clever, doing sums in his head as he crams toast into his mouth with two fingers. "They've never been out of Scotland."

To my surprise, there's a ripple of laughter. Generous, understanding. Whether it's a small town or another country, many people have brothers who never left home.

Then Reilly asks, "Where did you first meet this Mr. Johnson?"

This Mr. Johnson. I answer as if the question is in no way embarrassing. "In Maine. North Haven."

"Was he known as 'Red' Johnson?"

"His name was Henry Johnson," I say, rejecting the rakish nickname. "I believe his friends did call him Red."

"You and this Mr. Johnson started to go around quite a lot, didn't you?"

"Yes, we did."

"Ever go to a roadhouse?"

Look at the woman of low character, ladies and gentlemen. Running off to roadhouses with this "Mr. Johnson."

"No." Then I remember that silly, drunken night—Ellerson's black eye, Violet flirting with the truck driver—and add, "As a matter of fact, I don't remember. We had coffee in a café. Went skating."

"Did you ever go to Palisades Park with him?"

You're so beautiful. The sudden, blinding light through the window.

"Once."

"Was there any difficulty there that night?"

"No, I don't recall anything."

"Recall any conversation with any police officer the night you were there in the Palisades with Red Johnson?"

I see my way out. Reilly said "park," but Henry and I were in the wooded area of the Palisades that night, not the fairgrounds. I ask, "Palisades Amusement Park?"

"Yes."

"No," I answer truthfully.

Reilly sees his error. I watch him debate going back to correct his question. Instead he returns to my earlier slip, voice rising, as he says, "Is it possible that you ever went to a roadhouse and that you have forgotten it?"

I pause, as if I am searching my memory. "I did go to a roadhouse one evening in 1932 with Mr. Johnson. I do recall that."

"Do you know where Red Johnson is now?"

"Mr. Johnson is now in Norway."

"Have you communicated with him?"

"Not recently. About six months ago."

Nothing to be made of that. Wary, I wait for the next question.

"By the way, how did you come back to this trial? Who paid your expenses?"

"I came here to aid justice."

I didn't expect the question, and I answer without thinking. A murmur goes through the room. I can't sense the mood—appalled, disbelieving, surprised? But then Reilly shouts, "I move to strike that out as nonresponsive!" and I think, *Well, you don't seem to think that was good for you.*

Wilentz objects. For a few minutes, the lawyers argue back and forth: Must I answer who is paying my travel expenses? I realize: in addition to painting me as the woman who gave Charlie to her sailor boyfriend, Reilly is trying to imply that I am here because the Lindberghs paid me in the hopes of convicting an innocent man.

The judge rules I can be asked about payment. I say I have received $650 for expenses.

"Didn't the Colonel ask you what your price would be to come to this country and testify?"

"He did not."

"Well, how did you and he arrive at that sum?"

I am not to show anger. Ever, says Wilentz. But the thought that I have been paid to lie frays my nerves, and I say heatedly, "Because I cabled the Colonel I could not stand the expense on my own as I was losing employment on the other side through this, and that I couldn't see my way to come unless my expenses were made good."

"What employment were you engaged in on the other side?"

"I was . . . not engaged."

"Isn't it a fact that you haven't worked one day since you went back to Scotland?"

He means it to be a slur on my character. All I can think of is all those doors slammed in my face because they saw the Lindbergh Nanny. *I'm sorry, dear. It just wouldn't do.*

"That is a fact," I say.

"Yes, and isn't it a fact that you had no intention of working again?"

"Oh, yes, I have."

At his desk, Wilentz smiles at his papers. I have answered well.

Reilly asks me questions about the Whateleys. Did we meet in England? Have we corresponded?

"She is not an American citizen, is she?" he asks about Elsie.

"No."

"Neither was he?"

It takes me a moment to realize he's referring to Olly. "Neither was he, no."

He goes back to his table, picks up a folder. Returning, he takes out a photograph and shows it to me. It's Charlie and me in North Haven. I sigh against the impulse to cry.

"Is that your photograph, Miss Gow?"

"That is."

He moves it closer. "Take a look at it, please, Miss Gow."

I realize: it's not my image he wants me to see, it's Charlie. He's hoping I'll fall apart, crushed by guilt. Or go hard and uncaring, so the jury will wonder, what sort of woman would *not* fall apart at the sight of a murdered child?

"Yes, that is my photograph."

Reilly slaps it on the judge's desk. "Offer it in evidence."

Evidence? Of what, that I am who I am? Wilentz is also baffled, asking, "May I see it, please?"

Reilly switches, "Offer it for identification."

The judge is suspicious. Reilly has tried to make my identity evidence of a crime. Stern eyes on the lawyer, he says, "Well, for identification, it may be marked *for* identification."

I am marked Exhibit D-1.

Then Reilly places another picture in front of me. "This, Miss Gow, is also another copy of a picture of you?"

It's the woman by the car in Canada. The chorus girl with a criminal record. Small like me, dark like me. Smiling, her shoulder tilted flirtatiously toward the photographer.

"That is not my picture," I say.

He pretends astonishment. "It is not?"

"No."

He turns to the judge. "May I have it marked for identification?" I look to Wilentz, startled. What can this photograph identify if it's not of me?

The photograph of not me is marked D-2. Reilly puts both images in front of me. "Now, look at them please and compare them. See if one isn't a front view of you and one a side view of you."

It's bizarre; surely the jury will credit me with knowing my own face. But of course, if I show any doubt, Reilly will use it to suggest

Betty from Canada is Betty of Detroit, girlfriend of Scotty Gow the baby snatcher. And that all three are me.

I point to D-2. "That is not my picture."

Wilentz interjects, "Referring to D-2 for identification."

Reilly looks disbelieving at the jury. Turning back to me, as if he is saddened that I am telling such lies, he says, "The picture you have identified as your picture has the same kind of hair as the picture you say is not yours."

"I don't agree."

"The girl has the same smile, only a different pose, hasn't she?"

"I can't see that."

"You can't see it at all?" He peers at me. "Were you warned before you took the stand this morning that you should identify one picture and not the other?"

The question confuses me. Who would warn me of such a thing? "I was not."

Once again, Reilly has to change the subject. "Now let me get again, please, Miss Gow, the background of the Colonel's home . . ."

He asks how many staff the Morrows had. I answer between twenty and thirty. He makes passing references to Ellerson, Banks, and Violet, but doesn't ask much about them. He asks about the Whateleys; did they keep the Hopewell house open for the five months before the kidnapping? I say they did.

"You were supposed to be very fond of the baby, weren't you?"

"I *was* very fond of the baby," I correct him.

"He had a cold on Monday, but you didn't volunteer to go care for him?"

"I did. Mrs. Lindbergh said I needn't."

"But you saw Mr. Johnson on Monday."

"I did."

"And you told Mr. Johnson that the Lindberghs were not coming back?"

"I just don't recall."

"Did you tell anyone else that?"

All that running up and down hallways and stairs in the Morrow house. From the phone to Violet to Banks. Arguing with Whateley. Thinking what to pack. Marguerite at the door. The relief hearing Ellerson could drive me . . .

"I probably did."

"Why?" Reilly lets a touch of outrage into his voice.

"For no reason. In the house, I mean, I suppose it was a natural thing for anyone to ask me why the baby wasn't coming back, and I would reply that he had a slight cold."

"But you told no tradespeople, did you?"

"No."

"And you told no outsiders?"

"No."

"And you told no strangers?"

"No."

He points, thundering, "And you did not tell this defendant, did you?"

Careful to keep my gaze averted from Hauptmann, I say, "I did not."

"Now, on Tuesday, you were driven back to Hopewell by Red Johnson, weren't you?"

I have to stop myself from rolling my eyes, the trap is so obvious. "I was not."

"Who drove you back?"

"Mr. Ellerson."

"That is the Scandinavian you have spoken of, the second chauffeur."

Throughout, Mr. Reilly has been reminding the jury how many foreigners work for the Morrows and Lindberghs. "I believe he's of Scandinavian extraction. He was born in New Jersey."

"He's not the chauffeur anymore, is he? He's the gatekeeper, isn't he?"

"I believe so," I say quietly.

"Now, when Mrs. Lindbergh called, didn't she say, the Colonel will be detained in New York, he's making a speech?"

"She did not mention the Colonel to me."

"And yet, was it before or after the Colonel arrived that you and Red Johnson held this telephone communication that night?"

"Mr. Johnson and I held a telephone communication after the Colonel arrived."

"And at that time, there was nobody on the second floor but the child?"

"No."

"Where was the telephone call from?"

"Englewood."

Reilly manages to look aghast; if Henry called from Englewood, he could not kidnap Charlie within the next half hour. "Did you trace it?"

"No. It was what I understood at the time."

"Don't you know that it was from Hopewell?"

Wilentz shouts, "Just a minute!" as I say, "No, I don't know that."

Reilly collects himself. Swinging back toward the witness box with new energy, he says, "You had been out with Red Johnson the night before. What was the great importance of the second night?"

Wilentz objects again. Reilly withdraws the question. Then asks, "Was there any importance to the second night?"

"Yes, he was going to leave for Hartford the following morning."

"I suppose you wanted to say goodbye to him."

"Yes."

"Because Monday night's ride wouldn't suffice, would it?"

He sneers the word "ride," making its double meaning clear. I stare, letting him know I have no intention of answering the question. Thankfully, Wilentz says, "Your Honor, please."

"It didn't suffice?" tries Reilly, all innocence.

The judge says wearily, "That seems rather immaterial, Mr. Reilly."

Thwarted, the lawyer sighs, letting the jury see how he is abused in his quest for the truth. Watching him, I realize my nerves have stilled. My grip on Mother's handkerchief has eased. That last, bald insult has chilled me to the core. Mr. Reilly no longer frightens me.

He takes me through the evening again. The Vicks VapoRub, the layers of clothes, eating supper, going with Elsie to look at the dress, the location of the dog, the moment we realized Charlie was gone.

At one point he asks, "Had Whateley trained the dog?"

"With Mrs. Whateley, yes."

"Did they keep the dog in their quarters?"

"Yes, I believe so."

"Now, I imagine when the family is at the Hopewell house, more supplies are needed than when the Whateleys are there alone."

"Naturally."

"Did you deal with just one tradesman or many tradesmen in Hopewell?"

"I don't know."

"That would be the Whateleys' knowledge?"

"Yes." And think, *That was the answer he wanted—why?*

Then he takes everyone through the windows and the shutters again. I see a man in the front row yawn and a woman in the back toss her head in frustration as Reilly asks, "Have you any accurate recollection that the shutter was ever warped before that night?"

"No, I have not."

"Was there any handyman around the place who took care of repairs?"

"Mr. Whateley did all the small things around the house."

"He was well able to and could remedy a warped shutter."

I am unsure what he intends, and say, "I don't know that."

"But did you call it to his attention that night? That the shutter was warped?"

His purpose becomes clear: I am at fault because the remedy for the shutter was there, but I did not have it fixed. "It was too late then to do anything about it."

An odd question comes to me: How long does it take wood to warp? But before I can understand why such a question has formed, Reilly steers the questioning to the number of police and reporters on the grounds after the kidnapping, clearly hoping the jury will decide all the evidence is worthless. Then he asks about the number of sleeping suits Charlie had. "Did you ever see them after the child was kidnapped?"

I say I did.

"Where?"

"I packed them myself. In a suitcase to go back to Englewood."

Emotion strains my voice. Reilly acts the gentleman and gives me a moment.

"Now how about these thumb guards? How many did you have for the child?"

"I had two."

He picks up the one I found on the road, on the day I was sure Charlie was alive and coming back to us. "No springs or anything on this to hurt the baby's thumb, is there?"

"No."

"Would you slip it over your thumb and show how it is put on?"

He asks casually, but I can feel my knowledge of the thumb guard is controversial. "That is not the condition it was in. It was flattened."

"You found it on your way back to the house after a walk, one month after the baby was kidnapped."

Suddenly, his questions about the crowds at the house make sense. So many people, how did this little piece of metal go unnoticed for a month?

"That is correct."

"Did you drop it on your way down?"

"I did not."

He waits, then says, "Sure about that?"

"Positive about that."

Drawing closer to my chair, he says, "With *all* these policemen searching those grounds, you would have this jury believe that you could pick up in broad daylight this bright shiny thumb guard in the same condition it is—"

"It was in a much muddier condition when I picked it up."

"Who has changed this condition?" He turns, playing to the jury.

"It has not been changed," I say heatedly. "But it was more dull, I had to brush off the dust."

Whipping his finger at me, he shouts, "What do you mean by say-ing it was in a much muddier condition when you told the attorney general this morning that it is in the same condition?"

"It can't possibly be in the same condition when it has been han-dled by people."

Reilly hesitates, then realizes he can't refute such plain fact. "Now," he says slowly, "you are a very bright young lady, Miss Gow, aren't you?"

"I am."

I say it swiftly, without thinking. The courtroom bursts out laugh-ing. At first it is relief: a moment of drama, after all the tedious details of windows and time and phone calls. But there's something else: they are pleased. Happy I have fought back after two hours of attack. The first claps come from the back of the room, possibly the press. It becomes a storm of applause until Reilly looks helplessly at the judge, who bangs his gavel and shouts for order. I glance around the room, see open, ap-proving faces. They are on my side. Like the condition of the thumb guard, my intelligence—my integrity—is simple truth. Simple truth that does not change no matter how patronizing nor snide Reilly is. *I am.* The words echo in my head until I find myself smiling.

It takes quite some time for them to settle down. When the roar has dwindled into a low rumble, the judge says, "Now that demonstra-tion must not be repeated again. People must not applaud, and they must not laugh in such fashion."

Reilly is forced to ask for luncheon recess.

When we return, Reilly starts right in with Canada. "Miss Gow, when you were in Detroit, did you ever visit Canada?"

"I did, on one occasion."

"How long were you in Canada?"

"Oh, for about two hours."

The courtroom laughs again. The judge barks, "Silence, please."

Reilly asks if I know Nellie O'Connell, Abe Wagner, sisters named Paulette and Louise DeBoise. I do not and say so. He implies I know Dr. Condon more intimately than I've said. But he is exhausted. He's lost and he knows it. Still he tries one last time to create a lurid fantastical image for the jury, one that will distract them from the money and the ladder and his man's record of breaking into the second floor of houses.

He shows me a picture of Violet Sharpe.

She's sitting pert and eager, eyes bright, about to speak. No longer worried about how a show of emotion will look to the jury, I take a moment, hurting over how eager and open she was. I wouldn't want her here with Reilly tearing her to pieces. But she should be . . . here.

I hear Reilly ask, "And so you say you have never visited with Violet Sharpe any yacht or boat that was owned by Dr. Condon?"

I say it gently, as if sorry for him. "No, I didn't."

Reilly announces he has no further questions. Mr. Wilentz is allowed to make his last points. He asks, "You were quite fond, I take it, of Mr. Johnson?"

His voice is sympathetic. I think of Henry pointing around the Depression. *"Sitting room there . . . maybe a nursery just there . . ."*

"I was."

"You made no agreement with the Lindberghs that you wouldn't go out with any young men, had you?"

"No."

"He was a nice young man, too, wasn't he?"

All this to put a different image of Henry in the jury's mind. I say, "Yes," as if stating fact. It's not quite warm enough for Wilentz.

"A *very* nice young man, wasn't he?"

And other things, I think, as we all are. "He was."

Wilentz turns to the jury. "Mr. Hauptmann wasn't satisfied with murdering this child. Why, he wants to leave in the train wreck the lives and reputations of all these people. If they are not dead, they have to be crushed and Betty Gow is one of them."

Wilentz holds my gaze a moment. "Miss Gow, I am very much obliged to you."

It takes me a moment to understand that I am free. I can leave this chair. There are steps down to the courtroom floor, but nothing to hold on to, and I move carefully. I feel the solidity of the hardwood boards under me. But the courtroom is so full, it's not clear which way I should go. I step right, then head left. As I make my way toward the back, I am aware of . . . calm. Goodwill. I don't take in any of the faces; I've avoided looking at any one person in the crowd, terrified of spotting Colonel Lindbergh with a sad or disapproving look. I have allowed myself only the vaguest impression of Hauptmann himself; a blur of blond and clean-shaven face. So I am not even aware at first when I see him that I *am* seeing him.

That I have seen him before.

He is not sitting at one of the tables at the front, but just behind, in the front row of seats. The broad, handsome head, the bright hair that lies close to the scalp, the well-shaped mouth and nose.

"My sister is thinking of trying that kind of work."

The sister who never existed, the cold grin that let me know he knew I understood: his questions were all based on lies. His interest never in me. At least not as a woman.

"You're that nanny."

Animals know when they're being watched, they sense it. He does, glancing in my direction, meeting my eye. Something like a smile tugging at the corner of his mouth. Not smart to smile; people have already called him arrogant. But he can't help it. He got away with it, in every way that matters. I saw him before. I should have known. I did know. I knew he wanted something. But I never thought *Charlie*.

Those blankets were pinned. I pinned them. You didn't drop him. You . . .

My heart has leapt into a frenzied dancing, pounding so hard I can't catch my breath. My entire body is in thrall to that frantic, spin-ning pulse within me, whirling with it until I am dizzy. The hardwood floor tilts just as my legs become rivulets of water. I am dimly aware of noise rising like a wave, and it's just enough to knock me over.

The crowd closes over me.

Chapter Thirty

What do you think of those statements made by Reilly?" Alex wants to know.

A laugh escapes me. I am calling from the courthouse in Flemington—a phone call that must cost heaven knows how much—and Alex thinks it is a time to discuss legal tactics.

"Put Mother on, will you?" I ask him.

When the world stopped spinning, they brought me into a side room where I could catch my breath. The first thing I said after "I'm all right" was, "My mother will hear about this on the radio, she'll be so worried."

Wilentz said, "Why don't you telephone her?"

"Now?"

"Sure. We'll get the *New York Post* to pay for it. You're going to sell a lot of newspapers for them."

I laughed. "I suppose it would be good for her to hear I'm not engaged to Septimus Banks."

Now my mother's voice crackles over the wire. "Oh, Betty, is it over?"

"Well, it's all over as far as I'm concerned. I told them everything I knew. I kept nothing back."

"I'm so worried for you."

I almost laugh: *When have you ever not been?* "I know. It's been a tre-mendous strain. I thought my nerves would go—but I came through it all right."

I wait for my mother's response, but there's only the static noise on the wire. It seems we have lost each other. Anxious, I say, "Mother?"

Then Alex comes back, "Betty, hold on a moment, Mother has been taken faint. But look here, when Reilly said . . ."

When Mother has recovered and Alex has asked his question and Agnes has cried, "Well done!" and Izzy has said a careful "Hello?" only to go silent and bashful when I answer, so astonished is she that I am speaking from across an ocean, I eat the sandwich someone has brought me and consider what to do next.

Elsie fusses. As if I'd fainted an hour ago, rather than yesterday. Hav-ing come through my part of the trial, I can almost find Reilly's vision funny—all the Morrow-Lindbergh servants plotting and hopping in and out of bed with one another. Me with Banks, Whateley with poor Violet. "I don't know why it all has to be sex," Elsie says crossly and I laugh. Today it is her turn to testify, my turn to hold her hand and say she will be wonderful. The clown smile flashes now and again, but I can see: she is missing Whateley badly. Who if he were here would be chuntering at her, telling her not to get muddled on the time line, and don't be nervous, nothing to be nervous about. I would find it mad-dening, but—the thought comes to me only now—there was never any question, that she was the most important person in the world to him.

"Mr. Whateley would be so proud," I tell her. "I can see him now, grinning. Telling everyone, 'That's my missus.'"

"Making a nuisance of himself."

Before she goes in, I tug her jacket straight and tidy. Then, as I make to follow her, she says, "Oh, don't. If you wouldn't mind. I'm so nervous and it'll be easier if I can think of it as people I'll never see again."

"All right," I tell her. "I'll wait right out here."

Through the doors, I listen as Elsie is sworn in. Her nerves grow worse once she's sitting in the chair. Hauptmann's lawyer begins by saying, "It is obviously odd that the mysterious Violet Sharpe commits suicide; that Whateley gets a stomachache and dies suddenly; that Mrs. Whateley goes to England shortly after Betty Gow leaves for Scotland. All this, shortly after the Lindbergh baby disappears!"

I can tell, it's upset Elsie to hear Whateley's death being dismissed as stomachache, even more than the accusation against herself. Her voice is quiet, uncertain, the way it gets when she's deeply angry, but feels she must not show it. Reilly bullies her, insisting she speak up. Even the judge asks her to speak louder.

There is a long pause. I fold and unfold my arms in agitation. Then I hear Elsie loud and clear: "My husband did not go out with Violet Sharpe!"

The courtroom erupts with laughter. Forced to change tack, Reilly demands, "Did your husband know Dr. Condon?"

"No, indeed he did not know Dr. Condon."

"Didn't your husband and you know Dr. Condon in 1931 in New Rochelle?"

"No, he did not!"

You tell him, Elsie, I think. Then down the hall, I see someone familiar: Trooper—no, Corporal now—McCann as he gets ready to testify. He is anxious, pulling at his collar for air, sliding his hands down the front of his jacket.

"You'll be grand" is the first thing I say to him after nearly two years.

He breaks into a broad grin, then comes over for an impulsive embrace. Gesturing to me, he says, "Look at the act I have to follow." I wave my hand: *Go on.*

"No, really." He picks up a newspaper someone's left behind on a chair, gathers the pages as he searches for something. "You made every sob sister column in the country. Even Adela Rogers St. Johns."

Disbelieving, I look.

BETTY GOW'S POISE PRAISED

   Betty Gow impresses me as a highly sensitive, proud, dignified young woman and on the stand she was visibly nervous, obviously suffering. She has so often been described as "pretty" that it was a surprise to find her not pretty at all; her face is handsome rather, with big eyes that are somewhat prominent, a wide good mouth, well modeled cheekbones, a clear skin.

   Mr. Reilly showed indications of truculence early in his examination and Betty Gow didn't like it. I had suspected she was proud; she showed that she could actually be haughty. In good old Irish argot, Mr. Reilly got very short change out of Betty. No question seemed to faze her and once or twice there was the sharpness of actual reproof in what she said.

   We of the long press tables exchange opinions as the day goes by. We are none of us in sympathy with the effort the defense makes to hint that a truly good and affectionate nurse wouldn't leave a baby alone for two hours on a quiet Spring evening when he was snugly pinned into his crib, warm and fed, and blanketed securely. Those of us who have raised babies know that only a nervous or seriously sick baby would need closer attention than that, and this baby was neither.

It is her image of Charlie that gives me ease. She might think I am haughty or sharp, even snippy. Others will agree. But she leaves no doubt that Charlie was well loved. That he was cared for. That . . . we did our best.

There's another ripple of laughter from beyond the door. I say to Joe, "I think Elsie's doing all right. She was terribly anxious this morning, poor thing."

"Probably worried Reilly'll ask her about those tours Whateley gave for a buck apiece."

His tone is so light, the words so damning, I don't understand. "What tours?"

"The DOJ found out Whateley was giving tours of the Hopewell house to anyone who stopped by."

"What, inside the house?"

"Yeah. Lindberghs were never there, so what did it matter, is probably how he saw it. Make a little cash on the side. Good bet that's how Hauptmann knew the layout."

A little cash on the side. I think of the ransom money—nearly $3,000 of it exchanged in one place. It was Whateley, I remember, who knew the bills were going out of circulation. At the time, I thought, Oh, he always likes to know that sort of thing.

"Joe," I say, before I've fully decided to ask.

"Yeah?"

"The ransom money, the big chunk of it someone brought to the bank. Did the teller describe the man who brought it?"

He shakes his head. "Couldn't remember what he looked like."

I nod, thinking not all faces are memorable. "But now that you have Hauptmann, if you showed the man at the bank his picture . . ."

"The handwriting wasn't a match." I frown. "At the bank, you fill out a slip. They checked it against Hauptmann's writing. Completely different."

I don't want to ask. I want things to stay settled, the guilt and blame laid where they are.

". . . what name did the man give?"

"J. J. Faulkner."

Cricket, I think, bewildered. A man in white cracking a ball high and long through the air. Why on earth am I thinking of cricket?

One of Wilentz's assistants calls, "Corporal McCann." He stumbles reluctantly toward the door, saying, "It was really nice to see you."

"And you."

"I told you we'd get him."

"You did. You're a man who keeps his promises. Good luck to you, Joe McCann."

I keep the smile on until the door closes. Then let my mind focus on that man in white. My memory fails to give me a face. Because I have never seen his face. I have only heard his name.

"*G. A. Faulkner. Best all-rounder there ever was.*"

"G. A." "J. J." Say them out loud, there's barely a difference.

Drifting to the courtroom door I hear Elsie say, "Yes, Wahgoosh was very attached to my husband . . ." Her voice is more confident now, just as mine was when I felt the courtroom on my side. I think of Whateley calling, *"Here boy, good boy . . ."* Wahgoosh barking joyfully, knowing his master was the tall, portly Englishman, not the quicksilver American who was never home.

Reilly asks what Whateley's duties were about the house. "He looked after it," she answers. "Whatever needed doing."

"It was a new house," Reilly points out. "How much repair could it require?"

"You'd be surprised," she says. "Weak spots in the roof, damp in the cellar. Poor electrical wiring. Bad finish on the wood, it warps in the rain . . ."

That last awful day, the driving rain against the window of the car, the helpless waving of the wipers. Elsie saying, *"The weather's been so poor lately. Cold, wet, and damp for days on end."* Days and days, and yet the warped shutter was left as it was. Once I joked, "If you want something broken, send Whateley to fix it." Did he try to fix the shutter and fail? Or did he just . . . leave it?

Whateley so unexpectedly friendly when we visited, wanting to show Henry all round. *"I'll give you the full tour."* Henry admiring: *"He showed me how you find your way in and out, following the electric cables . . ."*

Not the first tour he'd given.

Elsie has made the courtroom laugh again.

Reilly asks her, "And had the Colonel been at home the evening prior to the night in question?"

"No, he stayed in the city that night."

"But the baby was always at the house with Mrs. Lindbergh on the weekends?"

"No, not always. The two weekends before that, he'd stayed with his grandmother in Englewood . . ."

It's not true, what I'm feeling. It's just another shadow created by the papers and men like Reilly taking advantage of our need to make sense of senseless things.

I think of the way Whateley explained Violet's despair: *"Far from home. Lonely. No real prospects. It can end badly, no question."*

No. It is true.

Chapter Thirty-One

I don't know how it comes up exactly, the idea of going to the Hopewell house. Like me, Elsie has been staying at Englewood. One day, she asks, "Have you seen the place since?" and when I say no, "Would you want to? I'd understand if . . ."

"No, I would like to," I say, surprising myself.

We are prepared to turn back. With the trial, the crowds of sight-seers have returned, both to the house and the spot Charlie was found. Elsie says some days, there are so many cars on the road to the house, "you'd think it was a fun fair." But today seems to be too cold and windy for the idly curious and Elsie and I have the grounds to ourselves. As I get out of the car, I look up at the quiet, abandoned house rising against the ring of forest. Hopewell. The name seems brutally unfair.

Elsie is quiet. I tell myself it must be painful for her to come back to the place where she and Whateley spent their last days together. She was out of the country when he died. At first she won't even look at the house, tugging for ages at her scarf.

"Are you sure?" I ask her.

She nods. "I'm fine, pet."

She uses her old keys to unlock the door. Inside the air is stale with dust and emptiness. Much of the furniture was left behind. It's been covered in cloth. The sofa, the coffee table, the grandfather clock—all bodies dressed for burial and eternal silence. Elsie and I part to explore the rooms we can bear. I step into the kitchen, which is empty, the cabinet doors all open for some reason. Peek into the servants' sitting room, where there is only a chair and the card table. One lamp with its plug pulled out. There are memories to be conjured if I want to. I find I don't want to. Better to leave these as blank, meaningless spaces. Like the sofa and the clock, cover the feelings in anesthetizing white cloth. And leave them behind.

I put a foot on the first step to go upstairs. The first memory that comes is me screaming on the stairs at North Haven—*"Then I quit! I quit!"* Desperate to get to Billy. Thinking I could just leave Charlie behind. Now, hand on the banister, I ask Charlie's forgiveness for that selfishness. The times I was bored, irritated by his needs. The time I took my arm away, let him fall. The time I was not in the room when the window slid open and that man came in. I ask his forgiveness for all of it.

"You going up?" Elsie appears from around the corner.

"Did you?" I ask, meaning the garage apartment.

"I didn't," she says. "I always hated it. So, I thought—why bother? They're not here."

"No," I say, turning to join her. "They're not."

"So you won't be staying?"

Elsie has her arm tight through mine as we shiver our way around the grounds.

"I won't," I tell her. "Mrs. Lindbergh offered me Marguerite's old place, which was kind of her, but . . ."

"Wasn't kind of her, it was smart. But I see why you don't want to. Home's best."

I'm about to be funny about how I've learned to enjoy my mother's fretting, even her hesitancy over any move in cards, when Elsie says, "I'm going home myself."

There is no cheer in her tone, no excitement. She is firm in her decision, but it's not been an easy one. For the first time, I see how she has aged since Whateley's death.

"You probably wanted to leave the same time I did," I say.

She glances at me. "I did. But I couldn't leave Mrs. Lindbergh. Not with the new baby and her still grieving. Poor thing going through the motions for his sake, didn't know where she was half the time. Not that he noticed."

After this small disloyalty, she straightens herself. "Anyway. It's time."

"Will you take a new position or . . ."

"I won't. I'm not well—" I exclaim; with an irritable wave of the hand, she dismisses my sympathy. "Mr. Whateley left me a bit. I'll be all right in that regard."

A bit. It is not like Elsie Whateley to talk about money. We are talking of something else. I have been undecided, these past few days, what to do with what I learned at the courthouse. Easy enough, I thought, to go back across the ocean, leave it behind. But now Elsie has put it before us, whether she meant to or no.

"I suppose he made something on those tours of the house." I try to smile as if she herself has told me this. As if it's the sort of thing any of us would do.

She hears the disapproval. "I did say to him, it's not right, bringing people into someone else's home. But he said, '*Someone else's home? We're the ones who live here, the ones who take care of it. If we want people in, it's our business.*' '*Nobody cares about Olly and Elsie Whateley's house,*' I told him. '*It's the Lindbergh house they're paying to see.*' But it made him happy, so I let it go."

I want that to be the end of it. Whateley showed the wrong person the house. As always, he would have talked too much, wanting to seem the expert. *Yes, nursery there, the Colonel's office right below . . .* I can see him as he pockets the money given as a tip. *Cheers, thanks very much.* He made a mistake. A stupid human mistake.

But that isn't how it happened. As everyone has said, the Lindberghs were never in Hopewell on a Tuesday. Someone had to be

told. By someone inside the house. Olly Whateley wasn't me or Violet
Sharpe, calling this friend or that to discuss a change in the family's
plans that meant a change in theirs. Steady, solid Olly and Elsie never
went anywhere.

And you can't make a call without a number. Which means on one
of those little tours, a number was given and a plan was made.

"Whateley's looking up the schedule, and he can meet you at the station."
He knew, probably earlier than any of us, that Mrs. Lindbergh had
decided to stay.

But why not on the weekend? Why not try then? Well, for one
thing, Charlie hadn't been at the Hopewell house the two prior weekends. He was at Englewood, well guarded. No chance there. And the
Lindberghs often had guests at the weekend. The house was full of
people, and you don't want a crowd when you're trying to . . .

What? What was the plan?

As if someone had ripped a hole in one of those placid white sheets
to reveal what's underneath, I see it, the image of Charlie and me in
North Haven. Me scowling at the camera. Charlie worried and peeping in the carriage. A picture of the baby.

"Growing so fast, I'd hardly recognize him . . ."

A new picture. A better picture. One that would show the world
the little boy he'd become, how much he looked like his famous father.

No harm in that, Whateley must have thought. One picture. As
Violet said: *"It was bound to come out."*

And so you make one phone call. *They're here. She'll be in bed, she's
got the cold. And he's staying in the city. It's just us and the nurse.*

The nurse who was careless. Letting the baby get photographed
the first time. She'll be distracted, brooding about her date.

But he wouldn't have called from the house. The police checked
all the calls and there was nothing suspicious in the Hopewell phone
records. Or Englewood. It would have been a pay phone. At a local
store. Some place like Clark's where it's crowded and the counterman
is too busy to notice all the faces coming and going. Whateley's wasn't
a face you'd notice anyway. Just another middle-aged man with thin-

ning hair who'd seen better days. The teller at the bank didn't remember him either. Despite the extraordinary sum of $3,000.

When did Whateley realize the real plan? That he'd been paid not for a photo, but a child? He was tense and snappish as it grew dark. Unusually harsh to Elsie over the dinner. His man hadn't come, but the Colonel had. When he wasn't supposed to. The horror he must have felt, as he went tramping through the woods in the dark with Lindbergh, one with a gun, the other with a torch. I think of his face the next day—gray, stunned. The way he kept rubbing a hand over his face: not real, it can't be real.

It ate him alive. The guilt became a steady drip of acid, harsh and corrosive, gnawing at him from the inside. March 1933, one year after Charlie was kidnapped, he sent Elsie alone to England, the first time they didn't take their holidays together. On May 1, he exchanged the gold notes.

Three weeks later, he was dead.

Did Elsie recognize Hauptmann in the courtroom, as I did? She'll never say, but I suspect so. He came at all of us. Me at the Peanut Grill. *"My sister is thinking of trying that line of work."* He said he knew Ellerson. That man who drove Violet into town—was it the strange other Ernie or was it Hauptmann? Or did Hauptmann simply approach her at the Peanut Grill when he was done talking to me the night I came back from Maine? He might have talked about missing Germany with Marguerite and Johannes. Hauptmann would have seen Henry with us at the bar. And Henry was always happy to talk with people. All it would have taken was the offer of a cigarette or a day's work.

But the Whateleys never went anywhere. So Hauptmann came to them. He read the reports in the newspaper about the Lindberghs' new house in a remote part of New Jersey, surrounded by woods, shacks, and abandoned houses. The house with no guards. The house the Lindberghs didn't live in yet, except the odd weekend. *I was driving by. Perhaps it's silly, but I am an admirer. Could I take . . . a little look around?*

Whateley could have said, I think savagely. When I was accused, Henry, poor Violet. The hell he could have saved us just by saying,

Hang on, a man came to the house one time, spoke with a German accent. And yet he never said a word. Possibly he consoled himself with the fact that the police already knew the kidnapper was of German extraction because of the notes. Condon had given them a description of the man. What more could he provide? Except a telephone number, which was almost certainly a pay phone in New York.

And he wanted the money. The hideous realization comes to me. No money if Hauptmann was arrested before the ransom was paid. And once Charlie was found dead . . . well, you'd be a fool to admit anything after that. Sit tight. Tell yourself you didn't know. Think of Elsie. Yes, best to just stay quiet.

Staring deep into the woods, I remember our visit here. How Whateley took Henry around the house, his pleasure at having someone to lecture—even about how to find your way in and out of the woods by using the electric cable as a guide. This is difficult land, thickly wooded with poor soil and bad roads. The town is Hopewell, but the terrain is the Sourlands. People have been broken trying to tend it, given up, left their houses behind. You can get lost here with no one to help or guide you.

Whateley's compliment—*"Nice looking, these coupes"*—nags at me. Later he told the police a couple in a green coupe had taken photographs of the house. Knowing Henry drove just that sort of car. Knowing—he must have—the police would make the connection.

If one needed to blame someone for, say, a burglary—the sort Mr. Hauptmann committed back in Germany—a poor young sailor not legally in the country would make a good scapegoat.

Which meant Whateley knew he would need a scapegoat. Just as he knew the money he was exchanging at the bank was the ransom money.

Which means I am wrong, and he knew Hauptmann wanted more than a photograph. He knew it before the ladder ever touched the side of the house.

The image of Whateley, not as dupe, but as someone altogether more cold-blooded, takes shape. He set Henry up by showing him the cables and telling the police about his car. Did he do something to the shutter? Certainly he never fixed it or asked the builders to replace it. Wahgoosh, who was so partial to him; would he have held him still in the servants' room, fingers around his snout so he didn't bark?

I remember what Lieutenant Keaten told me. That hundreds of children were kidnapped in a year, most of them returned safely. I want to think Whateley believed Charlie would be returned safely. He must have reasoned the Lindberghs and the Morrows could certainly pay. So much reward for so little risk. The Whateleys were nearly fifty when he made his bargain. He'd seen how some, like Arthur Springer, were given princely security by the family for their old age. While some, like Banks, were not.

I have learned some things about George Aubrey Faulkner. He was considered one of cricket's best before the war. Like Septimus Banks, he enlisted, serving with the Royal Field Artillery. He received the Distinguished Service Order. But he contracted malaria and no longer had the stamina to play cricket as he used to. His wife left him. He started a school, which struggled. Five years ago, just as we all came to work for the Lindberghs, Faulkner gassed himself in the storeroom of that school. He was said to have a wonderful smile.

It is not always the people you care for, that you fail to see properly. Sometimes it is the people you ignore. Whateley, blusterous and self-important; irritating, I thought, comical at best. Now I remember the grip of his jaw, how his lips went thin across his teeth as the Colonel demanded "Where were you?" the day Dorothy Lewes came. The way he looked just above Lindbergh's head so the younger man didn't see the rage in his eyes.

And I remember myself, on that very first day, my brief, intense desire to see that ostentatiously perfect chandelier crash to the ground.

It must have felt like a triumph of some sort, exchanging that money, getting the rewards denied him by others. So when he picked the name, he thought of a champion. A hero. Someone no one would know in America, where they don't care about cricket or the men who play it.

I look at Elsie. Her head covered by her scarf, she only shows me her profile. Her cheeks are slack, the flesh weary. Her eyes pouchy, broken through with red, the lashes sparse. Her lips, once loving and clown-like, are pale and set. She is an old woman. An angry old woman. I remember my hatred for the woman who thoughtlessly passed one of the ransom bills, that she was spending money we gave to the person who took Charlie without a thought for the agony attached to the bill. And now that woman is walking beside me in the chill February air, scarf over her head, great wobbling boots on her feet.

She has noticed, I can tell, that I haven't said a word since she talked of Whateley showing people the house. In my silence, she's heard the judgment, and now she snaps, "You're not to say a word against him. He couldn't know what that man was."

So she knows that Hauptmann came to the house. That he got the "tour." But that's all she will allow herself to know. Whateley made a bit extra. They saved. The money he has left her is not *that* money. I suspect she will never spend it. Just keep it locked away somewhere—proof that her Olly took proper care of her.

I find I lack the cruelty to accuse Elsie. Or her husband. In England and in Scotland, the words "not well" is how someone tells you they're dying. Nor will I tell the police. To reveal the inside accomplice will help Reilly who will use it to help Hauptmann. Who once asked if he would burn. Whateley burned. Whateley is dead. It is time for Hauptmann to burn.

But I will do one cruel thing.

"Do you remember?" I ask her. "That last day when Charlie came round the door? I said who's this who's come to see us and you laughed and said, *'Let's give him a cookie and see what he does.'* I always thought that was funny. He had his mother, but it was us he came looking for. Because he loved us. Trusted us to care for him. What we're put on this earth to do, isn't it?"

At the invocation of her old saying, Elsie nods vaguely, as if the memory is no longer clear. But then she slows. Stops. Her mouth trembles as if she's having a stroke. Her eyes are wide with despair. She raises her hands as if to stop herself from falling, turning a little this way and that, as if all she sees before her is there is nowhere to go.

"Come here," I tell her. "Come here." And for a long while we stand there. Elsie's right. There is no use in crying. You don't do it because it's useful; you do it because you must. Because that's all there is left to do.

I look back at the house. The shutters are closed, all the doors locked. We were careful, Elsie and I, to do that. Elsie from years of habit, me from an odd sense of ritual. Pointless, really. No one will ever live there again and there is nothing left to take. The whitewash is peeling and chipped. The grass around it is overgrown; where Mrs. Lindbergh had her garden is all just weeds. They've left, again, the Lindberghs have left. They'll never stop leaving, I think. They will only feel safe where there are no people. Or in a place where people can be kept in a place far from them.

"We have to go, Elsie," I tell her finally. "We can't be here."

As I pack my trunk, I lay Izzy's cowboy hat and Mickey Mouse doll carefully on top. The hat is not easy to pack, but it's the thing she wants most. If it doesn't survive the crossing, Mickey Mouse will have to do.

It's Kathleen Sullivan who comes to tell me Mrs. Morrow would like to see me in the library before I go. I say of course and follow her downstairs.

"Betty," she says when I enter and holds out both her hands. "I wanted to say goodbye. And to thank you." She grips my hands in hers; forceful. "I know it has been an ordeal."

"Well worth it," I tell her.

"How glad I am that you came to us. You were . . ." She presses my hands. "Oh, you were so good with him."

"He was a joy," I say with difficulty. "A lamb."

She nods in the shared remembrance. Tears touch the corners of her eyes.

"Thank you," she says again.

"Of course."

As she embraces me to say farewell, I can only feel the absence of her daughter and her famous son-in-law. They have not come to say thank you. That they are glad I came, that they know I loved their child. Perhaps it is too much to bear.

And perhaps, she still has doubts.

"Please give them my best," I tell Mrs. Morrow.

"You look swell, Beautiful. Better than ever."

"Still the gentleman."

I was right that first day. It was Ellerson in the little guard box at the gate. He smiles, only a half smile, because he is missing teeth. His body has grown fat and cumbersome. The merry face gone to flesh and broken veins. The eyes are still bright, but they flicker. He leans heavily on the stool they gave him. Standing is no longer easy, and I wave *no need* when he tries. From the small window of the guardhouse, I can see Alfred in the car. He gave me an odd look when I asked him to stop and let me out at the gate. I told him I wouldn't be long.

"How do you like my luxury digs?" Raising his arms, he touches the walls.

"About the size of a front seat of a car, when you think about it."

A flash of the old cheerful cynicism. "Come on, Beautiful."

The exchange of information—I am not married, nor is he, we both live with our mothers—is easy, taking little time. For a moment, I consider leaving it there. It's been years and perhaps he doesn't care. But I find I need to tell him; what happened will only feel real when I share the story with him.

"Do you know it was never Violet?"

There is a pause. This is not a subject he wants to revisit. But for my sake, he tries. "No?"

I shake my head. "It was Whateley. He gave tours of the house to sightseers. I think Hauptmann was one of them. That's how they made . . . the arrangement that Whateley would call when the family was alone at Hopewell without the Colonel."

"He was sort of a dunce, wasn't he?"

Remembering the Colonel's warning, I say, "Quite ordinary, certainly."

Ellerson shifts awkwardly on his stool. "I heard that when he was dying, Whateley made a confession of sorts. He told the reverend someone on the inside was working with the kidnappers."

He arches his eyebrow, and I guess. "Whateley said it was me."

"That's the rumor."

Why? I think sadly. We never got on, Whateley and I, but so spiteful a year later? After everything I went through? But perhaps he was worried for Elsie. What would happen to her if anyone began to suspect him or they traced the money. Better make one last attempt to place the blame elsewhere . . .

Thinking of blame and the harm people do, I will have to reckon with the harm I did to Violet. How I pretended to be her friend, all the while condemning her as a vapid, needy, careless girl. Out of guilt, I suspect, for my own carelessness and need.

Shaking my head, I say, "I'll never know why Violet didn't tell the truth. First she went to the movies, then she went to a roadhouse. Ernie Brinkert, no, it was the other Ernie, Ernie Miller. He called in the evening, then midday . . ."

"She didn't remember," Ellerson reminds me.

"How could you not *remember*?"

He sighs, the memory coming with pain. "You know how she told the police she was drinking coffee that night?" I nod. "Does that sound right to you?"

An image of Violet in the car, clapping her hands for the flask. "Later, she admitted she had a cocktail."

"Just one? She was seeing a hardened drunk—Banks. She liked a drink herself, and he probably got her used to more than was good for her. My bet? Miss Sharpe went through that whole evening in a state of blackout. Wakes up the next morning with a headache and a bunch of business cards and no idea where they came from. She knows she saw *someone,* thinks maybe it was the fellow who drove her into town. Beyond that . . ." He clucks sympathetically.

"The people she was with that night didn't say anything about her being drunk."

"Someone in a blackout can get through an evening walking and talking like anybody else. Maybe they sound kind of dizzy, but she always sounded dizzy. She killed herself because she thought maybe she did tell the kidnappers the family was in Hopewell, and that at some point, they would catch the kidnapper and it would all come out. You can't tell your employer you were so drunk you can't remember—not when you've seen other employees fired for drunkenness."

"And yet . . . you're here."

"Well, Mrs. Morrow doesn't let go of people so easily."

"She was the one who gave you the hundred dollars, wasn't she?"

He shows me the broken smile. "Didn't even ask why. When I got back to the house that day, I went to her. Said I'd gotten myself into a bit of a jam and needed an advance. Not a small one either. She probably had a pretty good idea why. But she handed it right over. Marguerite Junge, she was another one who liked to point fingers. She told the feds I was involved in the kidnapping. But Mrs. Morrow wouldn't hear of it. She's a . . . good person. Loyal lady. Even after I ran off, she let me come back." The smile fades. "No more driving though."

"No." As with the bequest withheld from Banks, Mrs. Morrow's generosity comes with limits. Nor is it universal. She fired Marguerite, supposedly for stealing food. But I suspect it was the secrets she stole—and shared with others—that got her turned out. It is a power of a sort, to know things about people, expose them, strip them of their mystique. Even the great Lindbergh.

I say, "Do you know, I never understood it? The flight. Why that made him . . ." I hold up my hands as if to encompass everything. "It's not that miraculous."

I expect Ellerson, hater of myth, to agree, but he looks sorrowful, as if I have missed out. "It was miraculous because he did it *alone*. For thirty-three hours. Everybody else who tried, it was a crew because they thought no one can stay awake and focused for a day and a half. More people. More weight. Too many people, too much weight—you crash. He took himself, some sandwiches, and a compass—that's it." He looks out at the Morrow gate from his box. "I'd have given anything to do it."

I glance out to the car where Alfred is waiting. Ellerson notices and says, "You take care of yourself, Betty Gow."

"If I said the same?"

He gestures to the box. "Well taken care of."

I take in the box: maybe five feet by three. "If you go wandering again, Glasgow's just across the ocean. I've heard it can be crossed by air."

"All you need is a compass."

"And some sandwiches."

With a hug, I say goodbye.

As the car turns onto the main road, I glance back, marveling at Mrs. Morrow's faith. In his vagueness and girth, Ellerson makes an unlikely protector. But she seems to understand he is not a man to betray. And maybe she also understands guards and gates only do so much. Every house has windows. Every house has doors. A shutter that won't close. People who don't have the strength to seal things tight. Tilting my head, I see the sky, a banner of blue above the trees. Vast and empty, uncluttered by people and their foolishness, it is a place you rely only on yourself—and perhaps one other. But our lives are always in the hands of others. Rather than soar above, you keep your feet on the ground, give kindness, and hope for the best.

For a moment, I can feel Charlie's hands in mine, eager fingers and soft palms. The little buttons of his knuckles. His wriggling excitement as I helped him make the leap from one place to the next, touching down, then up again. *"Come on, Charlie. England to France, over the Channel . . ."* You fly and you hold on.

Alfred asks if I want the radio. I say, if he does, that's fine. But not for me. I'd rather not hear other people's voices right now. Instead I turn to look outside and see myself reflected in the window. Two dark eyes, pale little face.

Why look, it's Betty Gow.

What do I know about Betty Gow?

I know her life has not turned out as planned. But very few lives do.

I know "pretty" is not the word people use to describe her these days—although it was once the first word that came to mind. I know she's got a sense of style. Knows what she's about, as my mother would say. She even has a job at Adairs Dress Shop. The telegram arrived yesterday telling her so.

I know she's not scared anymore. In fact, she's gotten rather bold in her later years. Intends to get bolder still.

I know she's going home. She may not be certain what that looks like yet, but she's going nonetheless.

And when she gets there, there will be people. Waiting for her.

The Real Betty Gow

In 1935, Betty Gow returned to Scotland, where she lived quietly for the rest of her life. Over the years, she spoke with several writers on the subject of the Lindberghs, remaining sharp, intelligent, and devoted to the memory of the little boy she called "my Lindbergh baby."

In 1993 at the age of eighty-eight, she was interviewed by Lindbergh biographer A. Scott Berg, who said of her, "She was smaller than I expected and there was something pretty about her. She was tough and feisty though. She was the one who was going to be in control here."

He told her that Anne Morrow Lindbergh sent her regards. At which point, "she just burst into tears." Decades earlier, after returning to Scotland, Betty had sent a letter to the Lindberghs. They never replied. For decades, she believed they hated her and blamed her for Charlie's death.

"She had been carrying this emotional burden for years and I had lifted it from her," said Berg. "She was sobbing. It was the opening of the floodgates."

As she vowed in the Flemington courtroom, Betty Gow worked throughout her life; her last job was as manager at Ilene Adairs Dress Shop. She never married or had children of her own. She died on July 16, 1996, at the age of ninety-two.

The Lindbergh Nanny:
Fact Versus Fiction

I have been fascinated by the Lindbergh kidnapping since I saw the 1974 film of *Murder on the Orient Express*. The film opens with a silent scene of the kidnapping of little "Daisy Armstrong." As the kidnapper makes his way through the darkened home—Long Island substituting for New Jersey—it is not the parents who encounter him, it is the servants. Most notably, the nanny who is seen tied to a chair, struggling fiercely, unable to protect her charge.

And yet except for Violet Sharpe, whose treatment and suicide provoked outrage in England, no one except for Lindbergh kidnapping scholars now remembers the Lindbergh and Morrow staff who came under such intense suspicion. When I first started exploring the identity of the actual Lindbergh nurse (the term then preferred over "nanny"), I was amazed no one had written her story since it first appeared in the headlines nearly a century ago. Unlike Violet Sharpe, Betty Gow was intimately involved with the event at almost every point. She was the last person to see Charlie alive; she discovered he was missing; and she was in the Lindbergh house throughout the investigation. She was a suspect. Her boyfriend was a suspect. She identified the body. She was defamed in the press and triumphant at the trial. Her testimony, letters, and interviews show her to be an intelligent, opinionated woman with a sense of generosity and humor. In short, she was the ideal heroine.

I am generally suspicious when it comes to conspiracy theories. I believe Richard Hauptmann was guilty. And yet I've never read a satisfactory explanation of how he, living in the Bronx, would have known the Lindberghs were in Hopewell, New Jersey, that Tuesday. The police immediately suspected someone on the inside had tipped off the kidnappers as to their whereabouts. That suspicion seems reasonable to me.

The Lindbergh Nanny is not a work of investigative nonfiction. It is a novel, based on biographies, histories of the case, and a range of sources including websites dedicated to the crime. I have no idea if Olly Whateley liked cricket. Or saw G. A. Faulkner in 1907. Or had any part in the kidnapping of Charles Lindbergh, Jr. As much as possible, I have tried to build the story around verifiable fact—at least as it was reported by the people involved. In some instances, I have drawn on rumor and speculation. Some instances, I invented. The police did strongly suspect someone in either the Lindbergh or Morrow household had alerted the kidnappers as to the family's whereabouts. Some of those people were investigated and remain people of interest on true crime message boards to this day. But the Morrows employed a staff of twenty to thirty people and their histories are largely lost to time. John Saunders, the gardener, could have passed as Betty took her phone call summoning her to the Hopewell house. Banks could have complained to pantry girl Margaret (last name not ascertained by the FBI) about having to find someone to drive Betty. Ida the cook (last name also not ascertained) could have been told not to count Betty in the day's meal calculations. The possibilities are many and varied as to who knew—and who might have told someone they shouldn't—that the Lindberghs were staying in Hopewell on Tuesday night.

However, federal investigators did learn Whateley had given tours of the Lindbergh home. Henry Johnson stated Whateley had shown him the power lines around the house. On May 1, 1933, a man who gave his name as J. J. Faulkner did exchange $2,980 in gold notes used in the ransom. He has never been identified and his handwriting did not match Hauptmann's. A few weeks after the deposit was made, Whateley underwent emergency surgery for a perforated ulcer. He died on May 23. The story that he accused someone on his deathbed and that someone was possibly Betty is less well substantiated and so is presented here as a rumor.

The second major invention of the book is the private life of chauffeur Charles Henry Ellerson. The real Ellerson was married with two children. There is nothing to suggest he was gay or bisexual. But he lived part-time at the boardinghouse, drank, had a gambling problem, and the odd girlfriend. He was described by Morrow secretary Arthur Springer as "a little wild, but harmless," which is possibly why Mrs. Morrow allowed him back as the gatekeeper after he disappeared for a time. He drove Betty to Hopewell on the day of the kidnapping, but another chauffeur introduced her to Henry Johnson. I added a different element to his story because I wanted one of the staff members to have a need for privacy that would be instantly understandable to the modern reader.

All the major events of Betty's life as related in the book—the circumstances through which she came to the Lindberghs, her time in Maine, her movements on the day of the kidnapping, media coverage, her role in identifying Charlie and testifying at the trial—are based in fact. The man Betty dated in Glasgow and Detroit was named William Coutts. I changed his first name to avoid confusion with her brother. According to a police report from Detroit, they did meet when she cared for his relative. But he was not appreciably older than she and he claimed they broke up due to her high standards. Her reasons for their breakup are roughly verbatim from her police interview. Betty's employment history before the Lindberghs is only loosely sketched in. She did work for the Lindberghs after the new baby was born. But it wasn't for long, so I have simplified her movements at this time. The letter Betty wrote to her mother immediately after the kidnapping is authentic; the rest are fiction. The newspaper article detailing Betty's mother's defense of her—*despite these she never hesitated*—is true. Betty's testimony is a condensed transcription of her actual words in court, including the moment when the courtroom burst into applause on her behalf. She did faint, but probably from the overall strain rather than sudden recognition of Richard Hauptmann. Her interviews with the police are a mix of transcript and fiction, although the key points of interrogation concerning her brother, Henry, and Scotty Gow are all accurate.

Her brother William died in a horrible accident while she was in Maine, and she later said she felt somewhat abandoned by the famous couple. She spent her own money to buy Charlie fresh clothes. She and Henry were cautioned by the police on the grounds of public indecency. (For more on that, see Lloyd C. Gardner's *The Case That Never Dies*.)

Anne Morrow Lindbergh's solo flight was done in strict secrecy. Only one *New York Times* reporter was given the story and Betty and Charlie were probably not present at the occasion. But I wanted her to witness Anne in the sky and to have the crushing experience of being followed by a media mob prior to the kidnapping, so I altered that event. Charlie did sleep in the barn and was left outside for times on his own. But the vision of him sleeping in a basket on the grass is mine. The routes that Betty and the Lindbergh family traveled to get to Maine have been simplified.

With regard to Charles Lindbergh, I have tried to stick closely to reported fact of him and his life during the years 1931 to early 1935. He was a complex man who not only held but promoted some extremely ugly views. Other aspects of his character are not so easily categorized, and because he was the father of a murdered child, I have tried to be fair both to him and to the reader. I relied primarily on A. Scott Berg's *Lindbergh;* Susan Hertog's superb biography *Anne Morrow Lindbergh;* and *Those Angry Days* by Lynne Olson. Where possible, I have paraphrased his words or quoted them, as I did with his defense of Violet Sharpe and his opinion of Hitler and Germany. (The headline he and Betty discuss is authentic.) One obvious invention: He did not teach Betty to drive, although his approach to driving instruction is described in his daughter Reeve's excellent book *Under a Wing*.

In later interviews, Betty referred to Lindbergh as a bit of a sadist. Several of the incidents that inspired that sentiment are included in the narrative. His views on breeding are alluded to here, as are his views on eugenics. But Lindbergh's involvement with America First and his views on race would have been outside Betty Gow's experience of him and beyond the scope of this book. It seemed reasonable to have Anne describe Lindbergh's work with Dr. Alexis Carrel. It would not have been believable for Betty to discover Dr. Carrel's grotesque racial views, some of which Lindbergh shared. For those who want to read more about those views or his work in medical science, I would recommend *The Immortalists* by David M. Friedman. *The Rise and Fall of Charles Lindbergh* by Candace Fleming is also excellent.

Anyone interested in the Lindberghs is indebted to the first and best chronicler of their lives: Anne Morrow Lindbergh. *Hour of Gold, Hour of Lead* is composed of her letters and diary entries from 1929 to 1932, covering the events of this book with astonishing wisdom and emotional rigor. Joyce Milton's *Loss of Eden* is one of the earlier portraits of the couple and has fascinating detail on the various threads the police followed in the kidnapping. Thomas Doherty's *Little Lindy Is Kidnapped: How the Media Covered the Crime of the Century* is a wonderful cultural history of the event and its aftermath as covered in the press. I am grateful to Professor Doherty for the information that Betty was unable to testify as scheduled.

The Lindberghs and Morrows had quite a few dogs. I have tried to be faithful to which dog lived where and when, especially Wahgoosh and poor Daffin. My apologies to any canine to whom I ascribed the wrong home or breed. Some of the human characters, such as baby nurse Marie Cummings, have been dropped for simplicity. The character of Trooper McCann is a composite. Some law enforcement officials have been left out for clarity, and their movements have been simplified in some sections, such as the day Charlie was found. I have tried to present them in a fair and varied way, albeit through Betty's experience. Whatever mistakes were made in the handling of this case, the effort by local and state law enforcement was tremendous.

The lives and characters of the Lindbergh and Morrow staff—the war service and marriage of Septimus Banks, Violet Sharpe's identity as Mrs. George Payne, the dismissal of Marguerite Junge—are all based in fact. Violet did have a sister, Edna, who returned home at the time of the kidnapping, but she worked for Constance Chilton and her personality as described in the book is purely fictitious. Their gossip about their employers is invented, but the details about the family it reveals have been reported in other works.

Henry "Red" Johnson married and had a second daughter. He never really recovered from his involvement in the Lindbergh case. He was prone to depression and fits of heavy drinking. He died in 1962 at the age of fifty-seven. For an excellent portrait of him as well as members of the Morrow and Lindbergh staff and other less well-known figures in the case, I highly recommend *Their Fifteen Minutes: Biographical Sketches of the Lindbergh Case* by Mark W. Falzini.

To those who want to delve further into the case itself, in addition to Lloyd C. Gardner's book mentioned above, I recommend *The Lindbergh Case* by Jim Fisher and *Hauptmann's Ladder* by Richard T. Cahill, Jr. *FBI Files on the Lindbergh Baby Kidnapping*, edited by Thomas Fensch, is also useful.

As I said earlier, I believe Hauptmann was guilty for all the reasons stated in the book. (Although there is no record of him ever connecting with the Lindbergh or Morrow staff and the vision of him at the Peanut Grill is entirely made up.) For those interested in works that offer an alternative view of who may have committed the crime, there are several, the most notable being Ludovic Kennedy's *The Airman and the Carpenter*.

Finally, despite my very best efforts, there may be honest errors. Hopefully they do not detract from the enjoyment of the novel or the reputation of Betty Gow, who was an exceptional woman. She faced extraordinary circumstances and a terrible loss with uncommon intelligence and grace.

Acknowledgments

Normally, I am a very independent writer. My thank-yous are usually to the excellent professionals at Minotaur and my agent, friends, and family. *The Lindbergh Nanny* is a book about a crime and a family that provoke controversy to this day. I needed help to write this book—and I got it. Now it's time to say thank you.

Due to Covid, the Lindbergh Archives were closed to visitors. This book could not have been written without Douglas Gaines Harrell, who generously lent me digital files for the 1932 New Jersey State Police reports. I very much look forward to Harrell's contemporary mystery on the subject of the kidnapping.

This book originally started with Betty as an older woman showing a writer around her garden. With the very first line, I got stuck: What flowers would you have in a suburban Glasgow garden? Happily, I asked the wonderful Dorothy Magnani, who comes from Scotland, and she asked her garden-wise relatives. Gratitude to Janis Tulloch, John Gynn, and Susan Gynn for their advice. I would also like to thank Ian Robinson and Simon Boughey for their excellent insights on cricket and the contributions of Aubrey Faulkner.

Anyone writing about the Lindbergh case owes a huge debt of

gratitude to Mark W. Falzini, the archivist at the New Jersey State Police Museum. Because the museum was closed, Mr. Falzini patiently answered scores of emails, addressing such questions as "Who was the DOJ informant?" and "Was Betty the oldest or youngest child?" I wish him great joy in his retirement. I would also like to thank the many authors mentioned in the author's note as well as Michael Melsky, author of *The Dark Corners of the Lindbergh Kidnapping*. I would also like to acknowledge the site www.lindberghkidnappinghoax.com.

Several writers read early drafts of this book, taking the time to give invaluable feedback and much-needed encouragement. I am enormously grateful to Clare McHugh, Jess Montgomery, and Susan Elia MacNeal, who asked: "Aren't parents always the prime suspects?" I am indebted to Karen Odden and Nina de Gramont for their support.

The Lindbergh Nanny has had no greater supporter than my agent, Victoria Skurnick. Thank you to my editor, Catherine Richards, who is that rare creature—a genuine editor, willing to talk through the smallest beat or character note of the story. As always, thank you to Nettie Finn for her insights and feedback. Thank you to Kayla Janas and Allison Ziegler. Special gratitude to David Rotstein for the gorgeous cover and his patience with my nitpicking about skirt length. I also thank production manager Catherine Turiano and production editor Ginny Perrin. Huge shout-outs to copy editor Justine Gardner and proofreader Terry McGarry.

This book is dedicated to my father-in-law, who, at a time when everyone was telling me what they thought about the case, asked the questions that helped me formulate what *I* thought. His willingness to engage and listen was a great gift, and this book is dedicated to him. I am lucky to have him, Peggy Florin, and Dana Florin-Weiss in my life. And no one has listened more or with greater patience than my husband, Josh Weiss.

To my son, Griffin—I promise, the next one is for you!

1. How does Betty change over the course of the novel? She loses many things through her involvement with the Lindbergh tragedy; does she gain anything?

2. What was your view of Charles Lindbergh before reading the novel? Did it change? In depicting Charles Lindbergh, the author has said she tried "to be fair both to him and the reader." Do you think she succeeded? Was it a satisfying portrait? How do you feel we should address the sins and misdeeds of a historical figure?

3. The novel offers a theory as to the identity of the "inside man" (or woman) who helped the kidnappers. Did you find it credible? Was there someone else you suspected?

4. *The Lindbergh Nanny* portrays the media frenzy around a famous crime and how people can be judged guilty by the public without trial. Can you think of similar cases in modern times? Has there been a case in which you were convinced of someone's guilt or innocence, only to change your mind?

5. The relationship between a mother and her child's caregiver can be fraught. How do you think Anne felt about Betty? How would you judge Anne's state of mind at the end of the book?

6. Violet Sharpe is a complicated character. Her words and actions are based on fact. Why do you think she lied to the police? Why do you think she committed suicide?

MINOTAUR
BOOKS

7. Bruno Richard Hauptmann was found guilty and executed for the kidnapping and death of Charles Lindbergh, Jr. Do you think it was a fair verdict?

8. What is your view of the Lindberghs' approach to parenting? Do you think both mother and father were equally dedicated to the "Watson method"?

9. Two key points of the novel were fictionalized, one involving a person's private life. Do you think a novelist has that right? Does it improve the story or hurt it?

10. The last line of the novel is "And when she gets there, there will be people. Waiting for her." Why do you think the writer chose that ending? Do we feel happy for Betty?

11. The novel starts with an image of a house Betty hopes to enter. What is the impact of starting with that image?

Read on for a sneak peek at
Mariah Fredericks's new novel

The Wharton Plot

Available Early 2024

Chapter One

Brownell paused in apprehension. In the afternoon quiet of the Palm Garden of the Belmont Hotel, his spirits were made uneasy by the sight of Mrs. Edith Wharton. As her editor for more than two decades, he had much to say to her, none of it what she wished to hear. Publishing was a genteel endeavor; but even in the sensitive realm of words, the brute reality of numbers could intrude. As it did in the matter of royalty payments, for example, which Mrs. Wharton wished to discuss. Also in deadlines, which he was keen to address. The number of books promised them: four. The years since her last novel: three. The sales for that novel, *The Fruit of the Tree* . . . well, being a gentleman, he would set that aside. For now.

Standing by the entrance, concealed by one of the extravagant palms that gave the tearoom its theme, he watched as Mrs. Wharton summoned a waiter to complain about the temperature of the water and the freshness of the linen. But she did so with none of her usual relish, and Brownell worried that she did not look well. She was a woman who collected maladies—asthma, nausea, flu, bronchitis, hay fever—as she collected small dogs. She was now nine-and-forty, and the features that one would have called moderately appealing in her youth were tense and strained. He took in the parched skin and hollowed eyes. The auburn hair, still piled proud and abundant atop her head, showed signs of graying and brittleness. There was nothing wrong with her face, he thought, save that there was too much of it for her small, unremarkable features. The jaw was heavy, the forehead prominent. As a man, she might have managed. He had seen pictures of her as a girl. As a child, she had resembled a pinched, sickly little boy with thin lips and miserable gaze—Oliver Twist. As a young woman, at her best, a handsome, sharp-eyed rogue.

Perhaps that was why she buried herself in clothes, barricading herself in a profusion of lace and furs, pearls roped like armor around her neck and wrists, her hands sunk deep in a muff of dark mink. Even her hats had a touch of the martial to them, giving the impression of a fine, plumed helmet.

In short, a woman you did not engage lightly in battle. One might have expected a woman of wealth to embrace the call of art for art's sake, eschewing all thought of commerce, certainly any hope of financial remuneration. Mrs. Wharton, however, did not merely hope to be paid. She expected it. She expected other things as well. With her very first book, she had written them, "I daresay I have already gone beyond the limits prescribed to a new author in the expression of opinion; but since you send me the title page, I shall consider myself justified in criticizing it." Another note read simply: "Gentlemen, am I not to receive any copies of my book?"

Brownell disliked meeting with authors face-to-face, preferring the cool distance of letters, where words could be considered at length. But Scribner's had been waiting for Mrs. Wharton's words for too long, and when they heard she was coming to New York in order to sell her house in the city, a meeting was proposed. He and the magazine editor, Burlingame, had tossed a coin as to who might have the pleasure of tea with Mrs. Wharton. Brownell had lost—and so here he was.

The waiter had returned, bearing a silk tasseled pillow of blue and gold. This he set down on the floor, and a Pekingese appeared, padding on tiny unseen feet to the pillow's edge, where it was lifted, then set down.

Settled on its luxurious cushion, it seemed to lie down; at least it quivered and looked lower than before. This was new. Previously, Mrs. Wharton had favored long-haired Chihuahuas. If it were possible for a breed to more closely resemble vermin, Brownell was not aware of it. The Pekingese at least had the advantage of volume, although the bright black button eyes were the only sign that it was a living thing and not a footstool.

Just then, those eyes moved in his direction; the thing seemed to pant. With the exquisite sensitivity of all pampered creatures, it sensed it was being observed. As if on cue, his mistress also looked up. Her expression told him she was aware that he had assessed her—and she was now assessing the assessment.

Bravely, he advanced. "Mrs. Wharton, my deepest apologies for being late. To atone, I bring you a gift."

Sitting down at the small table, which was laden with china and silver, he slid a red book in front of her. "The first printing of *Tales of Men and Ghosts*. We do hope you like it."

Immediately, he worried that he had overstressed the *you*, alerting Mrs. Wharton that Scribner's was less than thrilled by a collection of short stories that, in terms of content and style, bore little resemblance to *The House of Mirth*, her raging success of five years ago. When it was serialized, readers had buzzed for months over the fate of Lily Bart. Would she marry for position, for money, or for love? The public shock when the beautiful Lily destroyed herself had rivaled the clamor over the death of Little Nell.

Now Lily's creator gazed at the book over her gilt-edged Minton teacup of deep rose. Laying her gloved fingertips on the edge of the book, she opened it to the frontispiece and frowned.

Setting the cup aside, she sat the book upright, slid off the cover, and peered at the spine. Then she split the volume in two to inspect the typeface.

"Words fail to express how completely I don't like it. The ellipses alone. You could drive a coach and four between these dots."

He had expected this and gave her a game smile. "I should have been disappointed if you approved."

It was meant as an affectionate reference to their earlier quarrels, but the pained twitch of her mouth indicated indifference to her happiness felt all too familiar. He had heard that her marriage was in difficulties. There were rumors of her husband cavorting with young actresses, of missing funds. Even madness. There, he had doubts. Teddy Wharton was the most conventional of men, of an old Boston family, partial to dogs and golf and not much else. "Far too dull to be unstable," said Burlingame, and he, Brownell, had agreed. True, Mrs. Wharton had written to him that her husband's health claimed much of her time and energies, leaving her less opportunity to write. But he took that as a delaying tactic, much like her headaches and hay fever.

A rumble beneath the thickly carpeted floor set the silverware tinkling. Taking advantage of the diversion, he joked, "I suppose that is what comes of building a hotel directly above the subway."

"That is what comes of letting August Belmont build a hotel," she said, referring indirectly to the fact that Mr. Belmont was also the founder of the Interborough Rapid Transit Company. "As a child, I once saw his mistress in a bright yellow brougham on Fifth Avenue. My mother told me to avert my eyes." She raised an eyebrow, letting Brownell know that it was up for debate whether the formidable Lucretia Jones had been more appalled by the scandalous lady or the gaudiness of the carriage. Mrs. Jones, née Rhinelander, whose ancestor had gone riding with General Washington, had been deeply concerned by her child's passion for stories. Mrs. Wharton had told him that when young, she had to beg old brown paper wrappers from the kitchen staff to write on, as it was inconceivable that she should need writing paper beyond the stationery required for invitations and thank-you notes.

Which brought him to his first point. "We are tremendously excited about *Custom of the Country*. A beautiful young heiress makes her way in the glittering world of aristocrats and millionaires . . . a tale only Edith Wharton could tell."

She made a vaguely pleasant hum and fed the dog a macaroon. Brownell waited as she inquired if the macaroon was delicious, did the dog enjoy it, would it like some more, yes, yes, she thought it *would*.

She said, "I trust that means there will be a vigorous advertising campaign."

Queen threatens pawn, he thought. *Pawn moves to protect castle.* "Difficult to say until I've seen something of the book . . ."

"But you said you were so excited."

"Any work by you, Mrs. Wharton, is cause for excitement."

"Really?" She gazed at him, as if puzzled. "I can't say I was terribly excited by the promotion for *Fruit of the Tree*. My friends wrote to me, saying they couldn't find the book anywhere."

The Fruit of the Tree. A novel about textile mills. In New England. Heroic middle managers. Spinal injuries. Euthanasia. Response, both in-house and without, had been anemic.

She persisted, saying, "The reviews were excellent. The *Times* called it 'a powerful study in modern life.'"

The *Times* had also said "Central Incident Repels." Taking up his tea, he said carefully, "I think the exploitation of labor is perhaps not your subject. *Your* readers adore your ability to reveal the secret lives of the wealthy. You are their guide inside homes they will never enter, clothes they will never wear. They love your wit, your perception, the satirical portrait of the joys and cruelties of New York . . ."

"And I believe with the right support from Scribner's, they would love my portrait of joy and cruelty in rural New England just as much. I have another story in mind, the tale of a marriage. A poor farmer whose wife is an invalid . . ."

Rural? Farmers and invalids? *Poor* farmers and invalids? It was time, Brownell decided, to take things in hand.

"Mrs. Wharton, I feel strongly that *Custom of the Country* should be your next book."

"How strongly?" She looked directly at him, all pretense with the dog abandoned.

". . . How?"

"Five percent more strongly than you have felt about my work in the past?"

Breathing in deeply through the nose, Brownell contemplated the number of women he knew who were familiar with the word *negotiation*, much less its practice. Then he calculated the number of women he knew who were adept at figures, followed by those who would dare bandy percentages. He came up with a very small number. One, to be precise. Unfortunately for him, that one was seated across from him, in possession of a book he wanted very badly.

Lowering his voice, he said, "A twenty percent royalty is the top market rate."

She lowered hers to match his. "There are authors who get twenty-five percent."

He smiled. Broadly and at length until his face hurt. His mind groped for a decorous response but could not overcome the hurdle of outrage that Mrs. Wharton had asked for twenty-five percent. Twenty-five percent! What did one say to that? To a woman, in a public place where expletives were impossible? By letter, he fumed, this would have been far less aggravating.

Later, he would blame that aggravation for the error he was about to make. Had he been less riled by Mrs. Wharton's regal assumptions as to her worth, he would never have called out to that man. Never invited him to join their table. Indeed, had he not turned in his chair, frantically seeking someone—anyone—on whom to focus other than the percentage- and punctuation-obsessed Mrs. Wharton, he might not have noticed the gentleman at all.

Although it was hard not to notice David Graham Phillips. The writer wore a white suit in the city in late January and sported a large chrysanthemum in his lapel. As he moved through the tearoom, several people turned to look at him and whisper—whether in recognition, admiration, or approbation, it was hard to tell. Everything in his affect proclaimed him a man of higher purpose as he weaved in and around tables, arms swinging, legs leaping one after the other, eyes fixed upon the exit. And yet he pulled up short when Brownell said, "Why, here's David Graham Phillips, if I am not mistaken!"

Chapter Two

Mrs. Wharton at once perceived that her editor, having no answer to her request for increased royalties, wished to change the subject. She also perceived that the man before her in the blindingly white suit was not to her taste. At all. His upper lip—brutish, clean-shaven—appalled her; the gentleman's hairless perimeter was positively aggressive. *Adorn myself?* it seemed to say. *Sport plumage? Make an effort at style or elegance? For what? For* you?

There was vanity here; that ridiculous suit and the luxuriant sheen of his black hair told her so. His gaze, blue eyes slightly narrowed, invited, nay, insisted on the adjectives *piercing* or *keen*. The cleft in the pugnacious chin—obvious. The way he stood, restless, hands tensing to suggest fists, imitative of boxers, whom he no doubt affected to admire. As he gave her the briefest glance, then looked back to Brownell, she sensed his resentment as you would an odor.

She gathered from the male chatter that at one time Mr. Brownell and Mr. Phillips had both worked for the *New York World*. And that Mr. Brownell admired Mr. Phillips's articles in *The Sun*. Even more, he admired Mr. Phillips's novels, which he called "courageous" and "uniquely American." Mr. Phillips claimed to regret that Mr. Brownell was no longer with *The Nation*.

Casting an expansive hand in her direction, Brownell said, "Ah, but at *The Nation*, I would never have had the chance to work with Mrs. Edith Wharton."

It was the cue for deference, and she waited. At her ankles, she felt the brush of fur; Choumai in search of food.

Mr. Phillips grunted, "Well, that's true enough."

From this, Edith understood the following: Mr. Phillips knew her work and did not admire it. She was a woman, which he also did not admire. Further still, an *old* woman, whose age demanded he make a show of manners he no doubt found insulting to his *authentic being*.

Peering at the gentleman's lapel, she remarked as if she had just noticed, "A chry-*san*-themum."

Knowing an opening salvo when he heard it, Brownell said hastily, "Mr. Phillips is considered one of America's leading novelists."

"The," Mr. Phillips corrected him.

Brows raised to her hairline, Edith marveled. *The? The* leading American writer. Not James, not Dreiser, not Twain—although Twain had just died—*certainly* not she. And to insist upon it. *No, no, not* one of, *old chap*—the.

The! She repeated the word to herself until it rang with absurdity.

Phillips added, "By H. L. Mencken at any rate."

Sighing, "Well, Mr. Mencken," she plucked a champagne wafer from Brownell's plate and dropped it to the dog below.

But she felt Brownell's anxiety. For whatever reason, the editor wished to further his acquaintance with Mr. Phillips and he wanted her help in doing it.

She gestured to the vacant chair. "Won't you join us, Mr. Phillips?"

From Brownell, a waft of gratitude; from Mr. Phillips, condescension. Even the way he pulled out his chair was grudging, and she longed to say, *Oh, please don't if it hurts you so.*

But decades ago, as a newly made matron, she had applied herself to the art of that particularly bland form of charm known as pleas-antness. In parlor after parlor, dinner after dinner, she had murmured agreeably, asking only those questions that would allow the other person to flatter themselves. And while it had been many years, she could still discipline her features and voice in that style—blank yet ardently attentive—and she did so now, asking, "Are you also with Scribner's?"

"Appleton."

"An excellent house. And—forgive me, I've been abroad—I'm not familiar with your work."

Brownell said, "Perhaps you recall *The Great God Success* . . . ?"

Smiling serenely, she shook her head.

"*The Plum Tree? Old Wives for New? The Grain of Dust?*" And when again she shook her head, "Surely, *The Treason of the Senate.* In the words of President Roosevelt—'Here is the man who rakes the muck!'" Brownell swung his fist with a heartiness she found unconvincing.

"Oh, dear," she asked, "what did you do to displease King Theodore the First?"

She offered this light ridicule as she would insist that her guest take the last strawberry. The president was a personal friend; he had recently visited her in Paris. But she wished to show herself as someone who could laugh at those in her own caste.

Flinging one leg across the other, Mr. Phillips said, "I told the truth, Mrs. Wharton."

"The *truth*," she echoed as if amazed.

He heard the mockery and his expression hardened. "Yes, the truth, Mrs. Wharton. About how this nation's government is corrupted by money. About the hire and salary of the people's representatives by big business. Aristocracy has no place in a republic."

Edith was aware that many people had these views. She was also aware that these views did not interest her. At least not enough to be lectured by Mr. Phillips.

But he had more to say.

"I told the *truth*, Mrs. Wharton, about the stranglehold on our economy held by a parasitic class that does nothing, produces nothing except its own doodlewit descendants who will, like their forebears, simply *exist* on inherited wealth."

A great slam of his index finger on the end of the table to punctuate the point. Edith looked to Brownell; unless she was mistaken, she had just been called a doodlewit. Did he care to comment? Brownell, intent on splintering a meringue with his fork, did not.

She asked, "And these . . . parasites, are they the subject of your novels?"

"They're the subject of most novels these days, Mrs. Wharton." The legs unfurled and he turned to face her. "So many happy, silly stories about people tootling around in automobiles from one fussy house to the next, one showy entertainment after another. Dressing, chattering, playing at love. Those books are popular, I'll grant you that. But that kind of story doesn't make a bit of difference to the lives of real Americans."

He was so obtuse, she found it difficult to know: *Did* he understand that this could be construed as a criticism of her work? Her life and self? (She adored motorcars and could still remember the exhilarating stench of India rubber of her very first, a cream-colored Panhard et Levassor.)

She was pondering her response when Brownell stepped in, saying, "I actually feel Mr. Phillips's novels have something in common with yours, Mrs. Wharton, in the subject of the contemporary American woman, the, ah, perils of not knowing . . ."

Edith was about to disagree when Mr. Phillips laughed. "Mrs. Wharton hardly writes about the real American woman."

She paused. Gathered herself. "I don't?"

His head reared back in surprise. "A woman of your means? Who spends so much time abroad? What could you possibly know about the American woman of today?"

"But *you* understand," she said. "You, Mr. Phillips, understand this singular creature, the American woman of today. The real American woman."

"I think so, yes."

"You understand her thoughts and feelings. The world in which she finds herself, the difficulties . . ."

"Well, I think you and I might define those *difficulties* differently, Mrs. Wharton. I can accept that in America, most novels are written about women, for women—"

"Magnanimous."

"—but so many of these novels fail to tell women the truth they so badly need to hear. They perpetuate falsehoods, build up their illusions. No woman on earth has been so ridiculously deceived as to herself and so spoiled as the American woman. The worst of it is, she's bringing the American man down with her. Did you know that the rate of divorce in America is now two times that of the rest of the Christian world?"

Like a prosecutor, he leaned forward, and for an ugly moment, Edith fancied he had read the gossip about her own marriage.

She said, "Perhaps American women have higher standards."

"Higher standards, Mrs. Wharton, or *appetite*?" The legs recrossed. The fingers drummed upon the linen. "There is a certain kind of woman who toils not, neither does she spin. But she consumes, Mrs. Wharton, oh, does she. I tell you, a man is lost forever if he falls into the hands of a luxury-loving woman."

Folding a piece of candied lemon peel into her mouth, Edith nodded: *Go on.*

"While her husband labors, she spends. But not on the house that they share, not on the meals she provides him, not even on herself, at least not the part of her that a husband cares about. She grows fat. Slatternly. Rather than have children, she advances herself in society. She cultivates the art of leisure, drifting from one diversion to the next. Fashionable, ornamental, she seeks pleasure in New York, then pleasure in Europe. And lest anyone think her a mere sloth, she dignifies her indolence with nonstop fiddle-faddle about culture and *passion*. When what she really means is consumption."

What a joy you must be to live with, she thought. "Tell me, Mr. Phillips, does your wife enjoy your novels?"

She was pleased to see him retreat from the edge of the table. "I am unmarried. I work too much to have time for a wife."

"Yes," she said. "That *must* be the reason."

But it was a perfunctory sally; his spleen and determination to give offense had made her tired. She gave him her profile, her customary dismissal with bores.

Then she heard him say, "But you know this, Mrs. Wharton. Is not Lily Bart destroyed by her love of luxury? Are we not meant to feel that if she had given herself to Selden, a man of modest means, they might have been happy? I wish . . ."

Suddenly he seemed to be talking to her, rather than at her. Curious, she said, "Yes?"

"I wish you had given Lily courage. How much more powerful if she had made her choice—yes to love or yes to luxury—rather than drifting into self-destruction."

There was something wistful in his voice that, despite the criticism, drew her to ask, "And is that the *truth*, Mr. Phillips? Do you find that people are often courageous? Able to break the rules of their world and come through unscathed?"

For the first time, his eyes were open, free of scorn. "I admit, it's a rare thing to be able to burn one's spiritual bridges. But only love gives you the power to say farewell to your old existence and to take flight toward a new one."

Her first thought was *What absolute twaddle.* Her second was *Why did you not begin with this? I might have liked you better.*

Mr. Phillips, she wondered, *can it be you are in love?*

She felt Brownell was agitated. Well, he had brought this hideous man to her; let him suffer. Irritably, she turned to find the waiter; the table needed clearing. She listened as Brownell insisted they not keep Mr. Phillips any longer. Also that it had been a very great pleasure to see him again.

Then, almost shyly, Brownell said to Phillips, "One hears rumors that your next book is soon upon us. May I know the title?"

"It's called *Susan Lenox: Her Fall and Rise.* Taken me ten years to write, and almost as long to get the cowards at Appleton to publish. The public will not soon forgive me for this one." He grinned as if the prospect of popular loathing appealed to him.

"Explosive stuff, eh?" guessed Brownell.

"Let's just say if they're not scared now—they should be."

Pushing back the chair as if it were a dog that had gotten too familiar, he nodded curtly to Brownell and then to her, saying, "Mrs. Wharton, a pleasure."

She returned the pleasantry, matching his tone precisely. She and Brownell waited until Mr. Phillips had passed through the doors of the tearoom, staying silent as they imagined him racing through the vast Belmont lobby, shoving his way through its doors, and hurtling onto Park Avenue. Far below, the subway came and went, causing the table to tremble. Placing one hand gently on the surface, she took up the tongs and gave a sugar cube to Choumai.

"Forgive me," said Brownell.

". . . At some point. Perhaps next year. Around Easter."

"I didn't realize his views on women were so emphatic."

"And so *ignorant*!" She massaged her temples, then gave it up. What she needed was a cigarette.

She asked, "Are you trying to lure him to Scribner's?"

"He sells very well," said Brownell.

Rationally, she knew Brownell's talk of sales was not intended as an insult; she took it as one anyway. The ranting, successful, oh-so-American Mr. Phillips had left her with the feeling she often had in this country: of being profoundly inadequate and unfairly disdained, both abused and deserving of abuse. Looking at Brownell, she recalled his intense gaze upon her when he first entered the room, the way he examined her as if she were a manuscript. Was she to his liking? Perhaps she was too old-fashioned. Ridiculous, passé. Lacking the dash and energy—the *modernity*—of a David Graham Phillips.

Hearing shouting and the roar of falling stone, she glanced out the window to Forty-Second Street. It was an unlovely sight. Almost a decade earlier, it had been decided that old Cornelius Vanderbilt's

Grand Central Depot no longer served. With twenty million passengers in a single year, the station was judged to be filthy, overcrowded, even dangerous. So the old depot would be destroyed even as the new terminal was raised in its place. No more steam—all must be electric! Ever since then, they had been tearing up the street, blasting into bedrock, slapping tracks here, there, and everywhere. For years, they had promised a marvel. From what Edith could see, they had achieved only mess.

Hating everything, she reached down for Choumai. But the traitorous creature had sensed her mood and retreated under Brownell's chair. The table was cleared; there was nothing left with which to find fault. Still, she observed, "I've had better food at a French provincial railway station."

"When do you return to Paris?" Brownell asked.

"We are awaiting my husband's physician, Dr. Kinnicutt. He arrives from Massachusetts tomorrow. Mr. Wharton is setting off on a world tour; he yearns to see California. But I would like his doctor to see him before he goes. Mr. Wharton has had health difficulties. I think I wrote you in my last letter."

Brownell murmured sympathetically. "What do the doctors say?"

She attempted a laugh. "Which one? I could write a Molière play on specialists. This one says neurasthenia. That one Riggs' disease. It's senile decay. No, it's gout of the head. Then again, perhaps it's toothache. But Mr. Wharton's sister places great faith in Dr. Kinnicutt, and so it is to him I must appeal." What she did not say was that Nannie Wharton, if asked, would say Teddy's only difficulty was Edith and her "extravagances." Nannie would probably enjoy Mr. Phillips's novels.

The fingers of her right hand ached; she realized that she had been crushing them within the dark cocoon of mink in her lap. She longed to say something banal. Or literary. Something to prove that she was in control of her faculties. But her mind was fogged with misery. That was just one of the awful things about her situation. It made her mute. Not even mute, for she had nothing to say. Her mind was empty.

There were days when she opened her eyes in the morning and was not certain she even existed.

Briskly folding up her linen napkin, she revived herself with anger. How dare Brownell compare her to that repugnant man. How dare he say they had subjects in common. His skittish half-reference to the "perils of not knowing." How coy. How insufferably—

Another memory came, sinuous and unstoppable: the warmth of breath in her coiled hair as he whispered, "*That's* something you know nothing about."

Words spoken by a very different man under very different circumstances. Oddly, David Graham Phillips looked a bit like him. The commanding blue eyes. The flower in his buttonhole. The certainty and vigor as he demanded, "What could you possibly know about the American woman of today?"

To console herself, she seized on the most obviously ridiculous thing about Mr. Phillips: a *chrysanthemum*. In winter, for heaven's sake. Did he know its symbolism? A heart left in desolation.

She highly doubted it.

MARIAH FREDERICKS was born, raised, and still lives in New York City. She graduated from Vassar College with a degree in history. She is the author of the Jane Prescott mystery series, which has twice been nominated for the Mary Higgins Clark Award, as well as several young adult novels. She can be reached at mariahfredericksbooks.com.